THOMAS MULLEN's first novel, *The Last Town on Earth*, was awarded the James Fenimore Cooper Prize for excellence in historical fiction. A graduate of Oberlin College, Thomas Mullen lives in Washington, DC, with his wife and son.

Visit his website at www.thomasmullen.net

Visit www.AuthorTracker.co.uk for exclusive information on your favourite HarperCollins authors.

From the reviews of *The Last Town on Earth*:

'A subtle, robustly written novel of compelling contemporary resonance' HEPHZIBAH ANDERSON, *Observer*

'Thomas Mullen is an old-fashioned storyteller, and his epic novel dramatises the complex tensions between individual rights and group responsibilities . . . Mullen is both merciless and measured in his depiction of the natural forces that can drag idealism down to earth' *Daily Telegraph*

'In these days of anxiety over pandemics and terrorist "others" possibly in our midst, Thomas Mullen's novel of the Spanish influenza epidemic during World War I and its particular effect on a Pacific Northwest town could not be more timely or relevant, and eerily so. I promise you, while you're reading *The Last Town on Earth*, the mere sound of a cough will be enough to raise the hair at the back of your neck'

LARRY WATSON, bestselling author of *Montana 1948*

'*The Last Town on Earth* wraps its reader in its quiet power. As the characters become trapped by their town, we become increasingly trapped by our own fears and hopes. Thomas Mullen's debut is stirring, classic storytelling, with a deep resonance between the book's moment in history and our own times'

MATTHEW PEARL, author of *The Dante Club*

'In his remarkable first novel a brilliant series of plot twists is set in motion . . . Chilling parallels are overshadowed by the steady, nerve-shredding movement toward the story's climax . . . Time and again, Mullen's suspenseful storytelling pulls us forward. Time and again, his imagery . . . is devastatingly right'

New York Times

'Thomas Mullen's page-turner of a debut historical novel . . . [is] part morality tale, part coming-of-age yarn . . . Gripping . . . Psychological suspense, villains, victims, a conflicted hero or two, secrets and a mystery. In short, it's a grabber'

Washington Post

'Mullen provides a rich historical background and a well-drawn cast of characters . . . A fascinating account of a time and a place that most of us have never heard about' *Los Angeles Times*

'An engaging look at political and social isolation, and a vivid . . . study of human nature . . . The drama of the situation carries the book as inexorably forward as does the march of influenza through the area . . . If this novel teaches us something, it is that our history books can rarely portray the personal nature of political discourse in the past, or the sacrifices people make for their ideals' *The Lancet*

'Wonderful . . . Mullen has done a fine job with this, his debut novel, presenting an array of characters and showing with a deft hand their differing responses to the situation in which the town finds itself . . . [He] has created a fascinating microcosm and it's enthralling to watch . . . What makes this novel compelling is not only its hint of allegory . . . but the broader questions it forces us to ask . . . What he manages to do is leave the reader interrogating themselves as to what their own response would be and should be if faced with these same ethical dilemmas. And that's something to be valued in any novel'

Canberra Times (Australia)

THOMAS MULLEN

The Last Town on Earth

A NOVEL

HARPER PERENNIAL
London, New York, Toronto and Sydney

Harper Perennial
An imprint of HarperCollins*Publishers*
77–85 Fulham Palace Road
Hammersmith
London W6 8JB

www.harperperennial.co.uk

This edition published by Harper Perennial 2007
1

Fi[illegible] 2006

A catalog[illegible] ritish Library

ISBN-13 978-0-00-723500-1
ISBN-10 0-00-723500-3

Set in Adobe Garamond with Goudy Handtooled & Requiem display

Printed and bound in Great Britain by Clays Ltd, St Ives plc

This novel is entirely a work of fiction. The names, characters and incidents portrayed in it are the work of the author's imagination. Any resemblance to actual persons, living or dead, events or localities is entirely coincidental.

Perhaps the easiest way of making a town's acquaintance
is to ascertain how the people in it work,
how they love, and how they die.

—ALBERT CAMUS,
The Plague

An injury to one is an injury to all.

— *Industrial Workers of the World slogan*

The LAST TOWN ON EARTH

The sun poked out briefly, evidence of a universe above them, of watchful things—planets and stars and vast galaxies of infinite knowledge—and just as suddenly it retreated behind the clouds.

The doctor passed only two other autos during the fifteen-minute drive, saw but a lone pedestrian even though it was noon on Sunday, a time when people normally would be returning home from church, visiting with friends and family. The flu had been in Timber Falls for three weeks now, by the doctor's best estimation, and nearly all traffic on the streets had vanished. The sick were condemned to their homes, and the healthy weren't venturing outside.

"No one's been down this street yet?" he asked the two nurses he was traveling with, both of whom had husbands fighting in France. He was a thin, older man with spectacles that had been dirtied by the wet coughs of countless patients.

"No," one of the nurses said, shaking her head. Amid the swelling volume of the sick and dying, they hadn't yet reached those this far outside of town, a lonely street where the poorest derelicts and most recent immigrants lived.

Neighbors had reported unnerving sounds coming from within one of the houses, but no one had been willing to go inside and check on the family.

The doctor parked beside the house, a two-story structure at the base of a slowly rolling hill. The ground was all mud, the wheels sinking a few inches. It even looked as if the house were sinking into the earth, its roof sloping to the right. The house was the last of five narrow buildings that seemed to lean against each other in their grief.

Before leaving the car, the visitors fastened gauze masks to their faces, covering their noses and mouths, and pulled on thin rubber gloves.

The doctor knocked on the door. There was no reply so he knocked again, harder this time, and identified himself.

"Look," one of the nurses said. In the window to the left of the door they saw a face peering through the sheer curtain, a child no more than four years old. Her eyes were large and she appeared ghostlike, neither frightened of the masked strangers nor particularly interested in them. The nurse lifted a hand to wave but the child made no reply. The doctor knocked again, motioning to the door, but the child just stood there.

Finally the doctor turned the knob and walked inside. All the windows were shut, and the door clearly had not been opened in days. He noticed the smell immediately.

The little girl at the window turned to watch them. She was wearing an adult's flannel shirt over her dirty nightgown, and her thick blond hair was uncombed. She was frighteningly thin.

The parlor was a disaster, clothes and toys and books strewn everywhere. A rocking chair was lying on its side, and a lamp had shattered on the floor. As the visitors stepped into the room two other girls emerged from the chaos, one younger and one slightly older than the girl in the window. They, too, were oddly dressed, dirty, wraithlike.

The doctor was about to ask where their parents were when he heard coughing, dry and hoarse. He and one of the nurses followed the sound down a short hallway and into a bedroom.

The other nurse stayed in the parlor with the children. She knelt on the floor and took some slices of rye bread from her bag. The girls raced toward her, hands extended, fingernails ripping into the food. In seconds there was nothing left, and all six eyes were again gazing at her expectantly.

In the bedroom, dark curtains were pulled over the window. The doctor could see the two beds, both occupied. Intermittent coughs came from the figure on the right, whose head rested on a pillow stained a dark red.

The earlobes, nostrils, and upper lip were blackened with dried blood; the eyes were shut and the lids were a dark blue, as was the skin around them. The doctor saw a hand lying on top of the sheets, the fingers the color of wet ink. The small table beside the bed was streaked with blood, as was the Bible resting upon it.

The man coughed again and his eyes opened, unfocused, for no more than a second. The nurse knelt beside him to perform the meager duties her training dictated, even though she knew they were worthless now. It was better than looking at the figure in the other bed.

The woman lay on her side, facing her husband, her lips frozen in a rictus of pain. Her thin blond hair spilled across the pillow, some falling over the side of the bed and some caked in the dried blood on her face. It was impossible to tell how long she had been dead, as the Spanish flu's corpses looked unlike any the doctor had seen. The blueness that darkened her husband had fully consumed her, making it impossible to guess her age or even her race. She resembled the burn victims the doctor had seen after a horrific mill fire years ago.

She was probably about the age of the nurses, the doctor wagered, for the flu seemed to be taking only those who were in the prime of their lives. The children may already have been recovering, but the flu had smothered their parents. This was entirely the opposite pattern of most influenzas.

They heard more coughing, from another room. The doctor and nurse looked at each other, surprised, then followed the sound into a bedroom on the opposite side of the hall. Here the window was curtainless, and as soon as they entered they saw two bodies lying on a large bed, both of them coughing. They were young adults, the sheets bloody near their heads. They sounded exactly like what they were: two people slowly suffocating to death.

There was a sudden movement between the bodies, tiny hands. A raven-haired child no more than three years old had been napping between her dying parents. She appeared tranquil for a moment, but the instant the girl opened her brown eyes, she started to scream. Whether terrified by the strangers in the masks or her nearly motionless parents, the nurse wasn't sure. The girl kept screaming. It was as though the three silent children in the other room had found a voice in this one girl's horror.

The doctor was already in the parlor, telephoning one of the exhausted undertakers, though he knew it would be hours before one could arrive. Even the operators were sick, and he stood there for what seemed an eternity, silence on the line, waiting for a voice to aid him, waiting for an answer. The dead seconds stretched out before him like the arms of the starved little girls, beseeching him.

Part One

COMMONWEALTH

I

The road to Commonwealth was long and forbidding, stretching for miles beyond Timber Falls and leading deep into the evergreen woods, where the trees grew taller still as if trying to reach the sun that teased them with the paucity of its rays. Douglas fir loomed over the rock-strewn road like two warring armies perched on opposing cliffs. Even those travelers who all their lives had been reminded of their insignificance felt particularly humbled by that stretch of road and the preternatural darkness that shadowed it.

Some number of miles into the woods, the road curved to the right and the trees backed off a bit, the brown dirt and occasional stumps evidence that the woods had been cleared out only recently, and only with extreme tenacity. The clearing rose along a gradual incline; at the base of the hill, a tree that had recently been chopped down blocked the road. Into its thick bark a sign was nailed: a warning to travelers who didn't exist, a silent cry into deaf woods.

A crisp wind picked up atop the bare hill, carrying the combined exhalations of millions of fir and pine. Philip sucked in his breath.

"Cold?" Graham asked.

"I'm fine."

Graham motioned back to the town. "You need to get yourself a warmer jacket, go ahead."

"I'll stay."

"Suit yourself." Philip did look cold in his thin jacket and khaki pants—pencil-pusher attire—whereas Graham was clad in his usual blue overalls and a thick wool coat.

"Look like it's gonna snow to you?" Philip Worthy was sixteen, tall despite the limp that made people think he was shorter, but not as brawny as most of the men in that town of loggers and millworkers.

"It's not going to snow."

Graham, twenty-five, was what in many ways Philip aspired to be: strong, quietly wise, the man of his house. While Philip felt he needed to be polite and conversational to ingratiate himself with people, Graham seemed to say the minimum necessary and always won respect. Philip had known him for two years, and he still wanted to figure out how a fellow did that.

"Colder'n I thought it'd be," Philip said. "Sometimes that means snow."

Graham understood his companion's dread of snow. He shook his head. "It's cold, but it ain't going to snow. It's October."

Philip nodded, shoulders hunched against the cold.

Graham laid his rifle on the ground, then took off his coat. "Here, put it on."

"No, really, I'll be all right. I don't want you to get—"

"Put the damn coat on." Graham smiled. "I've got more meat on my bones anyway."

"Thanks." Philip placed his rifle beside Graham's. The jacket was big on him, the sleeves extending beyond his hands. He knew he looked foolish, but it was as good as wearing gloves. He wouldn't be able to hold the rifle, but that seemed fine, since he didn't expect he'd need to.

"Who do you think that was in the Model T on Sunday?" Philip asked.

"Don't know." Neither of them had been at the post on Sunday, when two other guards had seen a shiny new Ford drive as far as the fallen tree would allow. The guard post was too far away to get a good look at the driver, who never emerged from his automobile. The fedora told them it was a man, but that was all. The man had apparently read the sign, stopped to think for no longer than a moment, then turned around and driven away. It was the only sighting of an outsider since the town had closed itself off.

Commonwealth sat about fifty miles northeast of Seattle, or maybe a hundred—no one seemed to know except the town's founder, Charles Worthy, and those who transported the town's lumber. To the east were the jagged peaks of the Cascades, close enough to be seen on a clear day but far enough to disappear when the clouds were low and thick. On those days, the town seemed to be cut off from the rest of the earth. Miles to the west was the open sea, the confluence of Puget Sound to the south, the Strait of Georgia to the north, and the Strait of Juan de Fuca to the west, the point where all three combined and wrapped their cold embrace around the San Juan Islands. But the sea was just far enough away, blocked by the thick forest, that it might as well not have been there at all.

Commonwealth was no ordinary town, and that helped explain why it appeared on no maps, as if the rest of the civilized world preferred to ignore its existence. It had no mayor, no postmaster, no sheriff. It had no prison, no taxman, no train station, no rail lines. No church, no telephones, no hospital. No saloon, no nickelodeon. Commonwealth had pretty much nothing but a lumber mill, homes for the workers, plenty of land from which to tear down more trees, and the few trappings necessary to support the mill, such as a general store and a doctor's office. To shop for items the store didn't sell, to visit the moving pictures, or to attend traditional church services, people went to Timber Falls, fifteen miles to the southwest. But no one from town was allowed to leave anymore, and no one was allowed to come in.

"Think the driver will come back?" Philip asked. The wind blew his thin brown hair across his forehead.

Graham thought for a moment, his face appearing immovable as his blue-green eyes focused on the base of the hill. "No, not after he saw the sign. If it was someone who really wanted to come in, he would've tried. Probably just somebody on mill business who didn't know about the quarantine."

Philip nodded, appreciating Graham's certainty.

Philip had grown up with neither father nor siblings, dragged throughout the West by an itinerant mother until the accident that left him in the Worthys' care. And when his new family had moved to Commonwealth two years ago to start this bold experiment, he had quickly befriended Graham, who hadn't realized how much he'd missed his own younger brothers until he met Philip.

Graham, like many millworkers, had run away from his home too young, chased off by a drunk father with whom he had violently clashed one time too many. He had been about Philip's age when he'd left his home in Kansas, and sometimes when he looked at Philip, he was amazed that he himself had been so headstrong, so foolish, to venture out into the world at such an overwhelmed age. Somehow he had survived, survived bloody strikes and stints in jail and fights with cops, and here he was, a foreman at a respectable mill. Though he had his own family to care for now, he liked teaching Philip the things he'd learned from his older brother, to hunt his first deer, catch his first fish, navigate the trails that cut through the endless forest.

In truth, Graham didn't feel so certain that the man in the automobile wouldn't return, but the mere sound of his own calm voice was reassuring. This was why Graham had missed having younger brothers, he realized—they made you feel almost as strong as the image they looked up to.

Philip and Graham's first stint as guards, four days earlier, had been uneventful. They had stood there for the ten long hours, silent for stretches and chatting when the boredom became too great. Wondering aloud how long the flu would last, swapping stories of past illnesses and ailments. Philip had even proposed a small wager as to how long the quarantine would last, but Graham had lightly chastised him for being indelicate. Philip regretted the comment, felt young and stupid. But other than that the time had passed slowly, the sky gradually darkening, the mists descending from the formless clouds above, leaving the two watchmen damp and tired and longing for their warm homes, where they would have nothing interesting to share with their families over the supper table.

"So how's 'class' coming?" Graham asked, minutes or hours later.

"Class is fine. Ask me anything you'd like to know about interest payments."

"I would like to know nothing at all, thank you very much."

Philip was Charles Worthy's apprentice, being trained in the business side of the mill, bred for the same job that Charles himself had held in his father's mill, the one he had disgustedly turned his back on only two years ago.

"You honestly like sittin' in a chair all day?" Graham asked.

"Wouldn't know what else to compare it to."

Philip wondered if Graham looked down on his desk work, but with his damaged body, Philip was a bad candidate for labor of a more physical nature. He gave a surreptitious glance at Graham's missing finger, the one he'd lost in a mill accident some years ago, and figured his wasn't such a bad lot to draw.

Just the other day, Philip had helped calculate what the mill would save if it switched over from gang saws to band saws, whose thinner blades would mean losing less of the lumber to sawdust. It had been challenging work, but when he was finished, he felt he'd contributed something of value to the mill, and his father's soft-spoken compliment was still ringing in his ears.

"How's your little girl doing?" Philip asked.

"She's great," Graham said with a slight smile. "Been crawlin' all over the house lately. Amelia's gotta keep her eyes on her all the time now."

"How long till she talks?"

"A few months yet, at least."

"How long till she chops down trees like her old man?"

"Till hell freezes over."

"I don't know," Philip said, "she does look like a logger."

"How's that?"

Philip shrugged. "She drools a lot. Burps. Kinda smells sometimes."

Graham nodded, smirking.

"So you get any sleep, or is she still up all night?"

"I sleep when I can."

"Like when you're out here standing guard."

"I was not asleep last time. I was resting my eyes and ignoring you. It's an important skill a man develops after he has a wife and kid. Trust me on this.

"Speaking of which," Graham continued after a brief pause, looking at Philip from the corner of his eye, "I keep seeing you talking with that Metzger girl."

Philip shrugged unconvincingly. "She's my sister's friend."

"So how come I keep seeing you and her and no sister?"

It took an extra second for Philip to come up with a retort. "What, a guy can't talk to a girl?"

Graham smiled. "Boy, I hope you're less obvious with her than you are with me."

Minutes of silence had passed before they saw someone at the base of the hill.

They saw him through the tree trunks first, hints of light brown and tan flashing every other second through that tangle of bark. Each of them stiffened, breath held, as they waited to see if a figure would emerge or if they had imagined it, if it was some trick of light.

The figure turned the corner and looked up the hill, saw the town in the distance. Between him and the town stood Philip and Graham, though he seemed not to notice them.

"You see that, too, right?" Philip asked.

"I see it."

The figure started walking toward them.

"Read the sign," Graham quietly commanded the stranger. "Read the sign."

Indeed, after a couple of seconds, the figure reached the sign and stopped. Stopped for an unusually long time, as if he could barely read and there were one too many big words written there. Then the man looked up at them. Graham made sure his rifle was visible, standing up beside him, his hand under the barrel so that it was pointing away from him.

Philip hadn't looked at the sign in days yet he had memorized what it said.

QUARANTINE
ABSOLUTELY NO ENTRY ALLOWED!
On Account of the Outbreak of INFLUENZA
This Town Under Strict QUARANTINE.
This Area Under Constant Watch of ARMED Guards.
Neither STRANGER Nor FRIEND May Pass Beyond This Marker.
May God Protect You.

After reading the sign the man had some sort of brief spasm, one of his hands reaching to his face. Then he stepped up to the fallen tree and started climbing over it. It was an impressive tree, and it took him a moment to ascend its thick trunk. Then he was past it and walking toward them again.

"He's still coming," Philip said helplessly, trying not to panic. He hurriedly rolled up the sleeves of Graham's coat, wondering why he felt fidgety and nervous when Graham seemed to become even more still than usual.

The man walked with a slight limp, wincing when he moved his right leg. It made his progress slower but somehow more definite. His clothes suggested a uniform of some kind, with stripes on one sleeve. As the man approached, Philip and Graham saw the back end of a rifle poking up over his right shoulder.

He's a soldier, Philip thought, confused.

He was nearly halfway to them. No more than eighty yards away.

"Stop right there!" Graham shouted. "This town is under quarantine! You can't come any closer!"

The man did as he was told. He had dark and uncombed hair that appeared somewhat longer than a typical soldier's. He looked like he hadn't shaved in a couple of days, and there was a piece of cloth tied around his right thigh, colored black from what might have been dried blood. His uniform was dirty all over the legs and was smeared with mud across parts of the chest.

Then the soldier sneezed.

"Please!" The man needed to raise his voice in order to be heard over the distance, but the effort of doing so seemed almost too much for him. "I'm starving. I just need a little something to eat . . ."

What's a soldier doing out here, Philip wanted to ask, but he kept the thought to himself.

"You can't come up here, buddy," Graham replied. "The sign said, we're under a quarantine. We can't let anyone in."

"I don't care if I get sick." The man shook his head at them. He was young, closer in age to Philip than to Graham. He had some sort of an accent, not foreign but from some other part of the country. New England, or maybe New York—Philip wasn't sure. The man's jaw was hard and his face bony and angular, the type of face Philip's mother would have told him you couldn't trust, though Philip never knew why.

"I'm starving—I need something to eat. I've been out in the woods two days now. There was an accident—"

"It's not you getting sick we're worried about." Graham's voice was still strong, almost bullying. "We're the only town around here that isn't sick yet, and we aim to keep it that way. Now head on back down that road."

The soldier looked behind him halfheartedly, then back at Graham. "How far's the next town?"

"'Bout fifteen miles," Graham replied. Commonwealth was not on the way to or from any other town—the road led to Commonwealth and ended there. So where had the soldier come from?

"Fifteen miles? I haven't eaten in two days. It'll be dark in a few hours."

He coughed. Loudly, thickly. How far does breath travel? Philip wondered.

Then the soldier started limping toward them again.

Philip was rigid with a new mixture of fear, apprehension, and a sense of duty, the knowledge that he had a job to do. Although his job had seemed perfectly clear and understandable earlier in the day, he was realizing how completely unsure he was as to how it should be carried out.

Graham exhibited no such confusion: he picked up his rifle and held it ready.

Philip reluctantly did the same.

"Stop!" Graham commanded. "You've come close enough!"

It wouldn't be until later that evening, when he was trying to fall asleep, that Philip would realize he could have volunteered to fetch some food from town and thrown it down the hill for the soldier. Surely there could have been some way to help the man without letting him come any closer.

The soldier stopped again. He was about forty yards away.

"I don't have the flu," he said, shaking his head. "I'm healthy, all right? I'm not going to get anybody sick. Please, just let me sleep in a barn or something."

"For a healthy man, you sure are sneezing and coughing a lot," Graham said.

The man took another step as he opened his mouth to respond, but Graham froze him in place by raising his gun slightly.

"I said that's close enough!"

The soldier looked at Philip imploringly. "I'm coughing and sneezing because my ship capsized and I've been in the forest for two days." He sounded almost angry, but not quite—he seemed to know better than to raise his voice with two armed men. It was more exasperation, fatigue. "I'm telling you, I do not have any flu. I'm not going to get anyone sick."

"You can't control that. If you could, I'd trust you, but you can't. So I don't."

"I'm an American soldier, for God's sake." He eyed Graham accusingly. "I'm asking you to help me."

"And I'm telling you that I would if I could, but I can't."

The soldier hung his head. Then he coughed again. It was thick and phlegmy, as if he'd swallowed something in the Sound and was having trouble dislodging it.

"I don't suppose there's a sheriff in this town I could talk to?"

"Nope."

"What town is this?"

"Quit stalling, buddy. Hit the road. I'm sorry—I am—but my best advice is to head down that road fifteen miles, and when you do get to the next town, be mighty careful. Everybody's sick over there."

The soldier coughed again, then turned around. Finally. Philip closed his eyes for a moment, thankful. Already he had started imagining how he would retell this story to his family and friends.

But the soldier turned back around and faced them once again. Philip's stomach tensed at the look of focus in the soldier's eye, a focus that meant something had been set in motion. Philip tightened his grip on the rifle.

"So I guess you didn't get drafted," the soldier said to Graham bitterly, his eyes narrow.

"Guess not," Graham replied.

The soldier nodded. "Lucky break for you."

"Guess so."

The soldier started limping forward again.

Philip, wide-eyed, looked to Graham.

"I said you've come close enough!" Graham yelled, aiming the rifle dead at the soldier's chest. "Stop, now!"

The soldier shook his head awkwardly. His neck seemed rigid. "I'm not gonna die in the woods."

Philip aimed his rifle, too. He'd never aimed at a human being before, and it felt wholly unnatural, a forbidden pose. He hoped and hoped the soldier would turn around.

"I am not bluffing!" Graham screamed. His voice was different, more panicked.

The soldier was getting closer. Philip thought he could smell the man's stench, water-soaked and putrid from sleeping on mossy logs, lying atop damp twigs and slugs.

The soldier shook his head again, his eyes wet and red. He inched closer and closer to the two guards, to food, to a warm place to rest his weary bones, to salvation.

"Don't make me do this!" Graham cried.

More steps. The soldier opened his mouth and barely mustered a "please."

Graham shot him. The sound and the force of the shot made Philip jump, almost made him pull his trigger in a redundant volley. He saw the soldier's chest burst open, cloth and something the color of newly washed skin flying forward. The soldier staggered back a step and dropped to his left knee.

Then two things happened simultaneously. The place where the soldier's chest had exploded—which for a moment had looked slightly blackened—filled in with a dark red. And his right arm reached up over his shoulder and grabbed for the rifle slung on his back. Philip would remember in his haunted dreams the strangely mechanical motion of the man's arm, as if his soulless body were simply executing one last order.

Graham shot him again, and this time the soldier was blown onto his back. One knee crooked up a bit, but the rest of his body was flat on the ground, facing a sky so blank in its grayness that in that last moment of life he might have seen anything projected upon it: his god, his mother, a lost love, the eyes of the man who had killed him. The grayness was anything and nothing.

Philip wasn't sure how long he stared at the man, how long he kept his gun trained on the air that the man had once occupied. Finally, after several seconds, he managed to move his head and looked to his left, at Graham. Graham's eyes were wide, full of electricity and life.

They were both breathing loudly, Philip realized. But Graham especially: he was sucking in gulps of air, each one larger and louder than the last. Philip lowered his gun, wondering if he should touch his friend's shoulder, do something.

"Oh God," Graham moaned. "Oh God."

Philip didn't know if Graham had ever shot a man. He'd heard about what had happened to Graham in the Everett Massacre, but he wasn't sure if Graham had been a victim only, or an aggressor, too.

"Oh God."

Graham's breathing kept getting louder, and right when Philip was going to ask if he was all right, Graham swallowed. Held his breath and then swallowed that last bit of air, as if completely digesting the scene before him, the act he had just committed. When he started breathing again, he sounded almost normal.

A few seconds passed.

"We're gonna have to talk to Doc Banes," Graham said. Suddenly his voice was steady and serious, unlike his earlier cries. He might as well have been speaking about the condition of some of the machinery in the mill.

"I . . . I think he's dead." Philip's voice cracked.

"Of course he's dead!" Graham snapped, turning to face Philip for the first time. His eyes were furious, and Philip backed off a step. Then Graham's eyes returned to the body, and he paused for a moment.

"We should find out how long we need to stay away from the body before we can bury it," he said. "I don't know if dead bodies can still be contagious, and if so, for how long. We'll have to ask Doc Banes."

Philip nodded, slowly. Despite the wind, the rifle no longer felt cold in his damp hands.

II

The residents of Commonwealth had blocked the road and posted the sign one week earlier, the morning after a town meeting at which Philip Worthy was the youngest attendee.

He had sat there beside his parents in the front row of the fir-scented town hall, a building that had served many roles in the two years since its construction: a church on Sunday afternoons; a dance hall on the first Friday night of each month; a bazaar where the town ladies sold or traded quilts, blankets, and other crafts a few times a year; and a makeshift school until the growing number of children in Commonwealth had necessitated the construction of a schoolhouse next door. Philip's right knee bounced nervously as more men and women filed into the building. It had been cold when they had arrived in the early-evening darkness, but already it had grown warm in the room as people traded rumors and worries, the shuffle of feet and the twitches of fear.

Philip felt awkward at this meeting of adults, as if his presence would be questioned. But Charles had insisted, saying that as "a man of the mill," Philip had an obligation to let his voice be heard on so vital a matter. Philip turned his head to look for Graham in the packed hall, but he couldn't see his friend in the thick forest of faces.

Although Philip felt honored to be working in the mill office with Charles, he suspected the loggers and millworkers resented his easy ascension and looked down on him for his limp, for the wooden block in his left boot. He assumed they thought he wasn't cut out for the arduous labor that kept the town running, that fed everyone and kept them alive out here in the wilderness.

His adopted mother, Rebecca, looked at him and smiled shortly, and he realized he must have been showing his nerves. He sat a bit taller in his chair and stopped bouncing his knee. She reached out and squeezed his hand, then let it go. Her smile seemed forced. The look in her light blue eyes was watchful, as ever.

"How do you think people are going to react?" Philip asked her quietly.

She shook her head, some gray tendrils falling from her hastily arranged bun. Rebecca had been to countless suffrage and political meetings, not only in Commonwealth but also in Timber Falls, in Seattle, and in dozens of towns and cities along the coast. She practically had been raised on such gatherings, accompanying her father, Jay Woodson, a fecund intellectual who had written tomes little read by any but the far-left intelligentsia, provocative disquisitions on the country's coming economic collapse. Rebecca's father had passed away before she married Charles, but she had done her part to build upon her father's legacy, spearheading suffrage groups, antiwar organizations, and now this: the town of Commonwealth, a new hybrid of socialist haven and capitalist enterprise. And yet tonight's meeting was less about politics than survival.

"I don't know," she admitted to Philip. "We'll see."

Graham sat several rows behind the Worthys, having arrived only a few minutes before the meeting was to start. Amelia had stayed at home with the baby—she was more tired than usual on account of her being two months pregnant, a fact the couple hadn't yet revealed to their friends. He rubbed at his neck, the air too hot now that the room was filled to bursting, the movable wooden pews lined with men and women, the walls covered with people leaning, shifting their weight from foot to foot.

Finally, Rebecca whispered to her husband that he should get things started. Sometimes Charles still seemed uncomfortable in his role as head of the mill and de facto leader of the town, she noticed. All those years as the silent bookkeeper in his family mill, years of being overshadowed by his fast-talking older brothers and the domineering patriarch, had been difficult for him to overcome. He had learned how to emerge from the low expectations of others, had become an eloquent spokesman, rallying the faith of a town, but sometimes he needed his wife to remind him of this. Charles nodded without looking at her and stood up.

Charles's hair and beard had gone completely white over the last few years. He was tall and had the broad shoulders of a lumberjack despite the fact that he had spent all his days inside an office. Anyone could have looked at his fingers and seen that they were too free of blemishes, his palms too soft. At fifty-two, he was one of the oldest residents in this town of workingmen, and his eyes were calm and benevolent. His white collared shirt and gray flannel pants were slightly worn in places that he had either failed to notice or chosen not to concern himself with.

He was followed to the podium by Dr. Martin Banes, the town's sole medical authority, and as the two men looked out at the packed hall, voices quieted without a single raised hand or throat clearing. It occurred to Charles as he opened his mouth to speak that he had never heard so many adults so quiet. He stayed silent for an extra second or two, the first invisible syllable hiding somewhere beneath his tongue.

Charles was not the town mayor or its pastor, as Commonwealth lacked either civic or religious leaders. But the town was in many ways his creation, the realization of a dream he and Rebecca had shared years ago while suffering through the Everett general strike, its violence and madness.

Charles had been twenty-four when his father, lured to the great Northwest by stories of endless forests of Douglas fir, had uprooted his family from their home in Maine in 1890. Charles's mother and his younger brother had been buried less than a year earlier, taken by that winter's brutal pneumonia, and Reginald Worthy insisted that this new endeavor was exactly what he and his remaining sons needed. Their destination was the new town of Everett, established just north of Seattle with a well-situated port that, people said, would soon become the Manhattan of the Pacific.

The first years had been torture. Charles would remember with a pained wistfulness the busy streets of Portland—to say nothing of the crowded shops and festive parks of Boston—as he walked past newly constructed houses that looked like a strong gale might knock them down, the taverns whose floors were still covered with inches of sawdust, the streets thick with mud. And the stench of the place—the cows that townspeople kept in their yards as insurance against hard times, the sweat of the millworkers and loggers and carpenters, the poor experiments with plumbing. That far-western outpost of America was decades behind the New England that Charles sorely missed; it felt less like they had crossed the country and more like they had crossed back in time, slogging away in the preternatural darkness of a city without streetlights.

All the more reason to work ceaselessly, trying to forget the world around him by focusing only on what his father wanted him to master: the numbers, the cost of acreage, the price of lumber and the price of shingles, the pay of the millworkers. While his father and his elder brothers did the hobnobbing and the wooing, Charles remained at his desk in his small office, where the sounds of the mill would have made concentration difficult for a man less single-minded.

Still, to Charles, the great family narrative of amassing staggering wealth was a tainted one. He had never been comfortable with the way his family and all their rivals inflated their prices after the San Francisco earthquake of '06, profiting off the suffering and helplessness of others. But worse than that was the bust that had followed, when the mills miscalculated and felled too many trees. Prices had plummeted, men had been laid off by the hundreds, and accountants like Charles had searched desperately for ways to reverse the losses. It was busts like those that made his father's and brothers' unbridled avarice during good times a necessity, they told him: one needed to exploit advantages as a hedge against unforeseen calamities in the future.

To someone as conservative as Charles, this made sense in theory. What didn't, especially when business was thriving, was firing workers who asked for better wages, failing to fix machines until after they had maimed forty or fifty men, and charging exorbitant prices in the general stores they had opened in the timber camps. Certain things simply were not right, Charles said. But his brothers scoffed. You'd understand if you had your own family to care for, they would tell him, shaking their heads. Their wives and children needed clothes, food, tutors, maids. Perhaps a single man could afford to worry about the finer points of worker treatment, but they could not.

Marriage, as it turned out, did not mellow Charles's sentiments, especially since he had married Rebecca, an outspoken schoolteacher with radical leanings. The birth of their daughter only strengthened his belief in living a more moral life, both at the mill and at home. But it wasn't until 1916 that a decade's worth of family squabbles and jealousies finally exploded, as did the town where they resided.

It was the year of the general strike in Everett—the year the lines between the mill owners and the workers were drawn all the more starkly, even as the line between right and wrong was smudged. Charles found the unions' requests not so unreasonable, and he said as much to his father, who threatened to disown his son if he ever repeated such sentiments. Reginald and the other mill owners were enraged by the various acts of skullduggery and sabotage being hatched by the nefarious Wobblies—the Industrial Workers of the World, radical unionists who had chosen Everett as the next stop on their road toward revolution. The brothers shook their heads at Charles, brainwashed by his socialist wife. Rebecca wanted to leave the town, arguing that this was no place for their twelve-year-old daughter to become a woman.

The so-called Everett Massacre forever destroyed whatever creaky bridge had remained between Charles and the other Worthy men. Of course, his father and brothers insisted that it was the strikers who had fired the first shot and most of the following volleys—damn reds will try to burn down the town and rape and pillage their way across the country if we don't stop 'em now. But Charles knew that most of the guns fired at the workers had been paid for by the Commercial Club, a businessmen's group that his brothers chaired. If their fingers hadn't been on any of the triggers, they had pulled the strings from a distance. As the backs of the strikers were broken, the men returned to their jobs and the town stumbled back onto the rocky road from which it had briefly wandered.

But Charles and Rebecca believed the general strike and its violence had brought everyone's true colors to the fore. The couple made their decision. Charles let his brothers buy out his share in the Worthy mill, and he used the money to buy the land for Commonwealth—a distant plot that his father believed to be unworkable. Reginald, outraged by the defection and apoplectic at Charles's plan to build homes for workers and offer them higher wages, never spoke to Charles again. He died one year later.

Charles heard about the passing when he received a letter from one of his sisters-in-law three days after the funeral.

Now, barely two years after the Everett strike, Charles owned a successful new mill supporting a swiftly growing town where no one felt spat upon or cast aside.

Look at this, Rebecca, Charles thought. Look at what we've created—look at what we've done. It was amazing how people could toil so hard but only in extreme moments marvel at the accomplishment. He looked at the crowd, at the tense and nervous eyes—every person in the hall had risked so much by coming out to Commonwealth, taking a chance on a dream Charles had been foolish or stout enough to believe in. He would not let their sacrifices go for nothing.

"Thank you, everyone, for coming," he began. "We need to discuss the influenza that has hit so many other towns so hard."

By then everyone had indeed heard about the so-called Spanish flu, but it was hard to distinguish fact from rumor, truth from gossip, rational fear from paranoia.

What Charles told them was this: a plague that had apparently begun in eastern cities like Boston and Philadelphia had recently spread to the state of Washington. Dr. Banes added that he had received correspondence from a physician friend at an army base outside of Boston who attested to the disease's extreme mortality, its speed of infection, and the strong possibility that it would spread via army bases as young men from all across the land were shuttled to various training cantonments. Fort Jenkins was only thirty miles away, Charles continued, and he had heard from several purchasers that the surrounding towns had been especially hard hit. Businesses had been closed and public gatherings were forbidden. Physicians and nurses were working all hours, but still the disease was spreading faster than could be believed.

"The best anyone can figure is that this is some new form of influenza," Doc Banes told the crowd. He was fifty-six years old, with dark hair that had retained its color except for a shock of white at the front. He wore a bushy mustache that he once waxed into handlebars, but lately it had lapsed into a thick tangle. A good friend of Charles, he had abandoned the possibility of a comfortable but lonely retirement in order to join the Worthys here when they founded the town.

"It's similar to the flu that you know in many of its symptoms—high fever, headache, body ache, cough," the doctor explained. "It hits you quickly and can lead to pneumonia, and it's incredibly contagious. But it's far more severe than usual strains, and it's killing people faster than any flu anyone's ever seen."

Charles said that in his last trip to Timber Falls, he'd talked to several buyers with knowledge of the disease's spread. The flu seemed to have sneaked up on most cities and towns, but Charles could only speculate that Commonwealth had bought a temporary reprieve because it was so cut off from the rest of the country. They had been afforded a glimpse into the suffering of those around them while there was still time to defend themselves.

The hall was eerily silent as Charles and Doc Banes spoke. Many had heard rumors of such a flu but had hoped that the stories were embellished. Hearing the facts voiced by the soft-spoken Charles and the sober-minded Banes caused them to sit all the more still.

Charles told them he had heard that the War Department was even putting a halt to the draft because so many soldiers were sick, and that Seattle had passed a law mandating that anyone walking in public wear a gauze mask over his mouth and nose. Other towns had outlawed spitting and shaking hands.

Charles's voice gradually strengthened, filling in the empty spaces that had been created by the people's silence. "And as far as I'm concerned—as the manager of the mill but also as a man of this town, as a husband and father—we need to do whatever we can to make sure we stay uninfected."

"How do we do that?" A man called out. "You got a cure for us, Doc?"

Banes shook his head, but Charles spoke for him. "The only way not to get sick is to prevent the flu from getting into Commonwealth." He paused. "I propose we close the town to outsiders and halt all trips out of town. No more errands to Timber Falls or anywhere else, as that only makes it possible to catch the flu from people in those towns and bring it back here. No one leaves Commonwealth, and no one comes in, until the flu has passed."

For a moment the crowd was silent. Then came the sounds of hundreds of voices—some of them low murmurs between spouses, others exclamations, some of them disbelieving laughter. Charles saw Philip turn around and glance at all those heads nodding or sternly shaking, all those brows furrowed or eyes widening.

"For how long?" someone shouted above all the others.

Charles opened his mouth and the voices grew quiet, awaiting his response. But Charles stopped himself, deferring to the doctor.

"We can't be sure," Doc Banes said. "Probably no longer than a month—the flu moves quickly, and I would guess that after a month, the surrounding towns would have returned to health."

"You would *guess*?"

Banes looked back at Charles somewhat sheepishly. He wished he could be more certain, but he couldn't. No one could. What was happening seemed unlike any epidemic he'd experienced. He was already afraid that he had said too much, that he had given voice to fears he didn't fully understand. Now those fears would only be multiplied by the number of skeptical and frightened faces before him.

Charles held up his hands. "With the general store fully stocked, as it is now, we have enough provisions to keep the town closed off for nearly two months. If extreme measures need to be taken, some of us have livestock. Like all of you, I hope we won't need to wait as long as two months, or even one. But I believe in being prepared and not taking senseless risks. If we don't do something drastic, the flu will infect this town, and if it hits us as hard as it has other towns, there's no way we could keep the mill operational until it passes. To say nothing of the lives lost." He paused. "People, I believe that if the flu reaches Commonwealth, the mill will fail. And the town will follow."

"What about our lumber buyers?" a man called. "Can they still come in the town?"

Charles shook his head. "No, and that means not selling any lumber until we reopen the town. I will contact all our buyers and explain. I know they won't like it, but I also know that with the war demand for lumber being so high, they'll still be waiting for us when we reopen. Closing the town will make the mill's finances a bit tight, but it can survive."

The only visitors remote Commonwealth received were the ships that snaked along the river to the mill, picking up lumber, as well as some buyers who rode or drove into town for meetings with Charles. Both could be halted indefinitely. With no bank in town, most people subsisted on bartering and trades, in addition to visits to the general store, where their purchases were deducted from their mill paychecks.

If Charles couldn't travel to the banks in Timber Falls, he wouldn't be able to pay the workers at the end of the month, but they would have his assurance that he would do so as soon as the flu passed. And hadn't he already won their trust, giving each of them a house in return for the first few months of labor? Few residents had any savings, as most of their paychecks still went toward what they owed Charles for their homes, and those who did have bank accounts in Timber Falls would not have access to them during the quarantine. But to Charles, these seemed minor and necessary sacrifices.

"What if someone from Timber Falls comes in without hearing about the quarantine?"

Charles offered his idea about posting a sign, blocking the road, and stationing guards. He knew this might cause objections, so he tried to make light of it. "Guards would scarcely be necessary, as we have so few visitors. It would strictly be a precaution."

After a brief pause, someone else stood. "Mr. Worthy, I appreciate all you've done for us, and you've cert'nly given me a fairer shake 'n anyone else ever has. But, all due respect, havin' guards is just a bit too similar to the kindsa work camps I came here to get away from." The man sat down quickly, disappearing into the sea of heads, several of which were nodding in agreement.

Charles was unprepared for that remark. He had expected that some would oppose his idea, but hearing himself compared to the types of men who ran prisonlike factories wounded him. He felt his cheeks redden.

But before he could reply, a man in the row before Graham's stood up to speak, wool cap in his hands. He had a thick brown beard and hair that his wife had tried to comb earlier that evening, barely succeeding. "I lost my first wife to typhoid thirteen years ago," he told them. "Lotta people had it, and lotta people died. If something like that's happening again, I say we close the town." Several people murmured in response as he sat back down.

Charles nodded. He too lived with the memories of past epidemics, including the awful winter of '89, when he had lost his mother and his younger brother, Timothy. The sting of those deaths had faded, yet Charles had found himself thinking of Timothy more over the past few years, as the adoption of Philip had brought a boy of roughly the same age into his home. Soon Philip would be older than Timothy had ever lived to be.

A new speaker stood far in the back. "So if we close the town," he said, his voice a deep bass, "I can't see my family?"

There were a number of cautious husbands who'd initially come to work in the strange new mill but left their families behind, cared for by grandparents or friends in nearby towns. And some single men were courting women from Timber Falls, hoping to win their hearts and also their confidence in that mysterious hamlet deep in the woods.

"I understand your concern," Charles said. "Any man in such a situation can of course leave Commonwealth if he wishes, and when the flu has passed, I promise you will have a job to return to. But until the flu passes, you will not be allowed back in."

The man, who had remained standing, looked at Charles evenly. Charles knew, most likely, that he traveled to Timber Falls to see his family every Sunday, the most glorious day of his week. His choice was to abandon his family to possible sickness or turn his back on money that his family couldn't afford to lose.

Graham stood up suddenly, then paused, as if realizing he'd never spoken to so large a group before.

"I don't like the idea of being kept from coming and going as I choose," he said. "But I like the idea of seeing my family fall sick even less." Other men had sounded rushed, but Graham spoke slowly. Many heads nodded in agreement. "And I might not like the idea of guards either, but this ain't a bunch of Pinkertons and cops we're talking about—it'll be *us* doing the guarding." More nods. "I for one'll be proud to protect this town."

He sat back down. A man voiced a "Me, too." As did another and another. The hall echoed with the pledges.

Philip nodded. "Me, too," he was saying.

Rebecca saw Philip's lips move and she looked away, at her husband, who again seemed calm as a snow-swept field. The two of them had already argued about this at home, behind the closed bedroom door. To her, closing the town seemed the antithesis of everything they had worked for. The founding of Commonwealth had not been an act of rejecting the world, she believed, but of showing the world how it could be improved, so that others could follow their example. If they closed their doors—if they approved this reverse quarantine—they would seal themselves off from that world. She also worried about her family's health, and she had seen those haunted expressions of fear in Timber Falls when she accompanied Charles on his last trip to that suddenly desolate town. But she could not bring herself to support a quarantine.

She wanted to stand up. She wanted to say something, anything. She had spoken before larger crowds than this, crowds both supportive and hostile. But Charles had made his opinions plain, and the idea of making a marital disagreement public seemed untoward, if not downright wrong. She felt an uncharacteristic paralysis even as her heart raced.

Philip sat beside her silently as the meeting continued, more men and women voicing their concerns, but most of them in favor of a quarantine. After the silence between comments grew longer, Charles spoke again.

"I call for a voice vote," he said.

Rebecca's palms were sweaty; she rubbed one of them on her wool skirt. She wanted to stand. She wanted to stand. She stayed in her seat.

"All those in favor of the town closing its doors until the flu has passed," Charles proclaimed, "say 'aye.' "

The hall shook in response. Beside Rebecca, Philip voted quietly.

"All against, say 'nay.' "

In the hall were many dissenters, but they represented only a small fraction of the total in favor. The sound of the nays was heavy with defeatism, those voters having already realized that they were in the minority.

Rebecca voted nay, almost under her breath, aware that it barely mattered. The only person who heard her was Philip, who eyed her with concern.

Her husband nodded, the hall growing louder again as people spoke to one another, seemingly congratulating themselves on their decisiveness. To Rebecca, it was an empty happiness, for they had succeeded in an act of only ambivalent courage, some moral compromise whose weight, she feared, would begin to feel uncomfortable on their shoulders.

Next Charles discussed logistics: blocking the road and devising a schedule for the guards. After the meeting had adjourned and most people began exiting the stuffy building, a line formed in the left-hand aisle as men signed their names to volunteer for shifts. Rebecca wondered if as many men would have come forward if Graham hadn't thrown the gauntlet at their feet. Perhaps some did so out of a sense of adventure, while others did so out of fear of what would happen if someone less trustworthy were given such a responsibility. She looked at some of the faces and guessed that they were driven by a sense of shame that they weren't fighting in Europe. Some had registered for service but had been designated "essential war workers" owing to their duties at the mill; others had willfully turned their backs on what they considered a crooked war. Standing guard would prove to them and their families that they were indeed courageous men.

Beside her, Philip stood, and as he took his first step toward the line, Rebecca started to raise her hand instinctively to grab his shoulder, to pull him to his seat and tell him he was making a mistake. He was only sixteen! He should not stand out there and hold a gun against whoever might happen upon the town. But before she could grab him, he had stepped beyond her, into that long line, sidling up beside Graham, who nodded at his unofficial brother and patted him twice on the shoulder.

For many years Rebecca would remember that shoulder clasp and the way Philip's back seemed to straighten under the weight of Graham's hand.

III

What had the soldier's name been? How old was he? Where did his family live, and how recently had he written to them? Were they reading his most recent letter now, trying not to tear up at the end of it, hoping that another would soon follow?

Philip's mind raced. As much as he tried not to do this to himself, as much as he tried to focus on the supper on his plate, on his stepmother's voice, he could not stop himself from wondering about the man whose life he had helped bring to a violent and completely unexpected halt.

"Are you all right?" Rebecca asked.

If everything were all right, Philip thought, then there would be no need to post armed guards by the town entrance. There would be no need for the rifles, and there would have been no need to shoot the soldier. The soldier would be sitting beside him right now, happily eating Rebecca's cooking and telling them all for the tenth time how thankful he was for their hospitality.

"I'm fine."

They'd ask the soldier about the war and he'd shrug, act uncomfortable with all the attention at first, but once he started talking about it, he'd find it difficult to stop. He'd tell them about his training and the rumors circulating through the camp about where they'd be deployed. He'd tell them he wasn't in any hurry to get to the front but that once he got there, he'd be honored to do his duty for God and country.

Rebecca put her hand on Philip's shoulder. "Try to eat some."

"Sorry," Philip said.

"Don't be sorry. Just remember to take care of yourself. You have to eat."

He ate. It took effort at first, but the first few bites awakened his stomach. The stew was warm and heavily salted, and dark enough for Philip to be less than sure whether there was any meat in it or if it was just vegetables. What day was today? Was it Wheatless Monday, Meatless Tuesday, Porkless Thursday? Every grocery store in America displayed those signs. Save food for the soldiers, everyone said. "Wheatless days in America make for sleepless nights in Germany." Not that Philip would complain—he ate much better with the Worthys than he ever had with his own mother.

Outside it was already dark, the autumn sun chased away by the cold winds.

Philip tried not to think of the soldier. Instead, think of this house, the people inside it. Think of today.

"It's Wednesday," he blurted out.

"Yes?" Rebecca answered, her eyes watchful and warm.

He thought for a moment. "Are you sorry you can't be at your meetings?" Typically, Wednesday evenings were when Rebecca would be meeting with fellow suffragists in Everett or Seattle, or maybe in some of the smaller towns, hoping to build up the movement with new recruits.

She nodded. "I am, but we're all making sacrifices now." Then she found a way to smile at the situation. "I'm sure the groups can survive without me for a few weeks."

It was the second Wednesday since the quarantine had begun, so this would be the second week of meetings Rebecca had missed. She did not appreciate the forced inactivity; she sorely missed those suffrage meetings and rallies, as she had missed the rallies for the Woman's Peace Party, rallies they'd held in the months leading up to America's joining the war. She and other WPP members had made speeches and exhorted people to vote for the peace candidates, to fight against the pressures that the Preparedness Movement was exerting, those thinly disguised warmongers who wanted the country to build more warships and cannons and guns *just in case.* She missed those meetings especially, sitting with like-minded men and women, people who felt, like her, that no good could come of war, especially *this* war, fought for no justifiable reasons beyond those lies spread by the propagandists. But once Wilson had declared war and Congress passed the Espionage and Sedition Acts, suddenly the WPP was illegal—Americans weren't allowed to preach peace anymore. Now everyone was supposed to sing happy songs about fighter pilots and doughboys, hate the kaiser and love their president.

Philip nodded at her. "Hopefully you'll get to be out there again soon."

"In the meantime, I can always write plenty of letters," she said, smirking ruefully. "I just can't mail them yet."

"Maybe you'll get suffrage anyway," he said with a slight smile. "Maybe they'll pass the law during the flu."

She laughed. "That'd be nice, but I doubt it."

The door opened, and in walked Laura, Philip's adoptive sister. She was two years younger than Philip, with straight amber hair that might have been blonder had she lived someplace with more sunlight. She had brown eyes that could look incredibly mean when she wanted them to, which they often had in Philip's first few years with the family. Laura wasn't a bad person, Philip eventually learned, she was just used to being an only child. Having to accept an adopted brother—an *older* adopted brother, for goodness' sake—at the age of nine had been a difficult task.

She sat down on a chair opposite Philip and looked at him carefully, showing more compassion than she usually permitted herself.

"Hi," she said.

"Hi."

"I was thinking about making a cake later," Laura said.

Cake? This was something she did only on his birthday. Because everyone was conserving sugar until the war ended, the thought was downright treasonous. "Great. Why today?"

She looked away, as if uncomfortable with her own act of charity. "I just wanted to." A pause. "I thought you'd want some."

"Thanks."

Laura had not been told about the dead soldier. Their mother had explained that a man had tried to enter the town but that Graham and her brother had persuaded him to leave, and that the confrontation had left Philip exhausted.

"Welcome," Laura said. In the background, Rebecca tried to make herself invisible. "You don't need to help me with my math tonight, either."

"No, I said I would." Philip was afraid of changing his routine. It was awkward enough eating supper alone, but his guard stint had lasted until eight, and Charles was at an emergency meeting with the rest of the guards at the town hall.

After Laura went back to her room, Philip forced himself to finish his food. This stew would have saved the soldier's life, he thought. If it had been placed at the bottom of the hill moments before the soldier's arrival, he would have eaten it and then continued down the road. If they had known he was coming, if they somehow could have anticipated the day's events, he would be alive and his stomach would be full, and Philip's wouldn't be queasy.

When he finished, Rebecca told him she'd clean his bowl, which he politely tried to resist. Despite their years together, he still felt somewhat awkward around her. He had known that the way his own mother had raised him had been unconventional—taking him from town to town, scrounging for money, blaming him for their troubles—but he'd grown used to it over twelve years. Even the smallest acts of kindness from Rebecca left him somewhat unsure how to react, how thankful to be and how wary.

He sat back down at the dining room table as Rebecca cleaned the kitchen. The room was cold and quiet, and the windows strained against another gust of wind.

After waiting by the fallen soldier for nearly half an hour—long enough to determine that he didn't have any accomplices lagging behind—Graham had told Philip to head back to town and find the doctor, but not to tell anyone else what had happened.

Commonwealth was a small town, and most people knew each other—nearly everyone knew Philip and whose son he was—but fortunately, not many realized he was on guard duty that day. The few people he passed merely nodded to him, and he nodded back without meeting their eyes. For most of his quick walk through town, he saw only the soldier, his chest exploding and his empty body toppling back.

Philip was rushing down unpaved streets that were still thick and muddy from the previous evening's rain, past identical houses lining the road. Everything in Commonwealth was jarringly new. Due to the hastiness with which the town had been constructed, some porches leaned a bit too far to one side, and some buildings bore the spotty marks of a hasty paint job, but there were no dilapidated storefronts or vacant lots, no broken windows or collapsed roofs. The town was so freshly ensconced in the woods that it smelled strongly of the forest, the Douglas fir and red cedar, the salal and toadstools dotting the nearby riverbed. Mixed with this was the smell of so many men sweating in a stuffy mill, emerging at the end of the day breaded with sawdust, the scent of torn bark and wet wool. Moments ago the cicadalike thrum of mill saws would have echoed through the colonnades of trees, but the closing whistle had already sounded, and Commonwealth was so quiet Philip could hear the river dancing over moss-covered rocks.

And so quiet that Philip's voice, when he entered Banes's house and found the doctor alone, sounded deafening: "We shot a man trying to come to town. A soldier. He was sick. He's dead."

That was how it came out, the words a jumble, all the facts except the main one—we killed someone—seeming so unimportant. He was a soldier. He was young. He sneezed and coughed a lot. He said please. He started to cry right before Graham pulled the trigger. He had a limp, like me.

Banes followed Philip back to the guards' post, a good distance beyond the front of the town, past a row of fir trees that all but concealed the buildings from view. The doctor nodded when he saw how far away the body lay. All of his experience told him to go forward, to kneel down beside the body, but he knew he couldn't. He knew what the other people in his profession all across the country were going through right now, knew about the tired repetitions of futile acts, and he didn't want this to happen to Commonwealth.

"We'll leave him there for twenty-four hours," Banes decided. "Then we can bury him."

Philip was dreading the idea of burying the soldier, but at the same time, he wanted to be one of the ones to do it. He owed the soldier the respect of participating in a proper burial. Philip looked to his side, at the empty chair that the soldier could have been occupying, and he wondered what the man's family would have said at his funeral.

"I guess you were right," Philip said as he stood to leave the dining room. "I guess it was a mistake to go out there."

"I never said that," Rebecca answered after a pause.

"I know. I could tell you thought it, though."

Rebecca dried her hands on her apron. "I never thought you made a mistake. I thought you had a very hard decision to make—we all do right now."

Philip nodded, then excused himself to the bathroom, leaving her alone in the cold kitchen. She sighed, realizing she hadn't responded as well as she could have. But she was angry, and would it have been right to try and conceal her anger, to coat it with maternal sympathy and false warmth?

She hadn't believed what Charles had told her that afternoon about the soldier, had found it impossible to visualize Graham firing on another man—and with young Philip standing beside him! But then when she had seen the look in Philip's eyes, she knew it was the truth.

How could this happen? Years ago her two elder sisters had run off to join a commune, and Rebecca had hated them for running away, for cutting themselves off and never responding to her letters, even when she wrote to them of their father's illness. Rebecca and her younger sister, Maureen, had cared for their father in his dying days. Maybe their little commune had been beyond the reach of any postmaster, but that possibility did nothing to salve the pain she had felt, the loneliness she had seen in her father's eyes as he realized he would never see his girls again. Rebecca had hated them for their disinterest in the rest of the world, their silent shrugging at other people's plight. And now her own community was doing the same thing.

Rebecca wasn't sure if she was letting her anger at the country—at Wilson, at this horrible war—turn into anger about the town; she wasn't sure if they were separate issues or two sides of the same coin. She and her fellow suffragists had worked so hard, come so close, but they had failed. If only they had won the vote, used it in the 1916 elections, maybe they could have made the difference. Women never would have allowed this nation to turn to war, never would have let the politicians take their sons away for battles on the other side of the earth. All the letters they had written, the marches, the parades down the streets of Seattle, that feeling of absolute certainty that this was *right.* That incredible new word, *feminism,* still sounded strange to her ears but inspired her. It was a word she wanted her daughter to hold close to her heart as well. They had come so far and done so much, but they had still fallen short, and now this. The mothers were voteless and couldn't stop their sons from being fed into the meat grinders of Belgium and France.

Then again, maybe their votes wouldn't have mattered. After all, Wilson had promised not to drag America onto Europe's battlefields, yet here the country was at war, and the advocates for peace were being branded unpatriotic, radical. People were being jailed simply for speaking the truth, for proclaiming that this was a rich man's war, a war for the bankers who had loaned so many millions to the Allies that they couldn't stand to see them lose, couldn't risk the loans going into default. So feed us your workingmen, feed us your young boys who can barely read and write, and let us plug them into the trenches, let them die for J. P. Morgan.

Rebecca's last trip to the post office in Timber Falls had yielded a letter from her younger sister, and Rebecca still seethed to think of what Maureen had written. Maureen met twice weekly with other ladies in Seattle to roll bandages and prepare comfort kits for the soldiers, and she helped with the Liberty Loan drives, posting enthusiastic signs all over the city. She went to grocery stores to tell people the importance of food conservation, and just the other day they had told the police about a woman who was clearly ignoring the call, hoarding meats and sugar. Maureen and her friends met each week and made lists of neighbors who hadn't yet bought any Liberty Bonds, neighbors who might possibly be antiwar agitators, and turned the lists over to the authorities. Their lists had already led to seven arrests, she happily reported.

Ah, Maureen. Blessed with three daughters and a son not yet thirteen, thus safely insulated from the war. Of course Maureen was making sure her fellow ladies were enthusiastically in support of the war. Perhaps suffrage wouldn't have changed a thing. Maybe the Maureens of the world far outnumbered the Rebeccas, and this Great War would lead only to more wars, to be repeated infinitely.

Rebecca stood at the kitchen window, gazing at her own reflection and the faint shapes of the houses lining the streets. In other houses on streets just like this, children were sick, parents were sick, and beds belonging to young men were empty, perhaps permanently so. This was America, she thought, tears welling up in her eyes. This was what America had become. She dug her fingernails into her palms, willing the tears away.

Charles opened the front door, unbuttoning his coat and leaning forward to peck his wife on the cheek. Philip entered the kitchen and said hello as Charles removed the bowler that had once been black but had faded to gray. Rebecca left the room, knowing that Charles would want to talk to Philip in private.

Charles asked Philip how he was doing and received a shrug in response.

"I'm sorry you had to be a part of that." Charles had always had a soft voice, even when he was Philip's age. It was as if the rest of his body had aged all these years just so it could catch up to his voice, its calm tenor and weathered hue.

"It's all right," Philip said, though he looked like he was thinking, It's all wrong.

Charles nodded. He hadn't seen Philip look so vulnerable since the first time he'd seen Philip's eyes, in that hospital room nearly five years ago. Philip now sat at the kitchen table with his hands at his sides, as if he thought he might need to defend himself. His face was white and his eyes were slightly wider than usual, evidence that the shock of that afternoon hadn't worn off. Would it ever? Charles was becoming an old man; he had lost loved ones to disease and seen millworkers cut down by grisly accidents, had seen severed limbs and had touched frozen corpses and had heard the choking last breaths of his own mother and younger brother, but he had never seen anyone murdered. He had fought in no wars, had never needed to defend himself from some malignant aggressor. Though his association with his father's mill had caused him to feel somehow responsible for the violence of the Everett strike, he had never felt the punishing weight of an individual's death on his conscience. Fathers were never supposed to say that they didn't know what their sons were going through, but Charles was acutely aware of the fact that his son was stumbling through terrain where he himself had never trod.

So he nodded, closely watching Philip's eyes, which were avoiding his. Had the quarantine been a mistake? Charles should have known when he helped sway the town into this decision that it would so quickly come to roost under his own roof. It seemed some odd type of justice, centered there in the middle of a situation that until then had seemed to lack any sense of justice or irony or symbolism whatsoever, nothing but chaos and death.

"You two did the right thing," Charles said.

"I really didn't do anything," Philip replied. "Graham did everything. I was . . ." His voice trailed off.

"You may think so," Charles said, "but you helped by being there. I'm sure you made it easier for Graham."

Too late, he realized that was the last thing Philip wanted to hear.

"You did the right thing," Charles started over. "The man was sick, and if you'd let him in, half this town would be sick within days."

"He could've been sick just from sleeping outside all night. We don't know for sure he had the flu."

Charles shook his head, politely but firmly. "Right now nearly everyone in this country who's sick has the flu. Especially in Washington. I'm sure he had it."

I'm sure. Philip looked like he couldn't understand the concept of certainty right then. "I hope he did," he said.

"What you had to do out there was hard," Charles acknowledged, as if he had any idea. "I wish it had been me instead of you. But just because it was hard doesn't mean it was wrong."

Philip nodded again.

When Charles opened his mouth to say something more, Philip stood up too abruptly. "I should go to the store—Rebecca asked me to fetch a few things for her."

Philip clearly wanted to be alone. Charles waited a moment, feeling that he was abdicating some responsibility by letting his son leave before providing him with some nugget of paternal wisdom. But he let him go nonetheless because, God help him, he could think of nothing else to say.

IV

"And how is my favorite customer this evening?" That was how Flora Metzger greeted everyone who walked into Metzger's General Store, and she smiled at the sawyer who didn't look a day over eighteen.

"Jus' fine," he said. He gave Flora his order—molasses, cornmeal, potatoes, and any fruit she had—and she rummaged through the back shelves, whistling to herself.

"You look thinner, young man," she said when she returned. "Your wife ain't feeding you well?" Flora herself was well fed, with curly gray hair that hung down around her fleshy cheeks, and matching gray eyes that saw all that transpired within her store.

"She's a fine cook," the man said, holding back a smile.

"I hope you lie better to her than you lie to me." Flora chuckled as she scribbled a receipt. "Handsome man like you"—she winked at him—"I'm sure your wife has other skills."

"Good night, ma'am," the man said, blushing as he shuffled off.

Flora knew the way millworkers and loggers spoke among themselves—you could overhear quite a lot if you had a mind to—and she delighted in embarrassing them with the same sort of talk. Even the men who'd been shopping at her store for two years were hardly used to her banter; she always seemed to find the right comment for making the toughest of toughs turn red before he finished his transaction.

Up to the desk stepped Leonard Thibeault. Flora had known what he wanted as soon as she spotted his head looming behind the other customer. Leonard was a tall man, and he seemed to assume his height gave him an impressive air, that no one would think to doubt his strength or steadfastness. He had a long oval face and a bush of brown hair that added a couple of inches to his stature.

"How's my favorite customer this evening?" Her voice was thinner this time. His wry and somewhat off-kilter smile was all the answer she needed.

"Bottle o' whiskey, if y' don't mine." He had a low and rolling voice, the edges of his words dampened by a French Canadian accent that thirty years in the West had not erased.

She nodded and went to the back shelves. When she returned with the bottle, she noticed that Leonard wasn't wearing a jacket despite the cold, and that one of the buttons on his brown flannel shirt had been skipped so that the shirttails hung at different lengths. Such a sight normally would have won a gibe from Flora, but Leonard seemed beneath such remarks.

"You might want to slow down the frequency of these purchases," Flora advised as she filled out the receipt. Her eyes were on the paper, but she felt him swaying like a lone pine on a windy day. How he managed to drink this much without losing a finger or an arm to one of the saws was a mystery to her, some enchanted luck of the foolish. "You know we aren't getting any new shipments till the flu's passed."

She would've expected that someone who loved his liquor would learn to use it sparingly in times like these, to preserve the supply. But then again, someone like Leonard would probably figure a way to make moonshine out of pine needles if necessary.

When she looked back up at him, she saw him staring at one of the walls. He might have been reading a government flyer about sugar conservation if his eyeballs had been moving. He hadn't heard a thing she'd said.

"Thanks, Flora," he said, pocketing the slip and cradling the bottle as he swayed to the door.

Philip smelled alcohol on the breath of the tall man who nearly walked into him as he left the store. The man didn't apologize or even seem to notice as he veered off, busily opening a bottle.

"How is my favorite customer this evening?" Flora asked as Philip approached the counter. Behind her, Alfred Metzger had emerged from the cellar and was rummaging about in the aisles. He was always stocking and restocking and counting and recounting what was left on the shelves while Flora presided over the store. His height and thin frame made him his wife's opposite. Most customers saw his face only on the rare occasions when she wasn't manning the place.

"Fine, ma'am, and you?"

"I'm two days older than when you saw me last. That ain't good."

"But you look at least two days younger." Something about Flora Metzger brought out Philip's brash side.

She smiled and put her hand to her breast in mock flattery. "You always know how to make a fat lady's day." This was part of why Philip had wanted to visit the store, so Flora's forceful personality could make him forget about the soldier for a few moments.

"You look taller," she said. "You grown in the last two days?"

"Haven't checked. My pants still fit."

"Well, when they stop fitting, you come in here and I'll get you furnished right. I want my favorite customer looking sharp, you hear?"

"Yes, ma'am."

"Now, what do you want?"

Philip enjoyed this banter. One of his tasks as mill accountant was to visit the general store to collect production numbers and sales slips; trading goodhearted jabs with Flora certainly beat discussing volume with the laconic foremen.

"Flour and cornmeal, please."

She sighed mightily as she lifted herself from her chair. "How many?"

Philip thought. They really needed only one bag each, but with the town closed off, the store wouldn't be replenishing its shelves anytime soon. "Two bags each, please."

She heaved the bags onto the desk one at a time, then reclaimed her imperial position on the chair. After Philip signed his name by the cost in her book, she eyed him. "You preoccupied with something? You've already been in my store a full two minutes, and you haven't asked after my daughter yet."

Elsie Metzger was fifteen years old and one of the best-looking girls in town, as far as Philip was concerned. He tried to make his smile disappear, but it was impossible. "I . . . don't always ask after her."

"Oh, she's not good enough for you?"

"No, that's not what I—" He shook his head again, realizing he couldn't win. "So how's Elsie?"

"Lazy. She needs fresh air." Flora leaned her head back and called out, "Elsie! Come help Philip Worthy carry his purchases home!"

Philip shook his head. "No, please, I'll be fine." Could there be anything more insulting than needing a girl's help carrying groceries? He heard movement from one of the back rooms, so he started stacking the bags of flour and meal.

"Oh, hush. She's just back there twiddling her thumbs anyway. The walk'll do her some good."

"Mrs. Metzger, really, I don't need any help carrying this."

Flora raised one eyebrow. "I think you need help in more ways than you realize."

She'd barely finished saying that when Elsie came through the side door. Philip knew that most of the other young men in town didn't share his high opinion of the tomboyish Elsie, but that didn't make him question his judgment in the slightest. He knew her well because she was Laura's best friend. He knew what types of jokes she found funny and which made her blush; he knew that when she was playing cards, any faint wrinkles on her forehead meant she had a good hand and that a strangely serene expression meant she was trying to mask a bad hand. She hadn't been one of the prettier girls when she was younger, her thick eyebrows casting too dark a shadow over her eyes, her curly brown hair too disheveled. But she'd reached the age when some of the formerly overlooked were beginning to take their rightful places as the beauties they'd always been meant to be. Elsie's eyes glowed with an intelligent, mysterious light, and she was becoming vain enough to keep her hair more or less under control. She'd always had an uncommonly deep voice, but nowadays it seemed softer.

Philip had started to lift the sacks from the counter when Flora clamped her hands upon them. "I said Elsie's helping you, and that's final. I don't want anything falling and tearing open and going to waste—especially not while we're under quarantine."

He had once dropped a sack of flour, more than a year ago, and Flora had never forgotten it. But this was the first time she'd gone so far as making Elsie help him.

He finally accepted the inevitable. "I'll get the flour," he told Elsie, who lifted the meal.

"Tell Charles I said hello, and tell Rebecca she's not giving my daughter enough homework," Flora called after them.

With her back to her mother, Elsie rolled her eyes at Philip.

After Philip had followed her out the door, Alfred's voice rose from deep in the aisles. "You playing matchmaker, Flora?"

"Do you have a problem with Philip Worthy?"

"I only have a problem with your meddling."

"I don't meddle. I instigate. Big difference."

"My mom likes teasing you," Elsie said as they walked along Commonwealth's main street, dark except for the light emanating from people's homes.

"She likes teasing everybody."

Elsie nodded. "True, but you especially."

"Why's that?"

"I don't know. 'Cause you aren't a logger or millworker, maybe. You're not like most of the other fellows in town."

Philip's fingertips were already starting to tingle—they did that sometimes, a legacy of his accident five years ago. Damage he would have to live with, the doctor at the Everett hospital had said in an uninterested tone. At least the tingling meant they were still there, as opposed to his left foot, which had been amputated. The longer he carried the sacks, the more his fingertips tingled; soon the sensation would spread to his hands and up his arms, reaching his elbows. It didn't happen as often as it used to, partly because he was stronger and partly because he had learned how to function within his new limitations. The feeling was something between pain and numbness, but he knew from experience that if he pushed himself too far, his arms would grow unresponsive and the bags would come crashing down.

"I really can take those sacks for you," he told her. "You can head back if you want."

When had he started getting so nervous around her? He'd known her for five years: when he'd first been adopted by the Worthys, he had wasted many afternoons with Laura and Elsie, playing card games and taking bike rides, wandering along the river to collect driftwood. The three of them would sit on the stones at the water's edge, watching the river drivers walk across the gently bouncing logs as they floated down the river, calmly riding them like Aladdin on his carpet.

"Hey, this is my way to get away from my mother for a few minutes. Don't deprive me of it."

Philip nodded. "So my mom's not giving you enough homework?"

"Don't you dare tell her that. My mother calls me lazy if she catches me being idle for two seconds. Between school and the store, I do more work than she does, sitting there gossiping with everyone who walks in her door."

Although he liked working with Charles at the mill, Philip missed school, because he missed being around Elsie. He missed talking to her, missed looking at her while she concentrated on a test or stared out the window, lost. There were few girls her age in town, but even if Commonwealth had been overrun with young maidens he still would have plotted ways to accidentally cross paths with Elsie.

"So what happened out there this afternoon?" For all her criticism of her mother, Elsie did share her mother's hunger for gossip.

"What have you heard?" Because Mrs. Metzger hadn't asked him about the soldier, Philip had assumed the news hadn't gotten around. But maybe even she knew there were some things you shouldn't joke about.

"I heard some men saying someone tried to get into town."

Philip nodded. "Someone did. He was sick, so we made him leave—fired a couple warning shots, and he got the message."

That was what they'd been told to say. Charles's idea, and the doctor had agreed. No need to worry everyone, no need to complicate things. Only the guards needed to know. Charles had told Rebecca, so maybe it was assumed that the men would tell their wives and that their hushed and conspiratorial whispers would stay in the chamber of matrimonial secrets. But Philip sure wasn't supposed to tell anyone. That he knew.

"How close did he get?"

"Not close enough to make us sick." But Philip wasn't sure—what if he was carrying around a tiny piece of the soldier right now, in his lungs, his blood, his heart?

"What was he doing here? He didn't say if he was going to come back with more soldiers, did he?"

Philip and Graham had thought this question might arise, but Charles and Doc Banes had dismissed it. So Philip chose to belittle his own concern by smiling and lightly chiding Elsie. "I really don't think any soldiers are trying to take over our town. He didn't look like a Heinie."

She smiled, even though her grandparents had come over from Germany. Her parents had assured her that the incessant anti-German comments of the day didn't apply to them. "So who fired the shots?"

"We both did—Graham shot one, and I shot one." He said that quickly, twitching his head before he said it.

"I've just never shot at anyone, is all." Like many girls in Commonwealth, Elsie had fired a gun a few times, but she seemed to find the idea of firing at another person strangely thrilling.

Philip tried to clarify the lie. "We didn't shoot *at* him. We shot into the air. Just as a warning."

"Did he have a gun, too? He was a soldier, right?"

Damn, you have a lot of questions, he thought. "Mustn't've had one with him, I guess."

Elsie nodded. She planned on becoming a teacher in two years, when she finished her own schooling, and Rebecca had encouraged her to be curious and inquisitive, especially when things didn't make sense.

They walked on in silence. Philip's arms were aching, but he resisted the temptation to rearrange the bags and let Elsie see he was struggling.

"I heard in Seattle they aren't even letting people go outside without masks on," Elsie said. "If you don't have a mask, the trolley won't pick you up. You can even get arrested for it."

"I heard that, too. Not about the arresting, but I guess that makes sense."

"They've canceled school in most towns, and closed any other places people get together."

Philip nodded. "I wonder what teachers are doing, then."

"Getting sick, most likely. Or tending sick husbands and children."

"I guess we're lucky, huh?" But as his comment hung in the air, Philip thought how strange it sounded. He'd meant lucky that the flu hadn't invaded their town yet, but the flu was still laying siege to it, so that didn't seem so lucky. And what had happened today sure as hell wasn't lucky.

She seemed to know what he'd been thinking. "It's pretty rotten, isn't it? First war, and now everybody sick."

"They say we're winning the war." But by the time they could get another newspaper, Lord only knew what would be happening in Europe. Were the soldiers healthy? The one from that afternoon certainly was not. Philip had a sudden image of a gray battlefield bereft of explosions or gunfire but filled with the writhing bodies of the sick and dying.

"I know we'll win, but still," Elsie said. "Two rotten things happening at once. Makes you wish you could run away someplace where none of this is happening."

"It's happening pretty much everywhere, I think."

"I know. I just wish there was someplace to escape."

But as they walked in silence, they came to the same strange realization: the closed-off town of Commonwealth was precisely this place. There was no war, no pestilence. People around the globe were dying, dying from flu and pneumonia and aerial bombings and bayonets, but in Commonwealth, the last town on earth, people were safe. This was the place to run to, and they were already here. All they could do was wait.

By the time they reached his house, Philip's hands were almost completely numb. "Well, my lady, thank you for your kind assistance."

"You're welcome." He let her pile the cornmeal atop the stack he was barely holding on to. After a brief pause, he took a quick step toward the door right as she did the same. They smiled at each other awkwardly, and he stepped back to let her open the door for him.

"Thanks," he said.

"Sure. Be careful out at guard post, okay?"

"Okay." Their eyes locked for what felt like an uncomfortable amount of time.

"And if something interesting happens again, you'd better come tell me about it." She smiled again. "I don't want to have to carry cornmeal across town just to hear all the good stories."

She turned and hurried off.

Philip kicked the door shut and ran to the dining room table, dropping the bags with a heavy crash. He sat down and shook his hands to get the blood flowing.

It was quiet in the house. He sat there for a while, thinking about Elsie but also, inescapably, about what he and Graham had done. He looked at his hands and thought of Graham's four-fingered hand, wondering if Graham ever stayed up at night worrying that he'd lose more fingers on the job. One lost finger you could deal with, you could accept. Carry things with the other hand, learn to give an extra 25 percent of strength and dexterity to the remaining four fingers. But losing a second or third would be tougher, surely. Philip had seen many such men in Everett and Commonwealth, had caught glimpses of their horrible claws in the rare moments when they let their hands out of their pockets and exposed them to the world and the amazed gazes of children. He wondered if there was some end point, some line in the dirt, some amount of pain and suffering beyond which one could never continue.

Philip sat there and massaged his sore arms with his numb fingers, waiting for the feeling to return.

V

The body only felt light because six of them were lifting it.

On the doctor's orders, they'd waited exactly twenty-four hours, unsure whether Banes had cold hard science as his reason or if he was just superstitious. Maybe this was how you were supposed to bury vampires or the possessed to make sure they wouldn't rise again.

Philip had left the mill office to come down there, though Charles had told him he didn't need to. He had dreamed of the soldier the night before and had been thinking of him all day, and he knew it would have been wrong to run from this last duty.

The other gravediggers were men who, in addition to their jobs as loggers and millworkers, were serving the town as guards: Rankle, Mo, Deacon, and Graham.

"Vultures didn't get to it," someone remarked.

"Deacon wouldn't let them," Rankle said softly.

Deacon just nodded.

"You shoot at the vultures?" asked Mo.

Deacon shook his head. "They stayed away," he said in his raspy voice.

Indeed, Deacon, with his gaunt cheeks and flimsy limbs and coal-black eyes, looked like a scarecrow brought to wicked life. Philip could easily imagine wild, carnivorous birds keeping their distance from him—people did the same thing. Deacon had once trained to be a Catholic priest, so the story went, but he'd decided that God wasn't calling out to him after all. He was a man who usually kept quiet, allowing the demons to fight out their arguments in his head. Others noticed that when he thought he was alone, he swore like a madman.

Philip had never dug a grave before, though he figured the others had. This couldn't be the first burial for Doc Banes, nor could it be for Graham. And Deacon all but looked like an undertaker.

Jarred Rankle also had the air of a man who had dug his share of graves. A short but strong man whose brown hair had recently gone gray, he had eyes that looked as if they had been carved too deep into his granite face, and they seemed all the darker for hiding beneath those craggy brows. Rankle was one of Charles's favorite foremen, both for his efficiency and for his intellect. A former Wobbly of high rank, he often visited the Worthy residence to write political letters with Rebecca or read from her ever-growing pile of radical journals. He was an uncle of sorts to Philip and Laura and an irregular guest for meals, as he had no wife of his own. Rebecca had told Philip once that Rankle had a family years ago but had "lost" them. She had offered no further explanation and Philip had not dared ask, but her comment helped explain a certain look that shadowed the man's face at supper sometimes.

The earth was harder than Philip had feared. The first two shovelfuls were smooth and clean, as if the outermost layer of earth were a soft cushion to comfort all men, but after that it was dense, the tightly bound record of a million years barely held down by the trees and rocks. Philip's muscles would be sore the next day; his weakened hands were already tingling.

No one asked Philip or Graham any questions about the soldier. Philip didn't know if they were afraid of looking rude or if they simply didn't want to know, but he was glad they didn't ask.

The previous night, Charles and Doc Banes had called all the twenty-odd guards except for Philip to an emergency meeting at the town hall. They had told the guards about the soldier and asked that everyone keep quiet about it, but even they knew that some men were better at keeping secrets than others. Graham would certainly tell no one, except possibly his wife. But Mo, a talkative former boxer from Chicago, would probably find it difficult to keep quiet, as would some of the others.

Most of the guards were the same men who served as town magistrates, elected for one-year terms as members of a board that was the closest thing the town had to a police force. Four months ago the magistrates had met and voted to expel from the town two men who had been found to be thieves—the only expulsions in the town's short history. Other than that, the magistrates—who currently included Graham, Rankle, and Charles, with a lifetime appointment as the mill's owner—had spoken to a couple of violent husbands and the parents of some children who had pilfered from the general store, but nothing more. Everyone in Commonwealth seemed to want to be there badly enough that they did their best to live peacefully.

But now the guards were upholding an even greater responsibility, and the secretiveness surrounding the killing of the soldier struck some as wrong. Commonwealth wasn't supposed to have secrets.

The gravediggers chose a spot far enough away from the road to be unseen. They didn't want anyone to stumble upon the grave. None should know. No one needed to be killed to protect the town. All was well.

The trees here were close enough together to almost completely block the sun, but Rankle had managed to find a spot where they had enough room to dig without hitting unbreakable roots. In another hundred or thousand years, though, the surrounding roots would wrap themselves into the soldier's remains, feeding and somehow drawing life from this dead husk.

The body didn't smell yet, maybe because of the night's cold. For that Philip was grateful. Doc Banes had been the first to approach, had leaned over the body and done something the rest couldn't see. The body's right knee was still sticking up, frozen in the position it had first fallen. That amazed Philip. He wondered if it meant the eyes were still open, too, still pleading with the sky.

Then Doc Banes had thrown a blanket over the body and nodded to them, and they had proceeded to the spot where Rankle had started digging the grave. Philip wanted to say something to Graham but he wasn't sure what. He stole as many glances as he could at Graham's tireless face, but Graham never looked back. Instead Graham dug faster and deeper than anyone. The rest of the men took an occasional break to unclench their fingers and roll their shoulders, but Graham kept digging, a man possessed.

The previous day, after they had shot the soldier and Philip had run for Doc Banes, Philip and Graham had completed their shift in near-total silence. It had passed in a strange blur, perhaps the adrenaline from the encounter acting with some kind of amnesiac force. As far as they were concerned, the final thing they had done out there was shoot someone.

The men carried the stiff body, each surprised at how light it felt, and placed it in the grave. The blanket never slid off and Philip never had to look at the soldier's face again.

No one checked the body's pockets for any identification or other trinkets. No one wanted to know his name, and there was no way they could report his death to his family. The gravediggers couldn't afford to care about who the man was.

Mo, who normally found it difficult not to make conversation, whistled for a bit to break the silence. But even he seemed to realize it sounded disrespectful, and soon stopped.

Meanwhile, Deacon worked on the spot where the man had fallen, hacking at the earth with his shovel and turning it over and spreading the dirt around to cover the spots where blood had left its stain.

After the time-consuming and arduous digging, it was sobering how quickly they were able to fill the grave back up. "All right," Rankle said when the last shovelful had been moved back into place.

Every man thought to himself about finding a rock or a large branch to mark the spot, a talisman that would stand in as a grave marker. And every one of them rejected the idea without voicing it.

Graham turned around first, without bidding anyone good day. He kept his back to the rest of them and walked toward the town, leaving the shovel behind so no one would ask him about it. Philip realized he hadn't heard Graham speak a word all day. He followed Graham back to the mill, but from a distance.

Rankle joined Mo at the post, as they were on guard duty that day. When the others left and the two watchmen stared down the gentle slope of the road, the view before them was different than it had been before. Everything in their line of vision—the softly sloping hill and the dirt road and the thick forest beyond—was now forever defined by the fact that it was just a bit off to the left of the dead man's grave.

VI

Philip never would have volunteered for guard duty if it hadn't been for Graham. He wouldn't have thought himself capable.

Growing up with only a mother, Philip was accustomed to not understanding jokes that the other boys told, jokes they had presumably overheard their fathers or older brothers telling. Dragged from town to town throughout his childhood, he was used to being behind in his studies, relegated to the back of a new classroom while the teacher lavished attention on her familiar students and ignored the new kid. By the time the Worthys had adopted him, whatever lessons Philip had learned from his travels were buried deep beneath his grief for his mother and his difficult recovery from the accident. In school he was silent and at home he was distant, as if so convinced that this new existence was a dream that he was simply waiting to wake up. By the time he accepted the reality of his situation, he had already adjusted to thinking that his missing foot and difficult past made him somehow lesser than everyone around him.

It was Graham who taught him to revise these expectations of himself. Charles and Rebecca had provided what support they could, but that was their job as parents. It meant more to Philip coming from a man who had no obligations to him. He had met Graham when Charles invited the Stones to dinner during those first days in Commonwealth. When everyone else had left the table, Graham had matter-of-factly showed Philip his maimed hand, which he'd caught Philip surreptitiously glancing at several times.

Graham had invited him along hunting one afternoon, teaching Philip, despite his weak arms, how to hold a rifle, how to load it, what to expect when he pulled the trigger. Back when new buildings were seemingly sprouting from the earth in Commonwealth, Graham also showed him how to work on the frame of a house. Although Philip worried about being a drag on Graham's time, Graham seemed to enjoy teaching him all that he had been forced to learn from strangers on trains and in timber camps.

It had seemed perfectly natural to volunteer as a guard alongside Graham. But Philip wasn't sure it had been the right decision—not anymore.

Which was why, after supper on the day they had buried the soldier, Philip walked the four blocks to Graham's house. He needed to tell Graham his fear that standing guard had been a mistake. He had been dreading the thought of going back out to the guard post for his next shift, but he wasn't sure if that was because standing guard was wrong or because he was simply scared of another conflict. All day long, the only thing Philip had thought about was the dead soldier, and as bedtime approached he found himself dreading sleep and the haunted dreams it would bring.

True to the town's mission, the Stone and Worthy houses were nearly identical despite the gaping differences in the men's backgrounds. Both houses were two stories tall, with tiny cellars and roofs that pointed skyward like fingertips in prayer. Their chimneys exhaled smoke barely visible in the night sky. Charles's home was only somewhat larger, either a minor oversight in the town's egalitarian vision or a utilitarian acknowledgment of the fact that Charles and Rebecca had adolescent children.

The windows on the first floor were illuminated. Philip knocked gently in case the baby was asleep.

Amelia smiled when she opened the door. A few strands of her brown hair had escaped her bun and were hanging before her blue eyes. She was thin and not tall, with the light skin of a lifelong Washingtonian. Cradled in her mother's arms, the tiny head barely visible through the billows of blanket, was Millie.

"You here to get my husband involved in some kind of trouble?"

Philip hadn't quite lived down the time he and Graham had gone hunting and had temporarily lost a couple of friends' horses by failing to tie them down properly. The horses had panicked and fled after Philip fired his first shot. Of course, it was Graham who had taught Philip such troublemaking skills as firing a rifle and playing poker.

"Yeah, I was thinking of taking him by the saloon, maybe seeing if he wanted to rustle up some women."

"What saloon would that be?"

"It's a secret," he said, following her in. "Only the millworkers know about it. They said if I told any of the wives about it, they'd feed me to the machines."

"Um-hm." The baby started crying. "And why would you want to rustle up any women? I thought you only had eyes for Elsie Metzger."

"Boy, can't a guy talk to a girl without the whole town gossiping?"

"Can't a housewife gossip?"

Beyond the small parlor and the dining room, Philip could see that the kitchen was filled with jars—jars on the table, on the cutting board, jars crammed on the floor, leaving only a narrow path to walk through. Amelia was in the midst of the autumn canning frenzy, particularly important this year.

"Looks like you've been busy," Philip said.

"Oh, no more so than usual," she said, blowing a few strands of hair from her face. Amelia always seemed to be working on several projects at once—she was in charge of the town's community gardens, in addition to the impressive one in her own backyard, and whenever Philip stopped by, she was making preserves, sewing or knitting clothes for her family, or tackling the type of home repair work that many women reserved for their husbands. Amelia had lost her mother when she was seven years old and had inherited early the homemaker role in her family, which had included three younger brothers. The immense amount of work necessary for sustaining her new family in a frontier town perhaps seemed, in contrast, quite manageable.

"Aren't you happy to see your uncle Philip?" Amelia asked the baby, who was still crying.

"Doesn't sound too happy."

Amelia walked toward Philip and, too quickly for him to refuse, put the baby in his arms. "Cheer her up."

In his arms, Millie stopped crying, gazing at him wide-eyed, her forehead furrowed.

"You did it again," Amelia marveled. "You're like magic. Quite an effect on the young females."

"Last time she spit up on me."

Amelia laughed. "I forgot about that. Anyway, Graham's upstairs. I'll go get him." She stopped on the second stair and turned. "Oh, and no poker tonight. I don't want him losing any more of our money to you."

Philip smiled. Though a novice, he had picked up the game quickly. "We've only bet with real money once. I think we used walnuts last time."

"That explains why I couldn't find any when I was baking last weekend."

As Amelia went upstairs, Philip walked the baby in small circles. Millie was five months now, still impossibly small to Philip's eyes, but she felt heavy, as if a baby were somehow denser than other human beings. Her eyes were huge, and Philip wondered if the rest of her would grow into them or if she'd always have large eyes like her mother. She stared at him intently.

"So what are you looking at, exactly?" he said to her softly. Did she even recognize him, or had the event with the soldier changed him so much that even a baby could see the difference? He tried to laugh at himself when he realized he was reading too much into an infant's blank expression, but the laughter wouldn't come.

She was warm against his chest. His fingers had regained their feeling a few hours after burying the body, but they began to tingle slightly beneath the cotton enveloping the baby. It was with a disquieting chill that Philip realized he had held that day first a dead body and now a smiling infant.

He looked up, rocking the baby softly, and his eyes as usual were drawn to a crooked stair at the bottom of the staircase, which always reminded him of the days after Amelia's stillbirth. At the time, the Stones had been living in a smaller house with two other families, as Commonwealth still hadn't enough buildings. Whenever Graham wasn't working at the mill, he was helping construct new houses, and he had encouraged Philip to join in. Graham taught him the basics, and Philip spent many hours that summer helping the older men build the town. After the stillbirth, Amelia was bedridden for days, and Graham barely spoke, his face a downturned mask of silent grief. He also barely slept, working late into the night on the new house, desperate to complete the job so he and his wife could move in and begin to grapple with the world that had just turned on them.

Every night for two weeks he was joined by Philip, who came after dinner and silently worked with Graham until his arms were too sore to continue. Philip's inexperience was the reason one of the steps was crooked, but Graham had insisted it was fine, after issuing a short laugh. It was his first laugh since the loss of his baby. Other men in the town had seemed uncertain in Graham's presence, never knowing what to say to a grieving man, but Philip had simply shown up and worked, usually in silence, as it was clear that Graham didn't want to talk. Philip suspected Graham's refusal to fix the stair was his way of thanking him for helping when no one else had known how.

Philip was stirred from his memories when Amelia and Graham descended those stairs. Graham looked groggy, but he was holding a pipe and smelled strongly of tobacco, so he obviously hadn't been sleeping.

"I've been forbidden from playing poker with you," Graham said as Amelia took the baby from Philip and laid her in the crib.

"Me, too. Maybe you need to teach me a new game."

"You'll just start beating him at that one, too," Amelia said.

"I can hold my own, thank you very much," Graham said. "He's just a good bluffer. With that damn innocent face, you can never tell when he's lying."

"Watch the cuss words, husband."

"Bluffing's not lying," Philip said. "I would never lie."

Graham rewarded the lie with a mocking smile, then wandered to the fireplace, teasing the fire back to life with swift jabs from the poker.

"So how's the family?" Amelia asked Philip while kneeling on the kitchen floor, scribbling labels for each jar. "I imagine staying inside the town must be hard on Rebecca, not being able to go to all those meetings and things."

"It is," Philip said, "so she's been spending more time than usual at the school. Those poor kids are probably going crazy with all the extra work."

Suddenly, Amelia coughed. A few times.

Philip felt himself stiffen and saw Graham temporarily stop rearranging the logs. Amelia reached for a cup with her free hand and sipped the water, and all seemed well.

Her coughing wasn't entirely unusual, not anymore. After the stillbirth, she had lost a good deal of weight, and her subsequent pregnancy with Millie had been difficult—she had been bedridden for the last two months before the birth, as well as the first three weeks afterward. Considering how many times she'd been laid up with colds over the past two years, her coughing fit in the kitchen didn't really mean anything unusual, Philip told himself.

"But the mill's doing real well," Philip said. "Charles keeps talking about it. Says we'll prove his brothers wrong soon enough."

"His brothers are wrong in a lot of ways," Graham said.

"Once we can open up the town again, we'll have plenty of good shingles and lumber to ship out," Philip said.

To Philip, their banter felt somewhat forced, as if they were all concentrating on the charade that everything was normal. As he thought about this he looked at Graham, seeking some acknowledgment of what they'd experienced together, and when they made eye contact something flickered in Graham's face.

"Help me bring in some wood," Graham said.

Philip followed him out, closing the door behind him. Graham was already in the back, retrieving firewood from the shed. When Philip caught up to him, Graham turned around and faced him, though Philip could barely see his features in the dark.

"When are you out there guarding next?" Philip asked.

"Tomorrow night."

"Overnight?"

"That's right."

Philip couldn't imagine standing guard all through the night, surrounded by nothing but darkness and increasingly irrational thoughts. "Who with?"

"Deacon."

Philip had heard that Deacon had volunteered to stand guard on many of the nights; the role of nocturnal sentinel seemed entirely in keeping with his Gothic demeanor. But Philip was surprised to hear that Graham, who usually turned in earlier than Philip did, would want to do the same.

"Are we still painting those porches Sunday morning?" Philip and

Graham had planned on finishing some of the newer, as yet unoccupied houses in town.

"Sure. Why wouldn't we be?" Graham finished stacking the pieces of wood in his other arm. Philip offered to help carry some, but Graham shook him off.

"I figured if you'd be staying up all night the night before, maybe you—"

"I can manage," Graham insisted.

Philip nodded, backing away as Graham emerged from the shed with his arms full of firewood. Graham was about to unload some into Philip's arms when their eyes met again, and Graham stopped.

"Why do you keep looking at me like that?" Graham asked.

"Like what?"

"Like I'm somebody you just met and don't trust."

Philip looked down instinctively. "I was just . . . wanting to make sure you were all right," he replied weakly.

"Of course I'm all right." Graham looked insulted. "Why wouldn't I be?"

A few seconds passed as Philip fumbled with how to respond. "Because of . . . what happened yesterday."

"I did the right thing yesterday." Graham's tone was strangely aggressive, and the dim light cast malevolent shadings on his face that Philip hoped weren't truly there. "There's nothing for me not to feel all right about."

Philip nodded. "Okay."

"I did what I had to do. If I hadn't been there, you would've done the same. You know that."

Philip stood there blankly.

"You know that," Graham repeated.

"Yeah." Philip nodded, though he didn't know if he agreed. "I know. I just—I just wanted to see how you were."

Philip had wanted to confide in Graham, tell him his confusion about standing guard, receive guidance from him. But now he was afraid to do so, afraid to admit his fear. Graham was right—they had done the right thing, surely. Philip was just scared. And fear was like the pain in his arm when he carried too much weight: something he simply had to accept and move beyond.

"It's about time Amelia and the baby went to bed."

Philip was being dismissed. "All right," he said to Graham's back. "I'll see you tomorrow."

Graham had never lashed out at Philip, though there had certainly been times when dark moods fell over him. Something about the sheer force of Graham's will left Philip in awe of his friend, as if realizing anew the stark difference between himself and a true adult.

As Philip walked home, he thought about what had happened to Graham in Everett. What little he knew, he had heard from Charles. Graham wasn't one to share those kinds of stories, and judging from what Philip had heard, he couldn't blame him.

VII

Hours later Graham sat at his kitchen table, roused from sleep once again by the sound of the gunshots, by the look on the soldier's face. He was breathing heavily and his fingers twitched—it was a miracle he'd been able to leave the bedroom without waking Amelia. He put his head in his hands, hoping to steady them.

Graham had never killed anyone before. Never even shot at anyone. He'd broken his share of noses and ribs, he'd tussled and come out on top more than a few times, but he'd never crossed that line. You did the right thing, he told himself. There are hundreds of people breathing right now who can thank you for those breaths. He told himself that the right thing was often hard, and confusing, and fraught with peril, but he damn sure had done the right thing, so he just needed to calm down, breathe slow.

Ain't nothing a man has can't be taken away. Damnedest truth there ever was. All that one has could vanish—whether in an instant, with frightening speed, or across a lifetime, with decay so slow no eye could detect it. But with Graham it had come as quick as a breathe, and he would never, ever let that happen again.

He had so much to protect. He thought of his wife and daughter, the warm weight of the baby in his arms. The way she slept so peacefully, it was as though all the strife that had preceded her birth had abruptly and forever ceased to exist.

He had never known what he wanted until that day on Puget Sound, with the sun reflecting off the waves and the mountains hovering like benevolent spirits in the background. He was twenty-three then, six years after he'd left home when a fight with his father had gotten out of hand. He'd been riding the rails for years, had picked fruit in California and seen the bowels of the earth in the Montana mines, had been beaten up by railroad bulls who thought he was at worst a Wobbly or at best another bum come to ruin their towns.

Not long after leaving his family in Kansas, he'd fallen in with a friendly bunch who taught him how to bum rides on the train, how to avoid the railroad bulls and the town cops, how to find out where the next job was and how to get there. Taught him which job sharks you could trust and which would only take your money and then drive you to some godforsaken field where there was no job at all, just a handful of other bindle stiffs who'd been shaken down. Taught him how to hide your money when you slept on a train car, how to protect yourself in a flophouse, how to keep the bedbugs from getting to those places you really didn't want them. After only a couple years, it was as if Graham had been doing this all his life, and soon he was the one teaching the younger runaways and roustabouts, showing them how to survive, how to take the punches and keep on walking, grinning all the while.

But the romance wore off fast, as the bosses got meaner, the pay got lousier, and the food at the work camps got worse. Graham remembered the time he ran out of Spokane after a strike got ugly, remembered sitting on the train as the sun was rising over the Sawtooth Mountains, the air bracingly cold and so clean. He remembered sitting there and taking in all the beauty that God had laid out before him and wondering just what he was supposed to be doing in it. Surely he had a purpose, a reason for existing in a place as maddeningly beautiful as this, but what? His life had been a series of responses and reactions, nothing more. He'd hear about a job and take it. He'd get some jack and spend it. A strike would hit the town and he'd leave. Somebody'd call him a name and he'd throw a punch.

Until Everett. The playground of second-tier timber barons who thought they were industrial magnates of the highest order, Everett was a quickly growing town with no shortage of jobs. Time had passed in an almost seasonless blur. After a year or so, Graham's buddy Matt told him how he could make more if he worked in a shingle-weaving plant; Matt could put in a good word with the foreman and teach him how to do the work without losing a finger or two. Graham was desperate to create something completely his own, and saving some money would be exactly that. So he made the switch to sawyer, but it was harder work, in its way. Rather than living out in the woods beneath the persistent rains and leaning in to his end of a crosscut saw, Graham was hunched in a stuffy building manipulating pieces of wood through those terrifying machines. Some days he manned the tall gang saws whose vertical blades ingested fat logs and spat them out as perfect strips of wood, and other days he navigated the band saws, long winding strips of metal thin as ribbon but topped with steel teeth that cut the strips down further. Just keep those teeth away, he'd think, while inhaling all that sawdust and getting it in his eyes and squinting and wanting to rub them clean but resisting because one false move would mean—

Losing a finger. One day he'd been seized by a dust-induced coughing fit so violent that his left arm flew out where he knew damn well not to let it go, and when his hand came back, it had only three fingers and the thumb. It wasn't even his—it was someone else's, some odd misshapen thing, the last knuckle looking so weirdly prominent. And then the knuckle spurted an explosion of red like some Cascade volcano erupting to hideous life, and the red ran down the rest of the hand and he finally recognized it—good Lord, that is my hand, and there ain't no pinkie.

The man next to him, who should have been concentrating on his own work and was lucky he didn't lose any fingers of his own, looked up and shouted something Graham didn't hear. Matt came over from his usual station, wrapped a rag around Graham's hand, and took him to see the doctor. Matt was saying things that Graham couldn't hear—he'd shut down so that his body could concentrate on the feeling of shuddering pain, waves of pain, an entire hideous universe of pain that sucked itself thin and jammed itself into the tiny hole that his finger had left behind. The pain cut through his hand, his arm, it made his shoulder throb and his back ache. The doctor hit him with some morphine and finally he could think, could get beyond the strictly animal instincts to which his mind had become subordinated. He concentrated on breathing while the doc sewed him up and told him how to take care of the wound and what to expect from his new, three-fingered hand.

"This happens a lot, huh?" Graham had asked. It was the first thing he'd said since the finger flew off.

"To shingle weavers? Yeah." The doc, an older guy who had sewn shut countless gaping knuckles, fidgeted with his glasses. "How long you been on the job?"

"Four months."

The doc nodded. "Usually happens sooner than then. Law of averages catches up to you eventually."

Graham didn't know what the law of averages was, but he didn't like how the doc was treating him as if the accident were something he deserved. Maybe it was just the morphine. Nothing seemed quite right, not the too-white pallor of the doc's skin or the too-dark indigo of the midday sky beyond the windows or the lack of feeling beyond Graham's left wrist.

The doc told Graham what he owed. It was roughly two weeks' pay, which was more than he had. Graham stuttered a bit, but the doc had heard this before and cut him off. "How much can you pay at the end of the month?"

They worked out a deal, a payment plan on the finger Graham no longer had. With that settled, Graham bade the doctor good day and headed outside.

The doc's house was on a paved road not far from the center of town, just a few blocks away from the rowdy saloons that had been the focal point of a town outcry a few years earlier, or so Graham had been told. What you need is a drink, Graham told himself, but he knew he needed to go back to the mill and explain himself. Find out how much pay he was going to be docked for leaving early.

"How's your hand?" someone asked.

He turned around and found himself face-to-face with a woman whose stare could have knocked down a few trees; although she looked like she'd skipped one meal too many, she seemed huge in spirit. She had long soot-black hair that curled in the constant mists of Washington, and she wore a long skirt, a gray flannel shirt, and dark boots—a masculine outfit for a woman, particularly one as beautiful as she.

"How's my hand?" Graham repeated her question, unsure how to respond. He lifted his arm a bit, as if to display the bandage. "It's a little bit smaller than it was this morning."

"They've been making you work faster lately, huh?"

"Guess so."

She shook her head. "Miracle you still have nine fingers."

They got to talking, Graham impressed with the fact that she had initiated a conversation with a man she didn't know, a fairly bold thing for a woman to do. And he was glad she'd done it, giving him permission to study that face, to talk to a woman he didn't have to pay, a woman who seemed to take some interest in him. It made him feel off balance, at first, but maybe that was just the morphine.

"You're not a member, are you?" she asked. "You don't have a red card?"

Graham held his tongue for a moment, the twin bodyguards of caution and self-preservation keeping him silent. He did not have a red card, but even the subject of Wobblies was so taboo that he was reluctant to discuss it with a stranger, albeit an attractive female one.

Turned out she was a Wobbly herself and had arrived in town only a few days ago from Chicago. There had been rumors of a planned general strike for a couple of weeks; the mill owners had announced pay cuts and the unions were not pleased. Graham knew all this but had been doing his best to ignore it. He hated the mill owners as much as anyone, he figured, but every time a strike flared up, he lost everything he had and eventually had to pull up stakes and move to a new job in a new state. He liked Everett—he liked the neighborhoods of family houses and the kids running around after school, he liked being a part of the armada of men heading to the mill in the morning as the sun rose before them, slowly illuminating the tops of the tall trees that loomed above every road, capping them with halos of light. This was a place where he could stay. He hadn't worked out the math yet, but he figured with the higher pay he'd been getting as a shingle weaver, he might be able to save enough to get his own place. Maybe get married and start a family.

Graham said as much to his toothsome inquisitor, skipping the part about marriage.

"So you want to keep slaving away till you don't have any fingers left?" she asked.

He looked at his right hand—then and henceforth known as his good hand—and extended his fingers. Then he looked her in the eye and said, "I just want to keep the other nine."

She reached out and handed him a pamphlet. "If you change your mind, this tells you when we're meeting next. Maybe we can help you hold on to what you've still got." She smiled when she said that, for the first time.

"What's your name?" he asked. She said it was Tamara. He told her his name and thanked her for the pamphlet, and she nodded and walked away, to someplace important, judging from the speed of her steps and the confidence of her stride.

It was worth losing a finger to meet her. He'd lose another one if that was what it took to see her again.

So it was neither political nor economic motives that inspired Graham to attend his first official meeting of the Industrial Workers of the World. As he sat in the crowd, listening to the speakers—some of whom were from Everett but many of whom were from Chicago and other distant locales, rebels imported from the sites of many a clash between worker and owner—he fixed his eyes mostly on Tamara, until she looked back at him and he switched his gaze to the floor, his cheeks reddening. It took a couple of minutes for him to work up the nerve to look at her again. Had he actually blushed? He was a man who had felled trees and even bigger men, and he was blushing because he had looked at some lady who dressed like a female logger? He put his left fist inside his other hand, massaging the knuckles.

He was nervous when he walked up to her afterward and told her he was buying that red card, and they talked more about the possibility of a general strike and what it might do to the town. He was nervous when he asked to walk her home; she declined because she'd come with friends, but thanked him just the same. And he was nervous at the next meeting when the situation pretty much repeated itself, except this time she accepted his invitation.

But strangely, Graham wasn't nervous the first time he kissed her—on the cheek, after the third walk home—maybe because nerves know when something is right. He had finally figured out what it was he'd been running from, or running to.

Any hope for a normal courtship, however, was thwarted by the strike that commenced two weeks into Graham's life as a nine-fingered man.

And what a strike it was—nearly every mill in town halted, the saws stilled and the trees standing proud and tall as if perfectly confident that not another Douglas fir within the town's borders would ever fall again. And all the men on the streets, men in lines, men holding signs, men shouting. And eventually men fighting: strikers fighting with scabs and with strikebreakers, strikers with no accent fighting strikers with thick accents, cops fighting strikers. Surrounding them.

Graham's scant savings were near extinction when the violence escalated. Sheriff McRae had started hiring thugs who were friendly to the Commercial Club, the mill owners who wanted to see the strike broken and the outside agitators sent back from whence they'd come. Strikers like Graham soon learned which street corners to avoid after dark and how to steer clear of any man who wore a handkerchief tied around his forearm—the mark of McRae's vigilantes, who wore them so the real cops would know who was who when fights broke out. Graham heard about how the cops were going to start arresting anyone who gave a public speech, which made him think of Tamara, who'd taken to doing exactly that.

"It ain't worth it," he told her. "They'll arrest you, and then Lord only knows what they'll do." He almost added, I ain't going to let no woman of mine be manhandled by a bunch of lousy cops, but he knew not to say that. She was only just barely "his woman," and she was not the type who liked to think of it that way.

As he'd expected, she was defiant. "They can't arrest me just for talking, and if they do, so be it." She told him about her idol Elizabeth Gurley Flynn, the original Rebel Girl and doyenne of "the cause." Gurley Flynn had been put in jail more times than you could count, Tamara said, but she never gave up the fight. Tamara proudly declared herself a rebel girl as well, so bring on the cops.

Graham had to admire her fire, but he wondered what this educated Chicago woman—she'd been in college when she first joined the Wobblies, she told him—really knew about anything. She talked a good talk, and she sure as hell never acted scared, but just to be sure, Graham tailed her to the street corner where she'd told him she'd give her speech that night. It was dark and anything but quiet—people were milling all around, chatter that exploded into laughter now and then but always highly charged—when the speeches finally started. First it was a hulking fellow with a thick beard and some accent Graham figured was Hungarian. After the fellow's final fist-shaking exhortations, Tamara took to the pulpit.

She started telling them about a recent strike in New Jersey and how things had looked bleak but everyone had stuck together. They had refused to submit to a few men in back rooms who controlled everything, and so will we, she said. The applause was so loud that it almost completely shrouded the sound of McRae's goons moving in from the edge of the street and swinging their unimpressed clubs. Then the applause was gone and all that could be heard were the sounds of fighting, of dropped bottles popping when they hit the ground, of bones breaking and feet stomping and kicking, voices shouting and crying and grunting in an ever-tightening mass of enraged humanity. Graham pushed some folks out of his way and headed for the makeshift stage, where he grabbed Tamara by the wrists and pulled her through the crowd. An arm with a handkerchief tied around it got pretty close to them, but Graham jabbed a fist into the man's nose and the goon dropped back. In a few frantic seconds they'd escaped not only the melee but also the notice of the cops who were standing beyond the crowd, supposedly to arrest anyone who tried to escape.

"This happen in New Jersey, too?" Graham asked after they'd walked a couple of blocks, heading in the direction of the rooming house where she boarded.

"Probably."

"Probably? You weren't there?"

She looked away, embarrassed. "It was three years ago. I was only seventeen."

"This by any chance your first strike?"

She answered with silence.

"Well, it ain't mine, and not one of 'em that I've been around has ended well."

"Then you've been around the wrong ones."

He laughed softly. "I don't think I've ever met anyone as sure of herself as you are."

She grabbed his hand, held it. "I wasn't so sure of myself once the cops came. Thank you for coming to get me."

This was an opportunity for him to say something romantic, to court her by telling her it would take more than a few cops to keep him from her. But he was unsure how she'd react, so he kept walking.

"We'll win this," she said. "I know it. The more people they arrest, the more we'll send in."

Graham nodded. He still wasn't used to her penchant for using "we," her constant and assured feeling of being part of some great and uplifting whole.

They were at the front door to the boardinghouse. The kindly old lady who owned it had no idea Tamara was involved with those awful Wobblies, and if she had, Tamara would have been out on the street in a minute. Nor would the old lady allow a man to visit one of her boarders in her rooms. Graham wondered if sometime he should propose walking Tamara back to his place instead, or if that would be too forward.

"You ever think about what'll happen after the strike?" he asked.

"You mean if we win?"

"I mean either way." He was trying to act nonchalant but finding it impossible.

She looked at him closely. He never studied anything—especially not her—like that. He'd only had to look at her once and he'd known all he needed to.

Then she smiled slightly, like she had the first time they'd met. "I wonder what it is you're really asking me."

He couldn't help smiling back, either out of embarrassment or happiness or excitement, he wasn't sure. "Does a rebel girl just follow the cause to the next strike? You off to Cheyenne or Coeur d'Alene or Walla Walla next?"

"I haven't thought that far ahead." Still smiling.

"I used to be like that."

"Then what?"

"I got smarter. And I met someone."

She'd only let him kiss her on the cheek before, but that night she leaned toward him as if giving permission for more, to do what he'd been thinking about damn near constantly for days. They kissed for a longer time than was proper for two people standing beneath one of the few streetlights on that side of town. He held her and was amazed at how fragile she felt, despite the steel in her eyes and her voice and her posture.

Despite his happiness, he thought how vulnerable she was. And how vulnerable he was, to have something in his life other than himself that he needed to worry about, and protect.

The violence got worse, and fast. The night after the cops dragged a group of strikers to secluded Beverly Park and beat them nearly to death, Tamara told Graham that the IWW office wanted to send her down to Seattle to meet with the local chapter and recruit more people to Everett. That sounded like a safer idea than wandering around the violent streets of Everett, and Graham invited himself along.

With some of his few remaining coins, he paid for ferry tickets. A midwestern boy who'd spent all his adult life in the mountain states, he'd rarely been on a boat, and he didn't know how to swim. As a storm moved toward them, the chop of the waves increased. By the time they neared Seattle, the skies had opened and it was pouring—the Sound an infinity of liquid explosions—and the boat was pitching from side to side. The moment they got off, Graham let out a long, slow breath and tried to steady himself. He was not looking forward to the ride home.

Tamara, who had apparently been on many a boat, not only in Lake Michigan but also on the Atlantic, as she had family in Boston and New York, was good enough not to tease him. Instead she told him more about her family, how she was the youngest of five sisters and had twelve nieces and nephews with more surely on the way. She loved and missed her parents, but the cause was worth the physical distance between herself and her family. Graham had nodded to all this, secretly wondering if one day he would meet this lawyer father and warmhearted mother, this gaggle of sisters and brothers-in-law with their Chicago and New York accents, their starched shirts and fancy cigars.

This was what he wanted. Not necessarily the family and their unimaginable strangeness, but the comfort of sitting beside Tamara and knowing she wanted to be with him. He would create a haven for the two of them, carve a better existence out of the strange land he'd been wandering through, create a more beautiful and rewarding world than the one they'd known.

In Seattle the rain continued to pour down, the city as gray and forbidding as a medieval fortress. Some Wobblies met them at the docks and escorted them to a ratty office located between the shipyards and some paper mills. All day it was conversation and strategizing about cops and jails, lawyers who'd helped out at past strikes, and how many folks could be recruited from Seattle to come north. Graham tried to make himself helpful, but mostly he felt like a laborer transported to a factory unlike any he'd ever seen, a revolution factory.

At six o'clock Tamara told him they'd need to stay till tomorrow, that dozens of folks were being rounded up and they'd all head back to Everett the following afternoon. One of the Wobblies had a room they could use, Tamara said. *A* room.

The Wobbly, a thin redheaded guy named Sam, with a similarly redheaded wife, lived in a small place in the eastern part of town. They made supper for Graham and Tamara and talked about the labor situation in Seattle. All evening Graham couldn't stop thinking about sharing a bedroom with Tamara. Then Sam announced they'd best be getting some shut-eye, as tomorrow promised to be a helluva day.

It was all so strange, Graham thought, the way he and Tamara headed to the room without having spoken at all about the fact that they would be spending the night in the same bed. They just proceeded as if this were the rightest thing in the world. And it felt that way. She held his hand as they walked into the room and as soon as he'd shut the door she was in his arms, the two of them kissing before his hand had released the doorknob. Graham was conscious of the fact that he was in a moment he would remember till his dying day, so with every breath he concentrated on making sure that his future memories of that night would be forever untainted.

He did not awaken the next morning with Tamara in his arms because she was already up and dressed. He was a deep sleeper, she told him with a smile, and it was time to get going. She kissed him before leaving the room so he could dress in privacy, and this strange feeling of familiarity despite unfamiliar circumstances thrilled him. Waking up with a woman in the room, a woman he'd fallen in love with. He hadn't quite thought this possible, yet there he was.

In a few hours they were back at the docks, along with about four hundred new friends. The IWW had hoped for a couple thousand, but this was an impressive number nonetheless. Two steamboats were needed to get them to Everett, the *Verona* and the *Calista*. Tamara and Graham and the Wobbly ringleaders got on board the *Verona,* which departed first, and though Graham hadn't been looking forward to being on a boat again, he was relieved to see the bright sun in a perfectly cloudless sky, the water laid out so flat before him it was like a Kansan field, the tiniest of ripples shifting in the wind like stalks of corn. The boat ride was smooth, though so packed with bodies that it seemed to rock slightly just from the Wobblies' singing, which grew louder with each verse. The *Verona* cut through Puget Sound, and the Wobblies serenaded the surrounding islands with their battle cries, their hymns of brotherhood and triumph, their odes to fallen leaders, and their righteous calls for a future of unity and peace. In the distance Mount Rainier watched over them like a mildly disapproving God, or so it seemed to Graham. But soon it and the wharves and cranes of Seattle faded into the distance.

The air over the Sound was cold, but there were so many people on board that few could feel it. The boat slowed as Everett came into view, all the mills silent, the sky above their smokestacks pure with inactivity.

But silent the dock wasn't. As the *Verona* pulled nearer to Port Gardner Bay, Graham was one of the first to see the crowd. Even more people lined the streets and the hill just beyond, looking down at the dock and the approaching boat like spectators at a boxing match. These throngs were not singing, and Graham noticed that quite a few of them were wearing handkerchiefs on their forearms.

The passengers grew quiet, perhaps remembering broken noses and cut eyebrows suffered at the hands of McRae's men, or similar assailants in some other town, different faces but always the same fists. The passengers who had knives in their pockets let their hands slip down and finger the steel as they watched the scene unfold before them. Waiting.

The songs started up again, this time even louder than before. *"We meet today in freedom's cause and raise our voices high! We'll join our hands in union strong to battle or to die!"* Hearts beat faster as the singers looked one another in the eye, trying to keep themselves from being intimidated by some two-bit thugs with a bottle of whiskey in one pocket and a .38 in the other.

Graham put an arm around Tamara and held her hip with his good hand. They were toward the bow, on the port side—the side that was lining up against that dock swarming with men. Graham couldn't see any knives or clubs or shovels or guns on the dock, but that didn't mean they weren't there.

The boat pulled alongside the dock and one of the Wobblies reached across to tie it down, but an angry-looking man with dizzy eyes stepped out from the crowd. It was Sheriff McRae, Graham recognized, and the stories about him seemed to be true, as he walked with the slightly staggered shuffle of the raging and belligerent drunk.

"Who's your leader?" McRae demanded.

"We're all leaders!" a handful shouted back, voicing one of the IWW slogans.

Graham leaned down toward Tamara's ear to tell her they should take a few steps back, but before he could speak, McRae raised his voice.

"I'm sheriff of this town, and I'm enforcin' our laws. You can't dock here, so head on back to—"

"The hell we can't!" someone shouted back.

Then a gunshot. It tore through the air and bounced off the still water, echoing throughout the harbor, off distant islands and near inlets. Everyone on the boat tried to move, but there was nowhere to go. People screamed and ducked for cover, tried to turn around, to escape. The shot echoed endlessly. But it wasn't an echo—it was more shots, some coming from the dock and some coming from the boat. Who had fired first was as impossible to determine as it was irrelevant. Between the popping sounds of shots and ricochets were the hard slaps of limp bodies hitting the water, men disappearing into the depths below.

Graham slipped, whacking his knee on the deck and sliding forward, since no one was between him and the rail anymore. Everyone was running to the opposite side of the boat. Men on the dock were pointing and shouting and screaming and some of them were brandishing guns and firing still.

He realized he wasn't holding Tamara—he must have lost his grip on her in the initial turmoil. He looked behind him at the Wobblies running to the starboard side, looked for long hair, for those black coils, for anything remotely female.

The boat started tipping. All the weight had shifted to starboard, and now the port side, where Graham stood, was lifting into the air. Two vigilantes who'd had clear shots at him missed when the deck beneath him rose, but Graham lost his footing again and stumbled back, sliding on the wet deck and tumbling back toward the cowering bodies on the far side.

The boat's captain, who didn't give much of a damn for either unions or mill owners, started hollering at them to disperse around the boat or it'd go under. He turned the wheel and hit the engines with a force he'd never before dared, and the *Verona* lurched away from the dock, a lopsided and badly wounded animal retreating from predators. The only people who obeyed the captain's orders despite the bullets were Graham and a small handful of others hoping to get a closer look at the water.

The guns were still firing but were more distant now, less threatening. Graham leaned over the railing and screamed for Tamara. Was she in the water? Was she back on the other side of the boat?

Bodies floated beneath the dock, but none looked female. The water was so dark that the blood was completely absorbed into its deep indigo.

There. Over there, by the dock's farthest pylon. Long dark hair, soot-black. Hair Graham had twisted his fingers in the night before. But no, it could be a woman who'd been on the dock, could be anyone.

Then a wave from the wake of the *Verona*'s quick retreat hit the body, roughly lifting it and turning its head. Graham screamed when he saw her face.

He pulled at the rail so tightly he nearly tore it from the ship's deck. His scream echoed over the bay, over the Sound, over every island and with more force than the earlier anthems. Folks from Everett who were blocks away from the water heard that scream, marveled about it for days. He screamed so loudly the dead surely heard him, Tamara surely heard him, screamed so loudly he wouldn't have been able to hear her answer even if she'd had one.

Then her face exploded. Two goons atop the dock were laughing themselves hysterical, hooting and hollering and stomping with glee as they fired round after round at the bodies floating in the water. They shot indiscriminately at every floating thing in human form, shooting the bodies of Wobblies but also shooting the occasional body of an Everett cop or vigilante, a body who only moments ago had been a man filled with pride for his town and hatred for these foulmouthed agitators and their foreign ideas about how the world should be run. One or two of those bodies had actually still been alive, but most had already been dead, and still the men fired as if they could somehow make them more dead.

Graham's scream was cut off by this sight. His breath too fled—he stood there gripping the rail, watching in mute shock and rage.

The *Verona* pulled away with merciful speed and the scene dissolved into washes of gray and blue with streaks of red, blurring with the distance and with Graham's tears. The sound of the engine soon overpowered that of the gunshots, of the bullets slamming into flesh and water. Graham crumpled to the deck.

Their safety ensured by distance, the passengers on the *Verona* began to fan out again as the boat headed back toward Seattle. Wounded men were tended, though the death toll would increase by the time they made landfall. There were men with broken bones, men who'd slipped or been crushed as they'd fled the path of the bullets. And there were men, their eyes still wide, who had seen their comrades fall.

Yet they all seemed to know that no one had lost as much as the man who lay in a heap by the front of the boat. His arms were wrapped around himself, his nine fingers digging into the thick muscles of his shoulders. The rest of the men kept a respectful distance, a wide circle of emptiness surrounding him.

I will never again permit myself to be in so powerless a position, Graham had long vowed.

Ain't nothing a man has can't be taken away.

He knew that then, knew how easy it would be for home and family and love to vanish forever. He thought of the dead soldier and he pitied him, pitied the randomness of fate that had placed him on that path in front of Graham, pitied him the way he had once pitied himself. But Graham had done what was necessary to protect Amelia and Millie. He lifted his head from his hands and wiped the tears from his eyes. No one and nothing would come into this town, into his home, to do harm to his family. And even if the devil himself should ride into town on a flaming beast breathing pestilence and death, then Graham would stand at that post, look him in the eye, and shoot him down.

VIII

"You know what I heard?"

"What's that?"

"I heard that maybe the reason Mr. Worthy wanted us to close off the town is to stop workers from moving on to other jobs."

"What other jobs?"

"I hear they got lotsa jobs on the coast, on account of the war. Hear they'll pay fucking shipbuilders more than we're making here."

"Nobody's making more than we're making here. They give you your own goddamn house at the shipyards?"

"How do we know they don't?"

"I'm just saying I heard—"

"And we heard you just fine. Hell, didn't we all vote on this? I didn't see you raising any ruckus that night."

"Just 'cause I voted for something doesn't mean I can't change my mind. Ain't a man free to do that?"

"Ain't much free right now."

"That's my point. We ain't free to move around and look for—"

"Goddammit, enough. If that's the way you're thinking, then as soon as the fucking quarantine's over, you can take your goddamn self out to those shipyards and see how much those military folk'll pay you. I for one don't buy any of that."

"I wasn't saying I'm buying it. I just said I heard."

"Elton's been coughin' a lot lately."

"Elton's *always* been coughin'."

"But how do we know it ain't from the flu?"

"Because he was coughing last year and there wasn't any flu, and the year before that, and the year before that."

"But how come that—"

"It ain't the flu. He's just a sick bastard."

"Hey, Yolen. You been by the gen'ral store this week?"

"No. Jeanine's fixing to go today, though."

"Well, get this—there ain't no alcohol left."

"What?"

"The store's all out."

"Hell Jesus. You sure?"

"Otto said they'd just bought as much food an' supplies as they thought they could handle before the quarantine, but they mustn't've ordered much hooch."

"Shit, Leonard. I only got one fucking bottle left at home."

"I got less'n that."

"Shit. You really sure there's none left?"

"You ever have the flu?"

"Yeah, when I was ten. Kept me in bed more 'n a month."

"Damn. It killed all four of my grandparents in the same winter."

"Kills everybody's grandparents, if they're lucky. Better'n wasting away slow with something else."

"Don't think flu is lucky."

"How do you think that girl a yours in Timber Falls is doing?"

"Wasn't sick last time I saw her. But some of her friends were."

"Sure she'll be fine."

"You're a lucky man, with your girl already here in town. This quarantine lasts much longer, I'm gonna go outta my goddamn head."

"Can't last much longer."

"What the hell kind of man does this make me look like to her, hiding away because I'm scared of getting sick?"

"Don't worry about that. She ain't thinking down on you—she's probably worried enough trying to stay healthy herself."

"That's supposed to make me feel better?"

"Sorry . . . She'll be fine."

"Yeah . . . I get tired of waiting sometimes, you know?"

IX

"I heard someone say it came in a black cloud over the Atlantic," Laura said as she and Philip ate some of the cake she'd made. It was the evening after Philip's visit to Graham and Amelia.

"A black cloud?"

"Like a mustard gas cloud, only dark. Something the Germans released from a battleship, and the wind brought it to Boston. That's why it started there."

"Do you really think the Germans made it?"

"Maybe. I don't know. Why not?"

"Then wouldn't they all be sick, too?"

Laura shrugged. "Maybe they don't get the flu."

"Then I guess Elsie's family has nothing to worry about."

"What's that supposed to mean?"

"I just mean they're German."

"But they're American now, Philip." She paused. "You sure do bring her up a lot."

That shut him up for a moment.

"Maybe it wasn't from Germany," she said. "I don't know. It's an idea, is all."

Two weeks ago, just before the quarantine, they had journeyed to Timber Falls to see a moving picture at the new theater. Philip had been only a handful of times, and already he was anxious to get back to the theater and see whatever was playing. He loved the feel of the place, the plush carpets up the aisles and the sleepy usher not much older than he, wearing the funny hat and tearing their tickets as they walked in. The picture they had seen, *The Phantom Operative*, had been about the war, in a way. There were no soldiers in it, but plenty of spies: the plot centered on two American businessmen who had developed a secret serum that could counteract any disease within two hours of the patient's ingesting it. But it turned out German operatives had developed the exact opposite—an odorless, colorless poison that could kill anyone who even came too close to it. The Germans had some crazy scheme to put the poison on the feet of houseflies and send the flies to the American heartland, where they would multiply and spread their lethal freight.

When the reels were changed, there was a message on the screen asking everyone to stay in their seats; a representative of the government was going to deliver an important message. Up on the stage jumped an older man, late forties or so, and before he even started, Philip realized he must be one of the so-called Four-Minute Men. The speaker looked snappy in his dark suit, and without introducing himself, he launched into his speech, starting out dark and sinister as he painted a picture of the Hun army and its senseless wrath. *People say the war's already swinging in our favor,* he said, *but that's no reason for us to be letting our guard down. The German army is still a mighty force, and without all the efforts of the fine and hardworking American people, the Hun would have claimed Paris by now, would have pillaged all of France and would be aiming his Big Berthas at Big Ben.*

Philip didn't much mind these speeches, but he knew how Rebecca loathed them, so he viewed the man with a skeptical eye. Toward the end of the speech, the man reminded them of the importance of registration for all men between the ages of eighteen and forty-five, saying how it was a great honor to fight for their country and defend their women and children from the fierce Hun. Philip looked down at his missing foot, ashamed—even if the war continued until he turned eighteen, he would never be admitted. The Four-Minute Man closed by telling the crowd about the Fourth Liberty Loan and exhorted them to buy more Liberty Bonds, then walked off at a hurried pace, his footsteps chased by hearty applause.

Then the picture continued, and the virulent houseflies were let loose on the German operatives after a climactic fight scene, and all was right with the world.

"Where do you think the flu came from?" Laura asked Philip now. She almost never asked him questions like that, never wanted to defer to his opinion. Proud of her own intelligence and too acutely aware of the fact that he was older, she didn't want him to start thinking that his age made him any brighter than she. It had stunned him a few months ago when she'd asked him to help her with some of the math problems, and soon they had developed a regular tutoring schedule. But for math only: it was understood that Laura was still smarter in other matters. Philip simply had the edge here thanks to his financial tutelage under Charles.

"I don't know. Hadn't really thought about it like that. It just is."

"Have you ever had the flu?"

He thought. "Don't think so. I was pretty healthy until the accident. My mom always said I had the constitution of a rhino."

"A rhino?"

"I think she liked the way that sounded."

"I think she was making fun of your nose."

He touched his nose. "What?"

"I was kidding. Rhino."

He smiled at her warily, hoping it really was a joke and that he hadn't been walking around all this time, unbeknownst to himself, with a pointy nose. He couldn't help looking at her nose more closely than usual, and at the rest of her face. This person is my sister now, he thought, yet we weren't born of the same people. I don't have her father's nose, and she doesn't have my mother's eyes. Are related people more likely to catch the flu from each other? Would it come for both of us, or just one? How tightly connected are we? And I wish my hair was as blond as hers.

They sat there in silence, then Laura leaned forward a bit. She lowered her voice. "I wanted to ask you . . . if you would let me look at one of your books."

"One of what books?" Philip too lowered his voice, though he wasn't sure why.

"Your fighter-pilot books."

A quizzical look. "I don't have any fighter-pilot books."

She rolled her eyes. "They're in your closet. Under the box with your baseball glove."

". . . What were you doing in my closet?"

"Look, I could have just taken them and read them if I'd wanted to, but I'm being good enough to ask permission."

"If Rebecca knew about them—"

"I know. I can keep secrets."

"If she catches you, they're yours."

"Deal. But she won't catch me."

They left the table and walked to his bedroom, in the back corner of the house, directly below Laura's room. He opened his closet door, reached down beneath a pile of extra blankets, and lifted out the box with his baseball glove and three baseballs, revealing the contraband beneath. The one on top was called *Hunt for the Baron,* and the cover bore an illustration of a plane with the German flag painted on its wings, firing its silver guns and leaving supernaturally blue and pink flames in its wake.

He handed them to her.

"Which one's the best?" she asked.

He was surprised that she was interested in war stories—she was a girl, after all, and not one with a lot of tomboy traits. Philip himself had been somewhat embarrassed by reading them—wasn't he too old for such stories? Somewhere in those European trenches, other sixteen-year-olds were fighting for their lives.

"I haven't read them all yet," he said. "I've read the bottom four so far. I liked *Attack of the Flying Circus* best, I think."

He had bought a few of them in Timber Falls last month. They were in a stack by the front register of a general store, and the vivid covers had caught his attention, reminding him of the stories of cowboys and train robbers he had read when he was younger. He must have left dozens of those books behind in various boardinghouses during his childhood, as he and his mother always seemed to be moving unexpectedly, running from an angry landlord or a jealous boyfriend. He had reached for a couple of the war books, flipping through until the clerk politely suggested he be a good patriot and buy them.

As soon as Philip reached the Worthy home, he ferried them into his room, temporarily hiding them under his bed. Soldiers were not viewed as heroes in this household, he well knew.

Attack of the Flying Circus detailed the horrific exploits of the recently slain Manfred von Richthofen, the legendary Red Baron, whose so-called Flying Circus was still tearing holes through the skies above France, strafing Allied soldiers and civilians alike. It was a short book intended for somewhat younger readers, and it took Philip only forty minutes to reach the end, where brave American pilots shot down the baron and half of the Circus, chasing the dwindling armada back to German airways, from which it would surely regroup to terrify the skies another day. Philip didn't know how much was true, but he knew the Baron had existed, knew there was real blood being spilled somewhere beyond these pages.

Another book, *Spies in the Harbor,* was about German spies who tried to blow up the Statue of Liberty. This one, too, though fiction, hewed closely to the truth: before the United States joined the war, German spies had set off a bomb in a New York harbor, blowing up a munitions facility with an explosion so great it scarred the Statue of Liberty and woke up people as far away as Philadelphia. Everyone in the country had been warned about spies by alarmed government announcements, excited newspapers, and the persistent Four-Minute Men. There were so many recent German immigrants, no one knew whom they could trust. According to the papers, spies were everywhere, keeping tabs on the soldiers at the camps and the workers in the shipyards, spreading wicked rumors of lost battles in France, hoping to discourage the lionhearted American people. Columnists wrote tips on how to spot a spy, on which behaviors were sure signs of the Hun, on what things not to talk about in public. There were even reports that Germany was sending spies to mill towns, hoping to sabotage one of the industries that was keeping American troops supplied for the war. But Charles had reassured Philip that such rumors were groundless fearmongering.

Still, Philip felt stupid for reading these kids' books. "You can take all of them," he said to Laura.

She looked at him strangely. "I don't need *all* of them." Besides, how would she sneak all of them to her room without risking being discovered by their mother?

He had offered because he didn't feel like reading about soldiers anymore, or perhaps ever again. The mere thought of a soldier in the woods nauseated him.

"I'm going to go read it in bed," Laura said. "I'll put it back tomorrow."

Holding the book in her right hand, she reached down through the waist of her skirt with her left. Then, in a motion so practiced Philip realized she must have done this before—and often—she passed the book from one hand to the other inside her dress. There she was, pinning the book there between her belly and the skirt.

"That's disgusting," Philip said.

"I'm wearing long johns."

"Still." He shook his head. "You can keep the book."

She rolled her eyes at him. "I'll put it back tomorrow."

They said good night and she was gone, and he was alone again. He sat down on his bed, hoping she wouldn't think less of him when she saw how childish the books were.

All the soldiers and pilots in those stories had girls back home, sweethearts. The doughboys wrote them letters and received perfume-scented stationery in return, and at night they'd talk among themselves about how after they beat the kaiser, they'd head back home and marry Susie or Mary Ann or Fanny.

Philip lay down and imagined himself as a soldier with Elsie as his sweetheart. Would she write him letters? She would miss him terribly and roll bandages with the other Red Cross ladies as a way of being close to him; she'd think of him constantly. And what would she write to him? Something about how she missed him the most at night, when she was alone in the dark and the bed felt so big and empty without him. But that would mean they'd already shared the bed, and so he imagined this, too, imagined the two of them lying together, and his imagination continued to work backward, seeing himself sitting atop the bed and watching her undress before joining him. He lingered on that image for a while. Then he let her back into the bed and his imagination raced forward again, stopping at those moments any sixteen-year-old boy would fixate on and skipping past those he didn't yet understand.

X

Charles was standing at the foot of his bed, looking in a small and faded mirror above his dresser as he removed his tie, when he heard the murmuring voices of his children coming from downstairs.

"I'm glad he's talking to Laura," Charles said to Rebecca. "He's barely said a word at the mill the last two days."

Rebecca stood up from the bed, putting down the journal she had been reading. "How is a person supposed to act after watching his friend shoot someone?"

Charles was still, surprised by her tone. Then he walked up behind her, wanting to put his hands on her shoulders to calm her, but thought against it.

"He never should have been out there," Rebecca said.

Charles waited a beat. "He volunteered."

She turned to face him. "You let him."

"I was supposed to forbid him?" His voice grew louder, but he was still enough in control to keep the children from overhearing.

Rebecca began tidying the bed.

"Do you blame me for this?" he asked.

Her answer, when it came, seemed less important to him than the fact that she didn't voice it for a full three seconds.

"No," she said. "I know you didn't want this to happen. I'm sorry. I'm just . . ." She shook her head. "I'm just *angry* that it happened." She sat down on the bed again, her hands clasped in her lap.

Charles didn't want any more arguments, any more debates. They had been arguing for months about the war, as his opinions were more moderate than hers. He had reminded her recently that the price of lumber was up thanks to the army's need of spruce for fighter planes and Douglas fir for constructing cantonments, and then Rebecca had all but accused him of war profiteering. *Have we moved deep into the woods and paid workers a better wage just so they could help the army kill more Germans?*

"I'll tell him he's not to serve as a guard again," Charles said. "It was a mistake to let him, you're right."

"I've already talked to him about that," Rebecca replied, "and he doesn't want to stop. He's afraid he'd be letting Graham down if he did. And I think he really means that he'd be letting us down, too."

That seems to make this argument moot, Charles thought. "So what do you want me to do?"

Maybe all she wanted was to hear that Charles did indeed have Philip's pain on his conscience, have the death of the soldier on his conscience. Even so, he wasn't sure he could say it, wasn't sure he could give voice to all the pressures bearing down on him. He had that one life on his conscience, yes, but he also had the lives of every person in the town. Every man and woman he had encouraged to leave their previous jobs and homes, to whom he had promised a better way of life, for whom he had vowed a stronger community, a land of safety and hope. He had to remember that.

The town was bigger than Charles, bigger than his paternal instincts for Philip's protection, bigger than his need to please his wife. He thought of his selfish brothers, how they had always used their families' needs to justify their own petty actions—that was why the workers were badly paid, why the strikebreakers could knock heads. He would not allow himself to fall into that trap, to use his love for his family to justify a moral failing. It didn't mean he didn't love Philip, Rebecca, and Laura any less—it meant that he loved them so much he would not compromise his vision of love for all.

That this was so incredibly difficult to do only convinced him that it was right.

Rebecca said, "I don't want you to do anything."

Charles sat on the bed beside Rebecca, who was gazing ahead at the wall rather than at her husband's large blue eyes. He put an arm around her and she did the same, and they sat there in a half embrace.

"I don't blame you," she said, hoping it was true.

Twenty minutes later, Charles had gone to pay a quick visit to Dr. Banes, and Rebecca was downstairs making tea. The pot was not yet whistling when there was a knock on the door.

Rebecca pulled the curtain aside to get a glimpse of the visitor: Jarred Rankle. She smiled and opened the door.

"Good evening, Jarred." She backed away and left the door open. "You're just in time for some tea."

Rankle held a hat in his hands, as well as some papers. His heavy jacket only added to the thickness of his muscular frame, and the floor seemed to creak a bit more loudly when he walked on it than when Charles did.

"I'm finally getting around to returning these journals," he told her. "They were very interesting—thank you."

"Better start reading more slowly," Rebecca said. "We'll have to make every printed word last until the quarantine ends."

"Is Charles in?"

"He's visiting Doc Banes."

Rankle blanched. "Is he all right?"

She smiled. "Not that kind of visit. Just to talk."

He nodded.

"Join me for some tea. You look chilled."

He paused, torn between decorum and perhaps something else. His heavy granite eyebrows shifted a bit, then he sat down at the table. "Thank you," he said. "So how are your little charges at the school?"

She smiled as she carried two cups to the table and sat across from him. "They're fine. I think I may have miscalculated, though. I thought the inactivity of having the town closed would bore them and lead to trouble, idle hands and all that. So I've been even stricter than usual lately, giving them extra work, but I wonder if I've gone a bit overboard. The more I give them, the more distracted they seem. I'm beginning to feel a bit guilty about it."

"Ah, it's good for 'em." He smiled. "I never did well at school, and look what became of me. Drive the little ones into the ground; they'll thank you for it."

They talked for a bit about one of the journal articles Rankle had read, something about the recent trial of the Wobbly leadership. Dozens had been sentenced to long jail terms for the crime of speaking out against the war.

"Wilson's just using the war as an excuse to jail all the Wobblies," Rankle said. "He's in a panic about what happened to Russia—afraid of having his own Bolshevik Revolution on his hands."

"Did you see some Democrats are calling the IWW 'Imperial Wilhelm's Warriors'?"

He smirked. "I saw it. I'd heard it before, too. They'll blame 'em for the war, blame 'em for not fighting the war, blame 'em after the war. It's nothing new."

He coughed then, a hoarse and forceful shudder that rocked the table. Rebecca didn't worry, as she was used to his coughing. Like many men in town, Rankle had the asthmatic cough of the shingle weaver, his lungs scoured by years of sawdust.

Jarred Rankle had been a young husband and father living outside Missoula when the lack of jobs forced him to take a six-month stint felling timber three hundred miles from home. He had missed his family terribly during those months, reading letters filled with news of their two-year-old son's progress. After four months, his wife's letters stopped reaching him, and Rankle blamed the timber town's crooked postmaster, to whom he had refused to pay kickbacks. After the job was finished, it was time to see if the situation back in Missoula had improved, but when he reached his house he found it empty. Some of their scant possessions had been left behind, but not many. He asked around but no one knew where his wife was, or his son. He contacted family but they didn't know, either. Rankle's wife and child had lived there only one year and had few acquaintances, so no one had noticed their sudden absence. The winter had been long and cold, and weeks had passed when people never saw their neighbors. He spent the next six months and every last penny he owned trying to find them, but there was no trail and no leads. He never saw them again.

After drinking away a couple of years and living in and out of small town prisons, Rankle made a friend, a Wobbly by the name of Rubinski. When he heard Rankle's sob story, he both empathized and told him the story was all too common. *You think you're the only bum's dragged himself to the ends of the earth to find a job to feed your family and come home to find 'em gone? You think you're the only one to wonder if they was killed by Injuns or horse thieves, or maybe they found a richer man and ran off with him, or maybe they died of the cold in the snow? You think you're the only one who's played by the rules and still had everything taken from him?* A thousand invisible and brokenhearted men walked alongside him, kicking their empty bottles and holding on to old love letters with blistered, work-weary fingers. Rankle applied for his red card that week and never drank again.

Rankle spent the next ten years following jobs in the Northwest and organizing for the Wobblies. He had been in Everett for the general strike, where his position made him a marked man. He'd been outnumbered by thugs and beaten up at the Beverly Park ambush, and was in the hospital recovering when the ferries had taken their ill-fated voyage, though he lost two friends that day. Tired of the violence and overwhelmed by the disappearance of more loved ones, he had parted ways with the Wobblies after that. He left Everett and bounced from job to job until he heard about what Charles Worthy was doing in Commonwealth.

After a brief silence, he saw a preoccupied look take hold of Rebecca. "Are you all right?"

She placed her cup on its saucer. "Worried."

"Once the war's over, the unions'll be back."

She smiled. "Not about that. About Philip. About the quarantine."

Rankle felt a bit uncomfortable, stepping into a family situation. "He won a lot of guys' respect, volunteering as a guard."

"I'm not much interested in him winning respect. I think some men around here overvalue that."

Rankle's heavy eyebrows shifted in acquiescence. "If it helps to know, he does seem to be in good spirits around the mill," he said. "And people like working with him. He's a good kid. I keep my eye on him." He felt another cough coming but stifled it with a sip of hot tea. He could feel the sweat at his hairline.

"Thank you. He is a good young man. That's why I worry—about him and Laura."

"I'll say this: if I could raise a family in any town in America, it would be in Commonwealth."

She looked down for a short while, her brows knit.

"I voted against the quarantine," she finally said. "I think it's wrong. I don't think we should shut the world out, cut ourselves off." She stared at her hands, folded into a tense knot.

It was the first time she had confided in him this way. But she felt herself becoming as cut off as she feared the town had become; she was telling him because she had to tell someone.

"Things will work out," he told her after a silence. An expression as confident as it was simple.

She shook her head again. "I wish I had done more to stop it—" Her voice broke, her eyes watering.

After a moment's hesitation, he reached out and put one of his massive hands atop hers, squeezing it a bit. His palm felt warm on Rebecca's fingers.

She looked up at him. He was a handsome man, the sharp edges of his jawline and cheekbone intimidating, perhaps, but the calmness of those gray eyes more than compensating. Surely he could have remarried, Rebecca figured—he probably could have had his pick of wives, even in towns where available women were greatly outnumbered by loggers. She didn't know if he had ever stopped mourning his family or if he had never stopped believing they were alive. Perhaps he had allowed himself to become married to a cause, first to the Wobblies and now to Commonwealth. If so, it was not a complete marriage, for Rebecca still sensed the loneliness inside him.

He removed his hand, his gray eyes turning away, as if to remind them both where they were, who they were.

"I'm sorry to put on a scene," she said, gently dabbing at her eyes with a napkin.

He shook his head. "Don't be. Everyone's feeling unsettled. But I know we'll get through this."

He thanked her for the tea and was on his way, and she sat at the table for a long while, her fingers still feeling the weight of his hand.

XI

It was dark when J. B. Merriwhether of Merriwhether's First Bank turned off the Ford's headlights and killed the engine in front of his house in Timber Falls. He reached for the door handle and paused, realizing that, with the windows up, he could not hear any coughing emanating from his house. The silence felt like such a gift that he stayed there a moment, waiting inside the Ford, breathing.

His daughter, Gwen, had been sick since Saturday, six days now. On Friday night she had been her vibrant self, though restless from being cooped up at home—the schools were all closed on account of the flu. But the next morning she'd woken up complaining of a headache, of pains in her knees and elbows, of terrible cold despite three wool blankets. By noon she was running a high fever.

Gwen will pull through, J.B. had told himself. She was about the hardiest girl J.B. had ever known—whenever J.B.'s son, James, had taken sick for a few days, Gwen would barely get a sniffle. But as the days had passed, his calm words no longer reassured him or his wife. Every time he opened his mouth to utter them, they were bludgeoned by the sound of Gwen coughing, a sound that grew more hoarse each day.

The flu had been in Timber Falls for over three weeks now.

He couldn't believe how many people had succumbed. Mayors throughout Washington were closing dance halls and forbidding theater owners to run their reels, banning public gatherings for fear of contagion.

J.B. had kept the bank open—how could the pillar of a town close?—but within days, all of his employees had called in sick. For the past week he had been the only man in the building, helping the dwindling number of customers who came in each day. It seemed like half the town was sick, and the other half was home caring for them.

The *Timber Falls Daily* hadn't been reporting the flu's death statistics at first, but families insistent on recording the passing of loved ones had finally cowed the paper into listing the deceased. Mill owners had told J.B. they were suffering through absenteeism of strike proportions, and men had to be awfully sick before they'd forgo a day's wages.

James, meanwhile, was now in France, or at least he was when he'd written his last letter. *Most recent* letter, J.B. scolded himself, not *last* letter. J.B. remembered the look on Violet's face when he'd finished reading the letter, a look of profound worry. Did she still blame J.B. for not doing more to keep James out of the war? But what could he have done? J.B. had volunteered to work on the registration board, had worked with the other upstanding paragons of social order in Timber Falls, had sat with them at their desk on the appointed day when all the men of appropriate age were required to register. Some friends of J.B. had pulled what strings they could, and the long arm of Uncle Sam had passed James over that time. But months later, in the second draft, James wasn't as fortunate. So off he was to Fort Jenkins, and from there to France.

His mind on his son, J.B. had spent the last two hours doing his patriotic duty as best he could. Since locking the doors of his empty bank, he had driven all over Timber Falls, hanging posters on lampposts and walls. In the passenger seat of the new 1918 Model T Ford coupe was a stack of Liberty Bonds, and on the floor beneath them, a few posters he would deal with tomorrow. His wife didn't approve of the image—a bloodred handprint above the words THE HUN—HIS MARK / BLOT IT OUT WITH LIBERTY BONDS—but he found it stirring. She preferred the ones with the valiant woman in the white dress, one hand extended to the sky like Lady Liberty herself, standing above the words VICTORY—LIBERTY LOAN.

J.B. had driven down empty roads and hung posters that no one would see save the doctors and undertakers who rode past. He feared he was wasting his time, but someone had to sell the bonds, do their part. And J.B. needed a task, sorely needed to *do* something. Anything was better than sitting at home, listening to Gwen's cough. Waiting for a letter from James.

One night the previous week J.B. had been at the Pioneers Club, one of the few gathering places in town that hadn't been shut down, since it wasn't exactly a public venue. He had been drinking with some of the boys when they were visited, unannounced, by one of the Four-Minute Men. The speaker looked just young enough that his sons, if he had any, weren't likely to be drafted yet, and maybe that helped with his sunny optimism. *The proud and patriotic American people are the difference in this here conflict,* the man said, *the difference between the Allies drowning in the mud of Caporetto or standing tall at Belleau Wood. But folks in Britain are still low on food, and the French are being raided from their homes by the Heinies, so more help is needed from good Christian folks like you gentlemen here.* When the man finished, J.B. vowed to spend his weekend selling Liberty Bonds.

So he had driven all over Timber Falls and the neighboring towns, but in two days he'd barely sold any. Sometimes he heard coughing or moaning from within houses he approached, and sometimes, after his knock, there would be footsteps approaching the door. The footsteps would stop and he would wait, but in most instances, no one would answer. He would knock again and the footsteps would recede, their gentle sound fading beneath the percussive assault of more coughing. A total of eight people had dared to answer their doors, five of them purchasing bonds after enduring J.B.'s appeal. The last person to answer had said no, that the only reason she'd answered was she had hoped he was the undertaker. She'd been waiting for two days.

That had been Saturday.

On Sunday, rather than subjecting himself to another round of ghostlike homes and hollow-eyed stares, he had decided to drive even farther from Timber Falls in hopes of finding a less ravaged population. Surely no one had thought to trek out to Commonwealth—no one ever went to that crazy town. Perhaps it was foolish of J.B. to do so, but he had figured that since no one else had tried it, he might as well be the first. And besides, he had always liked Charles Worthy more than he dared admit.

Because who but a socialist or red sympathizer—which J. B. Merriwhether of Merriwhether's First Bank most certainly was not—would dare say anything the least bit favorable about Charles Worthy? A man who had made all the lumber barons of Timber Falls and Everett roll with laughter when he suggested he could run a successful mill by paying his workers more, by sharing with them equally? A man who had started a mill miles from a viable port, on a tract of land that his own father had deemed unworkable?

But J.B. had known Charles before all that, had handled the banking for the Worthy family's mill in Everett before starting a new bank in Timber Falls. He knew the calm and quiet Charles Worthy was craftier than he received credit for, and though Charles was overshadowed by his guffawing, handshaking, cigar-smoking brothers, J.B. suspected the Worthy family mill in Everett would undergo a decline now that Charles was no longer the caretaker of its financial fortune. If anyone could make a mill like Commonwealth succeed, it was probably Charles.

And wasn't his son, Philip, only a year or two from draft age? Philip was the other reason J.B. liked Charles. A man who adopts an orphaned boy like that, a complete stranger—that's not a bad man. J.B. wanted to be the first to sell some Liberty Bonds in that crazy town, to shake Charles's hand one more time.

After the long drive deep into the woods, however, J.B.'s journey had come to an end at the tree that blocked the road and the sign warning him off. He had sat there for a good two minutes, his engine idling, his foot on the brake, as he tried to make sense of it. The sign had said ON ACCOUNT OF *THE* OUTBREAK, not ON ACCOUNT OF *OUR* OUTBREAK. Was the town healthy and hiding? And though his eyes weren't as sharp as they'd once been, he thought he had seen two men standing atop the hill, watching him as he turned the Ford to drive away.

He'd told a few friends about the experience, asked them if there was any news from Commonwealth. That had been nearly a week ago, and he'd heard nothing.

And here he was, back from another wasted effort, back to his sick daughter and his stark house. He exhaled deeply, his breath fogging the windshield. In the Ford he, too, felt quarantined, temporarily separated from the town's horrors, his daughter's suffering. Upstairs Gwen's window was dark—she couldn't endure the lamplight even while awake. He hoped she was sleeping, but lately the coughs had given her no rest. He looked at the mailbox, saw that it was empty. Violet would have checked it by now, and if there had been word from James, she would have telephoned him at the bank. Unless the news was bad. Each day it was harder to get out of his Ford.

J.B. said a brief prayer for his children. Then he gripped the handle and pushed the door open, stepping back into a world he had learned not to trust.

XII

"'Across the foam in no-man's-land I'll soon be fighting, / But I know your lips are no man's land but mine.'"

Elsie heard Philip singing to himself while he painted the porch of a recently constructed house. Because of the quarantine, the call for more workers had been temporarily muted, and many houses in Commonwealth were empty. As Elsie approached, she wondered how long it would be until the flu passed and new workers could fill this block of empty houses.

"Morning," she said.

"Morning," he replied, putting down his paintbrush. He looked surprised to see her there—the new houses were at the end of a block, not really on the way to anything.

"Are you painting alone today?"

"Graham's supposed to be helping. Must be late."

She nodded, unsure how to ask the question that had driven her there.

"Where are you off to?" he asked.

"Church," she said. Though Commonwealth's traveling Unitarian minister had been banned from the town along with every other outsider, his leaderless parishioners had decided to gather for Sunday-morning prayer sessions without him. They would carry on, asking God to make the flu pass so they could end the quarantine, welcome back their minister, and act like a real church again.

"Get a little lost?"

"I felt like going for a walk," she demurred, looking away.

Philip crouched to wet his brush again.

"You're a hard worker," she said. "Six days a week at the mill, all this painting today, all that digging on Friday . . ."

Philip left the brush on the lip of the bucket and stood up. "What digging?"

"I don't really know. I was hoping you'd tell me. What were you fellows digging on Friday?"

"Who?"

She smiled a bit. "Don't insult me, Philip. I saw you that morning. I saw you digging out there and—"

"What exactly did you see?" His voice was tight.

Elsie took a half-step back. She looked down for a moment, her confidence in this confrontation dwindling. "I saw you and Graham Stone and the other men. I'd gone out for a walk, and I heard you out there . . ." She cautiously met his eyes again. "It almost looked like you were digging a grave."

"Is that all you saw?"

She nodded. "I went home after that."

Philip closed his eyes for a second.

"Why, did I miss something?"

He opened his eyes. "There were a couple dead deer down there. Doc said they mighta died of some kind of disease or something, and that we should bury them where we found them. We didn't want to tell people because we thought they might get scared it was flu, but Doc says it wasn't."

Philip wasn't as good of a liar as he thought he was, Elsie thought. But why was he lying to her? She paused, wondering how far she should push him. But surely there was an explanation. "Philip, I saw what you buried."

Their eyes locked. Then Philip looked around—a couple of women were walking past on the corner a few houses away, but they weren't close enough to overhear.

"What did you see?" he asked, his voice quiet.

She stared back at him. He knew she knew. Why did she have to say it? "It wasn't a deer." Until then she'd felt almost powerful in her knowledge of a secret and confident there was some safe and rational explanation for what she had seen. But his obvious discomfort scared her. "What's going on, Philip?"

Philip motioned to the door of the house. She was so overcome by the situation that she didn't think how improper it was to venture with him into an empty building. He opened the door and shut it behind them.

Inside, the house smelled like wood and dust, the things every house would probably smell like if people weren't living in them. Even Elsie's breath seemed to echo.

"It was the soldier from the day before, wasn't it?" Even though they were alone, she said this in a lowered voice.

Philip could only nod in response.

"Did he get sick? Did he sleep out there overnight and die?"

He looked startled, then nodded sadly. "Yeah. The morning after Graham and I made him leave, the guys who had the next day's shift saw him there. He must have hid down at the bottom of the hill overnight, hoping the next morning we'd let him in or something."

"So . . . did he die of the flu, or from the cold?"

"I . . . I don't know. Doc Banes, I mean, he said he couldn't tell. But, um, we left him there for a few hours in case his body was contagious, then we buried him."

"So there's a chance he was actually healthy and he died because we wouldn't let him in." She said this calmly, thinking it through.

"Charles and Doc Banes said we shouldn't tell anyone, though, because people might assume he'd died of the flu, and panic."

As Elsie took this in, she saw that his eyes were welling up. "Are you okay?"

He nodded, looking away.

She stepped closer to him, her hands clasped before her. She wanted to reach out to him but feared it would be improper.

"I'm sorry, Philip. I didn't mean to suggest it's your fault he died. I didn't mean it like that."

His gaze was hard and fixed on something beyond the window, just something to stare at as the tears slowly and stubbornly dissolved in his eyes.

"He probably did have the flu. If you'd let him in, maybe everyone in town would be sick by now."

"Yeah," he pronounced at last.

Elsie felt horrible. Not only must he blame himself, but surely the thought of the soldier dying from exposure made him think of his mother's death, of his frigid night at the bottom of the snowy gorge. The last thing Philip wanted to think about was a person who had died from the cold, she figured. She longed to reach out and hold him, tell him it was all right for him to feel this way.

"I'm sorry I brought this all up. I can get too curious sometimes, I guess."

He nodded, still looking out the window, then turned to her. "I don't think we're doing the right thing."

At that she stiffened somewhat. "You're right; we should go back outside."

"That's not what I meant," he said. "I don't think we're doing the right thing with the quarantine. I don't think we're doing the right thing closing the town."

She exhaled. "Everything's so . . . confusing right now. I keep hoping this'll end soon, that we won't have to worry about it much longer."

They looked at each other for what began to feel like an uncomfortable amount of time.

"I'm sorry I lied to you," he said.

"That's all right. I can see why you did. And besides, I lied to you, too."

"You were pretty good at it," he said, smiling.

She smiled back. "I really don't have that much experience."

"I *know* that's a lie," he said, laughing, and for a moment they were just two kids again, teasing each other because they didn't know how else to show their feelings. They were miles away from the flu or the war.

But within seconds Philip brought them back.

"I'm supposed to be out there in a couple hours. At the post."

"If it makes you feel any better, I know that you being out there makes people feel safe. People talk about it."

"Really?"

"Sure. My mother, for one—after her being so sick last year, she's really worried about the flu. And my dad. Other folks talk about it, too. Everyone knows how bad it is. No one wants it happening here."

He looked as if a weight had been lifted from his shoulders.

"I should be getting to church," she said.

"Okay. And . . . did you tell anyone else about . . . the grave?"

"No."

"It's supposed to be a secret."

"I understand. I'll keep it that way."

"Thank you."

"Are you not coming to church?" Elsie asked as they walked back outside. The Worthys had become irregular churchgoers, she had noticed, and that was probably Mrs. Worthy's influence, as it was rumored that she attended only for Charles's sake and secretly did not believe in God.

"Oh, no, I can't," he stammered, reaching down for the paintbrush. "I have to finish the porch."

They bade each other goodbye, but as she walked away, she reflected on his response. After walking half a block, she looked back at him, saw his thin body bent forward, his eyes intent on the wet bristles gliding across the wooden posts. The fact that he was out there painting a house that could not be used as a home until the quarantine ended seemed odd, she thought.

She turned around, late for church. In the distance she could make out the singing, the voices projected farther than usual, as if the congregants were so nervous from the jangling tensions of the quarantine that they were yearning to cast something beautiful upon that barren landscape. She ran toward them.

XIII

"Good day to be out," Mo said.

"Look like it's going to rain," Philip disagreed.

"Nah, that ain't rain. That's just Mother Nature's gray blanket. It's comforting."

Mo was a talker. Where a man of Mo's size got his unceasing energy was a mystery to many loggers, not least those larger men who had tried to shut him up with force and had learned, to their detriment, that his prowess with words was matched by the dexterity of his indefatigable fists. Turns out the one story Mo seldom told was how he had been a boxer in Detroit, flyweight. If you worked beside him long enough, he would eventually tell you, late at night and a bit high from drink, how he had accidentally killed a sparring partner with some hard blows, though he wasn't swear-to-God certain it was accidental, on account of his having been insulted by the sparring partner earlier that day. Which is why he had run from Detroit at age twenty-five, hiding in the Upper Peninsula and then the forests of the West, aiming all his future blows at defenseless tree trunks.

He had gone bald rather young—he was in his mid-thirties—and the ridge of his oft-broken nose was a painful zigzag. When people asked about it he lied and said cops done it.

"Rain is comforting?"

"If you look at it the right way, it is."

After only a few weeks of his new life as a logger, Mo had realized there was nothing else he would rather do. Forget boxing rings, gymnasiums—he needed to be outside. The smell of the earth, the sun's embrace—even on those deadly cold days, the *feel* of the sun—rather than the stilled emptiness of a building without windows. Mo quickly became the least favorite member of every team he was placed on due to his interminable monologues about the glories of the outdoors, his praise of greenery and blue sky.

"The Hun's really running now. I hear an armistice could be just around the corner. Before the end of the month, even."

"Where'd you hear that?" Philip had barely been paying attention to Mo's earlier ramblings, participating only with the occasional "uh-huh," but this statement piqued his curiosity. Until then he'd been thinking about Elsie and the empty house and how he'd felt when he was alone with her in a place no one else could see. He'd never wanted to leave, wished he could live there forever.

"Around." Mo shrugged. "Folks are talking. Guess somebody saw a newspaper."

"Newspaper would have to be over a week old by now."

"So maybe the war's over already and we don't even know. Maybe everybody else in the country is celebrating. Soldiers and nurses are dancing in France. Parades in Paree."

"That'd be nice."

"I doubt it's happened, though. Doesn't feel like it."

"You think we'll know when it's over?" They weren't close enough to other towns to see fireworks or hear the roar of a crowd, the thump and wail of a marching band.

"Sure we will."

"How?"

"I dunno. The air, the sky." He scratched at his cheek, beside an ugly boxing scar.

"We'll be able to tell the war is over because of how the sky looks?"

"Pretty much."

"The sky here's gray every day."

"Exactly. Don't you think old man Sun would finally come out for that?"

Philip checked for a smile but saw none.

"I can tell things from the weather," Mo said. "Every real bad thing that's happened to me out here, I've known it was coming from the weather."

"Such as?"

Mo thought. "First time anyone on my crew ever got killed, it happened on an afternoon when we had lightning but no rain. We were just about finished with our shift when we saw the lightning start, but we were working for a real mean bastard who didn't care if his crew got struck or not, so we had to stay out there. Lightning ain't a good thing when you're chopping down trees."

"I know that."

"So we're out there working, and everybody's pretending not to be bothered by the lightning because we're all tough bastards, of course, but everybody's thinking about it. I was working with this one fella I didn't particularly like on account of he was one of those guys who thought that insulting you real bad was the way to get to know you. So the lightning is flashing, but there's still no rain—no thunder, even, it was almost like we were just imagining the lightning—and I decide my saw needs sharpening so I head on back to the shed. I spend some time on it, and when I turn around to head back to my spot, I see that my partner is lying there on the ground. And I get closer and see he's been stabbed straight through the heart, there's blood all over his chest and his eyes are dead as McKinley's. And pretty soon the lightning had stopped, and it never did rain."

"Who killed him?"

"Couple a guys he'd insulted a bit too much. They were from Poland, and he'd had himself a good time the night before making fun of Polish women—Polish mothers in particular—and they hadn't cared for that. I pretty much knew it was coming."

"Then it wasn't the weather that warned you, it was you knowing the guys were mad at him. That's why you were afraid something bad was coming."

"First of all, I never said I was *afraid.*" Mo looked a bit peeved. "Second of all, you can call it how you like."

As more of the day passed in silence, Philip thought about Elsie again—so much better than thinking of the last time he had been out at the post. Was Elsie at church still, or was she at home, or helping at the general store? Philip was probably the furthest thing from her mind, he realized. When he'd been talking to her, he had seen the concern in her eyes, had even had the sense that she was close to hugging him, but surely he'd been imagining it. He was just the adopted boy with the missing foot who hobbled around town and happened to live in the same house as Elsie's best friend.

His thoughts and feelings leaped back and forth between these poles of infatuation and abject despondency. The skies became somewhat darker, the clouds more thickly covering any evidence of the sun, which Philip had not laid eyes on in days.

And what about Graham? He had never shown up to help paint. Something about the way Graham had acted the other day had kept Philip from walking over to the Stones' house and knocking on their door, asking what the holdup was.

"Shoot," Mo said suddenly.

"What?"

"I told the Wachowskis I'd get them some firewood this morning but I forgot." Jay Wachowski was a sawyer who'd broken both his hands in a mill accident the previous week, and the neighbors had been pitching in to help his family get by while he recovered. "Eh, I'll do it after the shift."

"It'll be dark then. They'll need wood before the sun sets."

"Shoot," Mo said again, looking back toward the town.

"Go ahead. It'll only take you an hour."

Mo didn't like having to face a difficult decision. "But I said I'd stand guard, too."

"If you'll only be an hour, that's okay. I can handle things out here alone for a bit."

"You sure?"

"I'm sure. Go ahead."

Mo nodded, carefully placing his rifle on the ground. "Allrighty. Don't go shooting any deer or anything."

Once Mo had left, Philip sat down on the ground just before the tree stump, feeling that he could be more casual now that no one was watching. His shift would end at eight. That was when Deacon would take over, standing there to commune with the darkness until the sun began its ascent the next morning. Philip wondered what kind of person would volunteer for that shift, for standing beneath the sky's sheer blackness with nothing except the sound of owls and the twitching of branches and the occasional deep sound that might be a bear and might be one's imagination.

Philip hadn't looked at his pocket watch in some time—he had come to realize that the less often he checked it, the more quickly time escaped. He stared at his boots for a long moment, daydreaming about Elsie again, and finally looked up.

At the bottom of the hill he saw something move.

Like before. All too similar to that day with Graham. First the colored shadows of something, tiny glances of a moving object revealed only in the spaces between the trees. It disappeared behind the thick trunks and reappeared a few feet to the right, moving toward the clearing at the base of the hill.

Philip's fingers tightened their grip around the gun for what he hoped would be just a moment, a passing thought, a mistaken impression. But then he realized how right he'd been—and how wrong the situation was about to become.

A figure was emerging from the woods, walking toward the sign. Again. It was a man, again, and he walked slowly but with no limp. The figure's steady gait was all that told Philip he wasn't imagining this, that this was something new, something happening right now. The man stopped at the sign.

"Go away," Philip said to himself, for the man was still too far to hear. "Please, please go away."

How could there be another person *walking* to Commonwealth, another lost soul straggling the fifteen miles from the nearest town? Philip shook his head at his peculiar fate, wishing against all reality that the man would simply disappear.

The man looked up at Philip. The light was just dim enough, beneath the canopy of the trees, for the man's features to be momentarily invisible. No face, no mouth, no particular type of clothing. Philip wished very much to remember him that way: as a nothing, a wraith that appeared and read a strange sign and just as quickly—please, please—vanished into the woods. A creature that would not fraternize with men. A spook. Please, please go away.

But the man disobeyed Philip's inaudible plea. He climbed over the fallen tree and started walking up the hill.

He slowly solidified from wraith to fully realized man; he acquired dark hair and equally dark eyes and a small nose that seemed all but overtaken by a recent growth of unkempt beard. Soon he would have a voice. Then a personality. Mannerisms. Possibly a regional accent. Where the hell was Mo?

It was another soldier. He was dressed like the first soldier, the same khaki pants and the same jacket over the same shirt that had come untucked and hung over where his belt should be. The same boots covered in the same mud that smeared most of his legs. Still, he looked cleaner than the last man, like he was more accustomed to finding himself lost in the woods and knew how to take care of himself. Some of the mud looked like it had dried days before. It lacked the fresh wetness of the first soldier's, just as this man's gait lacked the limp—the limp of the victim, the limp of the guy who seemed to know all along that he would be shot. This guy didn't know any such thing.

Something in his eyes struck more fear into Philip than he had felt before. Shouldn't something like this get easier the second time? The man was looking at him now, and it was with an uneasy feeling that Philip realized he was being assessed, measured up, and found wanting.

Philip stole a quick glance behind him to see if Mo was coming or even if Elsie was hiding somewhere in the trees. But there was no one, just him and a soldier. Philip turned back around. He had already let the man come too close.

"You can't come up here!" Philip shouted. He thought that was what Graham had said, but it sounded so much punier from Philip's lips. There was weight behind Graham's voice, mass. Maturity and suffering. Philip sounded like a kid holding a toy gun.

The man kept walking, silently.

"I said you can't come up here! The town is closed off on account of the flu!"

More footsteps, still no voice.

Philip lifted the rifle, aiming it at the man. He had noticed that, unlike the previous soldier, this man did not have a rifle slung over his back. Nonetheless, holding his own weapon gave Philip not a feeling of strength or safety but one of imminent danger. As if the gun were pointed backward at himself. As if he knew that the weight of any violence he rendered would feel all the greater on his hands.

"I said," Philip spat through gritted teeth, his voice surprising even him in its ferocity, "you've come close enough."

The man stopped. He was perhaps thirty yards away, at about the same spot the first soldier had fallen dead. He looked down, shook his head. When he looked back up, there was a smile on his lips. He was a handsome man, his smile well defined even in the beginnings of a beard.

"C'mon, kid, put the gun down and let's talk like civilized men."

He looked about Graham's age. That would make him nine years Philip's senior, but Philip still didn't like being called "kid" by a stranger.

"We're under quarantine. No one's allowed in town. Turn around and head somewhere else."

"And what town is this, pray tell?"

"Commonwealth."

The man seemed thoroughly unimpressed by the situation, as if Philip were a yapping family dog whose presence the man tolerated only so as not to appear rude to his hosts.

"Kid, do I look like I have the flu to you?"

"Do I look like a doctor?"

The man thought for a moment. "Would you like me to do a handstand for you? Or fifty push-ups? I'll do fifty push-ups for you—that should prove I'm a healthy man."

"We're not letting anyone into our town." Philip was trying not to be disarmed by the man's smile, his ignorance of the moment's severity.

"What's your name, kid?"

"You need to turn around *now.* I'm sorry, buddy. I'm just protecting my town."

"And what happens if I come any farther?" He took a step.

Philip thought of Graham. Then he thought of Elsie.

"I shoot you."

Philip had said that evenly, hadn't tried to make it sound like a threat. Just matter-of-fact, an immutable truth. The sun rises in the east, the trees here are tall, and I shoot anyone who gets too close. It was this simple tone of voice that made the expression on the soldier's face change somewhat. It was as if the little yapping dog had become eerily quiet while staring intently at the man's ankles.

"I don't think you would."

They stared at each other. Philip thought of the way Graham's eyes had looked two nights ago when he stared at his fireplace, of his trembling hands by the woodshed, the coldness in his voice. I need this guy to leave, now. I don't want to shoot him. I don't know if I can. I need to make him decide to turn around.

"I've done it before." Philip said that slowly, each word carefully measured, each word hurting as it came out, like shrapnel removed by rusty forceps.

"Have you?"

Philip couldn't tell if the man didn't believe him or was just hoping to catch this tough-acting kid in a lie that would expose him as a coward and blowhard.

"Look to your left. About thirty yards in the woods. Look for the tree with the strip of moss on its trunk in a diagonal line." The man did as he was told. "See it?"

"I see the tree, yeah."

"Now look below it."

The man stepped to his side to get a glimpse of the earth between the crossing branches. He was silent for a moment.

"That a grave?"

"That's right."

The gravediggers had put the grave where no one was likely to stumble upon it, but it was still somewhat visible from the road if one knew where to look.

"Looks fresh."

"Just a couple days old." While the man looked at the grave, Philip kept his eyes locked on his target. "He was a soldier, like you."

This too caught the man unawares. He faced Philip again. "Another soldier?"

"That's right. So don't think I'm intimidated by the uniform or anything."

Philip's muscles were getting tight, aching. They pleaded for him to relax at least momentarily or switch to another position, but he refused.

"I just need a place to sleep, kid." The soldier had wisely decided to stop goading Philip and was trying a new tack. "And some food. I don't—"

"Stop calling me kid."

"Some food and a place to sleep, please, sir. That's all I ask."

Philip had thought of this, of the option he had overlooked when the first soldier had come around.

"I maybe can bring you some food if you stay back where you are and don't come any closer. After the other guard comes back. But you're out of luck on the shelter. No one comes into the town."

"It's going to be freezing tonight. The hell with your food if you're going to leave me out here to die."

"That's the best I can do. Take it or leave."

The man thought about this. He looked back at the grave.

"You must be a deadeye with that rifle."

"Good enough."

The soldier looked down, and though Philip could barely see his face, he knew the man was smiling again. Why was this so entertaining to him? The bit of fear that Philip had seen in his eyes seemed to have left him already.

He's going to take another step, Philip thought. He's not scared anymore. Maybe he's crazy. Maybe something worse happened to him in the war, and the last thing he's going to do is be sent away by some "kid." He's going to come closer.

If the soldier takes one step farther, I'll aim for the ground right in front of him, Philip vowed. *Make him jump. Scare him home. He gets one warning shot. One.*

The soldier looked up again. Philip saw the decision in his eyes, the imminent movement. The muscles in Philip's trigger finger were so taut they ached.

Philip thought the man's step would be slow and deliberate, but he was wrong. The soldier didn't step at all. His movement was this: the right hand that had been dangling by his side disappeared for a moment, into the low tails of his untucked shirt, and as soon as it reappeared it was holding a pistol and the air around Philip exploded.

Philip instinctively fired a shot and dropped. The two shots echoed each other, the sound of Philip's still startling to him. He was on the ground now, hiding behind the mighty trunk that had been envisioned as a post but certainly not as a shield. His breaths came fast. He took a quick moment to look himself over and determine that he had not been hit by the soldier's bullet.

But had Philip hit the soldier? He listened for a sound. Was the intruder dead? Or was he crouching closer, just on the other side of the tree trunk?

Philip's fingers were shaking. He had to look, had to see if the soldier was dead. He took a breath. Be quick. Take a look, no longer than a second, and hide again. He repositioned his feet under him, his legs crouched so he could spring up and collapse back down again. He frantically reloaded his rifle, took another breath. Now.

He turned and lifted himself just enough for his head and shoulders to clear the trunk. The soldier was gone. Or at least he wasn't where he had been a moment ago. Philip glanced to his right, to the thick woods, the direction of the first soldier's grave, and just as he saw something move he let his legs go out from under him and he fell behind the tree trunk.

"You sure you want to do this?" the soldier called out.

The enormity of the fact that someone had just shot at him was slowly sinking into Philip's panicked mind. The soldier had shot at him and would do so again. In a way, the soldier was making this easy on Philip—now Philip *had* to shoot him or be shot himself. Everything about standing guard was supposedly in the vein of self-defense, but only now, with a tangible threat so close, did it truly feel that way.

Still, he knew he was the sole defense the town had. This man could be on the verge of becoming sick, could be carrying the flu in his blood and lungs. He could stroll into Commonwealth and soon people would be coughing, would be in bed with fever, would be hallucinating as their foreheads burned and their eyes clouded over and their insides flooded with mucus and death. Philip had to stop the soldier.

"I'm not letting you into that town! Even if you do shoot me, there's plenty more men that'll keep you from getting in!"

Someone must have heard the shots, Philip thought. They weren't that far from the town. Someone would come so long as Philip could keep the stalemate. Unless the men were still working on those two buildings on the main street, hammering up a storm. Surely the sound of gunfire would be audible over the hammering.

Philip heard movement. The soldier was somewhere in the woods to the right of the stump. The woods ended about twenty feet from where Philip was crouching, so they were close to each other. The soldier could be pretty much anywhere by now, approaching Philip from any angle. Philip was alone on an island, a tiny one. If he waited much longer, the soldier would get a clear shot.

Philip rolled to his side, clear of the stump's protection. With the rifle stretched out before him, he fired a shot into the woods, at his best guess of where the soldier had been during the split second he'd seen him before. Then he sprang to his feet and ran as fast as his lame leg could carry him. He lunged the last few feet, landing awkwardly and painfully behind another tree. The rifle bounced from his hands and landed a few feet from him, but he was able to reach out and grab it as he sat up, leaning with his back against the tree.

He was surprised the soldier hadn't shot at him while he'd made his escape. Was the soldier so close that he didn't need to? Was Philip hiding the wrong way, was his side actually exposed to his adversary, wherever he was? The man was a soldier, after all—he had been trained how to do this. He would know how to overtake some sixteen-year-old with a rifle and only one foot. The soldier was probably nothing but a shadow now, slinking between the trees, wrapping around tree trunks and between branches, crawling closer.

Philip tried to make his breaths quieter. Tried to be silent. Tried to listen for the soldier, but he heard nothing.

There were bushes and thickets and low-leaning branches covering most of the ground; it would not be easy to sneak around here without alerting one's for. Either the soldier wasn't moving at all or he was doing so with extreme deliberation, calmly brushing aside a branch, taking a step, waiting.

Then, a sound. Something to Philip's right. He turned just as the sound was dying away. Something moving over there, against that tree with the poison ivy beneath it. The moving object rolled toward Philip: a rock. A rock?

It had been thrown there. A distraction. Philip realized he had exposed his position, was no longer as well hidden. The moves were coming to him now, he saw the steps, but each one too late.

And as Philip turned back around, almost but not fast enough, he saw more movement, real movement, a man coming toward him with speed he could not counter. Before he had turned enough to face the man, the movement changed again, became awkward, and there was a hard dull sound, then a whimper.

The soldier had tripped and fallen. He'd been moving into position, close enough for a sure shot, when he had tripped on one of the serpentine but solid trunks that slithered beneath them. He'd fallen forward, landing on his chest but catching himself with his hands. His empty hands. Philip saw the pistol skitter on the ground and land in the nook of another tree trunk, perhaps six feet from the soldier's head. The soldier looked up, his eyes wide with the realization that this kid was limping forward, closer to the pistol than the soldier was.

Philip also realized he had forgotten to reload his rifle. He immediately did so, his earlier mistake depriving him of a quick shot. But now the rifle was loaded and now he was standing with one foot on top of the pistol. The soldier leaned on his hands, slowly raising himself to a kneeling posture. After his earlier nonchalance, his face finally wore a look of concern, extreme concern.

Philip was aiming the rifle right at the man's chest. They were no more than three yards from each other.

The soldier swallowed. His eyes were large, the pupils seeming to shrink as the whiteness grew around them.

Philip knew he should pull the trigger right then, pull it quickly and end it all. Don't give the man a chance to open his mouth again and start talking. He thought of Elsie, thought of Rebecca and Charles and his sister, Laura, thought of Amelia and his unofficial niece, Millie. A baby might be the first to get sick and die if the epidemic made it to town. He thought of the baby dying and Amelia pacing the room nervously, her face blank with shock. He thought of Graham punching holes in the walls of his house, Graham being unable to suppress unmanly tears just as he had been helpless to save his only child. Philip fixated on Graham despite himself, thought of Graham and the first soldier and the two shots, one to put the man down and one to finish him off.

"So that's it, then," the soldier said, waking Philip from his free-flowing fears.

The rifle seemed so heavy.

"Just get up and turn around," Philip commanded. "Get out of here. Please."

He shouldn't have said "please." It made him sound weak or conflicted and he regretted it immediately.

The soldier shook his head. "I'd rather die quick than slow, freezing to death. Go ahead." He sounded something between spiteful and at peace with his fate.

"Just go," Philip pleaded.

"Here. I'll make it easy for you." The soldier opened the first two buttons of his khaki jacket and held them apart, exposing a circle of undershirt that was the only thing covering his heart. "Right there, kid. Can't miss it." His eyes were almost completely blank, but the skin around his eye sockets was tensed. Philip could see a vein along the side of his head twitching. The man's teeth were clenched and his jaw was rigid and his head and neck began to shake. All the muscles in his body seemed to be flexing in defiance of death even as their master was openly courting it.

He was so close that, from Philip's vantage point, the end of the rifle covered the center of the man's chest, the bit of white cotton shirt a perfect target.

They were so close. They were too close. They were breathing the same air, and the longer Philip stood there, the worse he was making it. Was it already too late? Was the secret, doomed fate of the town already in Philip's blood?

They stared at each other, motionless. They stared at each other and breathed.

Philip lowered his rifle slightly. It was such a tiny movement but it meant so much, for he had made his decision. Whether he did it because he felt backed into a corner or because he was unable to follow through was something he refused to ponder.

"If we cut through these woods," Philip said slowly, "we'll get to an empty building. There's a cellar, and you can hide down there. I'll get you some food, then you can sleep. But before the sun rises, you leave. You're gone before anyone else is awake." He swallowed. "Do you understand?"

The soldier nodded, eyes wide.

"You'll stay silent and be gone by sunrise?"

"Yes. Yes. Thank you."

Philip lowered the rifle. He bent down and picked up the man's pistol, looking at it briefly before putting it in his pocket. He'd never held a pistol before and he hoped to hell it wouldn't go off in his pocket, but he wasn't giving it back to the soldier.

"You got any more guns hidden in there?"

The soldier said no, but Philip made him stand and open his jacket, lift up his shirt, and empty his pockets to prove it. Philip noticed that the soldier's hands were shaking, and his eyes looked more reflective than before. He had truly thought he was about to die, and his recovery from this was not quick.

"Lead the way," Philip said, pointing ahead with his rifle.

Philip followed about ten paces behind, which he hoped was enough distance to keep him protected from whatever vile germs or malevolent spirits haunted the air around his captive. Maybe being a few feet away for only a minute or two hadn't made a difference? Maybe he hadn't ruined everything for the entire town?

He tried not to think about this—he was already so nervous and scared that he couldn't afford to. The forest became even thicker as the hill rose, but Philip knew that after a few hundred yards, they would reach a clearing where a few empty buildings stood. The buildings had been built by Reginald Worthy's mill years before Charles had bought the property and created Commonwealth; they originally had been intended to store excess wood, but they were poorly located, much too far from the river and the mill. They had never been used, a strange waste of space that made Philip wonder if Charles was deliberately avoiding these buildings out of self-righteousness. The fact that they were so removed, at the end of a barely used road, made them perfect for Philip's purposes. The soldier could sleep in one all night and never be near enough to infect anyone. Maybe it would be like he had never been there. Maybe this wasn't a horrible mistake.

Twigs snapped as they ascended the hill. Philip's view of the soldier was dimmed by the falling dusk. The dirt and bark and grass and needles were losing their color, fading into a dull gray that would soon disappear into darkness.

Where was Mo? Now, of course, Philip was hoping that his bald accomplice would take even longer to return. If Philip could stow the soldier in the building and tell him to wait there, he could return to the post before Mo got back. Then he would tell Mo he needed to leave briefly—he'd make up some excuse—and he'd get some food for the soldier and bring it to the empty building. He'd do his best to avoid other people that night in case the air around him was polluted by disease. But if he had been infected by something, wouldn't he pass it on to Mo, who would then pass it on to someone else, and on and on in a matter of hours? How exactly did this work? Philip would have to find Doc Banes, ask him a few innocent questions. Then again, if he was trying to avoid people, he couldn't ask the doctor. This was already too complicated.

Soon the trees thinned out and a small clearing opened. It was a partially man-made clearing, and recent at that, as stumps littered the ground. Just ahead of them were three buildings, and Philip ushered the soldier toward the one that sat farthest from the town. As they approached the building, he had a view of the road that linked these forgotten structures with the rest of the town. The road went straight ahead, with the woods to the right and a thinner stand of trees to the left. Just beyond was one of the main streets—this road was one of the many spokes off of it, and most of the others were lined with empty new houses. Surely, no one should need to come down here.

"Go inside," Philip said to the soldier, stepping back several feet to give the man and his possible baggage of disease a wide berth.

The soldier obeyed.

"Head for the cellar. The stairs are in the back, on the right."

Philip waited a few seconds for the bad spirits surrounding the soldier to dissipate before he followed. Inside was a large, dark, windowless room, musty with stagnation. It took his eyes a moment to adjust. Dust covered the floor and walls, mottling the dark wood. The soldier had left footprints, and Philip consciously avoided them, stepping to the side as if he could catch the flu though the soles of his boots. He closed the door behind him just as the soldier began descending the stairs. Philip figured he would walk to the top of the stairs and call down, tell the soldier that it might be as long as an hour or two before he could bring any food. He would warn the soldier again that if he poked his head out and walked around the town, the other townspeople would be far less forgiving of his trespassing than Philip had been.

But his plans dissolved when he heard the sound of the door opening behind him.

Philip turned around and saw the door slowly complete its swing back into the building, saw the light from outside seeping in, and saw Mo standing at the threshold. Mo had a handkerchief covering his nose and mouth like a train robber from a children's book. There was also a handkerchief wrapped around the hand he had used to turn the knob and open the door. His other hand held his rifle.

"Philip? What are you doing?" Mo's words came slowly, muffled by the handkerchief. Above it his eyes were wide.

Philip was stunned. Mo must have followed him, must have returned to the empty post and seen the two figures disappearing into the woods, must have tracked them here, careful to keep his distance. So much more careful than Philip, stupid Philip, cowardly Philip, who felt the weight of his mistakes piling upon him with terrible suddenness.

Mo was shaking his head in horror.

"I was just going to get him some food," Philip said, or thought about saying, or tried to say, but maybe his voice gave out halfway—he wasn't sure. Even if he had said it, it was so small and unimportant that it didn't matter.

Mo backed up another step.

"Stay in there, Philip." He spoke kindly, but it was clear that this was a command and not a suggestion. "Just stay in there and I'll get Mr. Worthy and we'll figure this out."

Before Philip could protest or think of anything else to say, Mo moved his handkerchief-covered hand out of view and the door swung shut, casting Philip in total darkness.

Part Two

Prisoners

I

J. B. Merriwhether sipped his whiskey slowly. He wanted only the one drink, but he was in no rush to leave, so he was determined to make it last.

His working day had ended and here he was at the Pioneers Club, delaying his journey home. Twice he had called his wife, Violet, checking in on their daughter's condition. It had not improved. Gwen had been bedridden for over a week now and her cough was loud and thick. And persistent—all day, throughout the night, torturing his sleep and making hers nearly impossible. That morning a worrisome new symptom had appeared: a dark bluish hue around her eyes. J.B. had been unable to reach the doctor, who was one of just a few local physicians who hadn't been called into war duty. At seven-thirty J.B. had driven to his office at the bank, leaving his wife to try to call the doctor.

Gwen seemed worse, Violet had told him at four-thirty. Her fingertips and lips were blue, her eyes even darker than they had been that morning. And the mail had brought no new letters from James.

One child horribly ill and the other fighting in France. J.B. lifted the drink to his lips, barely wetting them, then set the glass down and licked the traces of alcohol from his lips. He should be home, but what could he do there? Nothing. He could do nothing.

But here at the Pioneers Club, he could be of use. He had received a call from Joseph Miller the third-highest-ranking member of the club and one of the most successful bankers in the Northwest. Although J.B. had done work for the Worthy mill a few years back, he mostly handled the accounts of townspeople, whereas Miller dealt exclusively with large business clients. J.B., in his small-town bank, secretly wished to be more like Joseph Miller, a man who seemed to know all the important financiers not only in Everett and Seattle but all down the Pacific Coast. One day, perhaps.

Apparently, J.B. had not been the only man summoned by Miller, as others began trickling in. Nathan Hightower was the first, and for this J.B. was not grateful. Hightower, foreman at one of the mills, had never been an easy conversationalist in the best of times, and he was now living in the worst: J.B. had driven by his house five days ago and noticed that the blue-starred service banner hanging from the parlor window had been replaced by a gold-starred flag, meaning that one of the Hightower boys had been killed in France. The next day J.B. had heard that both the young Hightowers, age twenty and twenty-two, had been killed in action. Now, every night when J.B. returned home, he stared for a long moment at James's blue-starred banner, but when he blinked, he saw for a split second the reverse image behind his darkened eyelids, the banner appearing yellowish gold. The vision haunted him.

He had not seen Hightower since—the two knew each other through the club, and even there they barely spoke. Most of the Pioneers with whom J.B. was friendly were financial types like himself, other bankers and a few lawyers. The mill men were another circle entirely, one that only occasionally overlapped with his.

He knew nothing to say to Hightower, a large man who looked every bit the foreman with his barrel chest and huge arms. His red hair was disheveled, shooting here and there like anxious flames, and his bushy eyebrows hung low. His flannel shirt reeked of the mill, of sweat and sawdust.

They stumbled through awkward small talk but were soon rescued by the arrival of two other men: Lionel Winslow and Skip Bartrum. Winslow was the thirty-year-old son of one of the town's most powerful timber barons, and J.B. had always been impressed by his confidence, if not by his professionalism or maturity. Lionel was known to lash out at others, to assume too quickly that he fully understood this world in which so much had been given him. He wore his dark hair slicked back with some foreign substance (something J.B. found a bit vain), his thin mustache was neatly trimmed, and his suits were impeccable.

Skip Bartrum was the Timber Falls sheriff. He never smiled and rarely made an appearance at the Pioneers Club. His round face had a sanguine hue, as if he had just downed a few shots of whiskey, yet no one had ever seen him drink, and he was reportedly in favor of Prohibition. For a sober man, J.B. thought, he sure as hell had the face of a mean drunk.

It was quickly apparent to J.B. that these three men knew one another well, were used to meeting together. He distinctly felt that he was the odd man out as the men discussed the war and the flu and the price of lumber. The Winslow mill was producing a cut of wood that turned out to be perfect for the new fighter planes, so business was booming. Not only was the mill shipping record amounts of lumber, but because it was technically performing a vital military duty, the government had agreed to send agents to patrol the mill and make sure the workers didn't even think about organizing to request higher wages. Times at the Winslow mill had never been better.

Bartrum had a son in France as well. He and J.B. compared what they knew of their sons' locations, wondering aloud if they were together. During this part of the conversation, no one said anything to Hightower, each man in his small cowardice pretending the sufferer was as invisible as his dead sons. Their guilt paled beside their fear that their own sons would soon meet a similar fate.

J.B. took another tiny sip from the half-empty glass. He thought about Gwen.

"Sorry to keep you boys waiting," Miller said as he appeared at the front of the room, quickly striding over and shaking hands. He sat at the head of the table. The room was dark, its walls covered in paintings of bears and other game from the surrounding woods. Two men sat at a table at the other end of the room, but apart from that, J.B.'s table was the only one occupied.

Winslow removed a cigarette from his case, failing to offer a smoke to the others.

"Thanks for meeting with us, J.B.," Miller said. He was of average height, maybe two or three inches taller than J.B., and average build. He had an unremarkable round face topped with neatly parted brown hair, and the dark suit he wore looked just like any other businessman's. He was the type of person who smiled apologetically when he had to break bad news, grinned broadly when he made a joke, and guffawed loudly when he heard one. Miller was everyone's friend, but J.B. had heard that once he put you on his other list, he was a man to be feared.

"Well, J.B., as you may know, Sheriff Bartrum, Lionel, and I are part of the American Protective League," Miller continued. J.B. nodded—he had not known that, but it helped explain why this disparate group was sitting together. The APL was a citizens' enforcement league, deputized by the Department of Justice to make sure their fellow Americans weren't fomenting dissent, interfering with the draft, or disparaging the war effort. J.B. knew the APL kept watch over certain people, making sure no one was agitating against the war or hoarding food, and he'd read in the papers about raids the APL had carried out in other parts of the country, rounding up slackers who hadn't registered for the draft and carting them off to prison. It was news to J.B. that there was an APL in Timber Falls, but maybe its secretiveness was key to its success. "I called you here," Miller said, "because of what you mentioned about your trip last weekend to Commonwealth."

J.B. had told him of the sign, the quarantine, the armed guards. He nodded, and the other men rolled their eyes at the mention of that laughingstock of a town.

Miller's voice was smooth, calm, but it had an unmistakable tone of purpose. "This morning I got to thinking there could be more going on in Commonwealth than we realize." He made quick eye contact with all his listeners. "I'm afraid it might have something to do with what happened at Fort Jenkins last week."

The other men nodded, and J.B. realized again he was the only one on the outside. With his forefinger, he traced the cool edge of his sweating glass.

"What happened at Fort Jenkins?" he asked.

II

"What's going on?" Philip heard the soldier's voice calling from the cellar. "Hey, you there?"

"I'm here," Philip replied. Ever since Mo had closed the door, Philip had stood there, paralyzed. "We have to stay here for a while."

Footsteps. The soldier was climbing the stairs. Philip's eyes were still adjusting to the dark, but he could see the man's face, see his stubbled cheeks and his thick brows. The whites of his eyes seemed to shine.

"There a problem?"

Philip realized his legs were shaking. He decided to sit down, placing the rifle before him and lowering himself carefully lest the butt of the pocketed pistol jab his thigh. The floor was filthy with dirt and old saw-dust and sundry other grime, but he leaned back on his hands nonetheless.

The building stank of mildew, and the lack of any light unnerved Philip in a way he didn't want to admit. Each footstep was loud in the building's emptiness, a hollow sound that perfectly echoed the feeling in his gut.

"I was going to help you," Philip said. "Now we're both stuck here."

The soldier thought. "You're in trouble with your buddies now?"

"We have to wait," Philip said angrily. "We just have to wait here awhile."

The soldier nodded. "You live in quite a friendly town."

"I've already been too friendly to you." Philip tried to imagine the horrified or disappointed reactions of Charles, of Rebecca, of Elsie. He tried not to think about Graham.

Philip and the soldier were not far from each other at this point, but somehow it didn't seem to matter anymore. Philip was now tarred, just like the soldier. He too was an outsider, not to be trusted.

For the soldier, who, moments ago, had thought he was going to die, this new development seemed relatively minor. He sat down at the top of the stairs, clearly reveling in the new feeling of relaxation. He closed his eyes and it looked to Philip like the man would fall asleep on the spot.

It was growing dark when Graham saw them hurrying across town, rifles and kerosene lamps in hand.

He had been fetching more firewood from the shed—the nights were growing colder—and as he returned to the house, he saw Mo, Charles, Doc Banes, and Jarred Rankle, concern in their eyes. Mo was supposed to be on guard duty, Graham realized, and so was Philip.

He stepped back inside, the scent of Amelia's stew wafting over him. It was the last of the venison. Graham had hoped to go hunting soon to replenish their supply, but ever since the events involving the first soldier, hunting no longer seemed the best use of his time. They didn't *need* meat, at least not yet, but what they absolutely needed was to make sure the right people were standing watch. Whatever time Graham had, he committed to the guard post.

"What's wrong?" Amelia asked, seeing the look on his face as he retrieved his jacket.

"I need to head to the post," he told her.

"Why?"

He paused, unsure whether he should risk alarming her. "I don't know. I think something's happened."

On his way out, he reached into the closet and grabbed his rifle.

They were a couple blocks away already, but he ran after them. Mo stopped to explain everything while Charles and Rankle walked on.

"Why did Philip let him in?" Graham asked.

"I don't know," Mo said, looking ashamed.

"Did the soldier get the drop on him? Was he leading Philip at gunpoint or something?"

"I think I only saw Philip holding a gun," Mo said weakly, "but I might have missed something."

Mo had found Charles at home, he explained, just finished with supper. Laura was washing dishes and Rebecca was sitting in the parlor, writing suffrage letters with Rankle. Mo knew he should try to be discreet but wasn't sure how, and he wound up blurting his message in front of everyone. It had been difficult for Charles to convince Rebecca to stay home with Laura.

"You just wake up?" Mo asked, eying Graham peculiarly.

"Not really." Graham had stood guard all night and had slept for an hour or two during the day, between chores. "C'mon," he said, and hurried after the other two.

Soon they reached the street that housed the three old storage buildings. The far one was about forty yards long, a third that wide, and the height of most of the two-story houses in town. There were no windows, and in the front were two entrances—a regular-sized door and a much larger one designed for trucks or carriages.

"Just Charles and me from here," Doc Banes said to the others. "Everyone else stay back."

"What if the soldier tries to shoot his way out?" Graham asked. "You two aren't armed."

It was rare for someone to question the doctor's judgment, but Banes had won little of Graham's respect over the years. After Amelia's stillbirth, Banes had insisted there was nothing he could have done for the baby boy, but Graham was unconvinced.

"We'll be all right, Graham," Charles said, though he sounded otherwise.

Graham thought about handing Charles his rifle but reconsidered. If something did happen, it would be best for all of them if Graham were the one holding it.

Charles watched as Doc Banes reached into his pocket and removed two gauze masks. The doctor put one on, the thin material straining against his thick mustache, and then he handed the other to Charles. Lamp in hand, Charles followed as Doc Banes walked past the first two buildings. They could see Mo's tracks, his bootprints stamped into the soft earth. They stopped twenty yards from the door.

"We'll need to keep them in there for forty-eight hours, Charles." Doc's voice was low enough that only the two could hear.

"Are you sure?" Charles's son was in there, trapped with an outsider no one knew, a man who possibly carried the flu. Charles's heart was beating quickly, and his hands shook. He was always so clear-minded and sober, especially in town meetings and at the mill, but he felt he had been thrust into a situation beyond his control. It reminded him of Everett, of the riots, that terrifying feeling of helplessness.

Banes looked directly into Charles's eyes, as he always did when delivering bad news. "The incubation period for influenza—how long it can stay inside you without giving you symptoms—can be up to forty-eight hours. So after two days, we'll be able to determine if this man has the flu. If they stay in there that long and they're both all right, then they can come out. But until then it would put the town at risk."

"But what if—what if they're not all right?"

"Whoever this man is, he's probably healthy, or Philip wouldn't have let him in. And if he had the flu, it's doubtful he would've been able to walk to Commonwealth. He's probably no threat, but we still have to take precautions."

Charles's brow was deeply furrowed and his eyes wide and focused on nothing in particular, the ground, the darkness. He looked at the decrepit building, his son's prison.

"It's good that there are no windows in the building," Banes said. "This is an out-of-the-way street, so they're as well contained as we could hope for. Is there a back door?"

"No."

"Good. We'll keep someone positioned here by the front to keep them inside. That's the best we can do."

"We need to guard the building?" But of course they did, Charles realized. Still, the thought that now his son had to be guarded was difficult to take.

Banes didn't answer, seeing that Charles was answering his own question in his mind.

"What about food? He can't eat for two days?" Charles asked.

Banes thought. "We can bring food by. We'll tell him to wait in the cellar and someone can leave a tray by the front door. Then we'll knock and walk away. One minute after the knock, Philip can come to the door and open it, grab the food, and close the door as quickly as possible. He'll keep the used trays and dishes—under no circumstances should anyone touch them or retrieve them. We can just repeat that process for every meal: no contact, and no one touches any used dishes. That's the best we can do."

"Are you not even going to go in and examine them?"

The lamp cast an orange hue on Doc's face, throwing shadows beneath his brow and nose and chin and frown. "I shouldn't. This flu is so contagious that even doctors and nurses who've protected themselves have become ill and spread it to others. As much as I want to help them, I fear I'd only make things worse for everyone else."

"My son . . ." Again Charles shook his head. "We have to just leave him there?"

Charles's brother Timothy had died when he was barely seventeen, never celebrating his final birthday because he'd been sick in bed. When Philip had turned sixteen, Charles had thought of Timothy's forgotten birthday, and the link in his mind between the two boys had filled him with disquiet. He still missed his brother.

"Charles." Banes grabbed his friend's forearm, gripping it as tightly as a tourniquet. "You know we have to do this. And it's only two days—he'll be all right."

"Trapped in a dark building with a man no one knows?"

"You can bring him more clothes, blankets, write him letters, anything. We can leave it for him just like the food. And in two days this will be over."

Charles nodded slowly. Doc released his arm, patted him lightly on the shoulder.

"All right," Charles said, hoping to signal that he was as clearheaded as ever. "I just wish we knew more about who that man is."

"Philip!" Doc Banes's voice coming from outside broke the calm in the dark building.

Philip turned his head, and the soldier opened his eyes. They'd been sitting in silence for longer than either of them knew.

"Are you in there?" Banes yelled before Philip could reply. "Don't come out!"

"I'm here!" Philip walked toward the closed door.

"Are you all right?"

He was scared and overwhelmed with guilt, but he tried not to let it show. "It's a little dark, but we're fine!"

"Who've you got there with you?" Banes asked.

A good question, Philip realized. Before he could ask, the soldier spoke up, hollering through the thick door and into the night beyond:

"Private Frank Summers!"

There was silence for a few seconds. Then Banes's voice returned:

"You're a long way from your base, Private."

"There was an accident—our ship sank off the coast. I was just hoping for some food and shelter for the night while I made my way back to Fort Jenkins."

More silence. Philip wondered who was out there with the doctor and what they were talking about.

Finally, Banes told Philip they would soon bring food. He explained the system and mentioned that someone would be stationed outside.

"Everything make sense to you, Philip?" Charles asked.

That's the same thing he says after explaining an accounting method to me, Philip thought. The same thing he says after running through the way we get the lumber from here to the buyers or how one of those enormous machines works. *Everything make sense to you, Philip?* And no, absolutely none of this made any sense.

"Yes, sir."

"I'll be back soon," Charles hollered.

"All right." Philip didn't know what else to say. He felt he should apologize to his father, but he knew this wasn't the time for such a conversation, and he didn't want to look weak by acting scared in front of Private Frank Summers. He was grateful that Doc Banes and his father hadn't asked how the soldier had gotten in, grateful that he didn't have to shout out—for both the soldier and his father to hear—the details of his failure. But he knew this imprisonment was a sort of punishment, even if not deliberately so, for letting the soldier into town.

"Looks like I got you in trouble," the soldier said.

Philip glared at him, though the darkness had shrouded his face. He walked toward the soldier's voice. "You got what you wanted."

"I'm sorry it's landed you here, too," the soldier said. By then Philip was close enough to see that he had a slight smile on his lips, a macabre appreciation for the bizarre situation. "But like I said, this is an awfully friendly town you've got."

"This town is feeding you for the next two days," Philip reminded him, sitting down on the floor with his back against the wall.

The soldier yawned.

"Why couldn't you have just contacted your base or something?" Philip didn't mean to sound as whiny as he did. "Couldn't they have come to help you?"

"Now you're giving me soldiering advice? If you know so much about how the army works, why aren't you in uniform?"

"I'm sixteen."

"Thought you were a little young. And what's with that limp? You got a clubfoot or something?"

Philip glared at him. Then he reached forward and, with a tightly clenched fist, rapped twice on his right boot. The deep wooden sound filled the air between them.

The soldier shifted his eyebrows a bit and nodded. "Well, since you don't seem to be in a very conversational mood, maybe I'll just nod off till they come by with our supper." He closed his eyes and leaned against the wall behind him. "Don't forget to wake me."

The soldier seemed to be enjoying this—after all, it beat sleeping out in the woods and starving—but for Philip, it was the worst imaginable scenario. He had been entrusted with protecting the town, yet he had done the exact opposite. He had failed miserably.

Philip folded his arms. He felt tears well up in his eyes at the sudden feeling of abandonment, but he fought them back, not wanting the soldier to see or hear. He tried to think of some solution to his new problem, but nothing was forthcoming. He retraced his steps, trying to pinpoint where he'd made his mistake.

The soldier started snoring.

III

Doc Banes didn't sleep that night.

Maybe other people did, even those who had helped him quarantine Philip and the soldier, those who knew that the town's precarious position in this pestilence-filled world had been jostled. Maybe they found some way to shrug in the face of what might be an incoming enemy. But Dr. Martin Banes didn't so much as look at his bed that night—there was too much to do.

After leaving Philip behind, Banes had walked Charles home, assuring his friend that everything would be fine. He declined to describe Philip as being held prisoner; he tried to couch things in dry medical terms. *We'll just wait out the forty-eight hours, after which time we'll know the soldier is healthy and all is well.* Banes had walked into the Worthys' home and helped Charles explain the situation to his wife and daughter, had stood there and weathered their anxious questions and cries, their hesitant but unmistakable blame. Finally, they began translating their worries into action, Rebecca arranging a supper delivery for Philip and Laura deciding to bake him bread. Banes had shaken the hand of the shaken Charles, tried to smile, thought against it, and instead left him with a forceful nod. *We'll talk to Philip tomorrow,* Banes had said, hoping to convey that the hours will pass quickly. *Yes,* Charles had agreed, his voice conveying: I hope Philip sounds all right tomorrow, I hope we don't hear any coughing, I hope I haven't buried my son alive.

When Banes made it home, it was nearing his usual bedtime, so he turned on the lamp by his desk and lit his pipe. He lifted a volume from his bookshelf, leafing through to unfamiliar pages, diagrams of microscopic organisms that still struck him as bizarre, like abstract renderings of prehistoric monsters.

Martin Banes was fifty-six and had been a doctor for thirty-four years. In 1886 he'd attended a medical school that no longer existed—one of the many wiped out by the reforms of 1904, when medical schools started establishing academic requirements for incoming students and instituting lab work as a norm. Banes hadn't even been to college; he'd been a chemist's apprentice until the chemist died of typhus so early into Banes's training that young Martin was still unqualified to take over the man's position. So why not turn to medicine? Just sit in a lecture hall for two semesters, take some notes, and you're fully trained. They didn't even have written tests—two of his classmates couldn't read. But who needed to read? He knew how to feel a forehead, where to hold a wrist when looking for a pulse, how to cut a vein, how to bleed a patient to restore balance.

And Banes was a good doctor, he knew this, despite the many changes that had shaken the field in his lifetime. He had tried to keep up, even if he hadn't always understood the new ways. He had abandoned the miasma theory in favor of the germ theory, abandoned what he'd been taught in school about atmospheric putrefaction in favor of microscopic organisms. The discoveries of Pasteur and Koch had cast aside centuries of medical thought, and now diseases were thought to be caused by tiny bacteria and viruses rather than climatic changes and noxious fumes. It had been years since he'd last wielded his lancet and performed a venisection. Restoring balance of the four humors was no longer a doctor's duty. Despite the advances, Banes sometimes felt that his responsibilities were becoming ever more complicated, the world more mysterious and challenging, rather than less.

Banes knew how to use the new antitoxins for diphtheria and tetanus, had seen how they cut down on those diseases. He took careful notes, he reported outbreaks to the local boards, he worked whenever and wherever he was called upon. How many mornings had his wife, Margaret, awakened to find him gone after he had been called to someone's home in the middle of the night? She had been such a hard sleeper, Margaret. Slept through the telephone ringing, slept through him dressing and packing his bag, hitching the horses and heading out in his carriage. He missed her. Now the bed was always empty when he returned from a house call, always cold.

They hadn't had any children, and only now, alone in his old age, did he fully understand all those pitying looks they'd received from others who eventually realized the couple was barren. Margaret had died of pneumonia five years ago, leaving Banes to his patients and his books and journals. Their meaning passed him by often, but he tried to ignore that, tried to hold tightly on to that which his mind was able to capture. But unlike past discoveries that had challenged his ways of thinking, past breakthroughs that had required him to absorb some foreign bits of knowledge, his sticking point now was the opposite: an almost complete lack of information about this new disease.

The newspapers had been of little help. At first they hadn't reported on the Spanish influenza, and when they finally did, they wrote as if it were already being cured. Nothing but good news was allowed in the press during wartime. Thus the stories all portrayed soldiers feeling better after a testy bout with *la grippe,* doctors feeling confident and civilians being insulated against disease, even if it was all untrue. Medical journals also glossed over the subject, at least the journals to which Banes subscribed. The little he knew about the Spanish flu came via the letters from his former patient Jonathan Pierce.

Pierce was now Dr. Pierce, had vowed to become a doctor after he recovered at age twelve from influenza. A bad case indeed. But Banes had treated him, had told his family how to nurse him back to health, had prayed for him at night, and young Jonathan had recovered, matured, gone to college, and then headed off to medical school at Johns Hopkins, a world away. He had kept in touch with Banes, sending him letters describing his adventures in medical science, regaling him with stories of laboratory discoveries and tales of unknown scourges both discovered and cured. Banes always detected the hint of condescension in these letters—Jonathan the wise young clinician informing the old, undereducated country doctor of the new ways of Science. At the same time, Banes appreciated this window onto the brave new world of medicine, felt privileged to have the view, if occasionally dizzied by its heights.

But the last letter had made him only dizzy. Dr. Pierce—along with all the other young, intelligent doctors, it seemed—had been assigned to medical military duty at the start of the war. Pierce was one of the physicians in charge of Fort Devens, a large cantonment outside of Boston. His letter had been written on September 20, and Banes could tell by the uncharacteristic waver in the script that Pierce had written it late at night, after too many hours of work and too many nights without sleep. The camp had been hit by some new plague, Pierce wrote. The highest health officials and the most esteemed minds had already come to Devens to offer their aid, and they had walked away shaking their heads. First Pierce had thought it was cerebrospinal meningitis, but then the cases worsened and spread, and men were dying. They were dying of bronchopneumonia, it now seemed, pneumonic infection perhaps caused by influenza. But it was an influenza unlike any he had seen.

The first sign of danger was the speed of contagion. But the symptoms rivaled the breadth of the epidemic in their horror. Even if only a few people had suffered this disease, it still would have been a terror to be scarcely believed. Men bled from the nose, from the ears, some even from their eyes. Autopsies of dead soldiers revealed that their lungs were blue and heavy, thick with fluid, sometimes thick with blood. Victims became cyanotic, starved of oxygen—parts or all of their bodies turned blue, sometimes such a dark hue that the corpses of white men were indistinguishable from those of coloreds. They were literally drowning to death in their own fluids. And so quickly! More than one soldier had died within twenty-four hours of his first reported symptoms.

The camp was a madhouse, Pierce wrote. Against army regulations, the soldiers had been crammed into too-tight quarters as a result of the scale of the draft, and their dwellings provided the perfect powder kegs for an influenza spark to ignite. Men were sick in top bunks, coughing and bleeding onto healthy men below. Healthy men tracked in patients' spilled blood on their boots, their bare feet. Dozens of nurses and physicians were sick, and some had died; the call for more nurses had already gone out to the surrounding counties. Some soldiers—healthy at the time, but who knew for how long?—already had been transferred elsewhere. Surely this would spread illness to bases in other states.

Of course, by the time the letter had escaped military censors and wound its way across the country to Washington State, by the time the small post office in Timber Falls had received it and Banes had journeyed to town for it, weeks had passed and the flu had spread across the land, making Pierce's prediction both prophetic and pathetically useless. It was already too late.

Banes knew it was possible that the mysterious soldier was healthy, possessing some resistance to the same disease that, according to rumor, had infected a majority of those at the nearest camp, Fort Jenkins. But he also knew there was an equal chance that the soldier had brought the disease with him, symptomless for now but present nonetheless. Evil spirits or invisible germs? A decaying jaundice of the air itself or a microscopic agent of death? Miasma or germ? The two schools of thought warred in Banes's mind, and though he accepted the new theory now, he had believed the other for so long that it seemed more natural to him, despite what those medical journals were saying. Regardless, the solution was the same: keep it contained. Keep Philip and the soldier locked away, count the hours. Pray.

Was forty-eight hours long enough? That was what Banes remembered having heard in the past, but he found nothing in his piles of journals to confirm it. This flu seemed so different, so much more powerful, than any before. Perhaps it could incubate for longer periods of time. Sitting at his desk, Banes knew that if the person trapped with the soldier hadn't been his friend's son—if he'd been anyone else in town—Banes probably would have chosen to quarantine him for longer. Lock him up for four days, maybe even a week. Why not? Where was the harm in inconveniencing two men, one of them a stranger? But he knew Philip, knew how young he was, knew what the experience would do to Charles and Rebecca. So he had said forty-eight hours and would stand by it and hope to God that he would not regret it.

Banes read through his journals and through all of Pierce's letters, dating back so many years. He read and read until he wasn't sure if his incomprehension was due to the lateness of the hour or the density of the prose or the second Scotch he had drunk, perhaps ill advisedly, at half past four. He looked up when he felt the sunlight creeping through the gap in his drawn curtains, breaking through the clouds of pipe smoke he'd been exhaling. Dawn. Surely Charles would head out to speak with Philip first thing in the morning. Banes would wait to give them a moment of privacy, then go out and survey the situation.

A whistle sounded—six o'clock. The night had escaped him, and he felt no more the wiser. He must sleep, even if he only had two hours. Just enough to stay alert.

The bed was cold. He thought of Margaret, then of the soldiers bleeding through their eyes. Please let that scourge leave this town untouched, he prayed. But if it were to come here, at least Margaret wouldn't have to see it; at least he wouldn't have to see her turn blue.

No, he thought, succumbing to superstition. Don't think that way—never regard a past death as welcome. That thought can serve as an invitation to death, allowing it to visit again, make itself at home.

IV

After bringing food to the storage building, along with a lamp, blankets, and two pillows, Charles and Rebecca had returned home in silence. While Rebecca cleaned the kitchen, Charles had escaped to his small desk in the bedroom, writing a letter he planned on delivering to Philip the next morning, something he hoped would soothe the boy during his internment.

Charles had been sitting there for thirty minutes and had written two sentences. He put down his pencil as Rebecca carefully closed the door behind her. She stood against it silently.

"This has to stop," she told him.

Confused, he asked, "What has to stop?"

"The quarantine. First closing the town, and now locking Philip away? Charles, this can't continue. You must see this."

"You heard what the doctor said. You heard how—"

"Charles, this is *wrong,*" she interrupted, her eyes pleading.

"Why is it wrong to try and protect the town? Rebecca, I'm . . ." He trailed off, exasperated at having to fight the same argument with his wife that he was already having in his own head. "I don't like Philip being in there any more than you do, and I hope to God he forgives me for this, but . . . I'm doing what I can to protect everyone in town."

"This is our *son,* Charles." She held out her hands to him.

"Other people in this town have sons!" Charles slammed a fist onto the desk and stood. "Is ours more important than theirs? How can you say we should put everyone else at risk just so Philip can sleep in his own bed tonight? How is that a solution?"

He paced past her, and Rebecca was quiet. He did not often raise his voice, and even more rarely did he do so with her.

"I am only trying to do what's right," he said, turning to face her again. "What's right for the people in this town, the people who have sacrificed for us. The people who have given everything to make this town work. There is nothing I can do"—his voice wavered—"nothing I can do for anyone in any other town that is sick. But there *are* things I can do for the people in this town, and I am trying to do them as best I can."

He was breathing heavily, more riled up than he could remember being since the Everett strike. When he turned back to Rebecca, he saw that the imploring look on her face had faded, and in its place was a muted caution that suggested resignation or restrained anger.

"I understand what you're trying to do, and your intentions are good." She spoke slowly. Her voice, too, was shaking, and her eyes were wet. "But I am finding it harder and harder to stand by these decisions."

"This is not easy for me, either," he said. "I am barely holding on, Rebecca." He wanted to tell her how much he needed her to support this decision and help him through it. But instead of admitting that weakness, he said, "This town was as much your idea as mine. This was your dream, too."

She started at that, then backed up, shaking her head. "I never wanted this to be something so apart from the world. I wanted to show the world what it could do, what we could do. I didn't want to stand back and spit on them. And now we're spitting on our own son." She opened the door.

"Rebecca, don't—"

"I'm sorry. I need to be alone." She descended the stairs, Charles watching her disappear.

He paced for a while before sitting down at his desk. Philip was in a dark building right now; he would sleep on a cold floor beside a stranger. A stranger who might be sick. And if he was, that would mean Charles was being asked to sacrifice his son for the town. He put his hand flat on the desk to steady himself as he sat there. Suddenly dizzy, he closed his eyes for a moment and breathed.

It had been barely five years since the morning that had changed Charles's life, when he had been driving out of Everett for a morning meeting and discovered the tire tracks that ran off the side of the road and down a steep ravine. Later, when he'd learned how Philip had been abandoned by his father, Charles had vowed that he would never repeat that transgression. But if Charles's and the doctor's decision looked like abandonment to Rebecca, it must look even worse to Philip.

Charles opened his eyes. He stared at the letter he had started, then crumpled it and threw it in the wastebasket. He would start again. He needed to start again.

V

Sometimes in dreams Philip would remember that feeling of being suspended in the air, of taking flight, of losing all contact with the earth. As bad as the crash was, it was the instant before impact that was all the more terrifying, the realization that he had been released from the calm embrace of his normal life and was hurtling toward something unknowable.

Not that his life before the crash had been entirely normal. By the time Philip turned eleven, he had lived in more towns than most of the grown men in Commonwealth. He had no memory of his father—whether or not he had ever met the man was unclear, as his mother, Fiona, had given him so many conflicting answers that he finally stopped asking. His earliest memories were of sharing a bed with Fiona in the house of one of her cousins in Los Angeles. There, he would play with the cousin's many children while Fiona was out working for their keep, or so she told him. But the brief idyll was interrupted by an argument, the cousin outraged—Philip dimly remembered accusations of theft—and he and Fiona were tossed out of the house. When Philip told Fiona he missed his playmates, she warned him never to speak their dirty names again. *It's a big world,* she told him. *You'll find other friends.*

The pattern repeated itself with other cousins, second cousins, and even further removed relatives until Fiona had all but burned down the family tree. Philip's questions about why Cousin Shelly had thrown them out or why Uncle Ike's wife had called Fiona a tramp were never answered, and not until years later did he fit things together, forming a picture that was no less disconcerting than the pile of pieces that had confounded him for so many years.

Once their family options were exhausted, the travels continued. They would find a cheap room to let, Philip would sleep beside her in their thin bed, and Fiona would find some kindly lady who felt sorry for her and said she could use a maid, or a cook, or anything. Philip would start classes at a new school while Fiona would catch the eye of a leading man about town, single or otherwise, and their courtship would mean that Philip got the bed all to himself many nights, something Fiona assured him was a privilege for which he should be thankful. He often woke alone, hoping she was only in the bathroom. He would close his eyes and imagine her there.

Just when he was starting to feel at home, his home would dissipate like a much-cherished mirage. One night she'd wake him up—sometimes in the middle of the night, sometimes at the fragile moment before sunrise—and she'd anxiously tell him to pack all his clothes. He would barely be able to do so (many were the favorite shirts and books he left behind, realizing only when he was a hundred miles away), and then they'd be at a train station. Fiona would smile at the old man in the ticket window, her right hand tightly grasping her son's wrist. Off to a new town.

Whenever he complained, she would remind him he was lucky she took him with her at all, that most other women in her situation would throw him into an orphanage or leave him behind. That kept his complaining to a minimum.

Fiona promised him that their home in Redmond, Washington, would be their last. And she proved to be correct, though not in the way she had imagined. They had moved into the home of a paper mill foreman named Carl Jasper, living with him for just over a year—the longest tenancy in any one place that Philip could remember. Despite this new, tantalizing feeling of permanence, Philip was uncomfortable around Carl. A looming presence whose head nearly scraped against the top of the small house's doorways, Carl seemed immediately untrustworthy, his house often filled with late-night card games and cigar smoke, bottles clanging while Philip tried to sleep.

Many were the nights when Philip would walk into the kitchen to find the couple huddled over some papers, watching his every move, their voices hushed. *Just wanted to get some water,* he'd say, and after he'd taken the glass back to his room, the whispering would begin again. He didn't ask what they were talking about, and he didn't really want to know, but he was hurt by their suspicious glances.

A few weeks after the whispering had begun, Philip came home from school and saw Fiona and Carl hastily packing their bags. *Grab your clothes,* they told him, *we need to leave.* He started to protest, reminding her of her promise. He'd made friends—one boy's father had even offered him a job delivering newspapers and running errands—and there was a girl he had a crush on, Anna, with green eyes and freckles. Fiona yelled back, saying she didn't want to do this, either, but they needed to go, *now.* They would explain later. Philip refused, arms crossed, until Carl knocked him to the floor with one blow. The man's hand had been open, but it still bloodied Philip's nose, and he lay on the floor stunned and looking to Fiona for aid. She merely softened her voice and told him to pack—and hurry.

They drove a nice new Ford that Carl had bought the day before. It was a beautiful car, the sides and hood so shiny that Philip saw his tear-streaked reflection as he walked up to the door. It was less bumpy than a carriage but colder than a train car, and the air whistled as it came in through the tops of the windows. They drove all through the night, and Philip sat there seething, angry at Fiona for betraying him, furious at Carl for the blow, and enraged at himself for being stupid enough to have thought this wouldn't happen again. Eventually, he slept, his head leaning back against the seat that smelled like melted rubber and bobbing every time the wheels hit a hole in the unpaved roads.

He awoke sometime in the middle of the night, shivering with cold, to find the world outside turned white, as if some pillow the size of the moon had burst above them, showering its celestial feathers all around. They were almost there, Carl said, yawning. He was driving very slowly, muttering something about so much snow and how maybe they should stop at the next town, wherever that was. Fiona looked at Philip in the backseat and gave him a slight smile, one that was different from any he'd seen on her face before. It looked more adult, the kind of expression parents didn't normally direct at their children, and the smile might have been an apology and might have been a sign of affection and might have been, finally, an acknowledgment that this was who she was and he would have to learn to accept her, flaws and all.

Carl had been steering the Ford downhill around a sharp bend when Fiona had offered Philip that smile, and the smile disappeared when the Ford lurched sideways. Philip remembered hearing Fiona start to scream something; he remembered a sudden force pulling him deeper into his seat and then that unreal feeling of flight. An instant of weightlessness followed by its opposite, tumbling through the snow and into the blackness beneath them.

Later, he didn't remember what he saw, whether the world spun in circles, whether he found himself staring at the roof of the Ford or its floor—just the feeling of being tossed and slammed and beaten while trapped inside a steel box that seemed to be shrinking with every blow, collapsing upon him as if it were being hammered into the shape of his coffin.

From there his memories were sharp but discrete, an occasional stark image propped up amid long stretches of nothing but shadow. There was snow on his eyelids when he opened them; he remembered this because he wanted to wipe the snow away but couldn't move his arms. They were trapped by something, or they were broken, and so were his legs. He felt upside down, his head lower than his chest; maybe that's why it throbbed so much, but he could barely see, so he wasn't sure. I'm not dead I'm not dead I'm not dead, he told himself. This realization was almost as shocking as it had been to find himself flying through the air a moment ago. How long ago? What about his mother? He called for her, and his voice was so stripped away by terror into a tiny, jagged sliver that the sound of it scared him all the more. Without waiting long for a reply, he called for her again and heard her moan.

He called again and again, her first name for some reason, louder and louder, even though the sound of his voice was making the situation seem more horribly real. He screamed for her to wake up, because he couldn't move and he was frightened and cold and didn't know where she was and she couldn't talk and he needed her then and she needed to wake up. He screamed and screamed if for no other reason than he couldn't bear to hear the sound of her moaning. He remembered how white his voice sounded, remembers screaming himself into exhaustion or some weird kind of trance, because that was where the memory ended, interrupted by a long black space until he opened his eyes again.

At that point, he moved his neck, trying to get a better idea of where he was. The coffin that had once been an automobile was made of tangled pieces of metal that wrapped themselves tightly around him, some of them sharp and stabbing at his side. He tried to calm down, tried to free himself, but whatever was on top of his legs could not be moved. It was dark and he could barely see, even when his eyes had adjusted to the night, even when he'd stopped crying.

I'm alive I'm alive I'm freezing I'm alive I'm alive I'm getting out of here somehow, somehow.

During the drive, he had taken off his gloves, and his fingers were going numb. He was able to free his hands from where they had been trapped, but the metal around him was too strong to budge further. He balled his hands into fists, he breathed on them, he stuffed them under his arms. He tried to use them to free his legs but it was useless—why wouldn't his legs move? He couldn't feel them, but he wasn't sure if that meant he was paralyzed, or maybe they were broken and in so much pain they were beyond him, or maybe they were already frozen, all the nerves dead. The cold surrounded him and there was nothing he could do to protect himself.

He called out Fiona's name again but she didn't respond this time. He yelled again, preferring even the sound of his mother in pain to her silence. But he heard nothing. Then darkness again.

Later still he realized that part of whatever was pinning his legs was Carl's body.

Through a shattered windshield or a torn-off door, the snow continued to fall. First the flakes melted, and then they started clinging to his face, accumulating. He would wipe them away and wake up covered again.

His heart had been racing earlier, but it felt so much slower now. Is fear something your body adapts to? He was still scared but when he tried to scream Fiona's name his voice was like a soothing whisper, as if it were trying to tell him he shouldn't be so worried, that he should just be still and go to sleep.

The next time he opened his eyes he found that his mother had somehow moved from wherever she had been and was huddled around him. He wasn't shivering as much as he had been, and he said her name. She didn't respond, but he could hear her breathing. He remembers that. Her head was behind his, and one of her arms moved, wrapping itself around his head, protecting his face from the snow.

But her arm must have moved again, because his next memory was of being buried in snow, and when he tried to clear it off, his arms did not heed his call. He was shivering again, colder than before, but not even these spasms could shake loose the snow. He stared into the whiteness as if the power of his gaze could melt it away, he blinked furiously, but he was blind, the snow piling so high it began to glow, to burn into colors.

He tried to call for his mother a final time and realized he couldn't even talk. The snow was spangled with color, as if a rainbow had exploded into thousands of tiny teardrops. He squinted to make sense of things and the dots of color danced, revolved; he felt himself spinning. He couldn't feel anything, couldn't hear anything. His body, his whole being, had been reduced to nothing but his failing vision. That was all he was. The spinning made him feel weightless again, almost the same sensation as when the Ford had driven off the road, but this time it felt like a gift, bestowed on him, and the dots glowed until they were all gold, then they broke apart and washed over him.

Those feelings seemed so fresh when Philip woke up. He was in a hospital room, and Charles would soon walk in and explain what had happened, tell him that his parents had been killed. Philip would lie there and calmly tell Charles, *No, they weren't both my parents—she was my mother, but the man in the Ford was just some guy.* As if this were the most important fact, as if he needed to clear up any misunderstandings before he could begin to contemplate what had just happened.

Philip gradually realized the stiffness in his limbs wasn't from the accident but from sleeping on a cold, hard floor, and that he was not in a hospital but in the storage building. He was not eleven but sixteen, not in Everett but in Commonwealth. He sat up, the vestiges of his dream fading back into his memory. He hadn't dreamed about the accident in a while now, and he wondered if it was his uncomfortable sleeping quarters that had evoked the memories or the sense of isolation, so familiar to him from his earlier life.

He sat up, pressing his palms against the wood floor. It was pitch black in the building. He could hear the soldier breathing heavily in his slumber; it was the only thing to remind him he was not alone.

The previous evening returned to him. Half an hour after Charles and Doc Banes had left, Philip and the soldier had heard a knock on the door. After silently counting to sixty, as he had been told, Philip had opened the door as slightly as he could and discovered two trays of food, two blankets, a box of matches, and a kerosene lamp. Philip brought the items inside, and before he had even lit the lamp, the soldier had started eating. Philip had tried not to stare at the man and the way he tore into the meat, gulping it down, and the way he drained all of his water in one long pull. So this is what a starving man looks like, Philip had thought.

There was a fireplace at the far side of the empty building, so they had wandered about, collecting scraps of wood scattered on the floor, left over from the construction. It wasn't very good firewood, but it was better than nothing. Philip had held on to his rifle and kept the pistol in his pocket; that had impeded his efforts, but he didn't trust the man enough to leave the firearms lying around.

Moments after gathering the wood, the soldier had fallen asleep again in front of the fire. As time dragged on, Philip also grew tired, so he had pulled a blanket over himself and put the rifle beside him, half concealed by the blanket. A young man sleeping with his rifle. They probably told you not to do it this way in the army, but he wanted to reduce the chances that the soldier would be able to take it. The pistol he stuffed in his left boot, beneath the wood block, confident the soldier wouldn't think to look there.

Philip didn't know how long he'd been asleep, didn't know what time it was. He wished he hadn't dreamed of his mother—there were enough reasons to be feeling bleak at the moment; he didn't need to waste any emotion on her.

He lay back down, listening to the soldier's heavy breaths. The man didn't sound sick. The other soldier may well have been sick, but this one hadn't so much as sneezed or coughed, not counting when he drank his water too fast and choked a bit. So there probably would be no outbreak in the town—no one would be harmed, and, hopefully, Philip would not be punished for his mistake. But that also meant he was trapped in here for two days for no good reason.

He wondered what Elsie was thinking, if she knew about his situation at all. Maybe they had called an emergency town meeting. Maybe all the workers were shaking their heads at the weakling gimp for letting the soldier in. Maybe all the younger boys were thankful they had this bad example to look down on, confident that when their time came, they would pass their tests with honor. Maybe Elsie would never speak to him again. Maybe Laura would face the unenviable task of having to defend her brother's actions in the face of the other schoolkids' taunts. Or maybe what he had done was indefensible, even to a sister. Not really blood, of course, but family nonetheless. Perhaps that was the difference—that a mistake like this was what would make a family that wasn't really your family turn against you. The Worthys would cast him out of their clan, considering his brief time with them nothing but a regrettable error of judgment on their part, a story they would occasionally tell others after the passage of many years: *Oh yes, once upon a time we adopted a son. Seemed a nice boy—shame how it turned out.*

But would even his true mother have accepted him after something like this? She had always seemed so close to leaving him, had used that threat to cow him into obeying her. Maybe a transgression like this would have provided her the perfect excuse to take the next night train without him.

Philip closed his eyes, trying to remember her without anger. It was cold in the storage building, but he had certainly survived worse. It didn't matter anymore, he told himself. She hadn't left him—for all her flaws and all her threats, she'd never walked out. The crash wasn't her fault, nor was it punishment for any sins she might have committed. It had just happened. Sometimes things just happened.

The flu had just happened. So he would wait in here for two days, then he would be released, and normal life would resume. He clung to this hope more tightly than he could cling to wakefulness, and soon he was asleep again.

VI

While the rest of Commonwealth slept, Deacon stood guard outside the storage building.

The sky was clear and the glow of the nearly full moon seemed unusually powerful, as though that one tiny circle, if punctured, would flood the world with so much brightness that every last pine needle would be illuminated, all the trees aglow.

Beyond the storage building, Deacon could dimly see an outline of the Cascades' foothills. The trees beyond the building would have been too deep in the blackness to be visible if not for the moonlight, which coated them with an almost metallic shine. They glinted like blades in the distance.

Deacon was past forty, but when he was sixteen and living in Minneapolis, he had decided to become a priest, delighting his Catholic parents. They had thrown a party for him the weekend before he began seminary, and he felt he'd finally found a purpose in his life, even if he had been lying when he'd told the abbot that he'd heard the voice of God calling him. In truth, he'd only *wanted* to hear something. His parents, too, had wanted him to hear the voice of God, had wanted it when his grades in school had slumped and when the local druggist had caught him stealing cigars and tobacco, had wanted it when other parents had told him he was harassing their children, especially the girls. So he had prayed and studied the Bible for many a long night. He had lied about hearing God's voice because he was tired of waiting for it, and because he assumed he would hear something eventually, would hear that voice call to him, a voice or something like it, a voice disguised as the wind or the tolling of bells at church or the announcer at the baseball games he sneaked into.

But the silence dragged on, and it worried Deacon, and as the months stretched into a second silent year, he became angry. He grew quick to argue and lashed out at his instructors; he scared parishioners on the rare occasions when the diocese allowed him to participate in mass. The silence was mocking him, mocking his earnest studies and all the hours he spent on hard floors, his knees aching. The silence and the smugly devout looks on the faces of the other deacons finally drove him to rage, until he ransacked the seminary library and hurled a Bible at a priest, fleeing into the soundless night and jumping a train up north, someplace where silence would be expected, normal. Someplace where he could be surrounded by other men who neither heard the voice of God nor expected to.

At his first timber camp he had introduced himself by his given name, but once the other men had heard his story, they couldn't resist calling him Deacon, either out of misguided reverence or as a taunt. The name had stuck.

The silence again settled upon Deacon as he stood there, staring. The prisoners inside the building never coughed or sneezed, never spoke loudly enough to be heard. Occasionally, the silence was broken by the hoot of an owl, but that was all. Even the wind had fled the scene.

Deacon wondered if the man in the building had brought the flu with him, wondered if he himself was only a few yards from that bit of evil. It was the invisible things that were most dangerous in this world, he knew.

His watch had stopped that morning and he'd neglected to wind it, so not even its ticking could disturb the calm. The hours passed like an unnoticed procession of ghosts. He would stay there all night, until someone showed up to take his place, and the silence would follow him home.

VII

It was surprising how dark the inside of the building was even during the day.

Philip opened his eyes to the morning wake-up whistle. Another thirty minutes or so passed, the soldier still sleeping blissfully, before Philip heard a knock on the door. It startled him so much that his legs, folded beneath him, kicked out a bit, one of them smacking the butt of the rifle. So clumsy I'm going to shoot myself, he thought, moving the rifle a few feet farther away. Still the soldier slept, heavily exhaling as if trying to shuck off a great weight. Philip thought he could probably fire a shot and the man wouldn't wake.

Philip lit the lamp, illuminating the stark surroundings. The huge room was empty, save one of the far corners, where the possessions of Commonwealth's few enlistees to the American Expeditionary Force were stacked. The dozen or so men who had gone off to war more than a year ago had opted to move their belongings into the storage buildings so that their homes, where they had been living for only a few months, could house new workers during their absence. Boxes were stacked in the corner, and Philip could make out such objects as a banjo and a large ceramic jug. He wondered where the men themselves were, if they were hiding in a trench or nailed inside a box.

Philip waited the prescribed amount of time after the knock, then opened the door. It was indeed day, but barely. Two bowls of oatmeal, their contents still steaming, sat on a tray alongside two large pieces of cornbread, most likely Laura's handiwork. Coffee, even some lumps of sugar beside the mugs. No one had taken sugar in coffee lately—more of the war rationing. He needed a moment to register the magnitude of this act. He had expected to be punished, but the sugar seemed like an apology for keeping him in here. He felt a knot in the back of his throat, and his eyes watered.

He pulled the tray in and shut the door, head down, waiting for the tears to fade.

"Mornin'," the soldier said, sitting up as Philip carried the food toward him. "Nothing quite beats breakfast in bed."

"I'm not your waiter," Philip grumbled, sitting down by his own "bed" and placing the tray beside him.

The soldier stood up and walked over. Despite his cheerful spirits, he seemed almost menacing for a moment, hovering above Philip, who was divvying up the spoils.

"Why don't you get a fire started?" Philip said, to get the soldier to move away.

"Yes, sir. Just like being in the army again—taking orders. Thank you for keeping me in my place."

Philip had been getting cold, but the fire changed that. When he lifted his bowl and set it in his lap, he noticed that it had been sitting on top of an envelope. He picked up the letter and saw his name written in his father's hand. He placed it on the ground beside him and covered it with a bit of blanket.

The soldier sat back down, and Philip handed him one of the bowls and a mug of coffee. Philip used two lumps of sugar and handed the soldier the others.

"Coffee and sugar," the soldier said. "Haven't had two lumps in a while. I normally don't take it that way, but I might as well treat myself."

After a mouthful of oatmeal, the soldier noticed that there was a discrepancy in the portions.

"How come you get all the cornbread?"

"Because my sister made it for me." Philip replied without looking at the soldier, but still he sensed the man smiling.

"Awfully nice sister you got."

They ate in silence for a moment.

"Aren't you about old enough to be having a sweetheart cook for you instead of a sister?"

"What's it to you?"

The soldier's smile widened.

They finished their meal in silence. Philip still felt guarded around this man, uncomfortable in his weirdly dual role of being both the man's guard and co-prisoner.

Philip noticed while they ate that the soldier's right fingers were wounded, red marks gashed along the upper and middle knuckles. Scabs were just starting to form.

The soldier coughed suddenly. It started as a short cough, perhaps even a clearing of the throat, but it spawned several more, a long succession growing louder and more forceful. Philip turned his head away, considered standing up and walking to the other side of the room. Finally, the soldier stood, coughing still, and wandered over to the fire. His coughing grew calmer, and then he made a short retching sound. He spat something into the fire.

He walked back toward Philip, picked up his mug, and drained the last of his coffee. He seemed fine.

"Don't suppose there's a bathroom around here?"

"I don't think so."

"Should we pick different corners of the building?" The soldier smiled. "I'll crap in one side and you crap in the other?"

Philip smiled despite himself, unsure whether he was being joshed or if the man was serious.

"Hey, he can smile," the soldier said. "There's a start. Stop being so grumpy, kid, or I'll piss on you while you're sleeping."

"Check the cellar," Philip said, trying not to laugh. "Maybe there's a hole or something."

After the soldier had descended the stairs, Philip reached under his blanket and tore open the letter. Charles had written it the night before. Philip wondered if his father had had as difficult a time sleeping as he had.

Philip—

It pains me to think of how you must be feeling right now. I apologize again for the situation, but Dr. Banes has impressed upon us all the necessity of quarantining the soldier, and since you and he had come into such close contact, we felt we had no choice. The feeling of standing there talking to you through those walls was a terrible one.

It is still unclear to us what exactly transpired while you were at the guard post, but there will be plenty of time for explanations later. I have my suspicions as to why you acted as you did, but I want you to know that I do not rush to judgment. I feel I am to blame for putting you in an impossible and thankless position, and for that as well I apologize. You did yourself and this town proud when you and Graham defended us before, and whatever happened earlier today is something of which I am sure we can be proud as well.

Dr. Banes has assured me the chances that the soldier carries the flu are exceedingly slim. We are taking these precautions only because it would be folly not to. I have always marveled at your ability to continue unperturbed by any obstacles, and can honestly say that if there is one person in this town best suited to the unusual task before you, it is you.

Remember, too, that because there are guards stationed by the building, there are always people within earshot should you need help. Neither I nor anyone else knows who this visitor to our town is. The fact that he is a soldier makes me confident he is a man to be trusted, though it is regrettably true that not all of them are the doughty souls we would hope them to be. Also, I assume that you still have a rifle in the building with you—if the rifle's presence concerns you, you could always slip it outside the door. In any case, I trust that you will take care of yourself in the same steely way you always have.

I regret that Dr. Banes has forbidden us to retrieve any notes from you, but it will not be long before we can speak in person.

Your sister sends her love, as does your mother, as do I.

Father

Philip felt the knot in the back of his throat again. He was unfamiliar with hearing Charles express such sentiments. During his first few months in the Worthy clan—months of being treated with extra care as he recovered from his injuries, recovered from his loss, taught himself how to walk again—Charles had been especially attentive, helping Philip with his studies so he could keep up, showing him around the Worthy mill in Everett, teaching him how the whole operation worked. But once the novelty wore off and the family grew comfortable in its new shape, Charles became more distant. Many were the nights when he was at the mill past his children's bedtimes, fewer were the fishing trips or the rides into town to see a moving picture. And when Charles was at home, he expressed just enough interest in his son to show that he wanted him to succeed—were his studies going well? was he making new friends?—but nothing more. He seemed to see his role as shepherding Philip into his new life, and now that young Philip was secure enough to walk on his own, Charles could retreat back into his adult world, his books and charts.

Philip reread Charles's comments about the rifle. Ever since he had won himself food and shelter, the soldier had acted quite uninterested in causing trouble, but now that he was warm, rested, and well fed, perhaps he would become a threat again.

The soldier started ascending the stairs, and Philip slipped the letter into his pocket.

"Well, the good news is, I found a bucket. The bad news is, it's a small bucket. Lucky for you I haven't eaten much over the last three days."

"You've been in the woods that long?"

The soldier sat down and exhaled deeply. "Yes. I walked all over looking for shelter, unsuccessfully, till yesterday. I did find a cabin two nights ago, with some beans in the kitchen—about one meal's worth."

"Sounds like you're pretty lost."

"They don't really teach us tracking skills over there. Just how to follow orders."

The soldier certainly smelled like someone who had been wandering around for a couple of days. Philip was grateful for the smoky scent of the fire.

"You said it was a naval accident?"

The soldier nodded. "I don't know what happened, though—it was at night, and I was below deck. Suddenly, everyone was hollering, telling us to get to the lifeboats. Some people were saying it was sabotage, a German spy or something. I don't know."

"Like a U-boat?" People all along the Northwest coast had been worried about a naval invasion—a German U-boat or even a Japanese warship, the yellow menace deciding to use Europe's Great War as the perfect cloak beneath which to launch its long-desired takeover of the coastal states. There had already been several false rumors circulating about U-boats sinking commercial vessels in the waters off Washington and Oregon, and no matter how many times they were disproved by the patriotic press, the fears remained.

"I don't know. Maybe. I didn't see anything, though."

"What happened to the other soldiers?"

Philip had the sense that the man would rather drop the subject, but he wanted to know more. After reading those kids' books about doughboys and fighter pilots, after seeing the news clips before the moving pictures, here he was with a real, live, honest-to-God soldier.

"I don't know. Me and one other guy were in our lifeboat, and all the boats got separated. We were a ways from the coast, and the weather was bad. I don't know where the others landed. If they landed."

One other guy in the lifeboat. Philip fixated on that comment. Surely that was the soldier Graham had shot. And surely this man had figured that out, had realized it when Philip showed him the grave. Philip hoped they weren't good friends, that this man wasn't looking for vengeance.

"So how'd you lose that foot?" the soldier asked.

Philip looked at him carefully, as he often did when someone mentioned his injury. But the soldier didn't appear to be trolling for a weakness or looking for an easy joke or insult.

"Automobile accident," Philip said, looking away. "I was trapped in a snowstorm. It got frostbite pretty bad, so they had to take it off."

"When was that?"

"Five years ago."

The soldier nodded. "You walk pretty good for a guy with one foot."

"They gave me a block. I have to wear boots, so I can lace 'em up to my shins real tight. A shoe would come right off."

"So you're a guy who's lost a foot from being left out in the cold, but you were still going to make me sleep out in the cold last night?"

"You were going to *shoot* me, so don't think you can make me feel guilty."

"I could have shot you dead if I'd wanted to, kid. With my first shot. You'll notice I had a free shot at you, but I hit that stump. I'm not that bad a shot."

"You missed because I pulled my trigger, too. And you were going to shoot me again in the woods, only you tripped."

The soldier exhaled dismissively. "I could have done it if I'd wanted to kill you, but I didn't."

Philip looked at him closely. "Say whatever you want. I still don't buy it."

"Well, I guess we'll never know what the other was going to do, will we?"

"Guess not."

They sat there in silence for a while. At some point, Philip gave a quick glance at his rifle, gauging its distance from the two of them.

"Stop looking at the gun, kid. I ain't about to grab it. I've got shelter and two days' worth of free food, so I don't plan on shooting my way out."

"Aren't you worried about getting back to your base?"

"I'll get there eventually. My only fear is whether my commanding officer will believe me when I tell him I was taken prisoner by a town of crazy loggers."

"We're not crazy for wanting to keep the influenza out."

"All right, you're all perfectly sane. But you've taken an American soldier prisoner, and I'll be the one has to explain it when I get back."

For the first time, it occurred to Philip that someone in the town could get in trouble for doing this. "What are you going to tell them?"

"I don't know, kid. Maybe you should be a little nicer to me, and I'll have nothing but good things to say about the fine people of . . . where the hell am I?"

"Commonwealth. What did you say your name was?"

"Frank Summers. And you are?"

"Philip Worthy."

Frank leaned forward, extending a hand. "Pleased to meet you, Philip."

Philip hesitated only a moment, then shook Frank's hopefully healthy hand.

"I think the pleasure's been all yours so far. No offense."

Frank smiled at the riposte. Then he stood and wandered over to the fire, jostling it back to life. He threw two more pieces of wood on top of it and sat back down.

"Have many of the soldiers at your base fallen ill?" Philip asked.

Frank eyed him a bit. "Yeah," he finally said. "A lot."

"How bad is it?"

Frank shifted positions, sitting more upright. "It's damn awful. They say you go to bed feeling fine but wake up in the morning feeling like you've been hit by a train. Headaches, guys so weak they can barely sit up. A buddy of mine heard someone say it feels like you've been shot through both knees and both elbows. And you cough like hell." He stared off to the side. "You hear a lot of people coughing at night. Like wolves howling at the moon."

Philip imagined this plague visiting his town, imagined lying in his bedroom at night to the sounds of everyone around him slowly dying in their homes.

"Nobody too close to me has been sick. Guys in my barracks have had it, but no one from any of the beds near mine, none of the guys I eat with or drill next to. Folks are worried, though, and it's kinda gotten the sergeants to go easy on us. I think they're afraid of pushing us too hard."

"Sounds bad."

"It is bad. But it's not just at the base—it's everywhere. My mom wrote me a letter, said everybody back in Missoula's sick as the devil. It started one day with a few people and then just exploded. She said she was keeping my sister home from school until it's over, and that letter was written about two weeks ago."

"So how can you blame us for keeping people out?"

"I didn't say I blamed you. I just called you a bunch of crazy loggers." He grinned. "So, you born in this town?"

Philip shook his head. "I was born in Los Angeles."

"Long ways away. Ever been out to Missoula?"

"Nope."

"Well, after this war is over, I'll send you an invitation to Montana's finest victory celebration. I'll introduce you as the man who defended the fair hamlet of Commonwealth from a villain more feared than the wicked Hun: me."

"Now you're joshing me."

But Frank hadn't really sounded like he'd been joking—Philip had heard a curious edge in the man's voice. Frank looked back at the fire, his eyes narrow, and made no reply.

VIII

Charles was alone in his office when Graham knocked on the door.

Graham did not look well. The muscles around his eyes seemed taut, as if he was forcing them to stay focused despite his apparent exhaustion. Then again, Charles knew he didn't look his best, either. He had been barely able to sleep the night before. Twice in the night he had risen from his bed, resolved to march to the storage building and tell the guard to release Philip. Both times he had remembered his commitment not just to his own son but to everyone else in town. Beside him Rebecca tossed and turned, perhaps unaware how similar his struggles were to her own.

They had spoken to Philip that morning, standing a few feet away from Deacon, who had stood sentinel throughout the night. Doc Banes had arrived at the same time to call out questions, and Philip's answers had been encouraging: he still felt fine, no aches, no cough, no pain.

Charles had been pleased that Philip seemed in good spirits, but Rebecca said it was probably an act. "He wants to look good in your eyes, Charles. He may be terrified, but he won't let you see it."

Rebecca was the one who was terrified, Charles tried to tell himself. But in truth, so was he. He was terrified Philip would be made a martyr for the town. Charles would readily lock himself in a prison and give up his own life for this town—he would let the flu eat him away, let it satiate its ravenous hunger on his body. Give up his own life, yes. But could he give up his family for the town?

After telling Philip they would come again in the afternoon, Charles and Rebecca had separated, she to her school and he to the mill. Charles tried to lose himself in work but could not. He thought of his absence from church services the last few months and regretted it even more sharply now that the quarantine barred the traveling minister from the town. Charles had subjugated his will to that of the town, to his dream, but he felt an almost nostalgic need to subjugate his fears to something even greater, if such a thing existed.

"How are you, Graham?" There was an empty chair next to Charles, but Graham ignored it, as if he had too much energy to be still, or as if he dared not sit, lest he fall asleep.

Graham nodded shortly. "I'm fine."

"How are things on the floor? Does everyone know about . . . Philip?"

"Word's spreading." There had been no official announcement about the quarantine inside the quarantine, but neither had there been any attempt to keep things secret.

Charles was worried about people's reactions. If Philip were blamed for letting the man in, then Charles would be implicated too, either by family bond or by the simple fact that he had allowed his son to stand guard despite his age.

"I think I should stop working in the mill for a while," Graham said. "Now that there are two places to keep our eyes on, we need more guards. And I figure I can be more of a help by spending all my time guarding instead of working in here."

Charles frowned. "Do you really want to do that?"

"Wanting's got nothing to do with it."

Graham was right. Keeping the town safe and protected was more important than the amount of work slippage that would result from Graham's absence from the mill—the other foremen could cover for him. If the soldiei got loose or someone else stole in and infected the town and all the workers became bedridden, where would the mill be then? As a result of the quarantine, the mill was accumulating a vast amount of wood waiting to be shipped; there were stacks fifty feet high in the yards beyond the mill, and they were growing taller with every passing day. The trees were still falling deep in the woods, the timber was still rolling into the river and floating along, the river drivers were still breaking up logjams and guiding the logs into the mill, the sawyers were still cutting planks and crafting shingles. Once the quarantine ended, the shipping companies would need to send out all their vessels for days just to get everything out of Commonwealth. But all would be resolved. The town would survive this financial bottleneck—if it stayed healthy.

Charles said, "All right. I can find a way to cover for your absence."

"Thank you. And maybe we can try talking more men into standing guard. We're getting stretched thin."

"Yes, of course." Charles should have thought of that. Things were threatening to spiral beyond his control, and being distracted about his son was not helping.

"I was thinking I'd head over to the storage building now. Deacon has been guarding it all night and this morning—he's probably falling asleep on his feet."

"But . . ." Charles paused, surprised Graham was willing to stand guard on Philip. There were other guards for whom the task wouldn't feel so personal. But he saw no recognition in Graham's eyes of the dilemma. Finally, Charles nodded.

Graham turned to leave. Charles felt for him, seeing the weariness in his eyes, the vigilance, the obvious sense he had of himself as the town's protector. But Charles was haunted by the thought of Graham and Philip divided from each other.

"I spoke to Philip this morning," Charles said as Graham put a hand on the doorknob. "He sounds perfectly healthy, and doing quite well, considering."

Graham turned around. "That's good. He say why he let the soldier in?"

"We can ask for explanations later. I'm sure he had his reasons."

Graham just stood there, and Charles felt that he had somehow insulted him.

"I'm sure"—Charles spoke hesitantly now—"he'll be happy to know it's you out there."

"I don't plan on talking to him."

Charles was entirely unfamiliar with the coldness in Graham's voice.

"Graham, if the foremen are able to recruit more guards, then it might not be necessary for you to stand watch all the time."

"I'm not worried about me," Graham said. "And other guards haven't done such a great job." Before Charles could respond, Graham went on. "Are you sure it's a good idea to let them out after only two days?"

"Dr. Banes said it would be."

Graham looked away dismissively. "Banes is your friend, Charles, and he's a good man. But I don't have a lot of confidence in him."

Charles was not surprised by the comment—he had observed the quiet that descended upon Graham whenever Doc Banes was in his presence, or even mentioned, ever since Amelia's first child had been stillborn.

"I trust the doctor's judgment on this, Graham, more than I would trust yours or mine."

"He's said himself that this ain't like a regular flu, so how do we know two days is enough? Even if he does know everything there is about flu, this could be something different."

Charles shifted in his seat. So far he had been careful to speak calmly, trying to loosen the tension, but this was too much. "What are you suggesting? We leave them in there for weeks? This is Philip we're talking about!"

Graham seemed to realize he had pushed too far. "All right. I should be going. Thanks, Charles."

Charles sat motionless, staring at the doorway. The anger and fear pressed down on his chest. It was a good while before he was able to return to his account books.

IX

Remote as it was, Commonwealth had been shaken by America's entrance into the Great War.

The town was less than a year old in April 1917 when Wilson implored Congress to declare war and make the world safe for democracy. But everyone in Commonwealth felt they had finally found a place that was safe and democratic, so the thought of heading off to distant Europe to fight for the rights they had just established was perplexing at best. Because the town was so cut off from the rest of the state, there were no visits from the Four-Minute Men, no posters on street poles advertising the draft or advocating the purchase of Liberty Bonds. People got news from the papers they brought back from their trips to Timber Falls or Everett, but it was as though the articles were printed in ink that faded the farther from civilization it traveled, until it could barely be seen in the Commonwealth rains. The sounds of those war rallies and parades, the speeches and marching bands, echoed off so many trees, weakening to a murmur by the time they reached the town.

But the army needed lumber, and plenty of it. It needed wood for the new fighter planes that would hopefully swing the balance in the Great Powers' favor; it needed even more wood for the cantonments to be constructed all across the country. Ten months into its existence, the Commonwealth mill had been performing barely well enough to support its workers and to convince buyers to keep returning. But when war was declared and representatives from Uncle Sam began showing up at the mill—pockets overflowing with Liberty Loan-funded dollars, practically begging for more lumber regardless of the price—the mill had taken the bold leap that Charles had always known it could.

The draft threatened to ruin everything. In June 1917, Uncle Sam began conscripting men to the new army. Charles couldn't afford to lose his workers right when demand had shot up, but he soon learned that men designated as "essential war workers" could be spared from military duty. The draft boards would make exceptions for millworkers, and Commonwealth could continue to run at peak efficiency.

The men still needed to go through the formality of registration, though, and even that was no small task. Commonwealth was populated almost entirely by two types of people: workers who had fled the constant harassment of bosses, union busters, and cops; and fellow travelers like Rebecca. These two groups sometimes overlapped but just as often did not. Many were intellectual greenhorns who, never having worked at hard labor, had required careful training and strict oversight by men like Graham. What the groups did have in common was a reticence to join up with what many were calling a rich man's war.

Like a doting father oblivious to all but his children's finest qualities, Charles chose to believe that most of the men in town had followed the law, registering for the war and securing worker deferments.

Philip had been not quite fifteen when all the men about town were talking about the draft and whether they should register. Many didn't even want to add their names to the draft rolls, didn't want to dignify the process with their participation. Out here, they felt safely insulated from the rest of the country, cloaked in invisibility.

Philip, who was three years younger than the draft age, had asked Graham if he intended to register. They were sitting on Graham's porch at the time, while Amelia was inside.

"No," Graham had said after a pause, taking the pipe from his mouth. He told Philip that if he were a single man, he may well have, but he had responsibilities now. At the time, Amelia had been in the midst of her first pregnancy.

Philip had been glad to know that the war would be over soon, that by the time he turned eighteen, this debate would be moot.

The issue of the war had been broached in a Sunday sermon that summer. A traveling Unitarian minister named Inston, who had befriended Rebecca years ago during a suffrage march in Seattle, had volunteered to serve as the town's spiritual leader. Because he led services in a town thirty miles away, he didn't make it to Commonwealth until two in the afternoon most Sundays, an unlikely time for church. To the more devout residents, who previously had either traveled into Timber Falls on Sundays or guiltily abstained, Minister Inston's visits were a revelation, a sign that just because this town had a different way of going about business didn't mean it had to be godless. Of course, many of the town's socialists were indeed godless and were a bit ruffled by the minister's presence, but Charles, who had been brought up a strict Presbyterian, had raised Laura and then Philip accordingly and had happily accepted Inston's offer.

Those who silently grumbled about the Unitarian minister's lack of fealty to their particular denomination assumed that in ten or five or perhaps even two years, when Commonwealth had become the strongest mill in the Northwest, the town surely would be filled with the music of dozens of different church bells on Sunday mornings.

Inston was a portly older man with a thick mane of chestnut-brown hair and a youthful exuberance. The day of the war sermon, he'd begun by talking about the day's Gospel reading. Jesus, in reply to a snare laid by the wicked Pharisees who had asked him what he thought of Caesar's taxation, had told his disciples to give to Caesar what was Caesar's but to give to God what was God's. Inston veered off into commentary on the war. His was a conversational preaching style, in which he asked questions of his congregation. With a group of listeners who were used to sitting in participatory union meetings and labor rallies, this style often caused his sermons to degenerate into freewheeling, boisterous sessions.

"But how can we give to Caesar when what he asks of us is our very lives?" Inston said, his voice filling every inch of the hall. "Not coins but blood. Is Caesar asking us for something we can rightly give, or is he really asking for something that is God's?"

These words had not been planned, and they surprised the minister himself. He knew as soon as he uttered them that they likely would have landed him in a bit of trouble, perhaps even led to his arrest, had he done so in any other town. But Commonwealth was different.

"How could God want us to give our lives to a crooked war?" one man called out, unofficially beginning the participatory portion of the day's service.

"We need to ask ourselves why God might want that. Perhaps—"

"To protect the rest of God's children," said a tall, bearded redhead named Walsh. His forebears were Irish, but his grandfather had moved to England and renounced the Catholic Church. When Walsh had moved to America he'd left behind many friends and relatives. "To protect those who can't protect themselves."

"It's somebody else's war," a man in the middle intoned loudly and with a dismissive shake of the head. "It's not God's war, and it's not America's, either. It's Europe's war, and just 'cause Caesar Wilson wants in on it doesn't make it God's."

Walsh sat in silent anger, his face nearly the color of his hair, as Inston regained control. The minister talked for a long while, straying away from the war and back into Scripture, words safely written thousands of years before that day's contradictions. The voices from the congregation ceased, and the remainder of the service passed without event. But the die had been cast.

As people filed out after the service, Walsh sought out the men who had made the antiwar comments. He walked up to a tall Swede who worked in the mill just as his father had in Scandinavia.

"So you're fixing to hide here while the real men protect our country?" Walsh challenged. The two men were pinned together by the crowd squeezing through the narrow doors.

"I ain't doing any hiding," the man said, "but the boys in the army aren't protecting any Americans. It ain't our war."

"Any man that don't enlist is yellow," Walsh said, scanning the men's faces. "Essential worker or no, every man should enlist."

"Speak for yourself, buddy," muttered someone whose back was turned.

"The Germans are out there killing babies while everybody here is all proud of themselves for living in this nice new town," Walsh went on.

"They did it to Belgium, and they're doing it to France, and next they'll do it to England, then they'll come for us. You all heard about them raping nuns and little girls, but you don't care. You heard about—"

"Those are lies!" barked Alfred Metzger. "No German boy would do anything like that."

"I didn't know I'd come to work in a German town," Walsh said. "German town and German yellowbellies."

Jarred Rankle, who only recently had started attending services—he still had not forgiven God for stealing his family—slid through the crowd up to Walsh, eying him carefully. "I'm not German, Walsh, and I sure as hell ain't yellow. But that doesn't make me agree with a thing you just said."

Inston had been standing by the door shaking hands, but like everyone else's, his attention had been stolen by the war debaters.

"Gentlemen, you are in the house of God," he reminded them.

The stone-faced Rankle was one of the few men Walsh wouldn't want to spar with, so he cooled down a bit.

"I got cousins fighting for England," he said to Rankle in a softer tone.

"And Metzger's got cousins fighting for Germany," Rankle said. "I don't care to see you two fight your own little war here, all right?"

"That's why I'm going to fight in the real war." Walsh said that as if voicing it for the first time. Like anyone else in Commonwealth, he had been deeply conflicted about fighting. But here, in the house of God, he had made his decision. He stepped back a bit, as the crowd had thinned somewhat. "I'm enlisting, and essential worker or no, I'm fighting. If I have to quit the mill and leave this town, I will."

Other men nodded in agreement. Some shook their heads. Some just stood there looking at him, or at their feet, or away.

"I can't imagine I'm the only man who's gonna uphold his duty," Walsh said.

Metzger glared at Walsh but said nothing. Maybe Commonwealth was a safer place to show support for your distant relatives than other American towns—where they were attacking people with German accents or even German surnames, where they had renamed sauerkraut "liberty cabbage"—but you could never be too sure. Metzger kept his head down and walked out of the church, hurrying to catch up with his wife and daughter, who had made their way out of the building before the tensions had risen.

Metzger was followed by Rankle, who had already seen his fill of violence and would never enlist in any damned army, deferment or no.

After most of the other men had filed out past the still-nervous Inston, Walsh was greeted by ten other congregants, some of whom he knew well and some he did not. They told him they appreciated what he'd said and they shook his hand. Inston watched all this quietly.

Those eleven men became fast friends. One of them would quickly change his mind about the war, but Walsh and the other nine would register in Timber Falls and would all specify to the suit-wearing gentlemen of the registration board that they wanted no deferral on account of their jobs. *Move us up to the top of the list,* they said, *we want to fight.* Most of them had no families, but the four who did—among them Walsh, with a wife and two young sons—found friends who could help provide for them or were confident that the monthly government check would be enough. God would make a way, they decided.

They were indeed drafted. The single men had moved their meager possessions into one of Commonwealth's unused storage buildings, telling Mr. Worthy not to waste their houses, to let other men move into them. They would take new ones when they returned. Walsh and the three other men with families moved their wives and children out of Commonwealth, disgusted by their fellow residents' avoidance of their duties. The summer of '17 soon cooled into a surprisingly dry fall and the ten men were gone, training in Fort Jenkins as they awaited deployment.

No one had heard from them since.

X

Elsie couldn't believe the news. "He's locked up in a storage building?"

Laura nodded, her brow knit with concern. They were standing outside the school, the first two students to arrive, as usual. Mrs. Worthy was already inside, having said hello to Elsie and hurried along.

Elsie pestered her friend with questions, only a few of which Laura could answer. Charles had told Laura that Philip had let the man into town because he was starving, that he had refused to just stand there and let the man die. Charles had said he was proud of Philip, that he had surely done the right and Christian thing but that, due to the flu, he and the stranger would need to be quarantined for two days.

"So he might be sick?" Elsie asked.

"I don't know. My father said I was asking too many questions."

Elsie shook her head, still taking in the news. "He must have let him in because of what happened to the other soldier."

Laura gave her a peculiar look. "What do you mean? I figured this was the same soldier as last time."

Elsie remembered Philip's warning that the first soldier's death be kept secret. "No, you're right. I'm just . . . confused by everything."

"My mother told me I should try not to think about it and pretend it's a normal day. She said Philip will be home for dinner tomorrow night and everything will be fine."

"This just feels so . . ." Elsie couldn't find the right word.

"I know."

"Are you all right?"

"I don't think anyone in my house slept very much. I could hear my parents talking all night."

"Maybe we could go visit him?"

"We're not allowed," Laura said, and finally motioned to the school.

They walked inside holding hands.

Once they were in school, Elsie had no choice but to stew in silence. Mrs. Worthy had already scrawled an assignment on the chalkboard and was sitting at her desk, sifting through papers. Elsie, in her role of elder student and apprentice teacher, asked how she could be of help, and Mrs. Worthy described the day's lessons. At no point did she say anything about Philip.

"How does that sound?" Mrs. Worthy asked when she finished her instructions.

"Fine, ma'am," Elsie replied. She realized she hadn't listened to a thing her teacher had said about the lessons. She stood there an extra moment, confused to be in such an unfamiliar position.

"Everything is going to be fine, Elsie," Mrs. Worthy said in her typical calmly authoritarian tone. "But there's much to get accomplished today."

Mrs. Worthy was the embodiment of her own advice, proceeding as if it were a normal day. Once the students had filled the building, attendance was called, the lesson was read, assignments were distributed, unruly children were disciplined, and order was kept as it always was. The only difference, Elsie noticed, was her: her inability to concentrate, her uncharacteristic daydreaming, the snippets of a letter to Philip she jotted in her notebook while pretending to record Mrs. Worthy's lesson. When Mrs. Worthy called on her during the lesson on the drafting of the Constitution, Elsie stammered until her instructor seemed to have pity and called on someone else.

During recess, news of Philip and the soldier spread, and by the end of the day, everyone seemed to know the story, despite the fact that Mrs. Worthy never broached the subject. When she released the students for the day, they walked away in a mass, trading stories about what their fathers and mothers had told them, speculating about the soldier and whether either of the prisoners would become ill. Elsie snapped at a few of them, then walked back inside to help Mrs. Worthy clean up. The teacher was standing at her desk, placing some papers in her satchel.

"I'm going to leave early today, girls," she said to Elsie and Laura, who was busily erasing the board. "I'll leave you to finish cleaning."

Elsie said, "Mrs. Worthy, I was wondering . . ."

Her teacher looked at her patiently. She already seemed to know what Elsie was struggling to say.

Elsie continued, "Does Philip really need to be locked in that building all day? If the man he let in doesn't seem sick, maybe they could come out this evening instead of tomorrow?"

Mrs. Worthy sat down beside Elsie in one of the pupils' chairs, finally acknowledging that this was not a normal day after all.

She explained the doctor's instructions and reminded Elsie of that day's history lesson. "We all are a part of something larger than ourselves," Mrs. Worthy said. "Being in a democracy sometimes means we are outvoted. When that happens, we need to press on and trust that the decision the majority made was right. I know it's hard, but it's something each of us has to do."

Elsie thought for a moment, then nodded. There seemed to be two Mrs. Worthys—the friendlier one at Laura's house and the sterner one in the school—and right now Elsie was looking at Laura's mother, her eyes a bit larger than usual, a look of empathy on her face.

"But," Elsie said, stammering again, "but he's going to be okay, right?"

Mrs. Worthy smiled, but it was a strange half-smile, the outer edges cut off by tension. She reached out and grasped Elsie's hands with a reassuring squeeze. "I'm sure everything will be fine."

Mrs. Worthy explained that Elsie could always write Philip a letter and ask the guards to deliver it—she herself would write to him as soon as she returned home, she said. Then she released Elsie's hands and stood up abruptly, walking toward the door as if she didn't want anyone to see her face. She bade them goodbye and was gone.

Elsie and Laura tidied the building quickly, each in a rush to escape the chores. Normally, Elsie's mother expected her at the store as soon as school was out, but since Elsie was not staying late to further discuss the next day's lessons with Mrs. Worthy, as she normally would, she had time to return home and work on a letter to Philip. She read through what she had written during the day, displeased with how it sounded. She started over on a clean sheet of her favorite paper, a bright white with fraying corners.

Still, it felt wrong that she had to write him rather than visiting him. Despite Mrs. Worthy's words, Elsie clung to the hope that when she reached the storage building, the guard would let her in, or perhaps there would be no guard, or perhaps Philip would already be freed from the building, the town elders having decided they were wrong to keep him there.

Her hopes were dashed as she approached the building, letter in hand, and saw a lone figure standing there. His back was to her, and he stood a good distance away from the building, as if wary of its inhabitants. He was holding a rifle.

She felt herself grow nervous as she walked toward the man, embarrassed to be delivering a letter to a boy and awkward to have to do so in someone else's presence. She concocted a quick lie to explain herself, but her stomach clenched, and she saw the envelope quivering in her hand.

When she was a few feet from the guard, he turned around and nodded a silent greeting. It was Graham Stone. Elsie knew he was friends with Philip and Mr. Worthy, but she had rarely come into contact with him. She found herself intimidated by his wordless gaze, the solidity of his posture, and the rifle that lay across his arms neither casually nor rigidly.

"Um, the kids at school wrote this letter to Philip," Elsie said without looking him in the eye. "Mrs. Worthy asked me to deliver it to him."

"I'll see he gets it," he said, releasing the barrel of the rifle with his left hand, which Elsie saw had only three fingers, and taking the envelope.

He kept his eyes on her for another moment and, seeing that she had nothing else to say, turned back around. His shadow stretched across her feet and then it was like he was a statue. He seemed in no rush to deliver the letter, and she wondered how he would do it, whether there were proscribed times for deliveries or if he had lied to her. She blushed when she realized there was nothing she could do to stop him from opening it, and the thought broke her from her brief trance and chased her back down the empty path.

She had walked less than a minute when she stopped and caught her breath, then turned around. Graham was in the same spot. He didn't seem to be reading the letter, and he obviously trusted that she was walking home.

Beside Elsie, a narrow trail split off and led into the woods. She slowly began to creep toward it. She had tramped over the trails all around Commonwealth, had explored them when her family first moved here, and had continued the habit despite her mother's criticism that such wanderings were unladylike.

Elsie loved the woods. Her grandfathers had been loggers and river drivers, so perhaps this was them surfacing in her, some hereditary predisposition that made her feel particularly at home when tramping beneath Douglas fir and climbing over fallen branches and pungent pine needles, collecting pieces of driftwood by the river. The trails were where Elsie escaped when she was tired from the drudgery of school and the store and housework, when she needed to disappear. Her mother had hoped she would outgrow such jaunts, but they had become more intriguing to her since her family had moved to Commonwealth, which was so newly carved into the woods that the trails cut behind most of the town's homes. She could wander through the woods and wind up in someone's backyard, or reach the edge of a street where some men or women might be talking, letting the afternoon slowly drift by. She'd hide beneath the low-hanging branches, careful to stay in the shadows, and listen. Even the most boring topics were interesting when you weren't supposed to be hearing them. Often she didn't know what people were talking about, didn't even know who some of them were. But it was real life. She liked spying because she was such a good student, she told herself; she wanted to know everything that was happening.

Secretly, she loved knowing there were things she had seen that others hadn't. Like seeing the men bury the dead soldier. Not even Philip's own sister knew about the dead soldier. Did Mrs. Worthy? Suddenly, there were big secrets in Commonwealth, and she didn't know who held them, who was unaware of them, or how many secrets she had yet to discover.

So much had changed since the quarantine. People were terse on street corners, conversations by front doors were cut short, brief nods were replacing warm handshakes. No one was sick, but everyone was acting as if disease were stalking them and they needed to swiftly make their way to the safety of their homes. Kids weren't allowed to play outside as often as before—mothers called them in, asked the friends to go back to their parents' house. The quiet air of the men who guarded the town seemed to have infected everyone to some degree, and Elsie didn't like it.

She'd even spied on some of Philip's first shift of guard duty, when he'd stood out by the post with Graham for an uneventful afternoon. She had watched them, sitting beneath a fir tree and feeling the sun briefly poke out through a thin spot in the clouds as the two men shifted their weight from one foot to the other. How unlucky, then, that she had missed the most interesting events. She would have loved to see the confrontation with the first soldier, to hear what Graham and Philip had said to him, to see what an actual soldier looked like up close. Had they really fired a warning shot, as Philip had said, or had he embellished the story for her?

Elsie knew this trail wound to the other side of the storage building, where Graham wouldn't be able to see her. She crept forward, careful not to step on any twigs and give herself away. The forest was thick here, the low branches all but blocking her from view, but she noticed when Graham moved. She stopped, peering out through a break in the trees, and watched him walk toward the storage building. She saw him slip the letter under the door, heard him knock on the door and go back to where he had stood. Then he was motionless again.

Elsie walked on, and the trail dipped down a slight hill until Graham and the building were out of view. But after a minute's walk, the trail tracked up again. A couple hundred feet to her right was the back of the storage building. Graham wouldn't be able to see her, as he was on the opposite side of the building, but she was careful not to make enough noise to attract attention. The ground was still damp from the rainfall early that morning, and she realized her shoes would be filthy, necessitating a trip home to clean them before showing up at the store. But it was worth it, for there was the back of the building, close enough to toss a pebble at.

She was at the edge of the woods now. She could see that the building was in disrepair, with a few holes at its base. They were too small for a man to fit through, but she could probably do it. Philip might even be able to, she thought. Maybe she could throw a pebble at the building, attract his attention, coax him out. She stood there in a crouch, her posture the picture of guilt. She knew she shouldn't be doing this, but she hadn't been able to resist.

She picked up a small stone. All she had to do was throw it. She listened. She could hear something, murmuring. She couldn't pick out words or even voices, but it must be Philip and the soldier. What were they talking about? Was Philip all right? The stone started to feel slick in her palm.

Something snapped behind her and she turned around, panicked. She couldn't see anything; it was only the sound of the forest. But she realized that just because Graham had stayed in one place for the past few minutes didn't mean he wasn't about to start pacing around the building. She could be discovered. And just what did she intend to say to Philip? She thought it wrong for him to be trapped in there, but she couldn't take it upon herself to set him free. What would the town do if she were caught? And what if the soldier truly did have the flu?

More murmuring from inside the building. It sounded no different from voices she'd overheard in houses throughout town. She was no more than thirty feet from the building. So close to Philip. But only when she was close enough to hear his laugh—there it was, rising above the murmurs for a brief, glowing moment—did she realize how far they were from each other, how separate this new quarantine had rendered them. She traded the stone from one hand to the other and back again, over and over. Then she placed it on the ground, silently.

The trail seemed darker as she walked back home.

XI

"I see your two twigs," Philip said, eying Frank carefully, "and raise you three."

After requesting playing cards from the morning guard, the two prisoners had scoured the building in search of something they could bet with. They found plenty of twigs—enough so it would probably take many hours for either of them to bankrupt the other. They'd started playing at least two hours ago.

Philip was beginning to enjoy Frank's company, but Charles's warning about the guns still left him unsettled. Which was why, the next time Frank wandered downstairs to "use the facilities," as he called it, Philip had gathered the rifle and pistol, carried them to the front of the vast room, quickly opened the door, and placed the weapons right outside.

They'd been playing for hours when they heard the midmorning whistle, just as Philip was raising Frank three twigs. Frank took the bait, then each player traded in two cards. Philip took a three of hearts and a seven of clubs, which gave him absolutely nothing.

Frank bet a twig. Philip raised him three more.

Frank scrutinized his foe. Then he dropped his cards. "Fold."

Philip raked the twigs into his stash, dropped his cards facedown, and started shuffling.

"At least tell me what you had," Frank said. "I had two kings."

"Do I have to tell you?"

"Not technically. A gentleman would."

"Do gentlemen play poker?"

"Of course."

Philip kept shuffling. "I had nothing."

Frank slapped his thighs angrily. But he was smiling. "You're a hell of a bluffer. I thought you had a royal flush or something."

Three hands later, two of which Philip won, they were interrupted by a knock on the door.

"I was just thinking it was time for dinner," Frank said.

Philip put down the cards and walked over to the door.

"You're a regular ringer, kid. After the war, you and me should tour the West, take on some high rollers."

Philip put his hand on the doorknob. He was already tired of opening the door, quickly picking up the tray of food and bringing it inside, then closing the door. This time he took an extra moment to look down the street, squinting at the brightness of the outside world. In the distance, closer to the second storage building, was one of the guards. First he was just a silhouette before the glare of the sun, then Philip recognized Graham's face. And his scowl.

Philip closed the door, the image lingering.

"Everything all right?" Frank asked.

"Yeah," Philip said, then carried over the tray. He sat down and took his first good look at the tray, which held two chicken sandwiches, apples, cups of water, more cornbread, and an envelope addressed to Philip in Rebecca's handwriting. Philip put the envelope in his pocket.

"So how long have you folks been keeping people out of the town?" Frank asked.

"Almost two weeks now."

"You going to run out of food eventually?" Frank took a bite of his sandwich.

"They say we can go at least a couple months if we need to. But the doctor doesn't think we'll have to."

Frank's eyebrows shifted and he seemed to almost say something, but he opted for silence and another bite. Philip put one of the pieces of cornbread next to Frank's plate. Frank, his mouth full, nodded in appreciation.

After they finished their meals, they looked at the cards, somewhat disappointed. Poker had been a welcome diversion for a couple of hours, but the long day stretched before them.

Philip swallowed. His throat was not sore. He did not have a headache. He was neither feverish nor chilled. He had no cough and no sneeze. All seemed well.

"Your sister makes good cornbread," Frank said. "She pretty?"

Philip shrugged. "Yeah."

"How old is she?"

Philip saw where this was going. "Too young for you."

Frank smiled. "Relax, kid. I'm just teasing. I'm not interested."

"You got a sweetheart back in Missoula?"

"I do."

"What's her name?"

"Michelle."

A pretty name, Philip thought. He himself had once nurtured a crush on a Michelle in Portland—or was it Eugene? Those years were a geographic blur in his mind, but he remembered Michelle, the red dress she always wore, and the way she laughed at his jokes more than at anyone else's.

"When was the last time you saw her?"

"Two months ago. Two months, one week, and four days." Frank grinned ruefully.

"What's she look like?"

"As a matter of fact—" Frank reached into one of his pockets and pulled out a thin leather strap that looked like a billfold. He removed a small photograph and handed it to Philip. Staring back at him was an attractive brunette, closer in age to Philip than to Frank, with large brown eyes and hair almost as straight as that of the Chinook Indians who lived outside Everett. It was just one picture, but if that was how she really looked, she would have been one of the prettiest girls in Commonwealth, Philip thought.

"She's sweet," Philip said, handing it back.

"It was tough to leave her for this."

"You'll see her again soon," Philip said. "They say the war's almost over."

"Yeah," Frank said, his eyes clouding.

"Why didn't you marry her? You wouldn't have been drafted then."

"Yeah, I would have. They changed that law—anyone who gets married after the war started is treated like a single man as far as the draft is concerned. Too many fellas had gotten out of the first draft that way, so Uncle Sam got wise. Marrying her would only mean there was a chance I could make her a widow. I didn't want to do that." Frank looked at the picture again. His eyes were hard.

"So what's she doing now?" Philip asked, hoping to dispel the black cloud that suddenly hung around his companion.

"Rolling bandages with the Red Cross ladies. Saving peach pits." Pits were collected by the government so their carbon could be used in the production of gas masks. "Same as everyone else." Frank put the photo back in his pocket. "So after forty-eight hours of this, they'll let us go?"

Philip nodded. "Sure."

"They're not going to change their minds? Decide to leave us in here for a week? Or a month?"

There were so many other things for Philip to worry about that he hadn't even considered this possibility. He found Frank's question too horrible to ponder. "No. Just till tomorrow night. Unless one of us gets sick, I guess."

"Well, I don't aim to get sick."

"Me, neither."

They looked at each other, knowing their fate was bound together. *I could feel fine tomorrow*, Philip thought, *but if he starts coughing and shivering, we're in here to stay.*

Philip rushed to break the uncomfortable silence. "Want to play another hand?"

They played and Philip won again, his ace-high full house beating Frank's two pairs. He raked ten more twigs into his pile.

As Philip shuffled the cards for the next hand, he thought he heard something. He looked at Frank's hands, one of which was in his pile of twigs, which had diminished noticeably after Philip's last few victories. Frank's hand twitched a bit when he realized he was being watched.

Philip dropped his cards. "I saw that."

"What?" Frank feigned innocence.

"You snapped one of your twigs!"

"What?"

"You snapped one of your twigs to make it two twigs—you're sitting over there minting yourself more money!"

Frank decided to give up his act. "Okay, so I snapped one of 'em. You got me. It was too long anyway." He grabbed a twig and flung it across the room, as if this would make up for his embezzlement.

Philip was unsure how big a deal he should make of the fact that his opponent was a confirmed cheater. "I have to watch you like a hawk, I guess."

Frank sighed. "I won't do it again. C'mon, deal the hand."

Philip taunted him: "I thought this was a gentleman's game."

"Just deal the damn cards."

After another hour in which Philip's collection of twigs grew, Frank announced he wanted to lie down. He pillowed his head on a folded blanket and shut his eyes; soon he was breathing so heavily that Philip figured he was asleep. Frank certainly seemed to be enjoying his reprieve from military drills and push-ups, or whatever it was they did over at Fort Jenkins.

Philip walked toward the fireplace and threw more wood on the fire. It was warm enough during the day, but the previous night had been cold, and Philip wasn't looking forward to another struggle with sleep.

He sat down and read Rebecca's letter. It seemed to have been written the night before; she mentioned how difficult it would be to go to school the next day and said that both she and Laura were worried about him. But this short time would pass quickly, she assured him, and tomorrow night they would have supper as a family again.

Philip was about to read the letter a second time when there was a knock on the door. He stood up hesitantly—it was too early for another meal—and walked toward it. After the requisite wait, he opened the door. There in the light of day, just on the threshold, was an envelope with his name written on it. He grabbed it and stole a brief glance farther outside, hoping to confirm whether the guard was indeed Graham. But out in the distance the solitary figure had turned his back, and because Philip knew he shouldn't stand there with the door open, he looked back down and closed the door, the room falling prey to the darkness once more. The back could have been Graham's, Philip figured, but maybe not.

The handwriting on the envelope was a mystery. It looked feminine, though—certainly it wasn't from Graham or Charles. Philip paused, then opened it. The one-page letter on plain white paper was signed *Elsie.*

A letter from Elsie! He had tried not to think of her that day, had tried to focus on making it through those forty-eight hours, to concentrate on the soldier, to lose himself in the card game. But it had been all but impossible to keep her completely out of his mind, impossible not to wonder what she was doing, whether she was thinking of him.

He sat down beside the lamp. Embarrassed, he looked back to make sure Frank wasn't watching, then he unfolded the letter again.

Dear Philip,

I couldn't believe it when Laura told me this morning what has happened. It was so hard to have to sit in class for the rest of the day and pretend to concentrate on what Mrs. Worthy was saying. She never called on Laura all day—she must have decided to go easy on her—but twice I was called on and both times I hadn't been listening. I had been so preoccupied.

Everyone at the school has been talking about you and everyone is hoping you come out soon. I think this whole quarantine thing is so rotten and wrong, and now that they've done this to you I can't believe that no one else sees it but me. I know you must feel the same way, though.

I heard some kids at school wondering aloud why you let the soldier in, but I can imagine why. I know that standing guard out there must be so difficult and to be confronted with someone wanting to come in must have been unbearably hard. I know you feel bad about what happened a few days ago—I still have not told anyone what I know—but I do think you and Graham did the right thing. I also think you did the right thing by letting the new person in yesterday. I know that sounds contradictory, but I don't think it is. I think you had your reasons and I want you to know that even though it might feel that you are alone, you aren't.

We'll see you soon,

Elsie

Philip placed the letter back in the envelope. Elsie had been thinking of him all day; he couldn't believe it. He had wondered if she'd felt the same way, had hoped, but this was his first strong piece of evidence. Unless Philip was misreading her words. So he opened the letter once more and read them a third time, his heart still beating fast.

Elsie's reference to other people talking brought back his fears that the townspeople would blame him for betraying their trust. She seemed to have faith in him; hopefully, the others would, too.

He lay down on his blankets and stared at the ceiling, thinking of Elsie. If he had been anxious to be released from this prison before, now he was positively desperate.

"So, what exactly do you do at Fort Jenkins?"

After supper, they had played poker for another hour, then had taken a break to collect more wood for the fire. To preserve lamp oil, they had decided to kill the lamp for the night, and the fire cast an orange and ever-shifting glow on their faces. They had already talked plenty—Philip had learned that Frank was a carpenter who worked with his father, that his father had built most of the houses on one side of the river in Missoula, that Frank had a younger sister who was blind, that Frank loved to fish and that his idea of happiness was climbing to the top of Mount Sentinel and watching the sun set over the hay-colored peaks to the west. But Frank had spoken barely a word about his military service.

"What do I do?"

"Yeah. Practice shooting, marching, digging trenches? How does it work?"

Frank thought for a moment. "Believe it or not, we haven't been able to practice shooting yet because we don't have any guns."

"No guns?"

"I guess they're running short, and the first priority is obviously the guys in France, so they haven't gotten around to giving my company real firearms yet. We practice marching with broom handles."

"Really?"

"And we practice bayoneting with broom handles."

"You must be a dangerous man with a broom. How about a mop?"

"I could stab you through the heart with a mop. Don't let me anywhere near the broom closet or I'll go off on a rampage."

When Philip looked back at Frank he saw a different face, that of a man miles away, slogging through mud or staring into an unimaginably vast sea. The face made Philip deeply uncomfortable.

"So after this is all over, you're going to marry Michelle?"

Frank looked down, then at the fire. "Yeah."

"You tell her about that, or is it a surprise?"

"She knows. She might think I was just saying it, though—a lot of guys just said it before they left so they could get their girls to loosen up with 'em. They brag about that at the camp. But I didn't just say it; I meant it."

Frank reached into his pile of twigs and threw one at the fire.

"So how come you don't have a sweetheart making you cornbread?" he asked, apparently eager to turn the focus of the conversation away from himself.

"I've got a girl," Philip blurted defensively. He regretted the lie immediately but, more important, didn't want to be teased. Was it really a lie, or was it just a mild exaggeration?

"Do you?" Frank said, raising his eyebrows and turning to face Philip. "Here we've known each other so long and you never said anything. What's her name?"

"Elsie," Philip said, painting himself farther into the corner.

Frank threw another twig into the fire. "Tell me about her."

"What do you want to know?"

"I want to know," Frank said slowly, looking at the fire again, "if the thought of her keeps you up at night. If hearing someone else say her name makes you turn your head. If she's pretty."

"She's very pretty. And yes to everything else."

"Blond or brown hair?"

"Brown."

"My kinda girl."

"She's real sweet. Very smart but not, you know, snooty about it. Like my sister can be sometimes. I used to be in the same class as Elsie, and I'd see sometimes that when she was writing her answers to a test, she was making a fist with her other hand. Like she was concentrating too hard not to."

"Why were you looking at her—you copy her answers?"

"I just like seeing her when she's focusing like that."

"You kiss her yet?"

Philip started wondering just how far this interrogation was going to go and how honest he cared to be. "Not yet. But I will."

"You do that. You're a lucky man, still in the same town as your sweetheart. Lucky you didn't have to get sent away." Another twig into the flames. "As soon as you get out of here, you march right on up to her and give her the kiss of her life. She doesn't like it, you can tell her that crazy soldier made you do it." He smiled and looked back at his companion. "But she'll like it."

Philip nodded, grinning slightly with embarrassment. "Okay."

"You going to marry her?"

Philip shook his head, his smile widening. "That'd be rushing things, I think."

"The wedding proposal might startle her?"

"Might."

"You never know. Some guys wait too long."

"Did you wait too long? How old are you?"

"Twenty-five."

"Twenty-five and still single? What were you doing with yourself before Michelle?"

"Maybe I did wait too long. Maybe I'm trying to teach you a few things I learned the hard way."

"Such as?"

"Such as, an opportunity can be either the shortest-lived thing or the longest-lasting thing in the world. You take advantage of it when you have it, and it'll last forever. You sit on your hands, though, and it'll be gone before you can even blink a second time."

Philip fixated on that image—of something important disappearing before his eyes, leaving behind no trace. Even though he wasn't sure if he should ask, he did anyway: "Are they going to send you to France soon?"

Frank paused. "Don't know. Some guys say they aren't sending anybody until the flu passes, but that's just a rumor. We'll see." Then he thought of something. "Are a lot of boys from this town serving?"

"Some of them, but not many. Most of them registered and got worker deferments." Philip added, even though he knew he shouldn't have, "And some guys didn't register."

"Really? You can get in trouble for that."

"I think they're conscientious objectors."

"Huh." Frank's face clouded over.

"What?" Philip asked.

"Nothing," Frank said. "I just know that there are some C.O.s in the army. They get drafted—they just refuse to fight."

"So what do they do?"

"They build cantonments. They clean mess halls. They get the shit work."

Philip looked at Frank searchingly while Frank stared straight into the fire. Then Frank lay down and closed his eyes.

"I'm going to turn in," Frank said. "If the good people of this town are going to set me free tomorrow night, I want to be well rested." He rolled over, facing away from Philip.

Philip, alone for a moment, briefly considered seizing the opportunity to read Elsie's letter again. But something about what Frank had said left him feeling juvenile. He, too, lay down and closed his eyes, visions of men with broomsticks marching past.

XII

The morning whistle sounded different to Leonard Thibeault, one of the Commonwealth millworkers. First the whistle was quieter than normal, as though someone had stuffed cotton into Leonard's ears while he'd slept, and then it was louder than he could comprehend. Deafening. Piercing. It was two holes drilling into his skull from opposite ends, and when the drill bits reached each other in the center of his brain, he opened his eyes.

Then he closed them. That was the second thing he noticed—the pain in his eyes. Not in his eyes exactly, but behind them, in the part of the body that controlled the eye, the invisible mechanisms that told it where to move and how quickly, the levers and switches and pulleys that helped him squint or stare or wink. The whole apparatus seemed shot to hell. Just that one blink and the pain was a wave that rolled through his skull.

He was on his back. His legs and arms ached, the joints in particular throbbing. At this point the signs and messages were coming at him too quickly and all he knew was that this was a terrible, terrible dream. Or he had woken up too soon. Or he had drunk too much the night before. What the hell was it he'd drunk? Was it trustworthy? He tried to remember, but his brain didn't want to, didn't let him—like a recalcitrant librarian, it balked at the orders, refused to look up the necessary information. Whatever he had drunk had knocked him flat out.

There was another whistle, following far too quickly after the first one. This certainly was not real. But no nightmare had ever hurt like this.

It was incredibly hot in the small bedroom in his empty house, where he hoped one day to bring a wife. He was sweating and his nightclothes were damp and the blankets that pinned him were surely unnecessary, but he couldn't muster the energy to remove them.

He was dimly aware of the possibility that this was real and he was awake and therefore was supposed to be at the mill, working. But the mere thought of rising was an impossibility. He felt his mind wandering to the strangest places, scenes he had visited as a child, so long ago that he hadn't thought of them in years. He thought about girls on whom he'd nurtured crushes as a schoolboy, about two of his cousins who'd died in a farm accident when he was six or seven. He didn't even remember their names. But there they were, laughing at something he'd said.

At some point, either seconds or hours after the most recent whistle, he felt more lucid than before, coherent enough to concentrate on his breathing. He thought that maybe if he took deep breaths, he'd feel strong enough to get up. So he inhaled deeply, but he'd taken in barely any air when his stomach muscles seized on him and he coughed so hard that his head lifted from the pillow, coughed so long it was like a dream without end.

Until one day he wasn't coughing anymore. He was still there, still lying on his back, still neither daring to open his eyes nor even think about it. It was so hard to think, the damned librarian in his head was so adamant about not doing any work, that it was better to just drift off. He stopped thinking about the pain and stopped thinking about breathing, and then one of his dead cousins—maybe his name had been Louis—threw him a ball. Leonard lifted up his tiny arms and caught the ball, smiling gleefully, and tossed it back toward Louis, tossed it so far he couldn't see if Louis made the catch but somehow he knew that he had.

XIII

Graham was tired, but he refused to let his fatigue interfere. Interfere with his work at the mill, interfere with his guard duties, interfere with the vigilance of his thoughts. He felt how precarious the town's situation was—the balance slipping more with each passing hour—and he needed to steady it, steady himself. He had little choice but to press on.

Graham was not sleeping well. He hadn't told Amelia this, hadn't wanted to disturb her slumber. She snored—a most unladylike snore, in fact, but one that had only made Graham smile to himself in the weeks after they married. Their courtship had been brief and not without controversy, as the couple had not received the approval of Amelia's father, a mean old specimen named Horace whom Graham had never spoken to without smelling liquor on his breath. Having lost her mother at a young age, Amelia had all but raised her three younger brothers while her father disappeared on his season-long logging jobs in the woods. Amelia had told Graham that her father had never laid a finger on her, and Graham believed her, but still he wondered sometimes whether there were childhood memories she hadn't told him, didn't want to acknowledge.

He had met her at church, in Timber Falls. The first months after Everett had been bleak, and Graham had moved around a bit before landing in Timber Falls and forcing himself to get a new mill job. He needed the work to keep himself from turning into a hopeless drunk, one of those shriveled husks he saw so often, guys who said they'd once been brawny and tough and could chew on gravel until some viciousness had befallen them, something that not even the Hercules of their youth had been able to counter. Graham would not let that happen. Every night he lay in bed sleepless, but every day he worked, each day harder than the last. He hoped that through pain and sweat and self-denial he could reach some plane where his past suffering could never again reach him, never bring him down.

He had known Tamara so briefly; he chastised himself for having allowed naive daydreams of romance to sweep him off his feet. They had been so different, the educated activist and the hardheaded millworker. He hadn't felt comfortable with her friends, their political conversations and obscure references, and as time passed, he came to understand that his feelings for her had been colored by the events swirling around them. He had mourned her for longer than he had known her, and though he felt this made him silly and a victim and small, the pain never quite went away, never quite left him, just faded like that of a broken bone that kept you awake late at night until you noticed, bleary-eyed, that it was morning and that at some point you did indeed sleep. And here you were on a new day, so what were you going to do with it?

I got used to not having a home and not having a family, he thought. I got used to having only nine fingers. I can get used to this, too.

After years of neglecting his religious upbringing, Graham had begun attending church. His mother had loved Sunday mornings, and as he sat there surrounded by the congregation's striving voices, he found himself remembering his family back in Kansas—the quiet mother who never knew how to stand up to her belligerent husband, the younger brothers whom Graham would pick on at home but loyally defend in the school yard.

Graham knew something about mean fathers, and as he sat in church, he could tell from a distance that this man Horace was someone from whom his daughter, Amelia, was yearning to escape. Graham's eyes met Amelia's once, and he looked away, feeling unholy or guilty or something not right, as he knew that church wasn't the place to be eying women. But he found he couldn't help doing it again the next week, or the week after that, and soon he was going to church every Sunday like a good Christian, though he was barely listening to the preacher, hardly singing the hymns. He was there only to see her.

Amelia had ice-blue eyes and an almost too-white face—her skin seeming to glow in the sunlight as she left church—that seemed remarkably controlled for her eighteen years. She was beautiful, but what also drew him was the strength she seemed to possess, despite being held back by her family. Perhaps Graham was drawn to her for these reasons, so he could both save her from her situation and feed off that strength.

The first time he gave her a gift, she'd given him an even greater one. A week after they had taken their first walk together, he had handed her a small bouquet of flowers, so uncharacteristically nervous that he'd made the mistake of holding it in his left hand. As she reached for the bouquet, she saw that hand, which he normally kept hidden in his pocket, saw the mangled knuckle and the skin that still hadn't lost its reddish hue after many months. He saw her eyes on the missing finger, and he hurried to exchange the bouquet between his hands, but before he could do so, she took that hand in hers. Let her fingertips glide over his knuckles, tracing the bones of his wrist, all the while keeping those ice-blue eyes on his. If she had smiled or said something reassuring, it would have sound forced, wrong. She just looked at him. It froze him for a second, the fact that she hadn't flinched, hadn't recoiled, had wanted only to touch that one part of him. Then she thanked him for the flowers, when he felt he was the one who should be thanking her. They walked through town for the rest of the afternoon, she holding his left hand, which she had refused to release. Graham had known she was the woman he would marry, that she was someone who had felt her own pain and recovered from it, walked away new, and that with her he would do the same.

Here they were two years later, and everything had come true. They had a daughter and another baby on the way. They had a house, and Graham had a good job and plenty of friends, men who would come by and sit on his front porch, or he on theirs, and smoke together after repairing someone's fence or working on a roof or building a shed. Amelia, too, seemed to thrive in the new town, busily maintaining their home, helping new families get acquainted with Commonwealth, making friends easily. His life was finally one worth having.

Graham sat up in bed after lying there restless for what must have been an hour, maybe more. It was the middle of the night and cold in the room as the blankets fell from his chest. Every time he had felt the languid arms of sleep ushering him in, he'd seen the face of the soldier before him, had seen the man's eyes beseeching him, had felt the hook of the trigger pressing into his finger. It had been days now, and still the gunshots rang in his ears.

His movement stirred Amelia, who rolled onto her other side so she was facing him, and wrapped an arm across his stomach. She muttered something, and after trying to figure out what it was, he realized she was asleep, stringing together disjointed syllables in some elfin language that made sense only in the dream she was swimming through. The surprising amount of moonlight shining through the window illuminated her face, painting streaks of glowing whiteness around her cheekbones and eyebrows, outlining her chin and the earlobe visible through her hair. Graham saw how other men started to quietly disparage the appearance of their wives over the years, but he still was amazed at her beauty, amazed she was his. For the first few months, whenever he woke in the middle of the night, he would lean over and kiss her lips or forehead before falling back to sleep; he needed to express this gentleness that, he felt, no one thought existed in a man who wore such a saturnine expression.

Now he was plotting escape from the bed, maybe to pace in the kitchen or stare out the window until his thoughts calmed, but the arm she had cast across his chest stopped him. He didn't want to risk waking her, to deprive her of the sleep that had become so cruelly elusive to him. The baby was at last letting Amelia rest a bit, and he didn't want to interfere with whatever dreams were giving her that serene expression. So he leaned back into the bed and, rolling onto his side, put his arm around her, the two of them lying in a half-embrace. His hand was on her hip, and he felt the enticing fullness of her body beneath the thin nightgown, felt himself becoming excited in his confused and weary state. He kissed her on the forehead and told her he loved her, softly enough for her not to hear it. He closed his eyes and willed that there be no other world except this bed, at least for the next few hours, at least until sunrise.

When the morning whistle woke him, he saw that he was alone. From the backyard, he heard the sound of wood being chopped.

He had been granted only random snatches of sleep, like crumbs to a starving man. But now that he was awake, he forced himself to move.

After throwing on some clothes and quickly washing his face, he walked down the stairs and past the crib—Millie was asleep, miraculously—and into the backyard.

Another swing of the ax and Amelia halved a log. Beside her was a stack of wood Graham had brought there the previous day.

"Morning," he said, startling her from behind.

"Morning," she said with a short smile. "I didn't want to wake you."

"I thought I told you not to do that," he said to her, motioning toward the ax that stood in the piece of wood, the handle held aloft by the embedded blade.

"You said you didn't *think* I should do it." She was slightly out of breath, her forehead damp with sweat. "That's not the same thing."

"Think of the baby," he said.

"Graham, I cut wood for months with Millie. I'm sure I can manage."

He pulled the ax from the log. "I don't want to be taking chances we don't need to be taking."

He almost added that she wasn't the same as she had been then, that she was nearly twenty pounds thinner and more frail, but he didn't know how to say it without making it sound like a reproach. They had already been through that after the stillbirth—her guilt, his insistence that she was not responsible—but everything had come out wrong somehow, left her feeling worse than before. So he simply gave her a patient but hard look, one that sought to end the conversation.

She started to walk toward the house, saying, "As tired as you've been, you're liable to cut your own foot off."

He let the remark pass. Alone outside, the air cold around his underdressed body, he lifted the ax and swung away, easily splitting a log. He could do this with his eyes shut, they both knew. He could do it blindfolded and dizzy, and still he'd never so much as nick his boot.

But the ax did feel heavier than usual in his hand, his breaths deeper.

When he went back inside, Amelia was cooking breakfast while the baby lay in her crib, babbling airy nonsense. Three half-knit projects—a sweater, a scarf, and a hat—lay across a chair. With Millie growing as fast as she was and with trips to the shops in Timber Falls a temporary impossibility, Amelia needed to have clothes ready for winter. Some neighbors and friends had lent them some baby clothes, but they never seemed to be enough.

Graham walked up to her and kissed her cheek. "Still got both feet."

"And you still look tired," she said to his heavy lids, to his red eyes, to the marks where his fumbling hands had cut himself shaving the day before.

"Just waking up."

"I wish you wouldn't stand guard every waking hour, Graham. It's not good."

"Someone has to," he said.

"There were plenty of other men in this town, last time I checked." The barest trace of a smile softened her words.

"There are. And a lot of them aren't doing their part."

"I especially don't like you being out there at night with Deacon. The man's crazy."

"He's harmless. Barely says a word."

"My point—" she began, but he interrupted.

"I'll get more men to volunteer. That'll leave me with less shifts."

She nodded to that, not fully satisfied but aware that she'd at least won a concession. They sat down at the table and ate in silence punctuated by occasional babble from Millie. Amelia had been with Graham long enough to know that there were different kinds of silence: the peaceful silence of contentment, the amazed silence of love returned, the reverential silence of new fatherhood, the preoccupied silence of concern, the aching silence of regret. She knew that even though he had barely spoken of the dead soldier, he had been staring at the man for days now. Graham was afraid the dead soldier would come back somehow, afraid more dead soldiers would rise up against the town, corpses exhaling pestilential fumes. The man in the storage building was just another dead soldier to Graham, and he was terrified and determined to chase him back to the grave. Amelia hated that her husband felt the obligation to fight every last demon on his own, and she wanted to help him, but neither her silence nor her kind words nor her amorous movements seemed to engage him. This would pass, she had finally decided. It was the only conclusion that made her feel more than helpless.

"Do you think Philip's all right?" she said to him after they had finished eating and he was preparing to go.

Graham didn't turn around. "Charles says he is."

When he had first told her what happened with Philip and the second soldier, she could barely believe it. She'd expressed concern for their friend, and he'd stalked away. Later that night, he had held her and said what she knew was an apology: he had told her he felt bad for Philip, too, but they needed to protect the town. He had held her in a way that showed he feared his own coldness.

"Just . . . tell Philip we're thinking about him," she said, thinking it was a silly message to send but not knowing what other sentiment to express.

"He knows," Graham said. "I'll be back for supper." He opened the door and closed it quietly behind him.

XIV

The alarm spread quickly.

Charles had been sitting in his office at eleven in the morning, trying to determine how long the town could survive under quarantine. If it really was true that cities and towns across the country had closed down their meeting places and shuttered all their businesses, then the mill's circumstances were not unique. Of course, if Philip or the soldier became sick and somehow passed the flu on to others in town, then Commonwealth would lose its reason for remaining closed off to the world. But Charles did his best not to consider that. That night, at six o'clock, Banes would go into the storage room and perform checkups. Assuming Philip and the soldier were still healthy, Philip would sleep that night in his bed at home.

Charles's thoughts were interrupted by a knock on his office door. When he looked up, he saw Mo walking in uninvited.

"Yes?" Charles asked, putting down his thick reading glasses.

"There are men from Timber Falls trying to get into town," Mo said urgently. "They say they won't leave unless they've spoken to you."

Mo explained that he and Graham had been at the post that morning and had refused entry to the men, who had driven to town in two autos. Mo said they seemed polite so far but were firm about not leaving until they saw Charles Worthy. The recent misadventure with the second soldier had led the guards to keep a horse at the post, and the sweat on Mo's brow suggested he'd galloped the whole way here.

Charles hurried to his carriage and rode behind Mo, who sped on his horse.

It had rained earlier that morning, and tree boughs hung heavy under the weight of the water. The carriage wheels left deep impressions in the wet earth as Charles rolled past the last of the houses and around the final bend.

Mo had already dismounted and was standing beside Graham at the post; both of them held their rifles pointed at the sky. Standing about twenty yards away were five men. The man in front wore a derby and a dark suit, not an expensive one but still fine enough to make him appear out of place in the woods. Charles recognized him but could not recall his name. Standing a bit behind was Lionel Winslow, scion of the mill-owning Winslows who all but ran Timber Falls. Lionel was young but quickly becoming the public face for the family firm as his old man retreated into senescence. His suit was dirty at the knees, most likely from his climb over the tree that blocked the road. Beside Winslow was J. B. Merriwhether, a quiet banker the Worthy mill had employed until they decided his obsequiousness did not rival his brains. J.B. looked uncomfortable, shifting on his feet. The two other men Charles did not recognize: one had a round, well-shaven, incarnadine face, and the other, a taller man with an equally red beard, was obviously a logger or millworker. These two looked more truculent than the others, closer to anger.

As Charles descended from his carriage, he remembered the advice Banes had given him regarding strangers—advice that Graham and Mo had apparently forgotten. He reached into his pocket and took out a gauze mask, fitting it over his nose and mouth. Upon seeing this, Graham and Mo each tied a handkerchief around their nose and mouth, taking turns so they wouldn't have to lower their rifles at the same time.

Graham had scanned every man in search of firearms and concluded that no one had anything on display but that any and all of them could be carrying something.

"You have a cold way of greeting people, Mr. Worthy," the man in front said. "Doesn't make a gentleman feel too welcome."

"I apologize if it seems rude to you, Mr.—"

"Joseph Miller." The man touched the brim of his cap.

"Mr. Miller, but times being what they are, we need to protect our town."

Miller introduced the two men Charles did not know as Skip Bartrum, Timber Falls sheriff, and the foreman Nathan Hightower. He added, "We're not accustomed to having guns pointed at us."

Charles smiled slightly. "They're not pointed at you."

"But your man there tells me if we were to walk much closer, they would be."

"Unfortunately, that's the case. The sign you passed explained things—this town is unaffected by the influenza, and it's our intention to keep it that way. We mean no disrespect to you gentlemen, but we know how many people in Timber Falls and the surrounding towns have the Spanish flu and are dying from it. Until the epidemic has passed, no one can enter this town."

"Well, it is a free country." Miller spoke calmly, almost playfully.

"But it's private property. In fact, you've been standing on private property ever since you turned around the bend there. I and my fellows here own everything you're looking at, and it's our right to determine who can enter and who cannot. In ordinary times, I'd be honored to give you a tour of Commonwealth, but circumstances are what they are."

"The hell kind of a town is this?" Hightower said angrily.

Charles felt Graham and Mo stiffen beside him, but he paid the remark no heed. If he'd cared about the opinions other men held about him or about Commonwealth, he never would have made it this far.

"And why exactly have you gentlemen decided to venture out here?" Charles asked.

"We thought the fine people of this town might like to buy some Liberty Bonds," Miller said. "It seems you've been overlooked by the past drives."

"Well, regrettably, we won't be able to get close enough to conduct such transactions. In better times, perhaps," Charles replied. "But you seem a rather large group to be selling Liberty Bonds. I would think one or two salesmen would have sufficed."

"Maybe we're just curious citizens, heard about the strange way you were conducting yourselves out here," Miller continued in a soft tone. Charles couldn't tell if Miller was trying to defuse the situation or if he was being patronizing. "These are troubling times, Mr. Worthy, and we like to know what's happening in our backyards."

"This is not your backyard."

"Well, we are neighbors, in a sense. Far as I know, Timber Falls is the closest town to this one, so we see it as our job to keep informed about what's transpiring here."

"We're only trying to stay healthy, Mr. Miller, so that we can keep working. We've heard that Timber Falls and others have been hit so hard that you've had to close businesses. If we had to do something like that, as a new mill with little margin for error, we would fall on hard times indeed."

"We've heard some things about your mill," Winslow spoke up. "Heard you have some mighty strange ways of doing business out here."

"I haven't offered any opinion on how your family runs its mills, Mr. Winslow," Charles snapped back.

Miller gave Winslow a quick look, apparently considering such a remark off the subject.

"But walling yourselves off from the rest of the world at a time like this—that's not very Christian, is it?" Miller asked.

"Don't talk to me about Christian," Charles said. "Christian has nothing to do with this. The flu does not discriminate. It's taking everyone in its path, and that's why we aim to keep you off ours."

Charles's nerves were at attention. With his gauze mask and his arms folded before him, he knew he must look strange, knew that Graham and Mo with their handkerchiefs and rifles looked more like train robbers than noble protectors. Ruefully, he realized that to an uninformed observer, the visitors would seem the more benevolent group.

Miller fixed his gaze on Graham. "You look like a healthy young man. I don't suppose you've registered?"

Graham rewarded him with no reply other than a steely-eyed stare.

"There are no slackers in this town," Charles answered for Graham. "All the young men have registered."

"It would be a shame if we found out anyone in this town was dodging the draft, Mr. Worthy," Miller said. "You want to be law-abiding in a time like this."

Graham's fingers dug into the rifle's handle.

"We are law-abiding," Charles replied. "And you also know, gentlemen, that the draft has been suspended on account of the flu. The same reason why we're closing our doors to you, and to anyone else, until such time as it's safe to greet strangers again. Once that's occurred and the draft is back on, then anyone in this town who's come of age in the meantime will show up at the enlistment office bright and early. You have my word."

"That's not worth much," Winslow scoffed, quietly enough to seem offhand but loud enough to be heard.

"You got something to say, you step to the front and say it, buddy," Graham challenged him.

"I'll say this," Hightower said. "My sons didn't die in France so you slackers could hole yourselves up and live off the fat of the land."

" 'Fat of the land'?" Charles uttered a short laugh, then spoke in even tones. "We've taken the worst plot anyone could have asked for and are making it work through the sweat of our labor."

Hightower was unconvinced. "My sons didn't die so you could—"

"We didn't kill your sons," Graham interrupted. "German army did. You got a quarrel with them, you can head over there yourself. Leave us out of it."

Enraged, Hightower took a step forward. Bartrum placed a stern hand on his shoulder and muttered something in his ear, restraining him. But barely. Hightower stood there and seethed, his eyes boring into Graham's.

"Funny you should mention Germans, young man," Miller said. "You see, all the right-thinking towns in this area have been awfully stirred up by what happened at Fort Jenkins a few days ago."

He let that dangle until Charles admitted, "We haven't been reading the papers."

"Three soldiers were killed by German spies," Miller said. "The spies got away, and they're probably looking for a safe place to hide until the search is off." He made a show of looking from left to right, slowly, at the thick woods surrounding them. "I wonder where Heinie spies might hide."

Charles was knocked off guard, and his thoughts raced: was Philip locked up with a German agent? There had been much discussion about spies in the newspapers and magazines over the past few months; the Metzgers had closed their shop in Everett and moved to Commonwealth in part because they had tired of the harassment over their German surname, the increasingly dangerous suspicions. But this was the first time Charles had heard an accusation about an honest-to-God spy in their midst, and it chilled him. After a couple of breaths, he shook his head, hoping to show Miller he would not be swayed by strangers spreading rumors. "First we're not buying enough Liberty Bonds, and then we're not registering, and now we're harboring spies? I suppose we're also responsible for the assassination of Ferdinand?"

Miller was cool, keeping his eyes on Charles. "My question is a fair one, Mr. Worthy. This is an isolated community. If I were looking to hide from the army, this would be an awfully attractive destination. And you do seem to be hiding something."

"We're only protecting our health, Mr. Miller—I do apologize if that offends your sensibilities, but we're doing what we have to do. If a German spy were to come up this road, we would be just as inhospitable to him as we're being to you."

"Only more so, I would hope." Miller smiled thinly.

"Of course."

Miller appeared willing to leave it at that, as Charles thought he saw the man turn as if to leave. But Hightower refused to let them off that easy.

"Look, we know you're all just a bunch of damn agitators and reds anyway," he said. "And I don't like knowing you're out here hiding while the rest of us are doing our part."

"The only one agitating is you," Charles said. "We're minding our own business here, on our own land, and you're trespassing."

Graham took a step forward.

"Is that why you're really here, Mr. Miller?" Charles asked. "You don't care for the way we go about our lives, so you've taken it upon yourselves to frighten us out of it?"

"The way I feel about your town, Mr. Worthy, is irrelevant." For the first time, Miller's voice lost its finely polished veneer. "What is important is that we're at war, and all the right-thinking people of this country are standing together."

"We're all proud Americans in this town," Charles replied. "And I resent any implication otherwise."

"You're Americans standing alone, and you're behaving quite suspiciously. We will be watching you, Mr. Worthy. We'll protect our country and our families from any threat we find."

"And we ours."

Without bidding good day, Miller turned around and started walking down the hill, toward the autos they had stopped in front of the fallen tree. Winslow and Merriwhether followed, but Hightower and Bartrum seemed reluctant to do the same. They took a couple of steps backward but kept their eyes on Graham and Mo.

"If we ever come back, you better hope you have more than two guns out here," Hightower said.

Graham shook his head. "Next time you won't get this close."

They glared at each other.

"Go back home, gentlemen," Charles said. "Nurse your families. Get Timber Falls back on its feet. After the plague has passed, you'll see that this has all been a misunderstanding."

Miller was nearly in one of the autos by the time Hightower and Bartrum started descending the hill. Finally, there were the echoes of the doors slamming shut, the engines roaring to mechanical life, and the autos pulled away.

Charles, Graham, and Mo were silent as they listened to the sound of the tires on gravel receding slowly into the distance, until it had been displaced by the gentle sound of water falling from the heavy branches around them. Charles removed his gauze mask, the fresh air feeling colder on his damp cheeks.

He turned to the watchmen, their eyes showing concern above their handkerchiefs.

"You think those soldiers were spies?" Graham asked.

XV

The mill hummed beneath them and around them as they stood in Charles's office. There weren't enough chairs to seat them all, so they stood, the small room quickly growing warm.

Charles had called an emergency meeting of the town's magistrates, the men who had been appointed to oversee any disputes in the town. There were a dozen in total, but they were short a few, the loggers stationed too far from the mill to be called in on short notice. It was only an hour after the confrontation. There were ten people in the room and the open doorway, among them Banes, Rankle, and Graham, who had sent someone else to stand watch with Mo so he could attend.

Rebecca was the only woman in the room. She had seen Charles and Mo hurrying into town moments ago through the school's windows, right as she was dismissing her charges for the day. Although she was not a magistrate, she wasn't about to be told to wait outside, not by Charles or anyone else foolish enough to try.

"A German spy?" she said incredulously after Charles had relayed Miller's story to everyone in the room.

"That's what they said," Charles replied.

"If there'd been some kinda fight at the camp, that might explain why all these soldiers keep wandering out here," someone said. "Maybe they were on the run from somebody?"

"I thought of that, too," Charles said pensively. "But if that was the case, wouldn't the second soldier have told us all that? He said there was a naval accident, that he was shipwrecked."

"Maybe spies set off a bomb on the boat," Banes said. "We haven't exactly interrogated the soldier as to what happened. Did Miller say specifically how the men had been killed?"

Charles shook his head.

"We need to find out who this soldier is," Rebecca said. She was standing in the middle of the crowd, not by Charles's side. Rebecca felt particularly on edge, her jaw muscles tight, her limbs ready to lash out. "And we need to get Philip away from him."

Charles held up a hand as if to calm her. Everyone else shifted on their feet. Most avoided looking at either husband or wife, not wanting to take sides. But Rankle glanced at Charles, then met Rebecca's eyes. She had not spoken with him since the night she unburdened herself, confessing that she did not agree with her husband. His eyes looked sympathetic.

"I'm not inclined to believe anything Miller says," Rankle said.

"Do you know him?" Charles asked.

"I know of him." Rankle explained that Miller, though a resident of Timber Falls, had come to the aid of his fellow business leaders in Everett during the strike, when Rankle was with the Wobblies. The strikers had added Miller to their list of foes, as he had lent money and forgiven debts to some of the mill owners during their troubles, had rallied support for the Commercial Club and spoken out against agitators and reds.

"I don't see why they would lie about this," Charles said. "And why would they come so far if not for something serious? I think they do believe there's a spy out here."

"Has anyone else heard anything about spies?" someone asked. "Or sabotage at the army base?"

"No one's heard anything about anything since the quarantine started," Rebecca said sharply. She realized when she said it that she sounded critical of Charles, and was embarrassed. She told herself to be more cautious, to trust that the magistrates would make the right decisions, but her faith in them was dwindling.

Some of the men in that room had themselves committed acts of sabotage in the past, at Everett and elsewhere, destroying mill equipment during strikes. But when America had joined the war and the newspapers started warning of sabotage on the home front, the thought of German agents stealing into the country had seemed incomprehensible to them.

Not anymore. A spy could somehow break into a factory or mill, Rebecca supposed, and cause havoc there, hindering America's ability to produce new fighter planes, new ships. Neither Charles nor the doctor had said anything about the soldier having an accent, but plenty of Americans were against the war. Their voices were silenced by the Sedition Act, but that only made their muzzled emotions burn more intensely. Perhaps this was someone who had family in Germany, Rebecca thought, or a more radical pacifist than herself.

"Didn't you say the flu started at army bases, Doc?" another man asked. "Maybe spies brought it there. Maybe this guy has something to do with that."

After an awkward pause, Banes said he didn't see how something like the flu could be used as a weapon, not unless German scientists had made discoveries their American counterparts had not. It sounded as if Banes couldn't decide whether he was being stubborn to ignore such possibilities or was allowing himself to be swept away with public hysteria by considering them.

"Philip hasn't said anything that would lead us to believe he's suspicious of the soldier, has he?" Banes asked.

"How could he?" Rebecca asked. "Even if he did think the man was a spy, he can't shout that out to us without risking his safety. And we told him not to write us any notes."

A few seconds passed in silence. Rebecca felt more words pressing at her tongue. She tried to resist, but she had held back her opinions before and seen the result.

So she said flatly, "We need to get Philip out of there."

"Doc said forty-eight hours," Graham reminded her. "Still got two hours to go."

Rebecca looked at Graham, surprised. He was obviously tired, his eyes red and his face strangely puffy. But she couldn't understand his obstinacy, his apparent lack of concern for Philip. And how could Charles not want to free Philip immediately? Was he so afraid of appearing to go back on his word to the rest of the town? Was he confusing being stubborn with being noble?

"I think letting anyone out before forty-eight hours would be a mistake," Banes said, adding his voice to the chorus.

Rebecca saw that they took comfort in the doctor's advice. They didn't want to do anything that would endanger them, endanger *their* families. Philip would just be an unfortunate casualty.

Rankle looked down at his boots, as if shamed by the accusation in her eyes.

"At six o'clock I'm going in to examine them," Banes continued. "As per our plan."

"But what if this fellow *is* a spy?" someone asked.

"I have no quarrel with Germany," Rankle replied.

"If this man has been running around the country killing American soldiers and doing God knows what, then I do have a quarrel with him," Charles countered.

Rankle paused. "He hasn't tried to break out of there," he said, "so he probably doesn't have a gun or anything. I don't see why he'd try and hurt Philip."

His attempts at reassurance only angered Rebecca more. Hadn't he felt this way when his family had disappeared, when no one in the world could offer any clues or theories on what had happened to his wife and son? There could be no lonelier feeling than when evil befell you and the world turned its back.

"There's one thing we haven't considered," Charles said. "If he is a spy, then holding on to him implicates us. If the army is tracking him, what if his trail leads them here?"

"Then the men from Timber Falls will come back," Rankle said.

"They can't force their way in," Graham said. "They have no right."

Rankle tried to reason with his friend: "Graham, I think Miller's part of the American Protective League. The APL's deputized by the federal government, so they can come and go wherever they please, even arrest people. They're the ones who helped round up most of the local Wobblies. And they've organized slacker raids, rounding up men who haven't registered. I haven't heard of any raids in Washington, but they've been happening all over."

Silence for a moment.

"Maybe the soldier's a deserter?" Banes ventured.

"If he was a deserter, Miller would have said so," Charles said. "He wouldn't need to make up some story about spies on top of that."

"Unless this is just some other guy," someone said. "Maybe there *is* a spy crawling around the woods, but it doesn't mean this guy's him."

That hadn't occurred to some of them, Rebecca could see. Suddenly, the men in the room were making more sustained eye contact with one another, as if realizing for the first time that there could be another intruder in the town. What if someone were plotting to break into Commonwealth, either to spread flu or to tamper with the mill? The guards were a perfectly good deterrent to anyone who tried to wander into the town, but surely they couldn't repel someone who was determined.

"We're putting an awful lot of stock in what Miller said," Rankle pointed out. "The Protective League is rotten. They watch everybody: their neighbors, their so-called friends, their family. *They're* the spies."

"And what about the other soldier—the one from last week?" Banes asked. He avoided Graham's eyes when he said it.

Charles ran his fingers through his hair, exhaled, and looked at his watch. "Here's what I think we should do." And he laid out his plan.

Rebecca did not agree with the plan, but most of the men in the room seemed to, so she did not speak out. She had been outvoted once again, succeeding only in revealing to everyone how alienated she had become from her own husband, her own town. She stood there, arms crossed, staring hard at the floor as the men filed out of the room.

The last to leave was Jarred Rankle, who paused to look back at her.

"It'll all be over in a couple of hours," he said. "I'm sure everything will be fine."

"Then you share my husband's certainty," she replied ruefully. She looked up at him, this massive man filling the doorway. When he stood up against a wall, it looked like the wall was leaning on him for support. "Certainty doesn't make one strong."

"But having everyone stand together does."

"Is this what togetherness feels like? It seems rather different, from where I'm standing."

"Your family will be together soon."

She wondered if she only imagined the faint stress on the word *your,* wondered if he was contrasting her plight with his. For a moment she thought he might step toward her, but instead he nodded and walked off.

It was dark as Graham approached the storage building, rifle in hand.

The doctor's mention of the first soldier had not unnerved him—Graham had already thought of the dead man, but the memory now lacked its stinging effect. Because there was a new threat, he felt all the more focused on protecting the town, on assuring the magistrates didn't make any foolish decisions. He'd made it clear that he would have preferred they just keep Philip and the soldier or spy locked away for a while longer. He felt bad for Philip, and he saw that the boy would be made a victim of the unusual circumstances, but it was the safest option for the town. Nonetheless, he could see that Rebecca would never allow that, and Banes seemed to be sticking to his story about the forty-eight hours. Graham had noticed a tremor in the doctor's voice, however: uncertainty that the others had missed. All week Graham had alternated between being so tired he feared the world was racing past him, but then suddenly so alert and aware that he thought he could see the detail of every single branch in the forest before him, as if all the world's secrets had been laid bare. It was the lack of sleep, he knew, causing his brain to work in fits and starts. Keep focusing, he told himself. After all those hours standing and seeing nothing, he felt in his bones that something was about to happen, something of dire importance.

XVI

The first thing Philip had thought that morning when he woke up was: how do I feel? He swallowed. No pain. No thickness in the back of the throat, no suffocating tightness. He sat up and his head did not throb. His chest did not hurt, his lungs did not burn. His ears did not ache or ring. He was not dizzy.

Morning, and I'm still healthy.

Poker for breakfast. Poker for dinner. Poker for supper. Philip and Frank had played poker for so long that Philip suspected there were certain twigs that had circulated between them a hundred times. When he closed his eyes, he saw aces, clubs, royalty.

"I say we burn these cards when they let us out," Philip said.

Frank made a show of dropping the cards he had been shuffling. "We can stop. What time is it?"

"Five."

"So we only got an hour to go?"

"Yeah. Doc Banes said this morning he'd come in at six o'clock."

"But nobody's said anything since. What if they've changed their minds?"

"They said six o'clock. They wouldn't lie to me."

Frank nodded. "Since it's going to be night by then, I thought I might stay in town until the morning, if that's all right."

"If Doc Banes doesn't say anything against it, maybe my parents will let you stay at our house. No one can give you a ride to the cantonment, though. If we left, we wouldn't be allowed back in."

"That's all right. I can make it."

"How are you going to get there?"

"Anybody 'round here got a horse I could steal?" Frank smiled, but something about the way he said it made Philip wonder whether he really was joking.

"You going to be in trouble with the army for being away so long?"

"I don't know. Never been away before."

"Maybe it'll turn out to be a good thing you got stuck here. Maybe you'll miss the boat to France, and by the time they get around to the next one, the war'll be over." But then he felt stupid after saying it, for his child-like need to paint happy accents on an undeniably gloomy picture.

Frank looked away. "Let's talk about something else, Philip. I'll be getting all I can stand of the army by tomorrow. Let's pretend there's no war going on right now."

The knock on the door came at quarter past six in the evening. Frank had asked Philip twice for the time, at 6:02 and 6:13, and he seemed increasingly anxious. At the sound of the knock, he jumped.

Philip started counting to sixty in his head, but before he got to ten, he heard Doc Banes's voice: "Philip, I'm coming in."

For the first time since Mo had trapped Philip inside two days ago, the door opened from the outside. Philip hadn't realized how moved he'd be by seeing someone else stride into the building. Banes closed the door behind him, his medical case in his right hand.

As Banes entered the tenuous reach of the light from the lantern and the fireplace, Philip saw that he was wearing a gauze mask.

Philip and Frank were standing, tense, unsure what would happen next.

Banes nodded at the soldier, whom he was seeing for the first time. "I'm Dr. Banes. I thought I would examine Philip here first, Private, then move on to you."

Frank said, "Yessir." He stood there awkwardly, then sat back down on the dirty floor.

Philip grew embarrassed about the smell emanating from the cellar.

Banes told Philip to remove his shirt. He asked how Philip was feeling, how he'd been sleeping, if he'd had any chills. Philip told him he felt perfect. He had his temperature taken, and he stood silently while the doctor listened to whatever his heart and lungs had to say. Banes seemed to spend an awfully long time listening to the lungs, Philip thought, and for a moment he got nervous. Could he actually be ill even though he felt fine? What mysteries did his body contain?

Banes had Philip cough, hold his breath, inhale and exhale deeply, repeat. Banes listened through Philip's chest and through his back and through his sides. The stethoscope had felt painfully cold at first, but now it had warmed to Philip's body temperature.

Banes made his diagnosis: Philip was healthy. Or, more precisely, he was exhibiting no sign of disease. Hopefully, that was the same thing.

"Well, son, I think you're as fit as can be." Philip couldn't see the doctor's lips through the mask, but he could tell the old man was smiling from the way the wrinkles around his eyes lengthened.

Philip smiled back. "Good to hear it."

Banes gestured to the door. "Go on out. Your family's waiting."

Philip pulled his dirty shirt back on and grabbed his coat, but before he could head for the door, Banes grabbed him by the forearm.

"If you feel anything suspicious, anything at all—no matter how minor—you come to me immediately. Understand?"

"Yes, sir."

Banes seemed to judge that the look in Philip's eyes was sufficiently serious, and he released his arm.

The first thing to hit Philip as he walked through the doorway was how clean the air tasted now that he was free of the stench inside. The wind on his face brought the scent of the fir trees and the wet earth and the smoke escaping from distant chimneys. He was free.

The sun had set, and only trace amounts of light were filtering in from the bottom of the western sky, but still it seemed bright to Philip compared to the inside of the storage building. About twenty yards away stood Charles, Rebecca, and Laura. Off to the side and behind them stood Graham and Mo and their rifles.

Philip smiled, feeling self-conscious. It was then that he remembered his feelings upon first being locked in, the shame of failing in his duties, of putting the town at risk. That shame returned as he scanned the faces before him.

His fear of what the others thought was fleeting, however, as Rebecca took the first steps toward him and then Charles and Laura followed. Everyone was smiling, and Rebecca was embracing him. He felt Laura's hand on his shoulder as Rebecca said welcome back. Her voice was choked up, and he realized there was a lump in his throat as well; his eyes were watering and he felt happy and ashamed and loved all at once.

After Rebecca embraced him, he looked at Charles, who was smiling broadly and also seemed on the verge of tears. He stepped forward and embraced his son, for the first time that Philip could remember.

Philip looked over his shoulder at Graham, who had not approached. Maybe he didn't want to interrupt the family's moment, Philip thought. So he waved to his friend, and Graham nodded back.

"How you feeling?" Graham asked without a smile.

"Just fine. Doctor says I'm all right." Philip stepped toward Graham, but Graham and then Mo backed away. Philip stopped.

"I think we should keep away just for now," Graham said evenly.

Philip looked down instinctively, as if he had been scolded. He stepped back into the fold of his family and looked at Charles.

"He wants to be extra careful," Charles said quietly. "He has a baby at home."

Philip nodded as if he understood, but he was confused. Doc Banes had just given him a clean bill of health. So was he a threat or wasn't he? Philip saw that Graham continued to watch the storage room as if he still feared the soldier inside it. Charles, too, wore a look of concern, one that his smile and embrace had momentarily concealed. "Is everything okay?" Philip asked.

Charles nodded, then suggested that maybe Rebecca and Laura could head home and prepare supper. This seemed to be a coded message of some sort. Rebecca nodded, and the two were quickly on their way.

"Philip," Charles said once they were out of earshot, "what has the soldier told you about himself?"

Philip shrugged. "Plenty. We've been locked up together for two days."

Charles asked about the soldier's family, where he was from, what he did for a living. Philip answered as best he could.

"Is there anything about him that you've found . . . suspicious?" Charles asked.

Philip didn't understand where this was going. He thought of the times during the past two days when the normally jovial Frank would go quiet, the moments that had left him feeling cold.

"What do you mean?"

Charles told Philip about the morning visit from the APL, and though he didn't share all the details, he mentioned the possibility of a German spy in the area.

"A spy?" Philip felt betrayed, though he wasn't sure who had betrayed him. He liked Frank, even felt that they'd become friends. "He told me he's from Missoula—"

"Did he say anything about three soldiers being killed?"

"No. He said he was in a naval accident, and he and one other guy landed together. I think that was the guy that we—" He cut himself off. "What's going on?"

"Nothing—never mind. I didn't believe them, either." Charles patted him on the shoulder, offering a smile that looked forced. "Why don't you catch up with Rebecca and Laura? I just need to stay a moment and speak with Dr. Banes after he's finished."

Even though he didn't understand what was happening, Philip turned around and, without looking back at Graham, hurried off as quickly as his wooden foot would allow. Rebecca's and Laura's figures were barely visible in the fading light.

"That bodes well for me, I guess," Frank said to Doc Banes after Philip had walked out the door.

"Let's not take anything for granted," Banes replied, examining Frank as closely as he had Philip, inspecting his throat and ears, listening to his heart and lungs.

Within minutes, Banes had reached his conclusion: the man was healthy.

"Are a lot of the men at Fort Jenkins sick?" Banes asked, knowing the answer.

"A few. Not many."

Banes listened again to the man's lungs, which he had already determined were healthy. "That's fortunate. Other camps aren't so lucky."

"I've heard."

Banes stepped behind him and put the stethoscope on Frank's back again, asked him to breathe normally. He noticed abrasions on the sides of Frank's neck, as if he had been in a fight, wrestled to the ground. The marks looked like they had faded with time; they must have been quite bad a few days ago, though his shirt collar would have concealed them. His right shoulder was badly bruised.

"You said you were in a naval accident?"

"Yes, sir."

"You didn't fall in the water, did you?"

"No, sir. But it was pretty hairy out there."

"Why were you on a ship? I thought you were in the army, not the navy."

There was the shortest of pauses. "It was a landing drill. Everyone in the army does them, far as I know."

"What exactly happened?"

"I'm not too sure. Either we hit something or something hit us, and the boat started going down. It was at night, and I was below deck at the time."

Banes contemplated how far he should push this. His fingers had started shaking somewhat, which is why he was spending so much time at the soldier's back, where his nervousness would not be on display. But he wanted to see Frank's eyes when he asked the next question. He walked around and put his thumb on Frank's right eyebrow, pulling up. The idea of examining an eye in this dim light was absurd, but hopefully his patient wouldn't realize it.

"Is that how the three soldiers died?" Banes asked.

Frank's neck twitched, dislodging Banes's finger.

"What soldiers?"

Banes considered reaching for the eyebrow again, pretending to continue the farcical examination, but he chose against it. He felt unsafe now. He should walk away, but he felt tantalizingly close to discovering what he was looking for.

"The three soldiers who were killed at Fort Jenkins last week."

The soldier looked at him long and hard. "Is this examination over, Doctor?"

Banes stepped back. "You appear healthy to me, Private."

"Then I'd better be going." Frank gave Banes a final glance, then picked up his shirt, buttoning it as he quickly walked toward the door.

"Graham!"

Banes's shout was a shock to the soldier, who barely had time to understand what the word meant or why it was shouted when the door before him swung open. Frank had been less than ten feet from escaping his dark and stinking prison, ten feet from the night and the cold and the stars, when two men with rifles stepped in and pointed their weapons at his chest.

"Stop right there, buddy," Graham commanded. Charles followed right behind Graham and Mo; all three wore gauze masks.

Doc Banes stepped to the side, walking out of the rifle's sights in a large semicircle until he was standing alongside the guards.

"What is this?" the soldier asked, and despite the dim light, his inquisitors could see his face turning pale.

Doc spoke into Charles's ear, loudly enough for Graham and Mo to hear but not the soldier. "I don't believe him. He's hiding something." Banes paused. "But he does seem healthy."

"I'm a United States soldier," Frank declared. "You can't keep me here anymore. You let Philip out—"

"Philip hasn't been accused of being a spy, and he hasn't been accused of murder," Charles said evenly.

Frank shook his head. "I am not a spy." He did not seem to be startled by the accusation.

"What's your real name, and where are you really from? And what were you doing at Fort Jenkins?"

"My name is Frank Summers." His voice sounded choked, from either the strain of lying or something else. "I'm from Missoula, Montana. And I was doing what every other American man was doing—except some of the guys in this town, so I hear."

Charles folded his arms. "I find it strange that you haven't asked us to contact your base, Private. If this is all a misunderstanding, couldn't you clear things up with a quick telephone call?" Of course Commonwealth had no telephones, but Charles wanted to hear the man's response.

"Please . . ." Frank looked down at the floor, then back at Charles. Whether he was trying to find a possible weapon, an escape route, or an answer to Charles's question was unclear to his captors. "Please, just let me go. I'm not a spy, I'm just . . ." He shook his head. "I'm no danger to anyone."

He still hasn't denied the murder charge, Banes thought, somewhat amazed. The man before them suddenly looked so pitiful—a dirty tatterdemalion with uncombed hair, an untended beard, and a look of absolute despair. But if the guns weren't trained on him, perhaps he would be grinning behind their backs.

Charles took a breath and issued a slight nod. "Keep him in here," he said to the guards. "We'll get some chains."

Part Three

Sacrifice

I

The flu had only worsened in Timber Falls.

Sipping Scotch, Joseph Miller sat in his den with Chief Bartrum. They had made their journey to Commonwealth based on a hunch that everything Charles Worthy had said and done seemed to confirm.

"What do you make of it?" Miller asked.

Bartrum shook his head. "It's crooked. I don't know if they do have anything to do with what happened at Fort Jenkins, but there's something going on out there. All three of 'em looked guilty of something."

"They were acting strangely," Miller agreed. Bartrum had declined Miller's offer of a Scotch, which confirmed the rumor that the police chief didn't drink. But Miller noticed a peculiar look in the man's eyes. Maybe he just preferred drinking alone.

"Obviously, I don't like Worthy," Miller said. "I don't like his politics and I don't like his town. But I would have been inclined to leave them alone, let them live whatever crazy way they choose to." He sipped at the Scotch, felt the warmth in his throat. "If he'd invited us in and told us they had nothing to do with Fort Jenkins, then fine. But there's something wrong about them closing themselves off. Crooked, like you say."

"Want me to look into it some more?" Bartrum's arms were folded across his broad chest. He looked out of place in such a refined room, surrounded by leather-bound books and fine paintings. His days had increasingly been spent assisting doctors, transporting and burying dead bodies, and dealing with the petty lawlessness that the state of emergency had engendered. Bartrum didn't know what sights his son was being confronted with in the war, but he didn't think they could be any worse than all that he had seen the last few weeks. Focusing on Commonwealth would be a welcome distraction from being a garbageman of souls, collecting the dead and making them disappear.

Miller nodded. "I'm curious about their registration records. Men in Commonwealth would have had to register in Timber Falls, correct? So let's look up the records, see how many men from Commonwealth signed up for the draft."

Bartrum stood to leave. "That should be easy—Merriwhether was on the registration board."

Miller finished his Scotch. "Any news on his daughter?"

Bartrum paused. "She died this morning."

After Bartrum left, Miller sat back in his chair, feeling fortunate that he and his wife had no children. Girls in Timber Falls were dying of flu, and boys from Timber Falls were dying in France. Just a few miles away, the people of Commonwealth were hiding from all this, doing God knew what behind their locked doors. Miller poured himself a second drink, wondering what he would say to J.B. when he saw him next.

II

The next day Doc Banes woke up more refreshed than he'd felt in days. Whether from relief at the healthy diagnoses for Philip and the soldier, or from the cumulative exhaustion of too many near-sleepless nights, he had finally slept soundly. When he rose, he stretched his back, which always troubled him in the colder months, and tried to remember his dreams, one of which had been about his wife. Already they were fleeting.

He had eaten a full breakfast and enjoyed a second cup of black coffee when there was a knock at his door. He opened it to find a young woman with dark circles under her eyes; she obviously had not slept as well as Banes.

"Doctor, my husband's real sick."

In less than ten minutes, they were in her house. The shades were all drawn, she explained, because her husband had complained of the brightness. But it was barely light out—it was early still, and thick clouds hung over the town.

She told Banes her husband had felt fine the previous day. No sniffling, no coughing. But in the middle of the night, he'd been racked by coughs that shook the bed. When the morning whistle had roused her, her husband had remained motionless on his back, as if he'd been dropped there from a great height. When he tried to speak, he coughed for a minute before he could form words. He managed to say that his whole body ached badly. He would not sit up to drink, he would not roll over to try and get more comfortable, he would not move at all.

It was a small house, nearly identical to the others on that block. The kitchen was not clean, and it smelled of whatever they had cooked last night, beans, perhaps, or stewed cabbage. A few empty bottles huddled in a group at the edge of a table. She led Banes into the bedroom, where the scent of alcohol was stronger.

"How much did he drink last night?" Banes asked hopefully.

She looked off to the side. Her name was Jeanine, and she was petite, barely ninety pounds, with unkempt, stringy dark hair. "No more than usual."

Before entering the room, Banes put on a gauze mask. As soon as Jeanine saw him do so, she started fidgeting nervously.

"Morning, Yolen," Banes said. Yolen was the opposite of his wife—his Goliath feet nearly hung off the bed, and his head looked too small for his body. He inhabited the bed so fully that Banes wondered how Jeanine shared it with him. His hair was the lightest blond, almost the mane of an albino. Doc wasn't sure if his skin was always this white.

"Doctor," the sick man greeted him with effort, his voice as tiny as his body was massive.

In a few minutes, Doc had the following facts: Yolen had worked a full shift at the mill the previous day, he'd felt perfectly fine all night, he'd eaten no meat for dinner, and he'd drunk perhaps more whiskey than was wise but not nearly enough to lay flat a man of his size. His lungs sounded dreadfully thick and his throat was inflamed. He was clearly fighting a tremendous infection that had sapped all of his strength; he had a fever of 104 degrees, and he was badly chilled.

Banes asked whom they'd had contact with last evening, if anyone.

"Our friends Otto and Ray," Jeanine said, and Doc wrote down their full names on his pad. Then he left the bedroom, and Jeanine followed, closing the door without a sound.

"Is he gonna be okay?"

Despite all his years of medical service, Banes still never knew who would react well to bad news and who would lash out, who would beg and who would deny the cold facts before them. The one thing he had learned was that people would startle and surprise you until your dying day.

So he ignored her question and instead gave instructions: plenty of rest, plenty of fluids. If noise bothers him, keep the house quiet. If light bothers him, cover the window. Give him aspirin for the pain, but no food, though he probably wouldn't want any. Absolutely no liquor. Just keep him as comfortable as possible.

"Call me immediately if anything changes."

"He told me his friend Leonard never made it to the mill yesterday."

"Oh? Why not?"

Up until that point, Banes had still maintained hope that this was not the flu, despite the telltale signs.

She shrugged nervously. "He wasn't sure. He meant to go by Leonard's place last night to check on him, but he never got around to it."

Banes had told the foremen at the mill to report any absences to him, but this news hadn't reached him. Too many foremen had become guards, and too many instructions had been forgotten.

"Does Leonard live alone?"

Jeanine nodded.

Banes asked her for Leonard's address, and as he prepared to leave, Jeanine asked with a quivering voice whether her husband had the flu.

"It could be," Banes admitted reluctantly. "But maybe not. Just do what I told you to care for him, and he should pull through in a few days." He took a step for the door, then thought of one last thing.

"In the meantime, don't leave the house at all."

Banes knocked on Leonard's door, hard. He rapped again, three times, so forcefully it hurt his knuckles. There was no sound, just the noise of the mill in the distance. He tried to peer in the windows, but the curtains were drawn.

He had taken off his mask as he'd left the distraught Jeanine, but he put on a new one before opening the door to Leonard's house. The door was unlocked, as was the norm in Commonwealth.

Inside, it was dark and the air was stale and cold, as if the house hadn't been heated the previous day.

"Leonard?" No reply. "Leonard? This is Dr. Banes."

The small parlor was unkempt, the home of a bachelor millworker. Banes's footsteps on the wood floor were loud as he walked toward what he gathered was the bedroom. He noticed a sickening smell.

Banes had feared he was walking into a mausoleum the moment he had opened the front door, and his fears were confirmed when he reached the bedroom. Inside it, lying on the bed, was a still form, the blankets covering only the feet, as if Leonard had tried to kick them off in his final throes of agony. On the wall beside him was blood that had been coughed there or perhaps wiped by his fingers, which were also a dark red. There was blood on the pillow and blood on the sheets, and his entire jaw looked as if he had dipped it in reddish black ink. His eyes were white and opened wide, so wide Doc wondered if his eyelids had somehow been sucked into the space behind them. There was blood on the small table beside the bed, blood on the corner of a framed photograph that had fallen from its stand, an old portrait of a stern father and expressionless mother and three young sons in suit coats and shorts, blood on its lower left-hand corner and blood in the center, where he must have brushed against it one last time.

It had begun.

III

That morning Philip heard the first whistle, but something kept him from rising. It certainly wasn't the pleasantness of his dreams; indeed, he'd suffered nightmares in which he was chased by various pursuers—people from the town, his mother's ex-boyfriends, ex-schoolmates living all across the West, people he'd never met. They came after him for different reasons: for shooting the first soldier, for not shooting Frank, for reading those silly fighter-pilot books, for failing to grasp all that Charles had taught him at the mill, for reasons he didn't understand.

Despite being intermittently awakened by those unpleasant visions, Philip stayed in bed because the outside world seemed so much less welcoming than he'd expected. He had thought the previous evening would feel somehow triumphant as he was reunited with his family, a free man. Instead, it felt like he'd walked into some altered rendition of his life, painted by a malevolent artist intent on revising Philip's most halcyon memories. As if not the flu but some other plague had descended upon the town while Philip was away, robbing everything of its warmth and casting a sinister hue on every familiar sight.

Rebecca had served supper even though Charles had not yet returned from the storage buildings; when Philip had asked why they weren't waiting, she had replied in an odd tone that Charles would probably be late tonight. His words were still ringing in Philip's head, the accusation that Frank could be a spy, something about three dead soldiers. Laura had asked a few innocent questions about how Philip had passed his time in there and what the soldier had been like, and Philip had felt Rebecca's eyes on him as he answered. Charles still wasn't home an hour after supper, but when Philip had asked Rebecca, she changed the subject, commenting on how tired he must be and saying perhaps he'd like to lie down early tonight. He felt strangely scared by her manner and by the look he'd seen in Charles's eyes and in Graham's. So he had obeyed Rebecca and retired to his room, closing the door and feeling even more alone than when he'd been locked up with a stranger.

A knock on the door finally roused Philip from bed. "It's getting late, Philip," Charles's voice importuned from the hallway.

As Charles walked away, Philip sat up. Waking up in his own room was reassuring, as was the ability to use an actual toilet, wash, and put on fresh clothes. When he walked into the kitchen, he saw that Rebecca and Laura had already left for school. Charles was sitting at the dining room table—normally, he would have left for the mill an hour earlier.

"I'm sorry I overslept," Philip said.

"That's all right. I'm sure you needed it."

They spoke briefly about the mill, Charles catching Philip up on who had taken over which of his jobs during his absence and which tasks had gone incomplete. But they were talking around something.

"I'm sorry I let him into the town," Philip blurted out. "I know I shouldn't have." He wasn't at all sure he knew that, actually, but he knew it was the right thing to say.

"It's all right," Charles said. "You shouldn't have been left alone at the post."

Philip recapped the events of his last guard shift for Charles, omitting certain facts. He and Frank had shot at each other, Philip said, though he was vague on how the shooting had started. They had run through the woods trying to hide from each other, but Philip had managed to sneak up on the intruder and take his gun. He had realized then that he and the soldier had had such close contact that the quarantine was effectively broken, so he hadn't known what else to do.

"I'm sorry," Philip said again. "I know there are things I should have done differently, but right when it was happening . . ." He let his voice trail off. He still barely understood what had happened in the woods, whether Frank really had gone easy on him, as he'd claimed, or whether Frank would have killed him if not for stumbling and losing his gun.

"I blame myself," Charles said. "We all assumed no one would try to come to Commonwealth, and that if anyone did, they would surely heed our warnings. I never imagined any confrontations like the two you've had."

Philip thought. "Where is Frank, anyway?"

Charles shifted in his seat and put his palms on the table. "Philip, we can't let that man go. We need to hold him here until we can allow someone from the army to take him back."

"Why can't we just let him leave? He's afraid that if he doesn't get back to his base soon, he'll get in trouble."

"Did he say that?"

Philip shrugged. "I guess he—"

"Did he seem anxious to get away?"

"Neither of us were very happy being stuck there, sir." Philip went on, "Do you actually think he's a spy? He seems like a good fellow. He's just—"

"The army is looking for German spies who killed three soldiers. It happened just a few days before he showed up here. We asked him about it and . . . I don't believe his answer."

Philip sat there, taking the information in. "Why don't you believe him?" he asked.

Charles explained that Frank came from the army cantonment but claimed to have been in a naval accident. Even if that was true, Frank would have to be a very poor soldier to trek from the Sound all the way here to Commonwealth, rather than in the direction of the cantonment. And surely he would have passed some other town; if he was so anxious to return to the base, why didn't he stop in the first town he came to? Why had he stopped here, at a town far removed from all others? Charles was certain Frank was lying; the only question was whether he had come to Commonwealth solely to escape his pursuers or if there was a deeper plot at work.

"We offered to contact the base and straighten everything out, but he asked us not to. Why would an innocent man do that? He lied to you when he said he wanted to go back to the base. Now, we don't know much about what happened there, but clearly he's . . . done something."

At those two hollow words, Philip folded his arms over his chest as if for protection. He looked away and spoke softly. "Graham and I . . ."

"You did the right thing then."

Philip shook his head, gritted his teeth. "How could I have done the right thing both times?" His voice was shaking.

He had never challenged Charles before, and he feared that his father, though slow to anger, would chastise him. But he did not.

"Philip, if these men were both spies, then that means that what Graham did last week was shoot a German spy. That changes things, you see?"

It doesn't feel any different, Philip thought. He looked up at Charles. "Maybe I should talk to him."

"No." Charles's voice was forceful, and he said that with a brief shake of his head, as if punctuating it with the fall of a hammer. "I don't think that would be wise."

"Maybe I can straighten everything out if we just talk a little while. This is all wrong—it's just a misunderstanding. No one's been acting right since the quarantine started, and now—"

Charles opened his mouth as if to speak, and that was enough to stop Philip. Philip didn't even know what he was saying, really. He was just flailing about, looking for something: explanations, justice, order. He wanted Charles to be able to deliver those, wanted it so much that he sat there mute, hoping that whatever Charles was about to say would make everything right. But Charles didn't continue, and they sat there looking at each other for a moment.

Finally, Philip looked away. He felt a cruel headache fumbling with his forehead, trying to gain a firm hold of his temples. "Are people angry at me?"

"No. People understand."

"Graham didn't look too happy to see me."

"Graham has been working very hard. He's a bit worn down at the moment, but I'm sure he'll come around. Don't take it personally if he doesn't want to see you yet—he's worried about his family."

Philip's best friend wanted to avoid him, and the man he'd been playing cards with for two days was supposedly a spy. The man Graham had shot was also a spy, a murderer himself. None of this made any sense.

Charles was about to tell Philip to get dressed for work when a knock came at the door.

It was Doc Banes, and he'd been running.

IV

News of Leonard's death spread like a forest fire through the town. Charles and Doc Banes decided that despite the risk of hysteria, people needed to know the truth so they could take precautions against infection.

They quarantined Yolen's house, with a guard assigned to the front door. It was as if everyone in town were slowly being divided into guards and the guarded.

Charles sent word through his foremen, letting them know more guards were needed and that they must report any absences immediately.

Philip, who had gone to work at the mill while Charles and Doc Banes made their plans, felt a special dread as he headed out for his daily errands that day. It was eleven in the morning when he left the office, walking down the long plankway that overlooked the mill, breathing in the sawdust and pine. Below him a group of sawyers was manning the gang saws, taking out the fresh-cut wood and separating the tie cuts and shingle bolts. The first time Philip had accompanied Charles to a mill, he'd been stunned by the constant buzzing that seemed to wrap itself around his head. Now it fit as comfortably as the wool cap he donned as he walked outside.

It was getting colder, with a stiff wind coming in from the river. To his right was the gaping mouth of the mill, opening up to the river beyond. A long and continuous supply of logs floated into the building, ordered by the chained booms that the river hogs controlled. And there was the river, alive with movement: hundreds of logs floated upon it, many of them giving ride to the river drivers themselves, men armed with peaveys and spiked poles and cant hooks. From a distance, it seemed like those medieval devices were an extension of the men's arms, as if the drivers themselves had become constructions of metal and wood. They jabbed and poked at logjams, they jostled recalcitrant drifts that were on the verge of straying downstream. What looked at first glance like chaos was in fact orderly and smooth, the gently bobbing traffic completely under the river drivers' control.

Philip had been stunned when Graham told him that many river drivers didn't even know how to swim, but after months of watching them work, he understood that they didn't have to. An experienced river hog was as likely to slip into the depths as a tree squirrel was to plummet to the earth.

Philip saw the narrow skidways cut into the hills that rose from the riverbanks, saw fresh wood that had been firmly planted in the ground a moment ago sliding down the chutes, disappearing beneath the chilly surface for a second or two, then reemerging, the light yellow of its cut wound poking up first. From where Philip stood, the loggers were invisible; the constant procession of logs floating down the river was the only evidence of their existence.

Despite all this activity, the sight was still unusual for the absence of boats navigating to the mill and hauling off stacks of timber, the absence of draft horses painstakingly dragging carriages of cordwood to the pull-ups. As hard as everyone was working to maintain the mirage that all was normal in Commonwealth, the lack of buyers and shippers—of outsiders—was jarring.

Philip walked out to the narrow dock built alongside the sorting gap. The water below was shallow and clear, and beneath the glassy surface, Philip could see deadheads lying on the river bottom, useless wood that had sunk and would be cleared away only when the pile threatened to rise above the waterline.

Philip had found that river drivers were the least conversational of millworkers, their jobs requiring them to operate at an apex of concentration and equilibrium. The river chief was a laconic man named O'Hare, a lanky redhead who would have been tall even if not for the two-inch spikes on the caulked boots that he and his fellow river hogs wore.

Philip's steps were silent, but O'Hare felt him coming from twenty feet away, felt the extra weight on the deck. When he saw Philip, O'Hare reached into his pocket and used a handkerchief to cover his mouth and nose.

Philip stopped several feet away. "M-morning," he stammered. "How are the numbers today?"

O'Hare eyed him with suspicion, then bent down and reached into a small metal box with his free hand to pull out some papers. Behind him, some of the river drivers had allowed their attention to stray from their duties and were watching.

The river chief read the figures to Philip, who recorded them in his book. The pencil shook in Philip's hand under the glare of so many squinting eyes.

"All right, then," O'Hare said, which was what he always said to conclude their brief interactions. But instead of turning back to his work, as he usually did, he stayed where he was, as if to watch Philip go.

"One other thing," Philip said. "Any unexpected absences?"

"Three guys haven't shown," O'Hare said, and told Philip their names. Then Philip, the mill pariah, walked back to the office as fast as he could.

"Where've you been, girl?" Elsie's mother barked as Elsie walked into the store. Elsie had stayed after school later than usual to help Mrs. Worthy clean up. Now that Philip was out of the storage building, she and her teacher had resumed their routine of discussing the day's events and planning for tomorrow's lessons.

Elsie apologized for being late. "I didn't think there'd be as much for me to do here." An unfamiliar sense of boredom had hung over her the previous afternoon as she'd helped her father with inventory. There had been less and less for them to do, as they were running out of stock to count, organize, and rearrange.

Elsie grabbed a broom and dustpan as a young woman entered the store.

"How's my favorite customer this afternoon?" Flora asked. Her voice sounded different somehow.

"Worried." The woman was one of the newest timber brides—she looked only a year or two older than Elsie. Pale blond hair, freckles high on her cheeks, thinner than most. "People are saying the flu got here after all."

"That's what I heard," Flora said. "Just a few people, though. Doesn't mean it has to get out of hand. What can I help you with?"

The woman bought some coffee and a bag of flour, one of the last in stock. "You got any more of those huckleberry jams or marmalades?"

Flora shook her head. "We're clear out of jams. Wouldn't mind some myself. Getting tired of nothing but butter on my bread." She smiled, an apology mixed with a reminder that everyone was in the same situation.

"Maybe I'll buy some extra butter while I'm here."

The woman was barely out the door when Flora started coughing. Elsie didn't notice it at first, but as she finished sweeping, the coughing intensified. She looked up.

"Alfred," Flora called out when she had the breath, "you mind interrupting your busy schedule and fetching me some water?"

But Alfred was in the cellar, so Elsie put down the broom and walked over to the spigot in the back room. Her mother was still coughing when Elsie handed her the glass. "Are you all right?"

Flora quickly drained the glass, but after she finished, she grimaced as if the water hadn't been able to wash down whatever was in her throat. She nodded. "Be fine. Just something stuck down there."

Elsie took the empty glass and filled it up again. When she handed it back to her mother, there was a distracted look in Flora's eyes.

By two o'clock, Philip had compiled the absence reports from the other mill foremen, most of whom were as wary of his presence as the river chief had been. There was no word from the timber camps, since the messengers hadn't made it that far into the woods, but there was a total of seven river and mill men unaccounted for. Doc Banes, back in Charles's office at noon to hear the report, shook his head.

"It moves fast."

Banes asked for the men's house numbers, and Philip looked them up in his account books, scribbling them on a sheet of paper. Banes grabbed the paper and his bag. "I'll be back in a couple of hours. Tell the foremen that if anyone else appears ill, they're to be sent home immediately. No one is to 'tough anything out' or 'work through it,' do you understand? If someone so much as sneezes, they're sent home."

Charles nodded.

"Philip, how well do you know Leonard or Yolen?" Banes asked.

"I don't," Philip said. "I recognize their names, but I don't think I've crossed paths with them lately."

"How about the men on the absentee list?"

Philip pointed out a couple of the names, men he'd met through Graham. "But I haven't spoken to any of them in days—not since before the quarantine started."

Banes pocketed the list.

"How could men I haven't even been near be getting sick, and I'm not even sick myself?" Philip asked, but the doctor didn't have time to speculate. Banes simply reminded them to keep track of anyone else who fell ill, and with that, he was out the door. All those late nights reading his journals and Dr. Pierce's letters were, alas, going to be put to use.

Philip slumped in his chair. Was he really the cause of the sickness in town? After enduring the glares of the river drivers, he felt trapped in his office, afraid to venture out and hear others' accusations. Worse, he feared that those accusations were justified.

He sipped his water, checking his throat again. He still had no symptoms. But would that soon change, possibly within the hour?

He kept his head down as he worked at the books. He tried not to touch anything that wasn't on his desk. He tried not to speak, not to breathe. He didn't want to make anyone sick, and he didn't want to catch anything from anyone else. He wished he could close himself off, a personal quarantine within the quarantined town.

Suddenly, the previous days' captivity didn't seem like such a terrible thing.

Jarred Rankle was walking home from the mill when he noticed Graham a few feet before him. Jarred called out Graham's name twice to get his attention. "Where you coming from?" he asked.

"Storage building," Graham answered. They continued walking as they spoke, each man hesitant to prolong his stay in that busy road. They sensed the fear in the town, in the closed windows and drawn curtains and in the wind that carried God knew what scourge.

"You hear about Leonard and Yolen?" Rankle asked.

"And the other guys who never showed up at work. Anything new on that?"

"I don't know about them, but three of my guys went home in the middle of their shifts. Started coughing like crazy, said they could barely stand up." Rankle paused. "Came from out of nowhere."

All day Graham had stared at that building, and the building hadn't twitched, and nothing inside it had moved, yet things were happening behind his back. The flu was sneaking past him, the dangers invisibly pooling at his feet.

They reached the street corner where they would need to part. They paused briefly, each conscious of Doc's warnings about lingering in public places. All around them, the tired men moved with wary purpose. Everyone wanted to get home, to close his doors. That was the advice the foremen had passed along—get lots of sleep and eat well. Avoid anyone who's sick. Stay home if you fall ill, and have someone notify the doctor. Already the men were avoiding eye contact, anxious to escape one another's presence.

Graham and Rankle were met by Mo, who hesitated before stopping to greet them.

"How's our spy?" Mo asked Graham.

"I didn't see him." Graham had been guarding the building with Douglas, a mop-headed blond fellow who had built many of the houses in town. Douglas had volunteered to be the one who went into the building to deliver the soldier's food, and Graham sure hadn't fought him on it. Even though Douglas wore a mask when he went in, and even though Doc Banes had vetted the soldier's health, Graham still didn't like the idea of getting close to the man while people in town were coming down with flu. He couldn't understand why other people didn't see what was so obvious to him: Doc Banes had been wrong. Quarantining Philip and the soldier for forty-eight hours had not been enough.

"I think more men are going to be sick tomorrow," Rankle said in a somewhat confidential tone. "I think things will get a whole lot worse before they get better."

"We don't know it's the flu yet," Mo said hopefully. "Doc hasn't said—"

"Doc's an old man," Graham interrupted in a low voice, looking at the legion of men walking past him, the dirty and stubbled cheeks, the furrowed brows. "Let's be straight with each other here—it's flu. The flu found us. The question is: what are we going to do about it?"

"Doc Banes told us to—" Mo saw from the dismissive look in Graham's red eyes that he was wasting his breath.

"It's the spy," Graham said, keeping his voice down so the passersby wouldn't overhear. "Things were fine till he got here."

Mo looked at Rankle, perhaps hoping he would disagree. Rankle considered something, then said, "We can't let him go, Graham. Charles is right: if anyone else caught him afterward and found out he'd been here, it'd be bad for us. It'd look like we harbored a soldier killer. The army would take over our town before we knew what hit us."

Graham looked away. Much of the past day had passed in a haze, the fatigue wearing away at the spaces beyond his vision, pulling the edges closer together, darkening them. But he suddenly felt energized. He would not be caught helpless; there was a solution.

"He's in there, and he's . . . he's breathing the stuff out on us." Graham struggled for the right words to convey what he thought was an obvious point. "He brought it into town with him, and now it's just coming out of him. The longer he stays here, the worse it'll get."

Rankle coughed, and Graham and Mo looked at him in alarm. After a second cough, he shook his head at them. "I'm not sick, fellas. Sawdust's been getting to me."

Mo said, "If it was the spy's fault, then Philip would've gotten sick, right?"

"I didn't say I understood how this all works," Graham admitted. "I ain't a doctor, and even though Banes is, I bet he barely understands any better'n we do. Everybody's calling it the Spanish flu, but for all we know, it's some kind of German poison or something. I don't know—all I'm saying is . . ." He paused, looking Mo in the eye, then Rankle. "You know that guy has something to do with this."

Silence. The ranks of passing millworkers had thinned, and now only a few stragglers passed them on the road. The first spittle of an approaching rain began to fall.

Rankle said, "Yeah. I think so, too." It was clear: no one had been sick before the soldier had come to town, and now contagion was rampant.

Mo didn't know what he thought, tell the truth, but he gave a sort of nod crossed with a shrug.

"So what do we do about it?" Graham asked.

"Graham," Rankle said, his gray eyes steadily aimed at his friend, "we just gotta hold tight and hope things turn out okay."

"You don't have any family that can get sick, Jarred."

Rankle squared his shoulders. "What's that supposed to mean? I'm not taking any stupid risks, Graham. I'm just trying to keep you from taking any."

Graham looked away again. "I'm not taking any risks. I just don't plan on standing around while everyone around me starts dying."

"*One* person has died. Even if more people do get sick, we don't know anyone's going to die."

Rankle and Graham looked at each other evenly.

"Wish this town hadn't dried up," Mo said to break the tension as the rain became steady. "I could use a drink."

But then he seemed to remember too late that both his companions had given up drink after their past tragedies. He stammered a bit, a brief and unintelligible mumble.

"Yeah," Rankle sighed, not seeming to mind. "Me, too."

"I should head home, fellas," Graham said. "I have to see to Amelia and the baby."

"All right," Rankle said, eying his friend with concern. "Take care of yourself."

"You two both." Graham nodded at them, then walked off.

It was dark when Elsie flipped the OPEN/CLOSED sign in the front window, her tired eyes reflected back at her.

The shelves in Metzger's General Store had never looked so barren. A couple hours ago she had helped her father bring up everything from the cellar, so whatever sat in the aisles was all that was left. At this rate, the store would be emptied in less than a week.

"I think everyone knows we're running low," Alfred said, apparently reading his daughter's thoughts, "so they're hurrying to buy what they can before it's too late."

"Do we have much at home?"

"We'll get by."

At the desk, Flora coughed again. She looked dazed, her posture less commanding than usual. She coughed again, cupping her hand in front of her mouth. After she stopped, Flora left her hand by her face, her fingers caressing the side of her nose, tracing the rim of her eye sockets.

"Are you feeling well, Mother?"

After a second, Flora responded, "No, dear, I don't believe I am."

V

Philip let out a long sigh, exhausted by his first day back in the world. It was after dinner and he was lying on his bed, staring at the ceiling, his fingers laced behind his head. As strange and terrible as that day had been, he found himself thinking neither about the flu nor about Frank. He was thinking about Elsie.

He wanted to thank her for the letter she'd left him at the storage building, for the bright light she'd shone on his dark stay in the prison. But he didn't know how he would say this, even as Frank's words about kissing her rang in his ears. She had written that she didn't blame him for letting Frank into town, but would she change her mind when she learned that the flu had been let loose in Commonwealth? Philip was too afraid to find out, which was why he hadn't ventured over to pay a visit to the Metzgers.

There was a knock on the door. "Come in," he said, sitting up.

In walked Laura, carrying a small satchel. "Hi," she said, closing the door behind her. Then she reached into the satchel and took out two of the fighter-pilot books, one of which Philip himself hadn't read. He would never read it, he had already decided.

"Thought I'd bring these back," she said. Philip shrugged, then rose from the bed and opened his closet door. After the books were safely buried beneath a baseball glove, Philip resumed his position on the bed. Laura sat on the edge.

"Everybody at school's scared," she told him. "Mom's even thinking about closing it down for a while."

"Are any kids sick?"

She shook her head. "But I heard Mom and Dad talking about which men from the mill are sick, and three of them have kids at school. The kids could catch it from them."

They were silent for a short while.

"Did people at school talk about me while I was . . . gone?" Philip asked.

"Sure, a little bit. It was pretty big news and all."

"Were people angry at me?"

"I don't think so. Why?"

"For letting the soldier in."

Laura shrugged. "I don't think anybody blamed you."

"But now people are getting sick."

She didn't say anything.

"Thanks for the cornbread while I was in there, by the way."

"Welcome."

"Frank says you're a good cook."

"So is he really a spy?"

Philip looked at her. "You aren't supposed to know about that."

"I can keep secrets."

"You keeping any other secrets I should know about?" He was thinking of Elsie.

She raised an eyebrow mockingly. "So tell me about the spy."

Philip thought for a moment. "I don't think he's a spy."

"Why not?"

"'Cause he's a nice guy. He's just a carpenter from Montana. He misses his girlfriend."

"Maybe he tricked you. Spies are devious—that's a requirement for the job."

Philip didn't like to think he'd been deceived. "I just don't think he is."

"Did he have an accent?"

Philip just rolled his eyes.

"Well, did he sound like maybe he was trying to *disguise* one?"

"*No.* But he did ask me if I knew of any good places to hide bombs, and he went on and on about how he loves sauerkraut."

"How am I supposed to know? Just because someone's a German spy doesn't mean he's actually from Germany. Maybe he's just an American who loves Germany or hates America. Maybe he has relatives in Germany and he's more loyal to them than to people over here."

"Elsie has relatives in Germany. Should we put her parents in prison, too?"

Laura sighed impatiently and got up. "You're impossible sometimes," she said disgustedly as she headed out the door.

"Good night, fräulein."

She closed the door just short of a slam.

Philip wished that joking with his sister meant things could be perfectly normal again. But people in town were sick, and Frank was locked in a cellar. Philip wanted to see him, to ask him more about who he was and where he'd come from—to exonerate him or to learn something that would cast new light on Charles's suspicions. Maybe Frank, guilt-stricken for deceiving Philip, would burst into tears and confess everything. Or maybe he'd be dead from flu in the morning. If Frank were to die, Philip would never know the truth about him. But if Frank died, maybe Philip would be next. Philip swallowed to see if his throat was sore.

He fell asleep with the light on. When he woke up in the middle of the night, he was so disoriented by the bright light that he thought he'd emerged into some transitory world where souls prepared for their final journey. Even after he had turned off the light, he lay awake for hours, staring into the darkness.

VI

Yolen was blue the next morning.

It had started in his fingertips, Jeanine told Doc Banes when he arrived. She had noticed it the night before when she had tried to give Yolen something to drink. He had fumbled at the glass and dropped it, pieces shattering across the floor. When she woke up this morning, her husband's condition had worsened: his temples were dark blue as well. The blue smear had spread to his cheeks and neck, and his lips, too, were the color of the sky minutes after sunset, as were his ears. He coughed violently as Doc Banes inspected him, nearly dislodging the thermometer.

His temperature was unchanged. That it hadn't increased was the only good news.

Banes knew that Yolen was drowning, slowly suffocating as his fluid-filled lungs failed to extract enough oxygen from the air around him. Banes had never seen such a thing. Even after he'd read about this in Dr. Pierce's letters, he had scarcely believed it possible. But here it was staring at him, eyes wide and helpless.

Banes put his hand on Yolen's forehead, trying to be reassuring. Yolen was disoriented and foggy; his mind could not escape from the blaze immolating his body. Banes told him to sleep.

Banes and Jeanine closed the door and went into the dining room, where she slumped into a battered wooden chair.

"Isn't there anything else you can do? What do those blue spots mean?"

Banes talked a bit about what caused the blue spots without telling her they might herald death.

"And why are people guarding my house? I'm a prisoner in my own home!" She stood up suddenly, as if prepared to fight Banes or whatever demon had cast its imprecation on her door.

"We can't let this spread through the town, Jeanine. It isn't you they're keeping in here, it's the flu."

Even as he said it, Banes realized that the need to guard this house or any other had already dissolved. As the previous day had worn on, he'd been forced to acknowledge that the flu was already spreading uncontrollably. Soon there would be more infected homes than the town could possibly quarantine.

"So I'm just supposed to stay in here until my husband dies?" Jeanine's eyes were tearing up, her momentary anger already displaced by fear. She had noticed that this time the doctor had put on the mask before he'd knocked on the front door. He was wearing it still, hiding behind it even as he tried to reassure her.

Banes said they shouldn't give up on Yolen yet. As bad as this flu could be, plenty of people pulled through. Leonard had died, but he'd had no one to take care of him. Jeanine could be the difference for her husband. Was there anything she needed, anything Banes could send over?

She shook her head and sat back down, staring at the floor and crying.

People should be here, Doc knew. Neighbors, family. Nurses. But the women who ordinarily served as his nurses in extreme times had all steadfastly refused to do so now—they didn't want to risk bringing flu home to their families. And the neighbors who should be cooking Jeanine's meals and visiting to keep her spirits strong were hiding as well, peeking at her house through closed blinds and praying that the scourge would not wander across their yard. Jeanine was as alone as her husband.

Most likely she would soon be alone without him, Banes knew.

Banes told her he would be back that evening. She didn't reply as he walked through the front door, past the guard with the gun. It was Deacon, who had been out there all night silently staring at those covered windows, wondering with a detached curiosity why the devil had chosen to strike this particular house.

It was the next patient who worried Banes the most.

Elsie Metzger had knocked on his door early that morning, requesting his visit. Walking into their home, he felt the noose tightening around Commonwealth's neck.

Flora Metzger had never been so silent in her life, he thought. Her voice usually rang through the house, but Banes didn't hear a sound as Elsie led him through the parlor, up the stairs, and into her parents' bedroom. When he finally heard her, a moment before opening the bedroom door, it wasn't her customary bright chatter but a cough, deep and husky.

Flora didn't look pale yet, but she probably would soon. Her temperature was nearly 105, and she was shivering uncontrollably, her hair damp with sweat. She appeared to be covered by every blanket the family owned.

"I want to take a look at your eyes," Banes said.

"Later. The light hurts too much."

Flora told the doctor she'd felt fine the previous morning, but at some point in the early afternoon, it had begun. Within two hours, she'd gone from perfectly healthy to miserable. And it had only gotten worse.

"I think my legs are broke," Flora whimpered after he'd listened to her lungs and peered into her nose and throat.

"Excuse me?"

"My legs. They're broken."

Banes paused. "Did you fall?"

"Don't remember."

Banes looked up at Elsie, hoping she might volunteer some information, but the girl's eyes were fixed on her mother's tensed face.

"I'll have a look." The doctor pulled the blankets up from the side, so Flora's chest and neck could stay covered, and slid her nightgown up to her knees. She winced through clenched teeth as he did so, in so much pain that Banes would have expected to see shattered bones poking through her skin. Yet her thick white legs were free of the slightest bruise or inflammation. He gingerly touched one of her knees and she gasped, which triggered another coughing spell. Aches were common with the flu, but her reaction was extreme. He pulled the blankets back over her.

"There's nothing broken. They're just going to be sore a while." He stepped into the hallway, Elsie following. "Has she been coughing much?"

"All night."

Banes nodded, thinking. "Run and get your father; tell him to just close the store for now."

By the time Elsie and her father returned, Flora was shivering so badly her teeth were chattering as loud as Elsie had ever heard. It sounded like rats gnawing through a wall.

Banes spoke to her father in the hallway, closing the bedroom door. He did not remove his mask. Elsie always felt somewhat unnerved in his presence, but now he looked particularly haunting.

He told them Flora had the flu, a bad case.

"Have any of your friends taken ill?" Banes asked. "Has anyone been coughing or sneezing in the store?"

Alfred's face turned pale. "Just her."

"How busy was the store yesterday?"

"Busy as it's ever been. Everybody's trying to get what they can."

Banes said, "I want you to leave the store closed. Stay here and tend to your wife. And Elsie's not to go to school." He reached into his satchel and handed them two gauze masks from his already dwindling supply. "Wear these when you're in her room. Wear gloves when you touch her, and wash your hands as often as possible."

Alfred looked stunned. From behind the door, Flora started coughing again. "Doc, I can't close the store. People are running out of food, and they need to—"

"Alfred, your wife probably caught this from someone who came to the store. God only knows who. Most likely it was someone who didn't know he was sick, someone who didn't feel it yet. If there's been sickness in that store, it means anyone else who comes there could get it, too. Just stay home for a few days, until she's recovered."

Alfred nodded. "All right. I'll just head back there and . . . put up a sign explaining things."

Elsie didn't like the defeated tone in her father's voice. And her mother's coughs were a tangible force, all but knocking on the closed door. She leaned back against the wall, hugging herself to keep from crying in front of Doc Banes, whom she never wanted to see again.

At first Banes tried to trace the emergence of the flu in Commonwealth, but every time he thought he'd found its path, the trail disappeared. Yolen was friends with Leonard, who had died within two days of falling ill. The night before Yolen had taken sick, according to Jeanine, he'd had a few drinks with his friends Otto and Ray, two rowdy shingle weavers. Ray had fallen ill the same day as Yolen and was in roughly the same condition, though not quite as advanced. Otto was one of the men who had reported to work at the mill the previous day but had left in the afternoon, overcome. By the time Banes made it to Otto's house, the man was lying in bed, coughing and delirious. At first Otto had thought Doc Banes was his long-dead father and had launched into some sort of apology for the old man's death. Banes had to interrupt him to ask about his symptoms.

Otto said he had felt fine, better than fine, that very morning. He had been standing at his position in the mill at about one o'clock and had abruptly felt struck down, as if by a blow square in the chest. His lungs were so constricted by coughs that he had doubled over and fallen to his knees. By the time he was able to get on his feet—with no help from his coworkers, who had backed away at the sight of his agony—his body was shaking and he felt so weak he could barely stand. *How could that happen, Dad?*

Banes wished he knew. He didn't understand how Leonard had become sick, and since the victim wasn't able to answer any questions, it seemed futile to investigate. Still, Banes asked Otto for a list of Leonard's friends in town and made a note to visit all of them, to find out if more of them were visibly sick and, if not, to warn them to keep to themselves in case they were on the verge of showing symptoms.

But now that Flora Metzger was ill, and so many people had come through her store the day before—signing the ledger book with her pen, standing there breathing while she went on and on with one of her stories—there no longer seemed a point to tracing the flu's spread.

Doc told worried families how to nurse their sick and told the afflicted to rest, unnecessary advice since the patients could barely raise their heads, let alone do anything else. Still, Banes wished he had a medical staff at his disposal, if only to visit each patient, but there was just one of him to answer their questions and to give them some reason to hope. He needed to see Charles and find out who else had left the mill due to illness, and he needed to get to the school and inquire about sick children and decide what to do about the youngsters with stricken parents. At the same time, there was little he could do but be a witness, a witness to events that were beyond his skill and beyond his reckoning.

Every time Banes knocked on a door, he saw people in the street watching him, faces peering at him through windows in nearby houses. Not a soul came by to inquire about their neighbors' health or to offer aid. They simply saw Banes's approach and retreated into the safety of their homes.

The gauze mask had become a permanent part of his face. Though he usually made his rounds on foot, using the excuse to get some exercise, he now drove through town in his horse-drawn carriage, aware that time was too precious and that, more important, he needed to maintain his energy; he could not afford to tire from too much walking back and forth across town. He wanted to see every sick person at least twice a day, but this would surely be impossible by tomorrow, if the infection rate continued at its current pace.

The symptoms were as ghastly as they were widespread. Some victims suffered nosebleeds that, combined with their coughs, often left them choking on their blood—which would explain the mess Banes had discovered in Leonard's room. Before noon Doc's shirt was stained by several patients' bloody coughs; he stopped at home to change, to avoid carrying the contagion farther in his travels.

Many people were nauseated, vomiting into buckets that their aggrieved family members could not empty quickly enough. Others had earaches and dizziness from middle ears so inflamed that Doc had already used his needles to drain the pus from four pairs of ears that day—finally, something he could do to alleviate symptoms, relieve pain. Hopefully that would quell the pounding, he told them, would cause the earth to stop wobbling around them, would ease the headaches so severe that more than one person had voiced fears that his brain was somehow growing beyond the capacity of his skull.

Banes was tired, but there were more names on his list. Again he felt a sick and surely immoral gratitude that his wife wasn't alive to see this. She had always been such a talker, and she had hated the days he would come home too demoralized or broken by what he had seen to chat with her. But what if she were still home now—what would she think if she saw him stumble through the door and slump into his chair, staring emptily at the wall, too overcome for any words at all?

But he wasn't home yet; there was still more to be done. And was it getting dark out already? Was this really night? Like the flu, it had come so quickly, almost without warning. Had he even eaten today? He couldn't remember. He was sweaty from moving in and out of hot, stuffy rooms, and his clothes were a mess again from so much blood and saliva. It was indeed dark out now, but there were still others to visit, others to console. What should they do about the school? And what about the mill?

And had anyone taken away Leonard's body yet? The town had one undertaker, an elderly man named Krugman. The small town had been filled mostly with people in the prime of their lives, and the undertaker's services had rarely been called upon. Doc feared that the next few days would more than make up for Krugman's prior inactivity. As Banes rode in his carriage along the river, he saw the many logs bobbing on the water's surface like corpses, and he realized he should tell Charles to set aside some of the lesser pieces of wood. The town would need coffins—many of them.

VII

"You shot your dog?"

"Damn right I did. And it was the right thing to do."

"I thought you liked him."

"That ain't the fuckin' point. Point is, dogs can spread germs as well as anybody else."

"Where in the hell'd you hear that?"

"It's the truth, dammit. Dogs, chickens, anything can have the flu. And dogs wander around, go all over the damn place. What's the point in keeping my family at home if the dog's poking through other folks' yards and getting sick?"

"Just can't believe you shot your dog."

"And you should shoot yours."

"Shoot Ransom? I love that sonuvabitch."

"Do you love 'im more'n you love your kids? Hell, it's your choice. But I made mine already. I can get another damn dog once the flu's passed."

"The general store's *closed*?"

"That's what I heard. Flora Metzger got sick, and now Doc Banes says the store's gotta stay shut."

"Shit. My wife was gonna head over there later today—we've damn near run out of everything."

"It sounds like your wife waited too long."

"When's it gonna open back up?"

"How the hell should I know? Go knock on Metzger's door if you want—I just wouldn't get too close to the poor bastard. Not now."

"Whiskey, you say?"

"Yep. A small glass of the stuff, every morning. That'll keep the flu away."

"Huh. Never woulda figured. How 'bout moonshine or beer?"

"Hell, no. It's gotta be whiskey. Works like a charm."

"Mientkiewicz's sick."

"Him, too?"

"I just saw him. He was walking to the mill but coughing up a storm. I passed him and we looked at each other—just looked. I knew it and he knew I knew it. I guess he was hoping maybe he wasn't so bad, you know? That maybe he'd be okay if he just tried to keep going."

"So what happened?"

"He was about two blocks away when I saw him, and he had this guilty look in his eyes. Then he just started coughing and coughing, all doubled over and everything, so I walked away. Didn't want to be too near him, you know?"

"I'm thinking I shouldn't be too near you now."

"I wasn't *that* close. And after I walked a block, I turned around and looked at him again, and he was in the same damn spot. Looking at me, but this time like I was the one doing something wrong. You know? Then he waved."

"Waved?"

"Yeah. He just kinda stuck his hand in the air, then turned around and started walking home. Kinda weird. Hope he's okay."

"What's that around your neck?"

"Shut up."

"No, what is it?"

"Garlic."

"Garlic?"

"My wife's idea. Says it'll keep me healthy."

"Does it work?"

"I don't know. We'll find out, I guess."

"Bullshit."

"No, I'm telling you it's the truth. That big ol' house of theirs has a goddamn giant cellar—I saw it myself one time when they had me over for dinner."

"The house ain't 'big'—it's just like everybody else's."

"First of all, no, the Worthys' house is not the same. It may not be twice the size, but it's definitely bigger than mine or yours. And since you've never been inside it, you'll have to believe me. And second of all, my point is that their cellar's so damn big they probably have more'n enough food stored away to last themselves the whole winter."

"I just can't see them doing that."

"I'm telling you, that's why Worthy wasn't as worried about shutting the town as everybody else was. We all were worried about running out of things, but he wasn't. He owns the mill, and he knows he has a cellar full of food and that his family'll never go hungry."

"Damn. That would explain a few things."

"Stop smearing Worthy over there. Don't believe what he's saying, Lars."

"Mind your own business."

"Think about it—he closes the town, forces us all to work even though other mills are giving sick folks time off. Now we're running short on food, and he's in his nice big house feasting and his kids aren't even finishing their plates. Their dogs are probably better fed than you are."

"Shut up over there. The Worthys don't even have a dog."

"You know what I heard about dogs?"

"Y'all should stop talking so much. Voices spread germs."

"Shoot. Good point."

"So do your work and shut up."

VIII

The following afternoon at least two people broke the doctor's rule about staying inside as much as possible.

But Rebecca and Amelia felt they had little choice. They were walking to the community gardens together, where they were to meet three other women who helped tend the crops. Most of the gardens had been harvested already, but some of the winter vegetables remained. Normally, the women would leave them until after the first frost, but pantries were bare all across town. They could wait no longer.

The gardens had grown steadily in acreage over the past two years, with more than three dozen households contributing, planting in the spring and tending the crops throughout the year. Everything was divided equally or traded at one of the swaps in the town hall. If only they had known back in the spring that there would be a quarantine, they could have planted more, could have made the garden a greater priority. Instead, they would have to make do with what they'd planted months ago, when something like an epidemic had seemed unimaginable.

Rebecca knocked on the Stones' door, a stack of wicker baskets in her free hand.

"I'm sorry I'm late." She smiled. "The children were rambunctious today."

"How are they?" Amelia asked as she closed the door behind her. She had answered the door in her coat, ready to go, the baby swaddled in her arms. Rebecca noticed that she was not invited in.

"They don't really understand what's happening, which is probably for the best," Rebecca said as they began walking. It was windier than usual as they hurried along the empty streets. She gestured to the baby. "Are you sure you'll be all right with her?"

"I'll have to be—I couldn't get anyone to watch her. The neighbors all had excuses. They barely even opened their doors when I knocked."

Rebecca nodded. They had made these plans three days earlier, right as the flu was twisting around them like some invisible choking weed. They were both nervous to be out despite the doctor's orders, but the garden was large, and the five of them would be separated by a great distance, going about their work in near-solitude. Only when they were finished harvesting would they be close together, dividing among themselves the kale and cabbage, the carrots and beets. Surely that wouldn't be enough time to catch something, even if one of them had something to spread. Of course, here she was walking beside Amelia, but somehow it seemed hard to imagine Amelia becoming ill, what with Graham being so protective of her. Rebecca knew that was a silly thought—no man could protect his wife from disease—but still she saw Amelia as safe.

"Are any of the children sick?"

It was unclear whether Amelia had asked this out of empathetic curiosity or out of fear that the woman beside her had spent the day in a sickroom. Rebecca scolded herself for being uncharitable.

"Three were absent today," she said. Included in that number was Elsie, who had been kept home to care for her mother. The school had seemed emptier without Elsie's eager presence, and Rebecca was worried about her.

They walked in silence for a moment. Rebecca thought she saw Amelia adjust her scarf so that it sat higher on her face, blocking her nose and mouth. But it was cold out, and a stiff breeze had preceded her action.

I'm thinking too much, Rebecca told herself. Her role as shepherd for nervous children had taken its toll on her today. She tried to focus on the good things. She cast a glance at Amelia's waist, made herself grin. "How have you been feeling?" she asked.

Amelia smiled. Rebecca was the only person other than Graham who knew that Amelia was pregnant now, though soon it would show. Rebecca had picked up on the subtle signs that men missed, and the two had whispered about it while washing up after dinner at the Worthys'.

"I'm well, thank you. I haven't been nearly as sick as I was with her."

"Are you eating well?"

"As well as I can, while trying to conserve what we have. Today will certainly help."

They had passed the last of the houses and were walking along the narrow dirt path that headed west, up a slowly rising hill bereft of trees. As they reached the crest, they saw the community gardens before them, neatly arranged in plots that they had helped lay out two years ago, when each of them had secretly wondered if the new town would survive long enough for the gardens to be harvested the next fall.

Rebecca thought something looked odd, but perhaps it was the wind blowing leaves and vines through the thin rows, throwing old fragments of pumpkins into the leeks, casting the purple-veined stalks of beets into the greens. But as she came closer, she understood. She dropped the baskets, and Amelia gasped.

The garden had been ransacked. While Amelia stood there, the oblivious child in her arms, Rebecca jogged forward into the carrot patch and saw the freshly torn earth, the discarded pieces of stalks and leaves lying about. She wandered on, saw a few shreds of cabbage but no heads despite the rows upon rows she had planted. The carrots and beets had been unearthed and spirited away, as had the leeks. The winter squash—which would have filled so many for so long, would have helped stretch out the small quantities of remaining meat—had vanished. There were but a few remaining, buried under the dirt that had been torn out during the frantic excavations.

Rebecca felt the prick of tears starting in her eyes as she hurried from plot to plot, hoping in vain that the scavengers had tired at some point, had left a section untouched in their hurry. But the entire garden had been plundered.

"Who would do this?" Amelia asked as tears came to her eyes, too.

Rebecca watched as the wind scattered her baskets. "Anyone."

IX

After standing guard outside the storage building from sunrise to sunset, Graham returned home for dinner. His wife had yet to start cooking, however, and was pacing in the kitchen. When she told him the news about the gardens, he nodded in sympathy, but he was not terribly surprised.

"People are panicking," Graham said. "More folks are getting sick—lots. Flora Metzger's one—they've even closed the general store."

"There must be some way to find out who did it, Graham. Someone out there has acres of vegetables in their house."

"I'm not about to go knocking on people's doors, not with everyone sick. We have to just leave it be."

Millie started crying from her crib in the parlor. Amelia walked over and reached a hand down to the baby but seemed too agitated to pick her up. Graham could see she was not satisfied with his response.

"We'll find out who it was eventually," he tried to reassure her. "Someone'll talk, things'll get out. But we can't worry about it now."

"This never would have happened before," she said.

"I can go hunting in a couple days. One deer'd last us a long time."

Amelia shook her head. "I feel like we should start locking our doors. People know how big our back garden is." She had finished harvesting the last of their own vegetables the previous day. "I don't want our cellar broken into." She laughed sadly. "Our doors don't even have locks."

He held her, and her nails dug into the back of his shirt.

"I'll build some latches on the doors tonight," he told her as she started crying again despite herself. He rubbed her neck and promised, "No one's breaking into this house."

Later that evening Graham was busily constructing latches for the front and back doors while Amelia knit another sweater for the baby. He knew he should be trying to catch up on sleep, but there was no end of things to do. He was tired, but it felt good to do something that soothed his wife, something other than standing all day or night with a gun in his hands. It had felt good to hold her and let her cry on his shoulder. She didn't do it often—it took a hell of a lot to upset her, he'd learned—and over the last few weeks, they'd had few quiet moments alone. They had not held each other like that since the day of the first soldier.

She seemed to regret having mentioned the need for latches, twice telling Graham that he needn't trouble himself after all, that he should let himself rest. But both times he shook his head. She was right about locking their doors, and he could sleep later. At one point she commented that this was one of the first times in days he'd been home in the early evening for more than a quick supper before heading back out to stand guard somewhere. She's right, he thought. I should probably see if any of the guards need to be spelled.

It was past ten when he finished the latches. As he put his tools away, he felt her walk up behind him and put her arms around his waist, her hands flat against his chest. He allowed himself to relax slightly, lowering his shoulders a bit so she could kiss the back of his neck softly. He closed his eyes. But then he took her hands away and turned around.

"I need to visit Mo," he told her. "I'm sorry."

She kissed him on the lips. "You have to see him this late?"

Graham wanted so badly to stay, but he knew what he had to do. "I do. I have to tell him he needs to stand guard tomorrow morning—the fellow who was supposed to is sick."

He was lying. He wasn't sure he had ever lied to his wife before, but even if he hadn't, this was a white lie. Tiny, microscopic. And it was a lie for good reasons. It was a lie with a halo atop its head.

She relented, knowing there was no way she could talk him out of anything relating to guard duty. "Will you be long?"

"I might be. I'm sorry."

"Maybe you should go to Philip's instead," she said. "His house is closer."

"I don't think Philip is working guard duty anymore. I have to see Mo."

As he walked toward the closet to retrieve his jacket, she found herself saying, "I feel bad for Philip. I've heard people saying it's his fault that people in town are sick, but I can't believe that. It doesn't make sense."

Graham put on his jacket and stopped for a moment before the door. "You don't think so?"

"I don't know." She shrugged, then her voice became lighter, as if she realized too late that it had been a mistake to bring this up. "Maybe we'll never know how it happened. He let a man in, but they're both still healthy, aren't they? Maybe he did the right thing letting that man in."

Graham was frozen, stunned. "It was not the right thing." His voice was as loud as it had ever been in his wife's presence. Amelia shuddered. "If that was the right thing, then what does it make what *I* did?"

He stood there, almost daring her to answer. He could not keep the anger from coloring his face, nor the pain, the pain that had left everything else exposed, raw.

She held up a hand. "Graham, I'm sorry, I didn't mean it that way." She stepped toward him, but he turned back around.

"I need to see Mo." He quickly moved to the door, closing it behind him as he escaped into the night.

It was cold out, but it could have been far colder and he wouldn't have felt it. He seethed, each footstep pounding into the earth. Did even his wife think he'd done the wrong thing? He tried to tell himself she was just confused. But what she had said made him realize all the more strongly that what he was about to do was the right thing. Was necessary. No one else seemed to understand, but he saw it now with a clarity he had not been granted in days, and the vision stirred him. There was something he could do to redeem himself, redeem Philip, redeem the entire town. He only hoped he wasn't too late.

X

The next day thirty-two sick men were absent from the mill, the timber camps, and the river crews. Many of those men had wives and children who were also ill, Doc Banes had told Charles and Philip that morning as he'd stuffed the newest list of addresses into his pocket and headed out the door. The numbers were growing at an astounding rate—Banes figured the sick could number more than a hundred within two days.

Depending on when Leonard had first become sick, this was only the fourth or the fifth day that people in Commonwealth had been infected. Leonard already had three companions in death, including his friends Otto and Ray, who had both joined him the previous evening. The speed with which they had succumbed—the ravishing violence of this flu—shocked Dr. Banes.

Right before leaving, Banes had said to Charles, almost offhand, that Flora Metzger was among the sick and that the general store was closed.

Philip froze. Then he interrupted the doctor and asked how Elsie and Alfred were doing.

"They seemed healthy when I saw them last night."

Philip faced his desk, too overcome to let Charles or the doctor see his reaction. He stared at the pages and charts before him, unable to think of anything except the fact that Elsie was now confined to a sick house, that she had to watch her mother suffer, had to fear that the same fate awaited her as well.

Philip was useless that day, unable to concentrate. He wanted to go straight to Elsie's door but knew he could not. There was nothing he could do, and Charles needed help in the office. Besides, Charles was friends with Mr. Metzger and with several of the sick workers; surely he was as worried as Philip was about Elsie. Philip thought about Graham, how he always seemed able to contain his emotions and focus on the task at hand, and tried to imitate that strength.

During the day, Philip collected reports from the foremen: twelve more men had reported sudden illness and left for home, bringing the total absentee number to forty-four. Each hour the ranks of the sick grew. Yet there was no companionship in it, as they were all isolated in their semi-delirious states, alone with their fevers and chills and strange waking dreams that seemed to talk to them like voices from beyond the pale.

That afternoon Banes visited the office again for a brief status report, and Philip asked if there was any more news on the Metzgers. Banes shook his head, saying only "Mrs. Metzger is much worse."

"Maybe I should go by and see if they need any help or—"

"Don't do that," Banes said, stopping even as he was nearly out the door. It was as though Philip had proposed burning down the mill. "Don't visit anyone who's sick. Don't try to help—all you'll do is get sick yourself."

Banes turned and left before Philip could say anything more.

Philip stayed at the office past the point where there was anything to do. He was afraid of bumping into millworkers on the way home, afraid of their suspicious eyes and stares of blame, so he waited until quitting time had long passed and he figured the streets would be deserted.

"Go on ahead," Charles had said, "I'll be home shortly."

Philip's stomach had been bothering him all that day—he'd been too nervous to eat since hearing about Mrs. Metzger, and as he walked out of the mill and down the long street leading to town, he felt a bit unsteady on his feet. With his hands stuffed into his pants pockets as protection from the surprisingly cold air, he kept his eyes on his boots as he made his way toward home.

He looked up when he heard voices. Five men stood on a street corner, their heads and shoulders illuminated by the streetlamp hanging overhead.

He recognized them as millworkers but didn't know their names—none were foremen, none had ever been introduced to him. Most of them seemed somewhat older, ten years or more beyond Graham's age, and each possessed a slight variation of the weather-worn, beaten-down look endemic to men of their station. Four sets of eyes were aimed his way, but one man stared at the ground, seemingly held captive by a vacant despair.

"'S him," one man said. Philip had intended to nod a polite hello, but he could tell from their tone that they weren't interested in pleasantries.

"He's the one brought the flu here," another said, and Philip sensed movement toward him.

One of the men was striding into his path, followed by two of his compatriots.

"You're Philip Worthy, right?" the man in front asked. His thick beard was dark, though the hair atop his head was dusted with gray, and his ears were oddly prominent. "I'd recognize that limp anywhere."

Philip felt his cheeks redden, and a sick feeling surged through his stomach.

The man stepped right up to him, closer than was friendly. "You're the one got Michael's boy sick."

Two men stood beside the bearded one. Behind them the other two remained, one of them still looking down at the ground with glassy eyes as he leaned against the streetlight and the other standing to that man's side as if protecting him.

"Who's Michael's boy?" Philip asked weakly, trying to sound interested and harmless.

"Leave it alone, Isaac," said the man staring at the ground. He had short brown hair, and on his chin was a sprinkle of light stubble. His voice was quiet and resigned.

Philip heard other voices coming from behind—more men emerging from the mill. He had thought everyone had left already, but apparently he was wrong.

"That's Michael," said Isaac, pointing back to the quiet one. "His son's so sick the doctor says he ain't gonna make it."

Someone mumbled into Isaac's ear, and he nodded. His eyes were filled with a barely contained rage, and Philip was afraid that if he looked away from them, the man would bare his teeth and let loose a piercing howl while lunging for Philip's throat. All Philip could do was keep looking at those eyes, as if he could pin the man in place with his gaze.

Isaac was a very large man.

"We should take him into the woods," said the third man, who had a long, thin face. The other men leaving the mill were approaching.

"What I want to know from you," Isaac said, still staring hard at his prey, "is what in the hell you think you were doing letting that man into our town."

"Leave it alone, Isaac," Michael repeated. He still had not moved from the streetlight, his head hanging so forlorn it looked almost like he had been tied to the pole and left there to die.

"I want to hear him answer for himself."

Philip hoped that Charles was part of the group of approaching men, but he could tell from the voices that he was not.

Isaac was waiting. His breaths were even but loud, as if he expected Philip to try running away and was ready to give chase.

Men like this were the people Philip had been protecting when he stood guard. But they had been different before. The fear of the flu had changed everyone. It had cut off everyone's breath, forcing their hearts to work twice as hard just to keep beating.

Philip was still afraid to look away from Isaac, but he shifted his eyes to the face of Michael and said, "I'm sorry about your son, mister."

"Don't even talk to him!" Isaac bellowed and stepped forward, forcing Philip to back up a step.

"What's going on, fellas?" one of the men from the approaching group asked.

Michael and his companion remained silent, and Isaac appeared too enraged to reply. "It's Philip Worthy," the thin man said.

"He's the bastard let the flu in," the fifth man said in a faint Eastern European accent. "We're trying to decide what to do wid 'im."

"Leave it alone," Michael said again, and again he was ignored.

"I ain't getting that close to him," one of the men from the new group announced, "and I say you're crazy to do otherwise."

Isaac backed off a step upon hearing this. These men blamed Philip and feared him all at once.

"I'm just trying to get home," Philip said.

"I'd let him go," another of the new men said. "It's not too wise to breathe the air around him."

"Get out of here," Isaac barked at Philip. Philip obeyed, one foot almost tripping over the other, an awkward stutter step that surely betrayed his fear. "Walk away and keep walking—walk straight out of town, you hear?"

Philip walked as fast as he could without running, passing the houses with the shades drawn, behind which families hid for silent suppers. As he put more distance between himself and the confrontation, his gait slowed. The charged shivers of fear were fading, giving way to a sickening anger—he was angry at himself for being scared, angry for looking weak and being outnumbered. Angry for not being as tall or as broad as Isaac, for not knowing how to answer the man's question in a way that would have satisfied any of them, or even himself.

The silence of the town was barely broken by his footsteps. The air smelled sweet, the fir trees seemingly more aromatic this time of year, the dirt and the earth releasing whatever spirit they had left before winter's grip suffocated them over the next few months.

It was so quiet he could hear footsteps approaching from several blocks away, before he could even see the figure in the distance. It took him longer than it should have to recognize her, since she was walking with her head down, and when she did look up, a gauze mask covered half her face.

It was Elsie, Philip realized. They made eye contact, but she looked back down as if hoping he hadn't noticed her, as if they weren't seemingly the only two people left in the entire town.

He froze and said her name, and she stopped, too, ten feet away. She was off to his left, as if she'd hoped to pass him without stopping. Philip had seen the doctor wearing such a mask, but it swallowed Elsie's smaller face, her eyes barely appearing over the top. Her hair was pulled back, though a few curls had escaped. They dangled in the faint wind.

"Hi," she said quietly, her voice muffled. "I'm just running by the store to get something. Doc Banes told us not to run errands, so I was hoping I wouldn't bump into anyone."

It hurt him to see her cowering that way, stigmatized by her family's new status. He stepped toward her, but she backed away.

"Doc Banes says I'm not supposed to get close to anyone," she said, looking down.

"Are you sick?"

She shook her head, and something inside him unclenched. "But my mother's not well."

"I'm so sorry. I just heard today. I wanted to come by and check on you, but Doc Banes told me not to."

She nodded, and for a few seconds they stood in silence. He thought of how he'd felt when Graham had backed away from him outside the storage building. How could he possibly keep away from her? How could he of all people justify treating her that way?

Finally, he took a step toward her, then another. "I'm sorry."

"For what?" She watched him approach, this time not backing away. "You shouldn't get too close."

"Most people think I'm the one who let the flu in," he said. "Best I can figure, if I haven't gotten it yet, I'm not going to."

"I don't want to be responsible," she said, but her voice broke off, cracked. He thought he saw her eyes water.

"I don't want to be responsible, either." He stopped a few feet in front of her, as close as two friends would normally stand. He could see the outline of her lips through the mask, see the gauze gently lean in when she inhaled.

"I'm just gonna run to the store," she said.

"You mind some company?"

He couldn't see her smile, but he could hear it in her voice. "I'd love some."

They walked together, Philip retracing the steps he'd taken from the mill.

"I haven't left the house since yesterday morning, when Doc Banes made me fetch my father from the store," Elsie said, looking around suspiciously, as if not quite sure whether she was glad to be in the outside world. "It's so peaceful out here."

"Everybody's hiding. You're not the only one who's been shut in."

"She keeps coughing and coughing." Elsie shook her head. "I've never heard anything like it."

"How are her spirits?"

"It's like it's not even her. She can barely talk—can you imagine my mother quiet? A couple times when my dad said something real obvious, she'd give me this look like she wanted to tease him for it, but she couldn't." Her voice grew quiet again as she walked up to the general store and unlocked the front door. "She couldn't even *talk.*"

Inside, she lit a small lamp as Philip closed the door behind them. She asked him to lock it.

"I don't want to light up the place," she told him. "People might think we're open and try to come in."

"You need a hand with anything?"

She said she'd be fine and disappeared into one of the aisles, carrying the lamp with her. Philip sat on a bench by the door and watched the light following her and turning a corner, leaving him in the dark. There wasn't much food left on the shelves, he noticed.

The light grew stronger again and there she was, a small satchel slung over her shoulder and the lamp in her right hand. She placed it on her mother's desk and sat beside him.

"Mind if we just sit her for a little while?" she asked. "I'm not in any rush to get back there."

"Sure."

He felt curiously excited to be alone with her again, behind locked doors. Mixed with this was his concern for her mother and for her own peace of mind, and his fear that he was to blame for what was happening. She didn't seem to be holding it against him, though.

"Is your dad okay?"

"Me and him both. It's only my mother so far."

"She's been sick two days?"

"Just about." They sat side by side, each facing forward. He stole occasional glances at her from the corner of his eye. Her face was still, her eyes motionless above the mask.

"She's getting through, then," Philip said. "First couple of days of the flu are usually the worst. I'm sure she'll be up and chattering away in a couple more days."

She turned to face him. "Has anyone else died?"

The fact that he couldn't see the rest of her face made her eyes look even more vulnerable.

"What have you heard?" Philip asked.

"That the first man died, the Canadian. But that was a couple days ago, and I can't get the doctor or my dad to tell me anything."

Philip breathed for a moment. He thought about lying but couldn't. "Three more men died yesterday, Doc said. I don't know about today."

She looked away again, and he saw tears welling up in her eyes.

"But a lot more people are sick than dying—those guys were probably the worst off, you know? I'm sure your mom's gonna be fine."

"Doc Banes said something to my dad this afternoon—took him into another room and closed the door. My dad wouldn't tell me what it was, but a couple hours later, I saw him in the parlor and he looked like he'd been crying. He still won't tell me." The tears fell down her cheeks and she looked down, ashamed.

Philip hesitated, then put his arm around her, squeezing her shoulder. "Doc Banes doesn't know everything," he said. "It doesn't matter what he said. He's been wrong about a lot of things."

He wasn't a good consoler, he figured, because her crying grew louder, and before he could say anything else, she collapsed in to him, her masked face on his chest and one of her hands behind his shoulder. He kept his left hand on her back, rubbing gently, not sure if he should say anything else. He felt his heart race as her back rose with each breath. But at the same time, he felt his own eyes welling up from the weight of so much sadness pressing itself against him. Those men outside the mill were right—this *was* Philip's fault, and all he could do was sit there and hold her and be thankful for the fact that she didn't blame him, at least not yet.

By the time the tightness in his throat had faded, Elsie was quiet.

Eventually, she pulled back. "Sorry," she said, sniffling again. "Now I'm all a mess."

"Don't apologize," he said, taking his left arm back. She reached into a pocket for her handkerchief and dabbed at her eyes. The mask was wet from her nose and the tears. "You can take that off if you want," he said, smiling slightly. "I mean, if you're only wearing it for my sake."

She paused, then pulled the mask down around her neck. It was the first time he'd seen her face since before he'd been placed under guard.

"All right," she said, then smiled back at him. "Though I'm not to blame if you sneeze later tonight."

"Deal."

He sat there silently while she wiped her eyes again.

"Thanks for sending me that letter," he said at last.

He saw an instant of confusion cross her face, as if the letter were something she had written many years ago and remembered only dimly. "Sure. Figured you must have been a little lonely in there."

"I think I read it ten times."

"Really?" She smiled.

"There wasn't much else to do." He had read it many times since, so boredom was no excuse. "I would have written one back, but they told me I couldn't send anything out."

"And now I'm the one trapped someplace." She rolled her eyes, somehow managing to smile at the situation.

You kiss her yet? Frank had asked.

"Maybe I could write you back then."

"That'd be nice." She looked back at him, and her eyes didn't seem as red. "I don't know how long I'm going to be stuck in there, so you might have to write more than one."

"I'd be honored."

"One a day."

He smiled. "Yes, ma'am. Should they be a certain number of pages?"

"You can decide that." Then she added, "At least one full page each."

"I can ask Laura to write you, too," he said, then regretted it, fearing that he'd shattered a moment he hadn't known how to handle.

"Okay," she said, looking at him calmly. "I'd be more interested in reading yours, though."

The way she said that made Frank's question echo in Philip's head again. Without thinking further, he leaned close to Elsie and she to him, and they kissed there in the dark building. It was quiet then, and all he could hear were the strange sounds their lips and mouths made. The kiss felt good, as if it were the first good thing Philip had felt in days, weeks, and it was worth any nervousness he may have suffered. She tasted like apples and smelled like something sweeter—he wasn't sure what it was, but he knew it was something he wanted to keep with him. At some point, he drew his lips from hers but kept his arm around her. She leaned her head on his shoulder and they sat there in the flickering lamplight, the shadows dancing in the aisles.

It was cold in the store and she felt warm, leaning against him. He didn't care if kissing someone from a sick house was unwise—he didn't see how what he had just done could possibly be considered a mistake. He knew he had done plenty of things wrong in the past two weeks, but this wasn't something to doubt.

Elsie shyly asked Philip how long he'd wanted to kiss her.

"Remember the time we were collecting driftwood and I found that piece that looked like a shield?" It had been a few months ago. He'd found a large, thin slice of bark that had somehow sheared off a tree's trunk. It was soft and brittle from its time in the river, and perfectly pentagonal, as if someone had painstakingly carved it that way.

"I still have that shield," she replied, smiling. "It's under my bed."

He smiled back. "I'm glad I gave it to you. I should have kissed you then." So they kissed again.

Eventually, Elsie said she should go home. "My dad's likely to think something's happened."

It was even colder outside than before, and Philip could feel the air's thin fingers prying through his jacket, sliding in through the buttonholes, and digging into the pockets where his fingers were bunched into fists. The reality of the flu seemed to return when Elsie fastened her mask back on. Philip regretted losing sight of her lips.

"You should probably let me go on ahead," she said. "If my dad saw us walking together, he'd be angry because of what the doctor said."

"Okay." Philip wanted to say something else, but nothing he could think of felt right. "I'll write you" was all he said.

"Okay." Just as he was wondering if she was smiling through the mask, she pulled it down again, stepping toward him to quickly kiss him on the lips. And then she did smile, for a full second or two before the mask returned, smothering her lips again, and she turned around to walk home.

He stood there buzzing for a moment, thrilling in his good fortune. He waited as the wind grew colder, until she had disappeared beyond the light of the streetlamps. Then he turned around and started walking, quickly, but not toward his house.

Philip felt wonderful and horrible, nervous and bold, excited and confused. He had imagined such a moment for longer than he could remember, and it had finally happened. Yet he had never planned on it being initiated by Elsie's need of consolation, had never expected his joy to be tempered by guilt.

He was amazed that she felt the same way about him as he did about her. That she had confidence in him. For months he had been too afraid to kiss her, so with his heart still beating too quickly and his nerves still shivering, he felt the courage to do something else he'd been afraid to do.

He walked faster, heading straight for the storage buildings.

XI

The town seemed even quieter than when Philip had first come upon Elsie, if such a thing were possible. And darker: there were no streetlamps, and he carried no light with him, all the better to stealthily make his way. Nearly every window was dark. As Philip walked farther, the occasional ominous sound he heard above the crunch of his boots was coughing. He heard it emanating from one house, then, a few blocks later, he heard another answering its call. Then another. It was as if the houses themselves were whispering to one another, spreading news of the flu.

Philip was close to the storage buildings when he saw a sign of life at last. Three blocks ahead, a carriage pulled by a fatigued horse turned a corner onto the road where he walked. Philip retreated to the side of a house. Why was he hiding? It was the flu, he realized, making every innocuous or mundane action seem freighted with new meaning, wicked purpose. But maybe what he was doing really was wicked—he wasn't honestly sure.

Philip saw a lamp bouncing lightly above the head of the driver: Doc Banes. Of course—who else would be out? The weary doctor was returning from a house call, apparently, with his ubiquitous bag beside him. By now he would have been performing house calls for over twelve hours. The old man's head hung so low that Banes might not have seen him even if Philip had stayed on the road. Philip both wanted and did not want to know what Banes had been through that day, how many patients he had tended, how many worried family members he had tried to pacify, how many fevered foreheads he had caressed, how many ominous verdicts he'd rendered.

In a moment Banes was gone, hurrying toward either his home or the next stop on his nocturnal tour. Philip thought about the list of sick men's addresses he had made for the doctor that morning and wondered how long the next day's list would be.

Philip walked back onto the road after the carriage had passed. The moon had disappeared and the black sky gone starless, his view of the heavens obstructed by invisible clouds. Here in the quarantine, they were cut off even from the sky.

The storage buildings gradually emerged from the darkness. Two lamps sat on the ground, and standing between them was a guard, a logger named Lightning. This was good news: Lightning was a hulking but gentle man and none too bright. Someone had once joked, "You're just lightning quick, aren't ya?" and the name had stuck.

Lightning's back was to Philip, and only when he was a few feet away did Lightning stir, cocking his head and then whirling around awkwardly. He pointed his rifle at Philip.

Philip held out his palms, stunned that Lightning would point the gun at someone coming from this direction. But then he understood—he had woken Lightning up. The guard blinked as if shedding the fog of his dreams, and his voice was slurred.

"Wha—whoozat?"

"It's me. Philip Worthy," he said, cautiously stepping into the glow from the lamps.

Lightning lowered his rifle. He was swaying a bit, as if sleep might conquer him again at any moment.

"You all right?" Philip asked.

"Yeah, yeah, fine." Lightning had a deep and thick voice. "You s'prised me."

"You the only one out here tonight?"

"Yeah. There're usually"—a slow yawn—"two of us here, but now too many guys are sick." Consciousness gradually returned to Lightning's large brown eyes. "So, uh, why are you out here?"

Philip swallowed, steeling himself once more. "I want to talk to Frank."

"Who's Frank?"

"The soldier. In there."

The gears in Lightning's head turned slowly. "You mean the spy?"

Philip nodded. He still couldn't refer to Frank that way.

"I can't let you do that. Nobody goes in and nobody goes out, except when we feed him his meals."

"He's not sick, is he?"

"Who, the spy? No, he's healthy. But—"

"I'm going in there. I won't be long. Don't worry about it." Philip took a couple of steps toward the door he had once been trapped behind.

"Philip, you can't do that." Lightning sounded neither stern nor threatening—he mostly sounded stunned that someone was disobeying the rules. It was as if this possibility hadn't occurred to him, and now that it was happening, he was powerless to stop it.

"Then shoot me," Philip said as he kept walking. Even if Lightning had been unarmed, holding Philip back would have been a simple task for a man his size. But the thought of using his strength that way probably didn't occur to him. Philip heard Lightning curse himself, bemoaning his bad luck that the rules should be broken on his shift. "I'll be right back," Philip promised.

Philip opened the door. Immediately, the smell of the place brought everything back: dead wood and twigs coupled with the odor of men locked up, of air that didn't circulate. And the darkness: as soon as he shut the door, it was as if a hood had been placed over his head by an invisible executioner. He stood there for a moment, hoping his eyes would adjust, and gradually saw a faint light trickling up the cellar stairs. He made his way toward it, shuffling his feet lest he trip over something.

"Hello?" he asked hesitantly, but heard no reply. They must be keeping him in the cellar, Philip decided. His deliberate footsteps made little sound, and he wondered if Frank was awake down there. When they'd been prisoners together, they had gone to sleep early, for lack of anything better to do. Now that Frank was completely alone, the boredom could only have intensified, laying slow siege to his mind.

Philip's footsteps on the wooden stairs were louder. "Hello?" he called out again.

"Yeah?" The voice was quiet, subdued by layers of anger, resentment, resignation. The face wasn't much better.

Frank was sitting on the ground, a few feet from the lamp, leaning against a wooden beam to which his feet were apparently chained. The growth on his cheeks had thickened into a full-fledged beard, and a mangy one at that. His hair was disheveled and looked darker than before, probably from the dirt he'd been sleeping on, and his forehead was sooty as a miner's. There was a blanket beside him and, in the corner of the room, the latrine bucket. The lamp cast its shadows upward, so Philip couldn't quite see Frank's eyes—they looked like dark holes cut into a mask behind which no man stood.

"Philip," Frank said, mild surprise in his voice. Philip couldn't tell if Frank had been asleep, but his overall demeanor and appearance was that of an eremite hiding in his cave, only recently stirred from a long hibernation. "Been a while."

Philip saw that Frank's wrists were crossed and bound by thick rope. On the ground a few feet away from him lay his billfold, containing the photograph of his beloved back in Montana.

"So what's happening in the outside world?" Frank's voice was cautious, with a hint of friendliness but no more.

Philip thought. "Well, for one, I kissed that girl I told you about."

"Attaboy. She slap you?"

"No, but she should have—her mother's real sick with the flu. Doc doesn't think she's going to make it."

"I'm sorry to hear that."

"She's not the only one. Dozens of people are sick, and a few have died already." He knew he sounded angry, and he was glad; he felt an urge to strike Frank. He stepped closer, only a few feet away, and that was when he saw that one of Frank's cheeks was bruised, a large welt gone yellowish beside his right eye. Maybe he had fought back when they'd first chained him up, Philip thought. The appeal of violence disappeared as abruptly as it had flashed through his mind.

"So why should she have slapped you?"

"People think I have something to do with the flu getting into town. For letting you in here."

Frank looked away. "You know I don't have anything to do with the flu."

"I don't know anything."

"Maybe you don't. Maybe none of us do." Frank's voice was calm, dreamlike. It sounded almost like he was talking to himself, or imagined that he was. "Maybe we're just here to run around for a while until we die."

"Or until someone else kills us."

"Yeah." Frank eyed him carefully. "You know, I really wanted you to kill me, Philip. Not at first, obviously, but after you got the drop on me. Down on my knees. I really wanted you to do it."

"Why? So you wouldn't have to try and kill me?"

"I did try to kill you. You were right when you said that—if I hadn't tripped out there, I would have shot you dead. You're a lucky bastard."

"Then why did you want me to . . ." Philip couldn't finish the question.

And Frank couldn't answer it, apparently. He swallowed, and when he spoke again, his voice was different, thicker but also weaker. As if he had just emerged from a nightmare, one that had left him badly shaken.

"You've gotta get me out of here, Philip." He sounded desperate, a tone of voice he'd never adopted before, not even when Philip had been pointing a gun at him.

"Why?" Philip thought of Elsie crying on his shoulder. "Why in hell should I help you?"

"Because otherwise they'll hand me to the army to hang."

"Because you're a spy?"

Frank shook his head. "They have you thinking I'm a spy, too?"

"All I know is what you told me."

Frank raised his voice. "Philip, I'm not a spy. I don't even know a word of German. I was doing my duty to my country, and now I'm being held prisoner by a town full of men who didn't even register."

"So what's this about dead soldiers and spies, goddammit? What in hell am I supposed to think? *Who are you?*"

"I'm who I said I was. My name is Frank Summers. I'm a carpenter from Missoula, Montana. I got a father and a little sister, and I'll bet they're shaking their heads right now, trying not to believe the lies the army's telling 'em about me. I need your help, Philip. If you don't let me out of here, I'm a dead man."

Philip was close enough to see a pleading light flicker in Frank's eyes.

"I mighta thought I deserved to die out in the woods," Frank continued, "but I'm not thinking of myself right now, you understand? I'm thinking of my girl, of my old man and my family. It's them that shouldn't have to mourn me, to hear those lies and feel shamed."

"What are you talking about?"

"I did lie to you—I wasn't in a naval accident. And if the wonderful people of this town had let me go after forty-eight hours like they'd promised, I wouldn't have headed back to Fort Jenkins—I would have run to Canada or died trying. I got some family out there, cousins of my old man. I figured I could hide there till after the war ended, then maybe . . ." He shook his head.

"So you're a deserter?"

"I am not a deserter." Frank said that with an angry pride. "I was ready to get to that goddamned front and kill as many Heinies as they could point me at."

Philip waited. Then: "So you're not a spy and you're not a deserter. Then why are you here?"

Frank sat in silence for a moment, head down. The shadows from the lamp crawled up his forehead. "Remember that other soldier you told me about? The one in the grave by the road into town?"

"Yeah."

"Well, I'm just like you, kid. I'm a murderer."

XII

The first time I saw the C.O. he was getting the hell beaten out of him by two Poles. I was leaving mess and was ready to collapse into my cot—we'd done extra drilling that day and had marched for hours through mud so thick you'd lose your boots after one step if you didn't lace them up extra tight. But as I passed the door I heard the racket coming from outside, the shouting and the ruckus, and wondered what the hell was going on. Was there big news from the front? Or an armistice? Or had they reopened the brothels just outside of town?

I walked out and saw a circle of men standing in the mud. One of them was a guy I knew pretty well, a blond kid named Ollie, so I sidled up next to him. He was smiling. Everybody was smiling.

Except the C.O.—the conscientious objector. He was in the middle of the circle, and he wasn't wearing a shirt; his stomach and chest were pockmarked with bruises, some dark blue and some a fresher shade of red. I didn't know the C.O.'s name but I knew what he was, had seen him cleaning halls and carrying garbage like the others. I didn't exactly know what was going on, but I knew better than to ask stupid questions.

"All right," one of the Poles said, handing a broom handle to his buddy. "Your turn."

The second guy smiled and held on to the broom handle the way we'd all been taught in bayonet drills. He stood in front of the C.O., who tried to back away, but one of the men in the circle stepped forward and gave him a push in the back, setting him up.

"Take out that Hun's liver!" one of the guys in the circle yelled, perfectly mimicking our drill sergeant. Everybody laughed at the impersonation, even me. We'd all been hearing that voice in our dreams for days.

The Pole lunged forward—using not just his arms but his whole body, just as the drill sergeants preached—and jammed the end of the broom handle into the C.O.'s stomach. If it had been a bayonet, it would've taken out his liver, easy. In fact, if I knew my anatomy right, then judging from the red marks all over him he would have already lost his liver, stomach, and large intestines. He would have been put out of his misery.

"Twist it!" somebody else yelled, echoing the drill sergeant again. "You gotta twist it on its way out!"

That wasn't possible, of course, because the handle didn't break the skin. Not that this helped the C.O., whose knees had buckled under him. Everybody was laughing.

The C.O. tried to get back up, but the guy with the broom handle pressed it against his back, keeping him down there.

"You know the rules, son," one of the others said. "You hit the ground, you do forty."

The C.O. painfully assumed the push-up position. "Count 'em off, everyone!" the Pole with the broom handle shouted.

Everyone counted. I moved my mouth but didn't really say anything. I was starting to feel sick.

The C.O. was too weak from the beating to do many push-ups. He barely made it to sixteen, then his right arm slipped out from under him, sliding in the mud. The laughter grew.

"You can't give us forty, you miserable little slacker?" one of them said, and as the C.O. tried to steady himself and pick up where he left off, the guy stepped forward and lifted his other boot. He placed his boot—softly at first—on the back of the C.O.'s head and pressed it down, slowly but steadily. The C.O.'s face was in the thick mud, and the Pole leaned forward like he was curious to see how far into the mud he could press him. Pretty far, it turned out.

The C.O. tried to lift himself up and, failing at this, started to beat hell out of the mud with his arms, splashing it all over the legs of the guys closest to him. After another second or two the guy with the boot stepped back and let the C.O. come up for air.

The C.O. breathed, but first he coughed and choked and then he vomited.

I had done my best to avoid him, along with the other C.O.s. They were targets, and it didn't make much sense to stand near a target. I had heard what happened to them sometimes, but this was the first I'd witnessed it.

The C.O. was wiry and about my height—he looked like he didn't need to be such a pushover if he didn't want to be. That I just didn't understand. Maybe if he'd been a scrawny little nothing, I would have empathized more, but wasn't he bringing it all on himself? He had dark hair that was longer than everyone else's, as though the army barbers had decided to make him an easy mark. And he had a mean face. Seems a strange thing to comment on or even remember, but it was a mean face—the eyes were small and the brows hung low over them, his mouth a constant frown. It was impossible to imagine him ever smiling. Not that he had much reason to, I guess.

Everybody in the circle was a private, far as I knew. The Poles had acted like the leaders of this particular mission, and no one had seen fit to challenge them.

One of the Poles lifted the C.O. up by the armpits. He tried to let him go but it became clear that the C.O. couldn't stand on his own anymore, so the Pole held on to him.

The other one walked up real close to the C.O. From where I was standing the Pole was in profile. He looked the C.O. in the eye, and the C.O. eventually looked back.

"You know you can stop this at any time, right?" It was the first thing the Pole had said that seemed intended just for the C.O. to hear, not some disingenuous comment that was really meant for the ears of the guys surrounding them, the motley chorus. The Pole's eyes had softened somewhat, as had his tone. He was leveling with the guy. "All you have to do is give this up, Hunter. Just get in line with the rest of us."

It was the first moment of the whole ordeal that seemed human. No, wait—what am I saying? The whole mess was human: the whole disgusting, violent circus had been human. Terrifyingly human. This new appeal to the C.O. was just another aspect of that humanity, another round in the chamber.

The C.O. looked down again and coughed. That appeared to be his answer.

The Pole stepped back and held up the broom handle. "Allrighty, boys, who needs more bayonet practice?"

I nodded goodbye to Ollie and headed back inside.

That was during my second month at the camp. By then I could march as well as any jackbooted Prussian warrior, like a true doughboy. I could reach into my pack and strap on a gas mask in under seven seconds. And though I had yet to hold a real bayonet, I could be as ruthless and exacting with a broom handle as those Poles could. Still hadn't held an army firearm yet—they kept saying we'd get them soon enough—but I knew I was a good shot, from the hunting I'd always done with my old man. I tried to imagine taking aim at a human figure rather than a deer or buffalo, but it was hard to picture.

The camp was a crazy mess. It rained all the damn time—nothing like back home—and the ground was mud as far as the eye could see. We marched and drilled endlessly in the muck, and at night we were holed up in barracks that weren't big enough to accommodate all the men they'd called in. Who the hell was running this war? we'd all wonder when we were sitting around jawing after supper. Why had they called us in if they didn't have any guns or bayonets for us yet, let alone cots?

I hadn't been called in for the first draft; I think the gentlemen on the registration board had passed me over for my old man's sake. But by the time they held the third draft it was pretty much impossible to stay out unless you were missing an arm or something. It had been hard as hell to say goodbye to Michelle, and I knew in my heart that she didn't believe me when I told her I'd marry her when I got out. All the boys were saying things like that, she said. She was right about a lot of the other guys. But I meant it.

The guys in the camp were a hell of a mix. Sometimes it seemed like I was in the minority for being born in America; there were guys from Sweden, Russia, Italy, Ireland, Serbia. There were even a handful from Germany, but they usually didn't admit where they were from. You could tell, though, based on which jokes they didn't laugh at. I was amazed at how many of the recruits couldn't read or write, let alone the one who didn't know right from left. Because I'm twenty-five as opposed to eighteen or nineteen, and educated, I had a lot of guys' respect pretty quick. I even wrote out some love letters for guys who couldn't write, in exchange for some smokes.

Every time I transcribed another guy's letter, I'd think about how that guy's sentiments sounded so similar to those I'd expressed to Michelle. So the next time I wrote to her, I'd concentrate on saying something unique. Every damned thing about the place seemed so two-faced to me, and I feared that Michelle would see it in my letters.

"You don't like the way they're always beating on the C.O.s, do you?"

Ollie had asked me that at supper the day after he and I had been smoking behind the barracks and had stumbled upon the same group of guys pushing around three C.O.s. This time they'd gotten themselves some water hoses and were blasting the naked C.O.s with cold water and making them sprint through the mud. Between sprints they flogged the C.O.s with the hoses, the metal ends leaving welts on the men's backs and chests.

"I didn't say that," I said between bites of supper.

Ollie was a good kid, twenty-one and with the blond hair and clean looks that would surely win him a beautiful bride and the respect of his neighbors. The son of a Lutheran minister from Tacoma, he said that after the war he wanted to go over to the Philippines and help set up a mission.

"No, but I can tell you don't like it," Ollie said.

I wasn't sure if Ollie's question merited a response.

"The more C.O.s there are," he added, "the more of *us* land on the front lines."

"Look, I'm not happy about being sent to the trenches while those guys stay here." I took a bite, washed it down. "I'm just saying it's hard not to feel sorry for guys who are always getting teamed up on."

"The C.O.s are rotten—they're all on the kaiser's side. I say we lock 'em all up."

"Why lock 'em up when you can beat them to death instead?" I said sarcastically.

"Nobody's getting beaten to death."

"Damn close. Look, I'm not saying I agree with those yellow bastards. I'm just saying it's a little rotten"—I arched my eyebrows as I echoed his word—"the way they let a few bullies beat the hell out of 'em every day."

I'd heard somewhere that the C.O.s were supposed to be kept separate from the rest of us, as a way of preventing the beatings we were talking about. But apparently the corporal in charge of Fort Jenkins didn't agree with those orders—he thought the best way to get the C.O.s to rethink their position was to thrust them up against the guys who soon would be shipped to the trenches.

"It works on some guys," Ollie said. He pointed at a redheaded Irish kid on the other end of the mess hall. "Look at O'Higgins—he dropped the act."

O'Higgins had been a C.O. because he said he couldn't support Britain, which was oppressing his family back in Ireland. But after a few weeks of beatings, he'd changed his tune, as a lot of C.O.s tended to do. Now O'Higgins was marching with the rest of us, learning how to survive a mustard gas attack and wield a broomstick like a weapon of vengeance.

"So maybe I'm wrong." I shrugged and swallowed some mashed potatoes. This wasn't a wise argument to be having, I knew, so I let Ollie win, and I changed the subject.

I wasn't against the war, but I didn't like anything that kept me away from Michelle. I wasn't alone—you could tell that a lot of the guys lacked the spirit that had oozed out of the fellows who'd reported with the first draft, about a year ago. The steady lists of war dead made us less excited to be there, but we had no choice, so we did our part.

The C.O.s acted like they had a choice, though, and that's what made everyone hate them. You still got drafted if you were a C.O.; they sent you to the camp along with everyone else and made you dig ditches or do laundry or clean toilets until you saw the light. And Ollie was right: the C.O.s would still be here scrubbing urinals while the rest of us were sent out to France to have our heads blown off in some rat-infested trench. That thought made scrubbing a urinal sound almost inviting.

After supper, I stood at the urinal pissing and thinking about the C.O., thinking about trenches and grenades and getting beaten by a water hose every night. Fuck them, I decided. They were getting off easy.

We drilled endlessly. Someone had said we would only be there for two months before we were shipped off, but eventually I'd been there three months. The latest rumor was that we'd be getting real bayonets in a week, but no one really knew anything.

We also learned they had called off the next draft on account of the flu. Fort Jenkins was too sick—and so were all the other camps across the country, apparently—so they didn't want to be sending any germs to the front lines. The formerly overcrowded barracks were becoming more comfortably populated as fellows kept disappearing into the infirmary.

The sick would soon be returning, we figured, but many were gone so long we started wondering. They never told us when a sick soldier died, but we knew it was happening. Word got around.

One night I was coming back from a game of cards at the YMCA and I saw someone sitting in the mess hall. It was late enough that we weren't supposed to be in there, so I took an extra step forward to see who it was. It was the C.O., the one I'd seen being used as a bayonet target a few weeks back. He was eating a bowl of oatmeal in the huge, empty room, crisply dressed in the white shirt that made all the C.O.s stand out.

For some reason I walked into the mess hall. The C.O. looked up right away, reminding me of a squirrel when it first notices you coming toward it. A darting motion of the head, followed by a second or two of paralysis while it assesses the possibility of imminent danger.

"Evening," I said with a curt nod, thinking I sounded harmless.

He nodded back and said the same, only more quietly. He had small eyes that hid beneath his brows, protected from the world by an angular face and a craggy jaw that looked like it'd cut your hand if you hit it.

"Mind if I sit down?"

"'S fine," he mumbled. There was plenty more oatmeal in his bowl but he made no motion to continue eating, as if afraid I would ram the spoon down his throat. He kept his eyes off of mine, just to the side.

"I'm Frank Summers."

"Lyle Hunter." He had an odd voice, some kind of second-generation accent I couldn't place. Hunter must have been a new name his family had taken when they got off the boat.

"How long you been at the camp?"

"'Bout two months."

I'd never been in the mess hall when it was deserted. Maybe the C.O.s were supposed to eat when others weren't around, but then again I'd seen them at regular mealtimes, too. All I knew was I was running a risk even being there, so I decided to cut to the chase.

"Why are you a C.O.?"

For the first time, he looked directly at me. Warily. "What's it to you?"

That sounded more testy than tough, especially given the way he averted his eyes again after saying it. His head was at a low angle, like he was too used to cowering.

"Maybe I'm just curious. Look, if I was interested in insulting you, I could always join in with the gang pushing you around every night."

I figured he would've been flattered I gave a damn, but to my surprise he uttered a short sigh, as if he'd been bombarded by well-meaning questioners such as myself.

"I object to this war. That's all I need to say."

"What, you think I'm a rat?"

No response.

"Why'd you even enlist? Why didn't you run off and hide someplace?"

"Just because I object to the war doesn't mean I have to be yellow," he said.

"You know they're going to keep riding you until they're sent off, right? And then new ones'll take their place?"

"Why do you care?"

I thought about that. "Maybe I don't like seeing guys get pushed around all the time."

"You think you're going to see any less of it in France?"

"That's different."

"Sure."

"Why don't you just give it up and drill with the rest of us? With any luck, the war'll be over before we ever make it to France. It's not like you'll have to do anything."

"I'm not compromising myself like that."

"For God's sake, a few bayonet drills aren't going to turn you into a killer. I've been drilling for three months and I'm not an animal."

He eyed me strangely. "You aren't?"

I waited a second to make sure I'd heard him right. Then I leaned back. "The hell is that supposed to mean? Jesus, I come here to talk to you, and you insult me. You're a real piece of work, you know that? No wonder you've got a target on your back."

I expected him to take it back, but he didn't say anything.

I got out of my chair suddenly, and he moved back a bit. As I walked out, I half expected him to call something out to me—I think I even wanted him to—but there was nothing except the sound of my steps echoing on the stairs, soon followed by the familiar chorus of the barracks before lights-out: the betting of cardplayers, yawns, laughter, coughing.

When you're told how your great-grandfather died fighting for the Confederacy, you start thinking you're the flag bearer for lost causes. Emmett Summers died at Antietam, I've always been told, leaving behind my granddad, who was ten at the time and, years later, wandered out west in search of God knows what. But what exactly was the lost cause here? I suppose the C.O. was fighting a lost cause, insisting on pacifism in the face of militarism. Maybe me thinking that I could make it through the war and emerge more or less unscathed—maybe that was the lost cause. Maybe Michelle was my lost cause. Trench warfare sure sounded like a lost cause, but you weren't supposed to talk like that, or even think it. Maybe there's just something deep inside me—some indefinable yearning, some deeply buried part of my great-granddaddy's soul—that wanted to find one more lost cause to fight for. That has to be the only explanation for what happened the next night.

I was returning from the YMCA, though I hadn't played any cards. Hadn't been in the mood. Instead I'd sat there pretending to read magazines, when really I had slipped letters from Michelle into them, so I could reread them without looking like a lovesick fool. Her last few letters had seemed less intimate, but I wasn't sure if that was in the writing or in my head.

I missed being with her, seeing the way she looked at me. One thing was bothering me particularly: if something happened and I did die in the war, or died of the flu before I even shipped out, Michelle would probably mourn me but would forever think that my wish to marry her had been a lie, something foolish and romantic I had said only because it seemed the thing to do. I wouldn't be around to prove that my intentions had been genuine, that I was genuine.

So I was in a rotten mood as I headed back to the barracks. It was nearing lights-out and it had started raining. I could easily hear the sounds coming from the back of the barracks as I walked past.

A cry of pain from somewhere out of sight sounds so unnatural, like a voice from another world. But I knew where it was really coming from.

I reached the door to the barracks and, since no one was behind me, I headed into the mess hall. I wiped my boots carefully on the mats at the threshold, careful not to track any mud on the recently scrubbed floors. The C.O. had been scrubbing them when I left. Now he was being tortured in the storeroom.

I walked through the empty mess hall toward the door leading to the storeroom. The sounds grew louder. It didn't sound like such a crowd this time, maybe only a few of them. Because it was a swivel door I was able to prop it open the barest amount with my shoe and peer inside. I saw something dark flash in the air, followed by a whipping sound and a whelp of pain. Then I saw the C.O., shirtless again, fall down. He was picked back up by one of the Poles, who turned him around again so that his back was presented to a guy whose back was also to me. The C.O.'s back was a vicious shade of red, some of the streaks three-dimensional. The other guy took a step and whipped him again.

"Damn, you got my fingers," said the guy who'd been holding the C.O. He said it with a laugh and shook out his hands. The C.O. was on the floor again.

They were standing in a narrow hallway beyond which was the storeroom, stocked with food and linens and the barracks' laundry facilities. Two dull lightbulbs glowed above them but the rest of the corridor was in shadow.

Then I saw that the rumor about the new firearms was true: there was a third bully in the room, and he was holding a bayonet. It was shiny and metallic and its long incisor smiled in the dim light.

"Pick up the Heinie bastard," said the one with the bayonet. He was a big Italian kid with dark hair and dark eyes; he was one of the few guys who never seemed tired after a full day of marching.

"Time for bayonet practice," said the one who'd been doing the flogging, whose name was Sepenski. His hair was sweaty and his sleeves were rolled up. He was a big kid, too, but not as big as the wop with the bayonet.

The C.O.'s chest and stomach were red from punches or broom handles.

"Just let me go," he choked.

It was the first time I had heard him beg during any of the ordeals I'd witnessed. Maybe it was the blade, or the fact that they were more secluded this time. Everything felt more sinister.

I put my hand on the door but something kept me from pushing it open.

The Pole who'd been holding the C.O. picked up his wounded prey again. He was no bigger than the C.O. himself, but he seemed to believe he was as big as his buddy Sepenski. He talked tough and always mentioned Chicago, where he'd grown up, so most guys just called him Chicago.

Sepenski backed away, giving the wop room. Chicago held the C.O. in a headlock, the C.O.'s arms jutting out at two o'clock and ten o'clock, his white and red chest exposed. Surely they weren't going to do this. The wop held the bayonet in the position we'd been trained to, his arms and back locked into the posture that I sometimes found myself adopting out of habit.

"Don't get me," Chicago warned his buddy in a somewhat quieter voice.

"Don't worry," the wop said. Like the two Poles, he had the barest of accents; he'd been born here and wanted everyone to know he was as American as guys like me. More, even.

Then the C.O.'s arms started flailing in a last desperate attempt to break free. But Chicago kept him in place and the wop lunged forward and grunted and his back blocked my view of what happened, but I heard the C.O. let out a high-pitched, muffled yelp through gritted teeth.

The wop's arms jutted to the right, dislodging the blade, and he stepped away. I could see the C.O. again and his chest and stomach were still red but no more so than before. Then I saw the gash in his right pant leg, filling with blood. They'd given it to him in the thigh.

For a few seconds I heard only the sounds of breathing: the bullies' deep breaths, in shock and awe at their own actions. The C.O.'s jagged breaths, choked off by pain and fear.

Finally I pushed the door open the rest of the way and walked in.

"Evening, boys," I said to them. "Everything all right?"

"Everything's jake," Sepenski said. They had all turned my way, but nobody wore a guilty expression.

"What say you call it a night? It's getting close to lights-out." I was a private just like them, but I was hoping my age would buy me some authority, that military discipline would kick in and they'd obey without stopping to wonder why.

But the wop said, "We have plenty of time. We have to break in the bayonet—he still needs something for the other leg."

"Where'd you get that?" I asked.

"What's it to you?"

I shrugged. "Just jealous. I've been waiting on mine for months."

He smiled, relieved to see I was no threat. My hands were in my pockets. I looked over at the C.O. Chicago had picked him back up. The wop handed the bayonet to Sepenski, who would apparently have the privilege of inflicting the second wound.

"Give me a shot at him," I said.

"I get the next one," Sepenski protested.

"I don't mean with that." I gestured to the bayonet and wrapped my left fingers around my right fist. "Just give me a shot at him."

The wop, who had stepped back, nodded. "Sure. Take your best shot."

I looked at the C.O., held up by Chicago. His head was hanging low, as if he'd passed out, but we all knew he hadn't—we could tell from his breathing, from his whimpers. The blood was running down his pant leg and pooling at the tip of his boot.

Maybe I figured if I could knock him out with one good punch, it'd end his misery for the night. If I hadn't walked in, they probably would have gone for the vital organs after the two legs, then the testicles. Maybe

I figured one hard punch could be forgiven if it would help the poor bastard keep his manhood. Such as it was.

"Hey," I said to the top of his head. "Look me in the eye, you sorry sonuvabitch."

A couple seconds passed, then he obeyed, lifting his head to face me. If he was at all surprised to see me, he didn't show it. I was just another one of the thousands of militants in the other camp. I was the enemy.

He did look like a sorry sonuvabitch. But his face was unmarked—they knew well enough to hit him in places that wouldn't show the next day when he was suited up and pushing his mop. They wouldn't like it if I gave him a shiner or broke his nose. We'd all have some explaining to do.

He was such a weak bastard, I thought as I inhaled, taking in the strength I would need for what I had decided to do.

"Pop the yellowbelly," Chicago said.

I made a fist and swung straight for Sepenski's ugly and smiling mug. Caught him square on the nose, so hard that his head snapped back and hit the wall behind him. He had only begun to fall down when I turned and drove the tip of my right boot between the wop's legs. His body crumpled, the bayonet falling out of his hands and clattering on the floor a second before his knees hit the ground. He rolled over to his side, howling an inhuman moan. I turned back to Chicago and the C.O. but they weren't there. They had disappeared. Then something caught me around the neck and I spun.

Chicago had dropped the C.O. and come for me, putting me in a headlock. I saw the C.O. lying there, saw the wop beside him, on his side and kicking his feet in this unnatural rhythm, saw the unconscious Sepenski off to the side, his back leaning against the wall and his face and jaw dripping with a steady stream of blood from his broken nose. Then the room started dancing before me as I swung around, trying to break free of Chicago. He wasn't as big as he thought he was and I sure as hell wasn't as meek as his last prey had been, and I was able to drag him behind me as I tried to shake him off. He had a good grip, though, and I couldn't break loose. I could feel my face burning.

I slipped some of my fingers beneath one of his arms and tried to pry it loose, but I couldn't manage it. So I stepped back with one leg and leaned forward, lifting at least one of his feet off the ground. We were off-kilter dancers, and I felt the balance of our union slipping from his feet to mine. I jerked forward even more, lifting both his feet off the ground, but he wouldn't let go. I twisted to the side and slammed his body into the wall. He still had me. My temples were pounding and my neck was on fire. I slammed him into the wall again, and again. Everything before me had gone black—I was as blind as my sister. Then I slammed him into the wall a final time and he squealed and his body went limp.

Very limp. The vise around my neck opened wide and his arms fell around me like those of a marionette, lifeless as wood and string. I heard him land behind me in a heap. I was about to turn and look at him when the vision now returning to my eyes struck me with all its gruesome horror.

The C.O., his face red and his eyes wide, was drooling with rage as he knelt there stabbing Sepenski with the bayonet again and again and again. The Pole's shirt was soaked through with blood and there was blood on the wall behind him and blood spilling onto the ground where he was sitting. Next to him the wop was lying not as he'd been before but on his back, staring up at those two naked lightbulbs through wide and motionless eyes. The C.O. had already dealt with him, had already torn his shirt into wet red shreds, had left him lying in a pool of his own wasted life, widening before my eyes.

The C.O. kept stabbing. The bayonet slid out easily, no twisting required. There were no broomsticks and no drill sergeants and no life before me, none. I was surrounded by death and I could barely move, could barely think, could barely cry: "Stop!"

I said it again, and the C.O. finally obeyed—after a final deep lunge with the bayonet that went so far in and stuck to something so solid that when he let go, it stayed there, hovering over Sepenski's chest like some horrific and final extension of himself.

The C.O. fell back onto his hands, then pushed himself against the opposite wall, staring at the body of his tormentor. His face was rigid but oddly shivering, as if at any moment he might scream or howl or bawl uncontrollably. With an unsteady hand he wiped away the spit that had dripped down his chin, but his eyes stayed on Sepenski.

I looked back at Chicago and saw that he was as dead as his buddies.

There was no blood, but his neck was bent at an impossible angle. It was as revolting a sight as that of his eviscerated companions. He was staring off above me, as if looking for the protector who should have stopped me from killing him.

"Oh my God," I said, or whispered, or thought, or moaned. The wop's blood was still flowing, its pool almost reaching me. I realized how much my right hand hurt, I felt the cuts and bruises on my neck, I bit back the pain I felt when swallowing. I could barely swallow, barely breathe.

I stood up, stepped forward, and vomited, resting my hands against the wall as I spat everything up. I closed my eyes and tried to will away the savage butchery that surrounded me. Coughing and choking on whatever was left inside me, I tried to steady myself, tried to think.

Beyond the C.O.'s shivers was silence. No sound of anyone running toward us, no one about to kick open the door. The whole ordeal had somehow been quiet enough to escape detection. Soon it would be lights-out; the quartermaster and maybe the sergeants would be patrolling the halls upstairs, would possibly even poke through the storeroom.

The shock was so overwhelming that not until later did I think maybe I could have concocted some story. Perhaps I could have cast myself as merely the luckiest victim of the C.O.'s deadly rampage. But right then all I was thinking was that I had killed someone, a soldier, and that the other two dead soldiers beside him may as well have been struck down by my hands. I had to get out of there.

I stood up and looked around. There was a door at the end of the hallway that was always locked from the inside. The C.O. had staggered to his knees, breaking free of his maddened state. He saw me looking at the door, then moving toward it.

"Where . . . where are you going?" he stammered.

I shook my head. Our barracks was located at the northeastern corner of the camp. Not too far away, trucks full of food and supplies were unloaded; surely those trucks had to go out, too. I didn't know the schedule or how I could get into a truck, but that seemed my best shot to get away from the cantonment.

I must have explained this to the C.O., or maybe he just understood it, because he threw on his shirt and tunic and followed me out. He followed as I walked through the dark camp, hiding in the shadows beside the buildings. I watched every window we passed, hoping no face would appear and spot us, hoping the silence would not be torn by an alarm, hoping I was the only one who could hear my thundering heartbeat, hoping the tracks we were leaving in the mud would not become an easily followed trail to our capture, hoping the bodies would not be discovered until we had escaped, hoping I would wake up in my uncomfortable army cot and shake my head at this horrible, tortured dream.

I remember him lying beside me in the back of a truck. I remember us overhearing the inane banter of the men driving it. I remember our bodies being jostled against each other as the truck made its way through the dark and uneven world beyond our base, a land defined for us only by the bumps in the road and the silence outside. I had no idea what towns the camp was nearest to, didn't know the roads or whether there were any railway lines nearby. I remember the C.O. wincing when bumps in the road jostled him, I remember smelling something that might have been his blood. I remember being cold back there, I remember hearing the C.O. put on a jacket that he found in the back, and I remember quietly removing a pistol from a crate and the C.O. finding a rifle for himself. He was a pacifist no more. He no longer had the luxury.

Sheer terror kept us from sleeping those long hours. I didn't know which direction we were headed, only that I was being taken farther from home. My neck ached and I touched my fingers to my throat, half expecting to feel Chicago's dead arm wrapped around me, but all I could feel was my pulse.

XIII

Long after listening to Frank's story, Philip still pondered it. A few blocks from the Worthy home, he sat on an old swing that he and Graham had hung from a fir tree a couple of years ago. It was cold out, and the swing wasn't the most comfortable of seats, but he needed a private place to think.

He believed Frank's story about the C.O. Frank had recounted his experience stone-faced at first, his voice calm in the manner of someone who had relived something a thousand times. The empty room perfectly complemented the hollow tone in his voice. He had killed a man and done it in a way that had amounted to killing himself, his tone seemed to be saying. Only now did Philip wonder how much of the despair came from the ramifications of his act—not being able to return home to his family, to Michelle—and how much was a reaction to the act itself, of feeling the dead body roll off his shoulders, of seeing the stillness in the other men's eyes.

As he spoke, Frank's cheeks were streaked with tears, though his face remained grave. Not until the end of his story did his voice thicken and his eyes turn red and his shoulders start to shake. Soon he couldn't talk, and the two of them just sat in silence, momentarily held captive by the weight of his memories.

I'm just like you, Frank had prefaced the tale, and that thought chilled Philip more than the wind that cut through his coat. It was getting late, and Philip was probably the only person in town who wasn't inside, except perhaps Doc Banes. Philip had felt a loneliness—a complete desolation—for days, ever since the encounter with the first soldier. Ever since seeing him fall to the ground as a result of what he and Graham had done. What Graham had done. What he and Graham had done. Which? Or both?

The loneliness had intensified each time he'd seen Graham walk past or stand there as if he did not recognize Philip as a friend, did not acknowledge him as a man who had been through the same terrors, did not want to accept the fact that they were somehow joined in this, awash in the same confusing swirl of emotions. Or maybe they weren't—maybe Graham's heart and mind were forever unknowable to Philip; perhaps the quarantine had forever separated them, driving them each down different paths that would never again intersect.

Yet Philip recognized what he had seen in Frank's eyes, and he felt a strange kinship. Perhaps it had been there all along, and that was why they had befriended each other. Each was trying to hide from something he'd done, some body they'd left behind, unsure of their reasons, doubtful of the purity of their motives. Philip hadn't seen that in Graham's eyes, but it was in Frank's.

Charles had said Graham was worried for his young family, that he had so much to lose. *But don't I have so much to lose as well?* Philip had wanted to shout. All his life, he had been dragged across the country in search of what he finally had: a family, a home. Now he had neighbors who knew him, a job where he could make something of himself, maybe even a future with a girl he was falling for. The thought of being responsible for the illness or death of Laura or Charles or Rebecca horrified him, had woken him up in the middle of every night over the past week. And now Elsie's mother was sick, the Metzgers shut inside their diseased home! He thought of kissing Elsie, and the rush of infatuation was rivaled only by the terror that it might be the last time he saw her healthy. Yes, he too had much to lose.

He had nothing to gain from trying to help Frank. If he somehow succeeded in letting the man loose, he risked the ire and possibly the punishment of everyone in town. He also risked Frank's capture on the way to Canada—a long and perilous journey, to be sure—and the captors learning that he'd been in Commonwealth. Surely they would pay the town a visit, asking questions. To aid him would be to risk everything Charles had created, everything the people in that town had sacrificed for. All to spare one man a trip to the gallows.

Philip thought of Elsie in her gauze mask, the way it cast her whole face in shadow. The last time he'd been faced with a decision to spare Frank, the result had somehow loosed the flu in Commonwealth. He wasn't sure how that was possible—Frank still denied ever being sick—but he couldn't deny the truth. Now he was thinking of helping Frank again, and wondering how this act might backfire as well.

The first soldier had been no spy but a conscientious objector. Not unlike Graham, who simply had not registered. The soldier had been just another victim of this rotten war, Rebecca would say. Philip kicked at a stone and then began to swing a bit, forward and back, the world before him arcing and bending like something elastic, something that could be distorted and reshaped to one's will.

It had occurred to Philip that every decision made by the town since the quarantine began had been somewhat selfish. They'd placed themselves on a pedestal above all outsiders, holding their value to be superior on pain of death. It seemed wrong, even when placed against the vision of Philip's own family falling ill. He didn't know how worthy a man he was or might become, what kind of skewed moral compass he had inherited from his mother, but he wanted to believe he was capable of selflessness. He needed to believe this.

He had looked to Graham for answers and found only silence. He had gone to Charles for explanations and found them too tortured, their logic too skewed by rationalizations. He'd find no guidance here, Philip had learned—the quarantine designed to block out the flu had only succeeded in cutting off the town from its previous ideals of right and wrong. It was a town in full eclipse, and Philip would have to navigate through the dark by himself.

"Okay," Philip had told Frank. "I'll get you out of here. But I need to figure out how."

The tears of grief that had materialized at the end of Frank's story were transformed to gratitude. *There's a set of keys somewhere*, Frank had said, *and they'll unlock these chains.* Philip told him he needed to think it through, devise a strategy. Frank had nodded, trying to understand, trying to restrain himself when for a brief moment he had thought he was only minutes away from freedom. *I'll come back,* Philip said. *Give me a day, maybe two. I need to think.*

He almost regretted having visited Frank, wished he had simply allowed the rush of kissing Elsie to carry him home. He could have fallen asleep content. Now he wanted to tell Elsie Frank's story, but he wasn't sure how she'd react, didn't know if she would understand why it was worth risking anything for this stranger. And he knew she had enough to worry about already.

Suddenly, as Philip sat on the swing, he was stirred from his thoughts by the sounds of coughing, loud and close by. He'd been sitting there for a while—he wasn't sure how long—and there had been no sound. And just like that, someone in the house was racked with coughs whose guttural bass notes throbbed against the walls, echoing in the world beyond. It can happen just like that, Philip realized. He knew who lived there: a mill-worker named Zeke who was only three years Philip's elder, and Zeke's new wife, whom he had courted in Timber Falls a few months ago. What was her name? Philip tried to remember. Red hair, pale skin, freckles all across her cheeks, a toothy smile. She was coughing badly. Then the window was illuminated, either she or her worried husband turning on the light. Fetching some water, or an extra blanket, or the Bible. The coughing became even steadier, the rat-tat-tat of a machine gun. The same sound and scene was most likely being enacted in the Metzgers' house, Flora coughing and Alfred holding a cool cloth to her forehead and Elsie praying. Philip tried to push those visions from his mind as he stood up and walked home, the coughs chasing him as far as the sound allowed them to travel, and then nothing, silence.

XIV

The next day passed in a blur for Philip, punctuated by the random sentences he scribbled to Elsie in whatever free moments he could find as he tried without success to focus on his work. He told her he was thinking of her, that the whole Worthy family, indeed the whole town, was praying that Flora would make a swift recovery. He told her how glad he was that they'd bumped into each other the night before, that he hadn't slept well because he couldn't stop thinking of her and what her family was going through. He told her he wished he could be in the house with her to help care for Flora, even though he secretly wondered whether he was a vector of illness, if his presence would finish Flora off. He told Elsie he was barely getting any work done, as if the length of the letter didn't make that obvious.

When Philip read the letter he saw that it was disappointingly disjointed, the product of the scattershot way it had been written. Whole sentences were repeated, and Philip's stomach went sour as he saw how little he seemed to be saying, how woefully inept his prose was at conveying his thoughts. But he remembered how much Elsie's letter had meant to him, so rather than tearing it up and starting again, he signed it, hoping his could have one half the effect as Elsie's had on him.

He slipped the letter under the Metzgers' door that afternoon, walking through streets so empty even the dogs had vanished. He had wanted to knock, to go inside, but knew he would be admonished for it, by Charles and by the doctor and perhaps even by Mr. Metzger. So he walked away, peering into a few windows on the first floor as he passed. The scant sunlight reflected off the glass and he couldn't see inside, didn't know if Elsie was there watching him or if she was in another room, tending to her mother. He heard no sounds from the house and wondered if that meant anything.

In the rare moments when he hadn't been thinking of Elsie, he was thinking of his promise to set Frank free. He mulled over every Houdini story he'd ever heard in search of inspiration—surely, if the Great One could escape from the jail that held President Garfield's assassin, then Philip could help Frank bust out of the storage building. Philip first needed to find out who had the keys to Frank's chains, or he would need to go into the prison armed with something that could break them. Regardless, he decided not to act that night, figuring his chances would be better the following evening when Lightning was scheduled to be on duty. He would tell Lightning he needed to talk to Frank again, then he would unlock or break the chains. Philip knew that some of the building's back walls were rotten—he and Frank should be able to find a weak spot in the back wall and create a hole big enough for a man to sneak through. Once Frank was out of the building, he would be on his own. Philip felt bad about waiting the extra day, but it seemed like the best decision.

Night seemed to fall more quickly than usual over Commonwealth. Philip's family went to bed early, everyone cautiously conserving strength. Philip sat in bed for a long while, staring out the dark window and wondering if the first snow would soon be upon them. He found himself thinking of his night in the ravine again, of Charles rushing down from the road to save him from freezing to death. Charles had trudged down the hill despite not knowing who was in the wrecked auto; he had somehow carried an unconscious Philip up the steep hill through a foot of snow. The thought of snow always left Philip quiet and anxious, but lately the memory seemed so much colder than usual.

XV

The sound that woke Elsie was one she should have been used to but wasn't: her mother's coughing. This time it sounded more like choking. Then she heard her father cry her mother's name.

Elsie ran into their bedroom. It was the middle of the night and the floor was cold on her feet. As she walked into the dimly lit room she saw the concern on her father's face, the pain in her mother's eyes.

Flora lay on her back, her head and shoulders slightly propped up on some pillows, but she was sagging from the weight of her coughs. Her hair was a disheveled mass of curls and her arms lay motionless at her sides.

When Elsie saw the gauze mask on her father's face she realized she'd forgotten her own, so she ran back to her room to fetch it. When she returned her mother was coughing again, and the sound was more horrifying up close. It wasn't a cough at all but more of a strangled wheeze, as if her throat and lungs had collapsed and she was struggling for air.

Elsie's father stood with a glass of water in his hand. "She can't swallow," he said, his voice pulled tight with worry, ready to break.

Flora hadn't spoken in over a day, had been unable to muster a single word as she lay there in the grip of her illness. Doc Banes had tried to control her coughing with codeine, to no avail. They had tried to believe that she hadn't grown worse each day, but this new change could not be ignored.

She started wheezing again, several staccato bursts followed by a mighty cough, as if she was trying to dislodge something. Elsie saw red spray in the air, saw blood on her father's mask and face.

Elsie stepped back. "Mama," she said weakly, wishing her voice could free her unresponsive mother from this spell.

She had heard that tuberculosis victims coughed blood, but flu? The doctor hadn't said anything about this—she had seen blood on his clothes a few times but had chosen to believe it was unrelated.

"She's having trouble breathing," Elsie said to her father.

"I know!" he snapped.

Now there was no occasional calm between breaths: either Flora gasped painfully or she coughed blood. Elsie put her hands over her ears to block the sound. She couldn't watch anymore, couldn't listen, but there was nowhere else to go. This was all she had seen for three days, each worse than the one before, and the nights were always the worst.

Alfred dabbed at his wife's lips, wiping away some blood with a handkerchief. The wheezing became higher-pitched.

Elsie swallowed. "I should get Doc Banes." She looked at her mother's face and wondered if it was turning dark or if that was just the lamp dimming.

Her hands were still so tight over her ears that she barely heard her father say, "Yes, hurry!"

XVI

It was dark when Graham rode on Mo's horse along the lonely road leading to the old storage buildings. Half a mile away Graham could hear the river faintly, the water running along the rocks by the riverbed. He felt as though the world around him had been nearly purged of sound but that he, an instrument of God or at least of his own decisive actions, was deafeningly loud, that the slow clops of his horse were shaking the earth and making the trees sway, that the deep rhythm of his heartbeat was chasing the nocturnal animals deeper into the woods. This was not nervousness, he felt—this was conviction.

Deacon was the lone guard at that hour, and he turned and nodded when he saw Graham approach.

Graham dismounted and tied the horse—which Mo had named Icarus because he'd thought that was what you called a horse with wings—to a post.

"Didn't think you'd be coming till later," Deacon said.

Graham replied that he'd had nothing better to do. "Why don't you head home," he suggested after a few minutes. "You've already been out here a while. I can stare at a building just fine myself."

"You sure?" Deacon did not sound surprised at the offer; he knew that other men didn't like being alone with him. All those years of silence, of not hearing God call out to him, had made him different. In a group he could be ignored or insulted, but when there was only one other guy with him, that guy would start to feel funny being around a taciturn ex-priest, especially an ex-not-quite-priest who invented his own cuss words and frequented prostitutes.

Graham insisted, reminding Deacon that he had already been out for a few hours, and Deacon complied. He said good night and started walking home, the silence following him.

Graham stood there alone. The wind picked up a bit, just loud enough to blanket the sound of the river.

The day before, Graham had guarded the house of a sick man for six hours. But today Doc Banes had told him that the guarding of sick houses was no longer necessary, that the sickness had spread so quickly across town that Graham's sentry duty the day before had been useless. Graham did not like thinking of himself as useless.

Doc Banes had given up—Graham could see it in the old man's eyes. Banes was not long for this world, and he probably wouldn't mind if all of the human race was wiped out in the next few months: all the more souls to escort him on his journey to the afterlife. Graham wasn't so sure he believed in an afterlife, but whether or not there was anything beyond, he was still determined to make this world as hospitable and safe as possible while he remained.

Frank had barely slept the last few days. There was nothing to tire him, nothing to tax his body or spirit, and long after eating the meager suppers they'd given him, he would sit there thinking, his mind more places than he could control. He thought of Sepenski and the other dead soldiers, thought of their laughter and their taunts, thought of the C.O. and his weak attempt at push-ups and the water hose and the broomsticks that had turned into bayonets. If only they'd stayed broomsticks. He thought of Michelle and wondered where she was, what she thought of him. He thought about his family being told that he was a deserter, which would have been bad enough. But a spy? Surely they would know better, would refuse to look those army officers in the eye as they spouted their drivel. They would steadfastly hold on to their vision of Francis Joseph Summers as an upstanding and patriotic and God-fearing man. The only thing Frank wasn't sure of was whether that vision was accurate any longer or if he had forever dispelled it with his actions.

His mind was doing things to him. He was certain one time that Michelle was there with him, that she was upstairs, that the people of this forsaken town had for some reason invited her in. Maybe they thought she could get him to confess to being a spy. She had stood at the top of the stairs and said she would come down only when he told the truth. He'd replied that he *had* told them the truth, but she chastised him for being dishonest with her. Finally he had screamed at her and she stopped talking, walked away. Another time he felt himself reenacting a conversation with his father, a long talk about duty and honor and all the reasons why enlisting was the right thing to do. It was a talk they'd had several months ago, and Frank had agreed with everything his father had said, only this time Frank found himself taking a contrary opinion. What the hell's so honorable about it? Duty to whom? To myself, or to the guys who would be fighting without me, or to the people here at home afraid of the Hun? Or duty to President Wilson, or to Carnegie, or to God, or to all the fallen soldiers before me, to Great-granddad Emmett and his bleached bones down at Antietam? His father had shaken his head at him and walked away—not at all how the conversation had ended the first time, when Frank's father had stepped forward and suddenly hugged his son, something he'd never done before.

But Philip's visit—that had been real, right? Frank had thought otherwise at first, had figured it was the latest trick of his mind. But at some point he realized that this really was an actual person visiting him and talking to him—unlike the guards, who always brought the food and never said a word, their dry lips sealed behind gauze masks. Philip wore no mask and wanted to talk, wanted to hear Frank's voice, to know him again. And the emotion that had been bottled up in Frank, then shaken and crammed into too small a space, had exploded, pouring out, and not until he had stopped shaking did he realize that it was the prison of his memories more than that of the chains that was so unbearable.

Philip's visit—that had been yesterday, hadn't it? Philip had said he would come back to free Frank. Had it been only a day? The absolute lack of sunlight in the prison was no longer bothersome to Frank; it had become expected. How long had it been since he was outside? Over a week, perhaps. He thought of the clouds and the sun melting the mountaintops in the distance beyond Missoula, of the vultures and buzzards that hung in the summer sky, of the kites he'd flown with his sister, who could not see them but loved the feel of the wind tugging at her hand as she grasped the roll of string, who thrilled at the knowledge that she was a part of something vast and overwhelming and beautiful, even if it was invisible.

Frank and the C.O. had escaped from the truck when it stopped at an outpost in a town they didn't know, had marched through the surrounding forest all through the remainder of the night and continued to march the next day. They didn't know where they were going, only that they would soon be pursued and therefore needed to create distance.

They found a place to sleep, a high spot that had stayed reasonably dry despite the rains. They had lain there beside each other, silent. At some point Frank had started crying and so had the C.O., and Frank saw the C.O. shaking his head over and over and saw him shivering and then Frank realized he was, too, and as they lay there in the cold they leaned in to each other and then clasped each other closer. Frank remembered the sound of the C.O.'s tears and the feel of the C.O.'s tensed fingers digging into his shoulders, remembered the feel of the C.O.'s tunic on his face as he buried his tears in it. They had lain there until they fell asleep, crying onto each other's shoulders and holding each other tight for warmth and for reassurance that they weren't completely alone in their fate.

They spoke little the next day. It didn't occur to Frank until later that the C.O. had never thanked him for his aid that night in the storeroom. Perhaps the C.O. knew that if Frank hadn't stepped in, his painful beatings may have continued but at least he wouldn't have been condemned to death, as he was now. Frank would still be an honorable soldier, waiting for the flu to pass so he could be shipped off to France. The C.O. had never thanked him and Frank didn't really feel like he deserved any thanks.

So maybe that was why Frank hated the C.O. so much. Maybe Frank blamed the whole situation on him. The morning after they had held each other, Frank had woken up and started walking. He pretended these were the woods outside Paris and that his pursuers were not the U.S. Army or police but the bloodthirsty, nun-raping Heinies, and he marched as fast as he could and never stopped, never looked back. He marched through the forest for hours, his feet sore and his stomach crying out for sustenance. He kept the road just barely in sight to his left, and when he finally took a break to relieve himself in the woods he saw that the C.O. was gone.

The sound of footsteps stirred Frank from his memories. The footsteps grew louder, tapping now down the stairs. They were heavy. Philip? The light from another lantern softly fell on the floor below, gracefully touching down without a sound except the footsteps, one and two more. And then a man standing before him, tall and strong, his face blank above the gauze mask but the skin around his eyes pulled tight in concentration. It was the man Frank had struggled against when he'd first seen the chains they meant to fix on his ankles, the man who had knocked him down with one blow—the man they called Graham.

"You're awake," the man said, sounding somewhat disappointed.

"Couldn't fall asleep with all the racket," Frank replied, making a joke despite himself. Always jokes when there was no reason, always stupid comments when he was in a dire situation, like offering to do push-ups to prove to Philip that he wasn't sick. There was a large man in the room and he had brought no food and there was no overt purpose for him being here.

"Well, it's your lucky day," the guard said. He reached into his pocket, and the hand emerged with something metal and shiny. "We're letting you go."

Graham was holding a key.

"Are you with Philip?" Frank asked.

Graham eyed him strangely. "Philip's at home." Then he stepped closer with the key. "Better back up a bit."

Frank lifted himself up, his knees aching as the stiff muscles and ligaments were forced from their positions for the first time in hours. He felt the blood rush to his feet, reminding them they had a purpose.

"Thank you," Frank said, backing away so Graham could bend down and reach the lock, and then Frank heard the click he had been dreaming about. He reached forward to untangle the chains, but Graham shook him off.

"I'll do it," Graham said. "Just hold back."

Frank nodded; he couldn't tell if this man still feared him, so he tried to act as harmless and compliant as possible.

After the chains were removed, Graham stood back up and took from his pocket a thick knife five inches long. "Better give me your hands," he said.

Frank stepped forward, closer to Graham, and lifted his arms, presenting his bound wrists. The rope was thick and he hoped Graham would be able to cut the coils without digging into his wrists, especially since they had been bound palms-up, exposing his steel-blue veins. But after Graham put one hand on Frank's wrists, the blade shifted in Graham's clenched fist and his arm lunged forward. Frank felt first a long pinch, as if the skin of his chest were being grabbed by a clawed beast, and then a hot and violent pain deep in his chest, flooding his entire body and causing every muscle to spasm. He reached forward with his nearly useless hands and tried to grab Graham's arm but the arm moved, pulling back and lunging a second time, driving the blade deeper. Frank finally grabbed hold of Graham's fist, trying in vain to break his grip on the hilt of the knife, the only part of it that wasn't jammed into Frank's muscles and bones and heart. Graham's other hand clamped down on one of Frank's. Frank slipped and his back was pressed into the wall and the blade sank deeper still and all the air was forced from his lungs. His fingers and Graham's interlocked like the opposing hands of a man praying. Frank's eyes fixed on Graham's, which were wide and determined as he forcefully exhaled and twisted the knife. Frank would never see Michelle again and never be allowed to argue his case before the military or at least his father, tell him that Dad you always said do right by God and do right by others and remember there's no difference between the two, the action that pleases one pleases the other, and Dad I swear I tried to do both even when it seemed they weren't the same, I swear I tried to do right and if I failed in that simple goal then I suppose the fault is mine, and mine alone.

Graham's fingers were still interlocked with Frank's. He finally let go and released the hilt, allowing the body to slide off the wall and onto the ground.

It had taken longer than he had thought it would; the soldier had suffered more than Graham had hoped. Graham would have liked to do it while the man slept but unfortunately that hadn't been possible. He turned around and grabbed the blanket, wrapping it around the soldier's body, covering him so most of the blood would be absorbed rather than staining the floor. There was already some blood spilled, but not much.

Graham also had blood on his fingers, blood that had seeped onto them as he'd held the blade in place and let it do its work, so he reached down and grabbed the end of the blanket and wiped them clean. He retrieved his gloves from his pockets and put them on, something he realized he should have done before. His mind had been on other things.

When he was a kid his father had bought two enormous hogs from a visiting trader, two behemoths that looked healthy as could be. But within days, the other hogs all became sick, some of them dying. Graham's father was not a rich man, and he couldn't afford to have swine fever kill off what few hogs he had to his name; nor could he afford to get rid of the two hogs that seemed to have brought the strange plague with them. Yet Graham remembered helping his father go out back one morning and slaughter those two giant beasts, killing them and burying their bodies right by the edge of their property. It was a lot of money he was burying, money spent in hopes of a good investment but costing him far more than he could have imagined. Young Graham had asked his father why they couldn't just release the two hogs—which had still seemed healthy the morning they were killed—or maybe put them in a separate pen where they wouldn't have sickened the others, but his father said it had to be done this way. They had disturbed the air somehow, and the only way to purge that disturbance was with blood. If he had let those two hogs go, the air would have remained foul, would have stayed that way forever and doomed all their livestock and possibly even the Stone family as well. His father had not relished this chore, and it would put the family in somewhat hard times for another year, but he'd had no choice, he told Graham. After the two hogs were slaughtered the remainder became healthy again, practically overnight, vindicating his father's decision.

Graham, standing over the dead man wrapped in the meager blanket, hated what he had done and hated that he'd had to do it, but that was the way it was and there was no point questioning it. Killing the soldier was what the town needed. He didn't understand why no one else could see this, or, if they indeed saw it, why everyone else had refused to act on it. This man had brought something upon the town, had fouled the air or carried a curse. He was slowly killing them off, one by one. Whether a spy or simply a soldier, he was indeed a murderer. Graham had done the right thing when the first soldier had approached, had saved the town, and by removing this soldier, he had done right again. This deed, though painful, would maintain the purity of his earlier act.

The dying would stop now, Graham knew. Maybe not right away, maybe not until a storm had washed the town clean or a good wind had blown away the rank air, but it would end soon. They would still uphold the quarantine, could still avoid the fate of Timber Falls and those other towns. They could leave those ridiculous gauze masks in a cabinet somewhere, a memento of a time they would try to forget.

Graham decided to leave the knife in the body rather than retrieving it and cleaning it. No more blood. He reached down and lifted the body, which was heavy but nothing he couldn't manage, and let it fold over his left shoulder. He grabbed his lantern and slowly made his way up the steps. Leaving the building and closing the door behind him, he carefully laid the body over Icarus. Graham climbed up behind the body and guided Icarus past the building and into the woods, along one of the old trails leading farther up the hill.

It had already been cold out, but now it felt like the temperature had dropped another ten degrees. Graham's fingers gradually lost all their heat through the insufficient gloves, and the haze of warm breath escaping through his gauze mask hung before his eyes. Icarus moved slowly and carefully, possibly spooked by the way the tree trunks looked in the lantern light, their bottom twenty feet illuminated but the rest fading into nothingness, nothing but the spirits of the forest hanging above them. Or perhaps the horse was spooked because he sensed he was carrying dead freight, that the faint wetness he felt along some of his vertebrae was the blood of a man who had been alive only moments ago. The earth crunched beneath Icarus's hooves, and Graham swayed as they proceeded along the uneven ground.

Graham rode until he reached the clearing he had been seeking. He dismounted and tied Icarus at its edge, then grabbed the soldier's body by the feet and tugged. The body slipped off the horse and landed roughly on the ground. Graham bent down and lifted the body on his shoulder again, walking to the outer circumference of the lantern's light.

The light barely traced the edges of the grave Graham had dug earlier. His shoulders and arms were still tired from the digging; each shovelful had been a painful extraction, as the earth had been wet from the recent rains and cold from the long nights. He dropped the body into the grave and looked at it down there, the way the blanket had rolled up, exposing the soldier's feet and hair. The sight of the partially covered body lying there in a filthy blanket in the dark and wet grave struck Graham in a way that even the act of killing had not. He wanted to apologize to the soldier, but he reached for the shovel and began to fill the grave.

Mo had agreed to lend Graham his horse with the understanding that Graham would use Icarus to ride the living soldier out of town, giving him a head start to someplace else. Graham had said he would ride over the back trails a few miles, far enough to get the soldier away from Commonwealth but not so far that Graham would risk bumping into anyone from the outside. The next morning Rankle and another man—who were not in on the plan; Graham knew that Rankle would not approve—would take over guard duty, and when it was time to bring the prisoner some food, they would discover him gone. They would also discover a hole in the back of the building, which Mo had secretly made that morning. No one would ever figure out how the soldier had let himself out of those chains, but it wouldn't matter—he was gone, he was part of the past.

Mo assented to the plan because he, too, was beginning to think the soldier was the problem. In truth, Mo hadn't quite understood the reasons for keeping him captive these last few days, the reasons Charles and Doc Banes had presented and Rankle had echoed. So when Graham had told him the plan, Mo had agreed, clearly pleased that all he had to do was make a hole in a wall and lend Graham his horse, then play dumb the next morning.

By the time the grave was filled, Graham's arms were so heavy he wouldn't have been able to lift them above his head if he had tried, wouldn't have been able to reach up to the heavens even if he hadn't been scared to do so. He patted down the freshly turned earth, hoping that no one would cross this way for some time, at least not until after several good rains had flattened the dirt. This was a seldom used trail, leading only deeper into the forbidding woods and hilly terrain, away from the river and the timber camps.

Graham dropped the shovel and took off the gauze mask, which had made his work all the more tiring, as if it were smothering him, his mouth and nose trapped by the wet second skin. He untied Icarus, picked up the lantern, and took a final look at the fresh grave. Then he rode back to town, past the storage buildings and beyond, back to Mo's house, where he returned the horse to the stable. The town was dark and peaceful, not even Doc Banes anywhere to be seen.

Graham's steps were slow as he made his way back to the storage buildings, where he would stand for the rest of the night, guarding a building with no one inside it, waiting for the foulness to pass.

XVII

Charles walked to work early the next morning; his sleep had been brought to a premature conclusion by nightmares about the mill failing, the town in ruins. But the waking world proved no more peaceful.

The roads were filling up as men walked to the mill, but conversations seemed especially muted. If people kept getting sick, it would be difficult for the mill to operate on its normal schedule. Charles was worried—the quarantine had already taken a financial toll on the mill, but if sickness limited production even after the quarantine ended, the mill would be in for hard times. He told himself not to worry. The mill had a massive amount of lumber ready to ship, a backlog that had been steadily building. Even if they needed to slow down production for a week or two while the men fought illness, shipping out all that lumber would pay immediate dividends. Because there was no bank in Commonwealth—something Charles hoped to remedy by persuading some Timber Falls bankers to open business in town—he had been unable to issue end-of-the-month checks to his workers. They had received IOUs that shamed Charles nearly as much as they irritated the men receiving them. Though everyone had known such IOUs were a possibility back when they had voted on the quarantine, the problem had seemed abstract at the time. With every passing day, however, it became more real.

Now that Commonwealth was infected, its residents were frightened and suspicious—people were no longer interested in communal sacrifice.

Meals were becoming smaller and less frequent as everyone dug into the recesses of their pantries and cellars. Those men who owned cows or chickens as hedges against tough times were finding that the tough times had arrived, and each day someone heard the squeal of a neighbor slaying his animals.

Still, Charles refused to believe that the flu's arrival meant the quarantine had been ineffective and should be ended. Commonwealth still wasn't as ridden with the illness as Timber Falls and other towns seemed to be, so perhaps the sick people could still be isolated; perhaps the flu could be contained.

The entire town had worked too hard and had enjoyed too many successes to be defeated by something as meaningless as an illness. Charles had created a town that his children would be proud to inherit, a town where one day his grandchildren would grow up in peace and safety. He had not allowed his brothers to ruin it, he had not allowed competing interests in Timber Falls to undercut him, and he had not allowed the logistical challenges of starting a town in a distant land to disturb the tangibility of his dreams. The flu would not stop him.

But something did stop him on his morning walk to work: broken windows at Metzger's General Store. Charles increased his pace until he reached the door, which was slightly ajar. Silence. He paused, wondering if an intruder was still inside. But then he heard a sound: a loud curse, in a voice he recognized but had never heard at such volume.

Charles stepped inside. Alfred Metzger stood in the middle aisle between bare shelves. Some flour and cornmeal had been spilled on the floor, amid empty boxes and torn sacks.

Metzger turned around when he heard Charles's boot crunch on a shard of glass. Charles hadn't seen him in days, not since Flora had taken sick and the doctor had recommended isolation. Metzger looked terrible: his hair was uncombed and his eyes were red, on the verge of tears. One of his boots was untied, laces trailing after him, and shirttails poked out from beneath his jacket.

"Look at this," he said, his voice as empty as his ransacked store.

"This happened last night?"

Metzger shrugged. "I don't know—I haven't been here for two days. I didn't have much left, but now I have nothing."

First the community gardens and now this, Charles thought. Prior to the flu, there had been only two thefts in Commonwealth's history, and both of the perpetrators had been expelled from the town. Now theft was becoming the norm, it seemed.

"Who would do this?" Metzger said almost to himself, his foot nudging aside an empty box.

Charles remembered that Metzger was potentially carrying the flu, and he felt an urge to remove the gauze mask from his pocket. But doing so would have felt like turning his back on Alfred. He let his hand fall to his pocket, but he couldn't bring himself to move any further.

He saw the blood on Metzger's shirt. "Are you hurt?" Charles asked.

Metzger gave him an utterly confused look.

Charles gestured to his shirt, and Metzger glanced down. When he looked up again, his face was unchanged, and Charles realized the look wasn't confusion but shock. "Flora died last night. She couldn't breathe."

Charles felt a quiver in his gut. For the past few days he had known Flora's life was in danger, but still he reeled from the news. "Alfred, I am so sorry."

"And now this." Metzger turned back to the empty shelves.

Charles wondered for no real reason if the two events had happened at the same time. Had Flora's chair by the front desk been knocked over just as Doc Banes had tried sedating her? Had the store windows been shattered and the last of the food stolen just as the doctor, conceding defeat with his modern methods, had taken out his knives and tried to bleed the sickness out of her? Had the thieves concluded their work here, not even bothering to close the door, just as Flora issued her last breath?

"There's nothing left," Metzger said, sifting through the debris. "I barely have any food left in my own home."

"If you want for anything, I'm sure your neighbors would help."

Metzger shook his head. "Which neighbors would that be? The ones who stopped coming to visit when they heard Flora was sick? The ones who hold their breath when they walk past our home?"

Charles looked down.

"Open your eyes, Charles! My neighbors *did* this! No one is going to feed my daughter and me but *me*!"

"*I* will feed you. If there's anything you lack, you know you can come to my home and we'll share whatever we have. You know that."

Metzger glared at him.

"I'm . . . I'm sorry I didn't visit while Flora was ill, Alfred. I was only following the doctor's instructions." Charles realized how pathetic that sounded. "I'll visit tonight, and anything that you need, I'll pro—"

"I do not want your help," Metzger spat. "You've done enough already. Calling a town meeting that panicked everyone. Locking down the town so people would have to rob me to feed their families. What's the point in keeping the town closed if everyone's sick anyway? This"—he gestured at the store—"would never have happened if people had been allowed to come and go as they pleased!"

Metzger was right, Charles realized. And that only underscored a more horrible truth: that the town, having quarantined itself for over two weeks now, was particularly ill equipped to deal with the flu's onslaught. If the town hadn't been closed all month, at least people's pantries would have been filled when the illness hit. Now they had little left to eat and were weakened by meager diets. Perhaps the flu had been inevitable, in which case closing the town was the biggest mistake Charles had ever made.

More crackling of boots on broken glass caused Charles to turn around. Two more millworkers had walked into the store, slowly taking in the scene. Their eyes seemed too weary for surprise; they were merely saddened by the inevitability.

"Have mercy," one of them said.

"We'll get this cleaned up," Charles said to them, feeling the need to show that things were under control. "Don't worry, I'm sure—"

"Is everything gone?" the other man asked, completely ignoring Charles. "Ain't there a storage room or a cellar or something?"

"That's empty, too," Metzger said.

Three more men had poked their heads in.

"There ain't nothin' left?" One man's eerie calmness disappeared. "How can there be nothing—"

Charles held up his hands, hoping to calm the man, as well as those behind him, who were cursing. "Please," Charles said. "We'll set things right."

"Who the hell did this?" a man in back yelled. The gathering was attracting an even larger crowd as men passed the store on their way to the mill. There were half a dozen millworkers inside now, with still more crowding the doorway behind them.

"I'm gonna kill the bastards that did this!" someone vowed.

"Forget killing 'em," another man said. "Let's just steal the food back."

Charles wondered if he should call a meeting of the magistrates, launch an investigation. Whoever had stolen from the store and the community gardens likely had volumes of food. But the thought of searching house to house did not sit well with him. That would lead to more confrontations and conflicts, would turn Commonwealth into precisely the kind of police state he had abandoned during the Everett strike. He wondered if that transformation had happened already.

"What the hell are you so angry about, Mike?" a man with a long scar down his left cheek said with a sneer. "You got enough food at your place to feed an army."

Heads turned.

"The hell I do!" said an older man with a thick black beard flecked by white hairs. "I ain't got no more'n you!"

Even though a cold wind was blowing in through the broken windows, Charles felt sweat roll down his back.

"You're the one with the two cows in his backyard," someone else said to the man with the scar.

"Do you see, Charles?" Metzger said softly into Charles's ear as they watched the millworkers' argument intensify.

Charles finally saw a friendly face, that of Jarred Rankle shouldering his way in through the crowded doorway. Rankle interposed himself between the scarred man and the bearded man, who seemed on the verge of blows. Charles could see Rankle reasoning with them, and he envied his friend's lack of hesitation at striding right up to men poised at the lip of violence.

Another man stepped away from the mob to approach Charles. "How can the store be out of food, Mr. Worthy? I've about run out myself." He was young, barely older than Philip, and one of the newer workers at the mill.

"I'll visit your house later today," Charles promised, putting a hand on the man's shoulder. "You can tell me what you need then." He hoped that this was reassurance enough, even though he wasn't sure what he would be able to offer the man.

The man looked less than hopeful as he turned to leave.

"Let's everybody get to work!" Rankle called out after clapping a few men on the back. "We don't have time to be feeling sorry for ourselves. Let's keep this mill going."

The men were still grumbling, but Rankle seemed to have called their bluff: no one wanted to fight, no one wanted to riot. They just wanted things to be back to normal, and for now, hearing one of the town's respected foremen insisting that things would indeed work out seemed to be enough. But it was clear that the men's tensions would not be eased for long.

The workers began filing out, and Rankle walked against the tide toward Charles.

"This isn't good, Charles," he said quietly.

Charles nodded. "I know. We just need to press on as best we can. This can't last long." He saw a lack of conviction in Rankle's gray eyes.

"I need to get to the storage building. I'm supposed to relieve Deacon this morning. I'll come by your office after my shift's over." Rankle left, and Charles and Metzger were again the only people in the building. Charles closed the door, hoping to prevent another scene.

Metzger was standing behind the desk where his wife had always sat. Even if the shelves had been filled, the room would have felt empty without her. He leaned forward, his palms on the desk, his head hanging down as if he might collapse.

"Alfred," Charles started, "I can't pretend to know how you feel right now. If anything that's happened is the result of my choices, then I will carry that regret with me to my dying day." He paused. "In the meantime, you're right: the quarantine should be called off. If you need to go to Timber Falls for food, you of course have my blessing. I'll tell the guards they are no longer needed. And I'll go to the banks on Monday to get what money I can. I only hope the stores in Timber Falls have opened back up."

Metzger kept his head down through Charles's speech.

"Rebecca and I will come over tonight, and if there's anything we can do—"

"There is nothing you can do." Metzger still would not look at him. "You are not welcome in my home."

XVIII

Rankle was surprised to find Graham standing guard at the storage building. He'd thought Deacon had manned the night shift.

"Deacon looked tired," Graham said. "I sent him home early."

"He have the flu?"

"Naw, seemed okay. Just tired."

"Anything happen last night?"

"Heard some wolves. First time this year."

"Maybe you should get yourself to bed. Sleep the night off."

"Sounds good to me." Graham smiled.

"You cut yourself?" Rankle asked, gesturing at Graham's right hand.

"Huh?" Graham looked down and saw that dried blood darkened the space between his thumb and forefinger, running down across his wrist. "Oh. Must have beat up my hands cutting firewood before I came over here. Getting clumsier in my old age, I guess."

"Get to bed, old man."

"'Night."

"'Morning."

Soon Rankle was joined by a short Pole named Wozniak, and half an hour later, Wozniak's wife came by with a bowl of oatmeal and some water for the prisoner. Wozniak stayed outside, grasping his rife, while Rankle laid his on the ground and went into the building with the prisoner's breakfast.

He was met at the bottom of the stairs by the pile of chains. He dropped the bowl on the floor and spun around in case the soldier was hiding in a corner waiting to jump him. But the soldier wasn't in the corner. He wasn't anywhere in the building.

Philip knew something was wrong as soon as he walked into the office.

Still nervous about being confronted by angry millworkers, he'd taken a less traveled route to the mill and had arrived half an hour after Charles. When he walked in, he saw a doleful look in his father's eyes, as if Charles had already had a long morning.

Philip sat down. "Are you all right, sir?"

"I just spoke with Mr. Metzger. His wife died last night."

Philip felt hot, the blood rushing to his face. The room was very still. Even the mill beyond seemed quieter than usual, reluctant to shake off the night's slumber. "Did he say if Elsie was sick?"

"He didn't, so I assume she is well. As well as can be expected for someone who just lost her mother."

"Maybe I should visit them later," Philip said. "See if there's anything I can do to help."

"That wouldn't be a good idea. I know it sounds like the right thing to do, but . . . they aren't in the mood for visitors just yet. Maybe tomorrow."

Philip suspected that Charles was prevaricating and simply didn't want Philip in their house, didn't want him to risk getting sick. He was beginning to hate his father's fear, and wanted to say as much, but he could see in Charles's eyes that this wasn't the time to talk back.

"You should go to the foremen," Charles said. "Doc Banes will be here shortly, and he'll want an absentee report."

Philip hurriedly walked out of the office. He needed some air, and he needed to obey Charles, but he couldn't endure the look in the foremen's eyes, not yet. So he stopped, frozen on the long plankway that overlooked the mill. He realized he was shaking. The saws seemed louder than usual, accusatory, sneering. He leaned over to steady himself, his hands on his knees and his back against the wall. He breathed. He hoped no one was looking at him but he figured someone must be, and still he stood there. *Breathe.* Soon he would stop shaking, and he would do his job, and he would write down the next list of the sick and dying.

Twenty-three more men unaccounted for. Philip returned to the office and added the new names to his master list, now two pages long.

He wanted to write another letter to Elsie, but he didn't know what he could write that wouldn't seem trivial. All he'd written this morning were the names of more dying men, so the thought of conveying love or hope or sympathy with the same pencil seemed heretical.

"We should close the mill," Doc Banes said to Charles after seeing the list. It was late morning and he had just walked in, hours later than the previous three days. The circles beneath his eyes seemed darker than usual, his eyes redder, his mood darker.

"Are you sure?" Charles asked.

"Charles, look at that list." Banes's voice was calm and sober, but extreme tension welled unmistakably beneath the surface. "At this rate, half the mill will be sick in two days. And it will be worse after that."

There were already too many sick people to see in one day, Banes explained. Even when he did see people, there was little he could do. The reality was that the numbers were increasing steadily, and the only thing that might slow the progression of the epidemic was to insist that everyone stay home to avoid contagion.

Charles had not wanted to admit it had come to this, but he hadn't seen what his friend had. Perhaps closing the mill was for the best—considering the near-violence at the general store, maybe the men needed a respite from the compounded stress of work and illness. After a few days of seclusion, everyone would remember why they had come to Commonwealth, why this town must succeed.

Or perhaps Charles was deluding himself.

"I was also thinking," he said, feeling shattered, "that we should call off the quarantine. The guards haven't been able to keep the flu out, so there doesn't seem to be any reason to prevent people from coming and going as they choose."

This statement was nearly impossible for Charles to make, even though he had said much the same thing to Metzger that morning. But Banes only nodded.

"Philip," Charles said, "call in all the foremen."

A few minutes after Philip had left, Rankle joined Charles and Doc Banes. He was breathless, and he had news—the soldier had escaped.

An hour later, Philip walked up to the Metzgers' front door. Charles had sent him home minutes ago, after meeting with the foremen and telling them to pass on word of the mill's closing and the quarantine's end. Charles had stayed behind to finish some paperwork, and Philip was hoping to get a head start on the millworkers.

But he could not bring himself to pass by the Metzgers' door, despite what Charles had said. He took off his cap, holding it as he knocked.

On the third knock, Mr. Metzger answered, still looking like he hadn't slept.

"Philip." He had always been a quiet man, but his voice was weaker than usual.

"Mr. Metzger, I just wanted to express my condolences for your wife." Philip hadn't planned out what to say. He tried to look at the man's face but found it too difficult. "Coming by the store and hearing her tease me has always been the best part of my job, sir. I'm . . . really going to miss her."

He finally dared to look back at Metzger's face, and he didn't like what he saw.

"Go home, Philip."

Metzger shut the door.

Philip stood there, stunned by the abrupt dismissal. He put his cap back on and wondered if Elsie had been nearby, if she had heard Philip's voice. He stayed by the door an extra moment, in case she might throw it open and call out to him. But the door stayed closed, and he finally headed for home.

XIX

During the meeting with the foremen, Rankle had stood there with others, nodding patiently. He had told Charles and Doc Banes of the missing soldier while Philip had gathered the foremen, but that fact seemed almost trivial compared to the enormity of the mill's closing. Whether or not the soldier was indeed a German spy who had spread disease seemed hopelessly irrelevant now that each man had before him the task of saving the sick and protecting the healthy. The people of Commonwealth could no longer concern themselves with anything other than the flu.

Which was why Charles hadn't even thought to tell Philip of Rankle's discovery until hours later. The thought of leaving the mill felt as horrible to Charles as if he were abandoning a child on a city sidewalk, and the guilt and the fear that this was a terrible and irreversible mistake clung to him. He reviewed his notebooks and charts and tried to calculate the impact of a day's closure, or a week's, or three. Now that the quarantine was broken, perhaps Charles could contact his buyers, could invite the boats to once again wind their way down the river and begin taking the huge stockpile they'd amassed since the quarantine had begun over two weeks ago. Metzger would be able to replenish his store, and even if his mourning delayed him a few days, families who were still healthy would be able to shop for necessities in Timber Falls. Perhaps the healthy could shop for the sick, arrange deliveries to make sure those most in need of sustenance would not go without. Perhaps breaking the quarantine would actually help the town when it needed it most.

Then again, with the mill closed, there would be no workers to load the boats. And what if those other towns were still so sick that their businesses were shuttered? And how could Commonwealth's current mood give Charles any faith that people would start delivering food to one another despite the profound risks such altruism carried? Charles sat in his office for a full three hours after everyone else had abandoned it. Finally, he stood up and gazed through the window that looked out onto the main floor, all those inert machines and the stunning silence. He turned off his lamp and put the mill behind him.

The afternoon was silent as a Sunday. There were no sounds of distant saws, no echoing *thooms* of heavy trunks landing on the wet earth, no persistent roar and clatter emanating from the mill. It was quiet and it was cold and it felt exactly the way weather should feel if it were trying to mimic death.

When Charles came home, Rebecca and Laura were playing cards in the parlor, as if it had been a normal day and not one on which Rebecca had announced that the school would close until further notice. Philip was in his room.

It was nearly time for supper when Charles remembered what Rankle had told him about the spy, remembered Philip's strange and unfortunate attachment. He knocked on Philip's door and found his son sitting on his bed reading some letter that he hurriedly placed beneath the folds of his bedsheet.

"He's gone?" Philip said when Charles tried to explain.

Charles nodded, still perplexed by his son's fealty to the man who surely was a spy—Charles believed it now more than ever—and told Philip what Rankle had discovered. No one knew how the man had escaped from his chains, but it didn't matter. The soldier was no longer their problem, and they had no shortage of problems at the moment.

After Charles left, Philip sat in bed, thinking. Frank was gone, trekking through the woods to Vancouver. Philip didn't understand how Frank had escaped, or how he could possibly make it to Canada now that it was growing so much colder. Philip had been planning to send him on his way with a bagful of food and some warmer clothes—how would he make it without them?

Philip suddenly had the thought that Frank might not have run yet—that he might have chosen to hide in someone's cellar or closet for one last night, waiting to steal some food and clothes and then make his escape. Philip latched on to this idea, determined to see the empty prison with his own eyes.

Charles was in the parlor and saw Philip donning his jacket. "Where are you going?"

"I left something at the mill—I'll be quick" was Philip's terse reply. He grabbed a lamp and walked out the door before he could hear a response.

It was cold, and the evening winds had begun to fling themselves at the town's closed doors and shuttered windows. The sky's color was draining away, revealing the darkness that had been hiding behind the clouds, crouching in anticipation of the bitter black night to come.

Philip walked as quickly as he could, and when he reached the dead-end street, he marveled at how different the storage building looked without a guard or two standing before it. He opened the door and the lamplight led the way before him, as did the echoes of his footsteps. When he reached the top of the stairs to the cellar, he saw light coming from below.

Someone was down there.

Philip felt his heart beat harder than before, and though he tried to control his emotions, he couldn't stop the pounding. For some reason, he didn't call out a greeting, choosing to let his footsteps reveal his entrance and trusting that whoever was down there was no threat to him. He walked down the steps slowly, and when he reached the bottom, the light from his lamp joined with that of the other lamp, which sat in the center of the room as if it had been left behind.

But Jarred Rankle sat on the ground, leaning against the wall. "Philip," he said, his voice calm. "What brings you here?"

"I just . . . wanted to take a look around," Philip replied uncertainly.

Rankle had a sad look in his eyes, and he wasn't wearing a mask. Rankle seemed to trust that Frank's germs or spirit or contamination had fled along with him.

Philip felt uncomfortable—Rankle was a trusted family friend, but his presence here was a mystery. Still, Philip walked toward the post where Frank had been chained. The chains lay in limp coils as if they'd never had the strength to contain a man and had simply given up the ruse. Philip was taking it all in when something caught his eye.

It was the photo of Michelle. Philip picked it up and stood staring into her eyes as if hoping she would explain. Philip would have expected Frank to leave behind his boots before this picture. Could he have been a spy all along, and the photo no more than a prop to lend shading to his false character?

Rankle didn't ask what Philip was looking at—he must have already picked it up himself, already had these thoughts, already dropped the photo back on the ground. Then Philip's eyes were drawn to something else. He crouched back down and inspected the strange red stain on the floor by the wall, a darkness that seemed to bleed from the earth itself. He had actually stepped on it a moment ago, and his foot must have kicked away some of the dirt that had apparently been brushed over it. He reached forward and swept away more of the dirt, revealing an ever larger, reddish black stain that Philip knew could be only one thing.

Philip stood up and took several steps back. He still held the picture. He looked at Rankle, who met his eyes evenly.

"I don't know anything more than you," Rankle said. "He was gone this morning. We saw the break in the wall upstairs, figured that's how he got past us. Then I came back and looked around some more."

Philip felt a quiver in his gut that he could contain only by forcing himself to breathe slowly.

"What did you do to him?"

"I just told you. I didn't do anything."

Philip swallowed, steadied himself.

"Who was on guard duty last night?" Philip looked at the floor when he asked this, but when no reply came, he shifted his gaze back to Rankle, who was also staring at the blood. Philip repeated his question.

"Deacon was supposed to be," Rankle answered with apparent reluctance. "But when I showed up this morning, Graham was here instead."

"What do you think happened?"

The gravity of Rankle's stare was his only reply.

Philip froze, overcome. "I need to see Graham," he finally said, although he could feel his legs shaking. He put Michelle's picture in his pocket.

"You'll do no such thing," Rankle said, standing up.

Philip was surprised at the command. "I need to see him." His voice shook with fear and rage and the tears he was barely withholding.

"If I have to carry you back to your house right now, I will. Graham's home protecting his family, and you'll respect that." Philip remembered the stories about Rankle's own lost family. Though his words were harsh, Rankle's voice was shaking also, evidence that this was no easier for him than it was for Philip. "You'll tell no one about this. You'll leave Graham alone, and you'll go home and stay with your family until this has passed."

As badly as Philip wanted to see Graham, he was terrified of doing so, and he felt himself withering before Rankle's orders. He nodded, anxious to escape. He felt disoriented by the same dizzying mix of nauseated fear and confusion as when he was first trapped in the prison, and again when Charles had asked him if he had any reason to suspect that Frank was a spy, and again when he had realized that the flu had come to Commonwealth.

Rankle said he was going to stay and clean up, so Philip left alone. He could have disobeyed and visited Graham, but he no longer felt the desire to do so, at least not right away. He walked home and told his family, gathering at the table, that he was not hungry and felt unwell. Knowing that any mention of sickness was alarming, he reassured them that he was just tired.

He lay in his bed for a long while, haunted by thoughts of Graham and Frank and the C.O., haunted by the sounds of coughing. And though he thought he felt as bad as he could, he was wrong. For at least he was still healthy when he closed his eyes.

Part Four

Specters

I

Violet Merriwhether couldn't look at her husband anymore. If she did not look at him—if she stayed in her room behind a locked door, the drawn curtains keeping her in darkness and protecting her from any evidence that there was a world beyond—then she could exist there quietly, alone. It would be the saddest existence possible, a woman in a dark room slowly starving to death, yet it would somehow be bearable. If, however, she looked at J.B., she would remember her husband and the love between them, would remember the existence of love, the possibility of hope, would recall mornings when the two had sat on their porch holding hands and playfully bickering over what to name their children one day. If she looked at J.B., she would remember that she had once been a mother, that she'd once had two children, that there had been a part of her that was beautiful and alive but fragile, so painfully and worryingly fragile, and that this part of her had ventured into the unforgiving world and been struck down. And this she could not accept, could not even fathom.

If she looked at J.B., she would shatter. She had already shattered at the sight of Gwen suffocating to death, and again at the sight of that telegram lying on the kitchen table. She had shattered so many times that each minuscule piece had itself shattered, her former core becoming bits of dust blown through the air. At Gwen's wake, Violet had heard some of her friends asking one another how she was holding together, and regardless of what they thought, Violet knew that she was not held together anymore, that the pieces of her had long since dispersed. Yet she still existed—how could that be? She stayed in that room, in the dark, and whenever her husband knocked at the door she pretended not to hear him. She knew the sound of the knocks would eventually fade away, and they always did.

J.B. was sitting at the dining room table when he saw Joseph Miller park in front of his house. He sat at the table even though it reminded him of the day the telegram came, the telegram he had placed on the table unread and had stared at, message side down, for what seemed hours. It had been a Saturday afternoon and Violet was out visiting with friends, well-intentioned friends who were trying to keep her mind off the death of her daughter, however briefly. J.B. didn't know if he should wait for her return before reading it. How do you face death, how do you face tragedy? Alone or with your beloved by your side? What can a man say when he faces things he cannot protect his wife from, cannot protect his family from? He had been the smallest man in the world, sitting at the table on that Saturday.

Every night since James had been sent to France, J.B. had prayed to God, asking that the Lord spare his son. *Please protect James and keep him safe always* were the words J.B. used night after night. But he had been raised to be a caring and empathetic man, and he realized how shallow it seemed to ask the Lord to protect only *his* son, realized it meant putting James's life above the lives of all those other boys who had been sent into the chaos of war. So J.B. would follow those words with a plea that God spare all the other boys as well. *Please keep all the boys safe,* J.B. prayed. But that meant he was asking God for something impossible. This was madness, and he felt that God in heaven was shaking His head at J.B., at the smallness of a man who wants one thing but asks for a larger thing instead, a wish that he cannot have. And the Lord had punished him for it.

J.B. had slept the last two nights in the parlor, lying on the cold floor and staring at the ceiling. Above him was the bedroom where his wife was hiding. He had woken up each morning with that same awful feeling, the dawning realization that those recent horrors were not dreams, that they were real and had followed him into this next day. Each morning his son and daughter died again, Gwen in his arms, her body flailing while tears streamed down his face, and James simply disappearing before his eyes.

Gwen had been the most beautiful young woman in town; the suitors had already been lining up. J.B. would never again turn away one of those eager young men from his door, would never again see the look of disappointment in their eyes, never again hear the stammers and see the dashed hopes of young invulnerability that so reminded him of himself long ago, of young James Barrows Merriwhether knocking on the door of the beautiful Violet Casey's parents. The Merriwhether porch would never again host such excitement, such unbridled enthusiasm.

Yet now Joseph Miller was standing on the porch. He looked at J.B. through the window, but J.B. did not rise to admit him. Miller motioned to the door as if to let himself in, and J.B. nodded.

Miller entered the dining room, and J.B. hoped that the man would not offer any condolences, but those hopes were dashed immediately. J.B. nodded and looked away, tired of seeing men appear so deeply uncomfortable in his presence. It was the way he had once felt around people like the foreman Hightower, father of the two dead sons in France. J.B. hated that he had anything in common with that man, hated that the two of them were now confined to the same circle of Hell.

Miller cleared his throat, as if the unpleasant air around them could be so easily dispelled. Then he told J.B. of his plan. He asked if J.B. would come with them.

J.B. nodded. "Just tell me when."

II

When exactly Philip woke, he wasn't sure. He knew only that the painful and fuzzy transition from sleep to wakefulness was accompanied by a striking pain in his head, starting from his temples and burrowing deep into the back of his skull. His eyes had been open for a while and his room was slowly coming into focus when he realized what this meant. He gingerly lifted his head from the pillow and propped himself into a sitting position, leaning on the cold wall behind him. This only made his head throb more. He tilted his head back to look at the ceiling and beg God that this wasn't happening, but tipping his head that far triggered something inside and he lurched forward again, coughing violently. He leaned over the side of the bed, hoping that position would clear his throat or his lungs or whatever it was that had become so polluted while he'd slept.

He sat up again, still coughing, his eyes tearing up from the pain and the fear and from something in the back of his mouth that seemed to be drying out his throat but flooding his chest. He reached out for a glass of water but found none there. He'd retired to bed so hurriedly the night before that he hadn't brought any water with him—hadn't even changed out of his clothes, he now realized. Even in his flannel shirt and wool pants, he still felt cold beneath the thick blankets, and although leaning against the wall made him colder, he lacked the strength to move, or the necessary drive to force his body to rearrange itself, or the capacity for rational thought that such a decision required. So he just sat there coughing until someone opened his door.

It was Rebecca. The concern in her eyes was altogether different from the usual maternal empathy. Instead, it was a mixture of fear and denial.

"Are you all right?" She asked that quietly, as if she knew noise would pain him, which it did. She took a couple of steps into the room.

"My head hurts," he squeezed out between coughs.

She nodded, and the furrows in her forehead grew more pronounced. She told him she'd be right back with some water, and he closed his eyes and opened them again and there the glass was, with the water whose coldness was both soothing and oppressive. He drank and it eased his throat a bit, but it caused him to shiver all the more. Rebecca, seeing this, said she'd make him some hot tea. She reached for his forehead and asked if he felt hot or cold. Both, he said. She asked if he was hungry and he thought about this as if it were some abstract question, something he had never before considered, then uttered a no. He coughed again.

Rebecca rearranged his pillows so he could sit up without pressing against the cold wall, then she went out to get him another blanket. In the hallway she met Charles, who had been in their bedroom but had been stirred by the ominous sound of coughing from below.

"Get Dr. Banes," she told him, whispering in the hall. "He looks terrible."

Philip's head was pounding, and the aspirin Rebecca had given him didn't seem to be working. It was like throwing a glass of water on a forest fire. He felt weak and his legs ached. At first he had tried to rearrange them, to keep them perfectly straight or bend them just so, but he soon determined that no matter how they lay, they would ache as if they were being pummeled with hammers.

He tried to cough harder and dislodge something in his throat, but the coughs only made the something hurt more intensely. He wanted so badly to reach into his own mouth and find the something, to scrape around at the back of his palate and appease it. But gradually he realized the something was nothing—or perhaps it was his throat itself. It wasn't going anywhere, and he had to breathe around it, breathe despite it. He sipped at the tea, which was now lukewarm, and tried not to choke.

"Is it flu?" he asked Doc Banes weakly as Charles and Rebecca looked on with worried eyes that seemed so large, since the rest of their faces were covered by gauze masks. The doctor said yes, it was influenza. Flu had a habit of taking you by surprise, he said, so maybe if Philip had felt himself coming down with something the day before, then it could be just a bad cold. But Philip had felt fine—physically, at least—the day before, and then woken as if someone had poisoned him while he slept. Rebecca started to ask what they could do for him and Philip coughed so she stopped midsentence, as if the exact cadence and tenor of his coughing were something they needed to heed and study. Then he was silent and she finished her question. Philip missed the doctor's answer, ignoring it because his head hurt and Banes's voice was grating. Philip closed his eyes because he was angry at the doctor's sad and tired demeanor, angry at the gauze mask that served only to accentuate the distant look in the man's eyes. Philip sat there with his eyes shut and concentrated on breathing. When he opened his eyes again his mug was filled with steaming tea and his visitors had fled.

What time was it? His watch was atop his bureau, and the headache had left him further disoriented. There was light peeking in through his drawn curtains, but not much. Still sitting up, he drifted off, his coughs mercifully subsiding.

He was dreaming about standing at the post with Graham when his eyes opened and he saw his tiny room before him, a sliver of light escaping from between the curtains and bisecting his bureau. Graham had been standing beside him a moment ago, telling him about Amelia and the baby. The first soldier had been there too, had said he'd like to meet Graham's family. Graham had nodded awkwardly at the man's polite comment, had looked away because he didn't know how to tell the man that he was already dead. Philip hadn't known how to tell the man, either. The man—the C.O., Philip now knew—had then looked at Philip inquiringly, his soft and wounded eyes searching for an answer to Graham's sudden coldness. Philip tried so hard to think of an answer that the pressure forced his eyes open and woke him up.

He had to see Graham. He felt lucid for a moment, more so than he had all day. But he did not feel better—his head pounded every time the blood vessels grudgingly expanded to let his virus-infested blood through, and his legs ached as he kicked off the blankets. It was cold outside of the bed so he needed a sweater, but his journey over to the bureau took a while, the movement broken down into small, discrete steps: stand up; wait; step forward twice; wait; close eyes; swallow and try not to cough; cough; step forward and grip bureau; wait; open drawer, grab sweater; collapse in sitting position back onto bed, holding thick sweater between sweaty fingers.

As he pulled the sweater over his weak frame he reeled at the soreness in his arms and neck, a pain he'd never felt before, not even after the recovery from his accident. This was excruciating, but he would rather collapse in the street than sit in that bed any longer and wonder what his friend had done.

He opened the door and walked into the hallway. Not until that moment did it occur to him that his parents would stop him from going. He tried to be quiet, stifling a cough even though it nearly made him double over in pain. No one was in the hallway or the kitchen. He heard soft voices murmuring from the parlor, Laura and Rebecca reading to each other or telling stories or doing something to keep the horror at bay. Would he get them sick? He had not thought of this before, either—the realization had been buried beneath the difficulties he'd faced in simply lifting his head from his pillow. He wondered how common it was for one person in a house to have the flu without passing it on.

When Philip passed the small mirror in the hallway, he averted his eyes.

His hands were in his gloves and on the doorknob, turning it as slowly and silently as possible, and then he was outside. The light hurt. It was startlingly light out—blue sky! Perfectly blue with no clouds in sight, as if some long-earthbound angels had flown up to the clouds with glinting rapiers, slashing away at that underbelly of gray. Philip normally would have appreciated the sun, but the light seemed so strong that he squinted and looked down at the dirt. He walked slowly, momentum gradually taking control.

If it had seemed cold in his room, it felt arctic outdoors. The air was impossibly cold. Surely there was something wrong—and there was: him. He knew his body wasn't working right, and he told himself it was just in his head, that the shivers sending his spine into spasms were not real, that the wind that seemed to cut through his clothes—the strangely aggressive cold—was not real. It was only a couple blocks more, and his legs were still working, and the dizziness he had felt at first was subsiding.

He felt frail and damaged, but he had to do this. He was scared of Graham, the man who had seemed like his big brother these last two years. But he needed to confront him.

There was Graham's house, right in front of him. It stood facing the main street, strong and proud as the day they'd built it. The curtains were drawn on the second-floor windows but not on the first, and through one of those he saw Amelia gazing outside. She must have been sitting on a chair, and as Philip walked forward, he saw the baby in her arms, little Millie perched between her mother's legs and staring wide-eyed into the world where nothing was happening. No one else on the streets, no sounds from church services at the town hall three buildings away, no children laughing. But the baby stared transfixed as if before her were colorful parades and painted dancers, elephants and zebras marching past. Death and desolation could still seem beautiful to eyes that didn't know what more to expect from the world.

Then Amelia wasn't there anymore and Philip was even closer to the house, almost at the steps in front of the porch, when the front door opened. Graham was not wearing a coat or gloves, yet he didn't look cold in the wind that was so mercilessly assaulting Philip.

"Philip," Graham said simply, letting it hang there while he stared. "What's wrong?"

Philip swallowed and concentrated on not coughing. Graham stood on the porch, and Philip stopped before the first step.

"What happened to Frank?" Philip asked.

Graham looked like he didn't understand; Frank was a meaningless name to him.

Philip said, "What happened to the soldier, the spy?"

Graham's expression changed. "Good God, Philip," he said softly. "You sick?" He raised his right hand to cover his mouth.

"What happened to Frank, Graham?"

"I let him go." Graham's body was rigid. "Philip, you should be in bed. You gotta rest."

"Why didn't he take his girl's picture?"

"I don't know." Graham turned back around to ensure that he had closed the door behind him. His hand still covered his mouth.

"Why was there blood on the ground?" Philip was seized with a wrenching cough. When it abated, he demanded, "What did you *do*?"

Graham stepped forward despite his desire to be as far away from this sick person as possible.

"I undid what you did!" he screamed through gritted teeth. He had looked so controlled at first, his shirt tucked in and his hair neatly parted. But now that they were closer and Philip was focusing better, Graham did seem a bit puffy in the face, a bit red in the eyes, and his face grew tainted by the emergence of feelings he had been trying to stifle.

The door began to open behind Graham, who twirled around to shout at it, "Stay inside, please!" His voice was harsh and strong, and the door shut before Philip could even see a person behind it.

"Where's Frank?" Philip asked again. He walked up a step. "Where's Frank?"

"You know where he is."

Philip could hear Graham's breathing as loudly as he could hear his own tortured gasps. Breathing was becoming more difficult, his chest tighter, and whether this was some new symptom or the price of exerting himself, he wasn't sure.

"How could you just—" Philip cut himself off. His eyes were tearing up again.

"Go home, Philip. Please." Graham had lowered his hand after warning Amelia not to come out, but again he lifted it to his face. "You need to rest."

"Don't tell me what I need to do!"

Graham's apparent desire to change the subject, to pretend that Frank had never existed, enraged Philip. He kept shaking his head, and when he finally stopped, when he looked into Graham's eyes, he shouted:

"You're a murderer!"

"*You're* the murderer!" Graham stepped forward again, the two of them separated only by a couple of feet. His hand-mask fell away and there was his full face again, his red cheeks and his lips curled back in a snarl. "You've killed this whole town from letting him in here! I did what I had to do to keep everyone safe, no thanks to you!"

Philip launched himself forward without thinking, and then he was upon Graham, his gloved hands reaching for Graham's neck or his face or his heart, he wasn't sure which. He only wanted to shake at Graham's certainty until all the events of the last few weeks could somehow return to the way they once were, when he and Graham had been friends and they both knew what they wanted out of life and it was the same thing.

Graham pushed him back easily and Philip fell, slipping back and hitting against one of the porch posts. They looked at each other for a moment, amazed to be fighting. Then Philip lurched forward again, this time leading with his fist, which caught Graham on the side of the face and swung him to the right. But Graham turned back and grabbed Philip's collar with his left hand to hold him in place, and he was about to sock him with his stronger hand, his full-fingered right hand, when something seized inside Philip's chest and he coughed in Graham's face. Graham froze and looked as if Philip had just poured a bucket of his warm blood over Graham's head.

They realized they were being screamed at from two directions.

Amelia had been watching from the window with Millie in her arms, and though she hadn't been able to hear the conversation until they had started shouting, she had hurriedly put down the baby and rushed to the door when she'd seen Philip attack her husband. She had started screaming for Graham as her hand grasped the doorknob.

"Stay inside, Amelia, please," Graham tried to shout, but it came out as a whimper. "He's sick—don't come out."

When Amelia heard Graham's plea she stopped, her hand pressed against the door.

The other person screaming was Charles, coming down the road after his son. "Philip!"

At his father's voice, Philip gave in to his body's agonized pleas and slumped down onto the porch, huddling there and catching his breath and coughing yet again. He closed his eyes and for a moment things were quiet, then humming at a low and steady pitch. He wondered where he was.

Charles was crouched above him and Philip felt a hand behind his back. Charles was wearing his gauze mask. "Are you all right?"

Philip nodded, and his father helped him to his feet. Philip leaned against the post again while Charles asked Graham what was going on.

Graham found that he couldn't bring himself to look Charles in the eye. He breathed in and out, and his mouth was tight as if trying desperately to prevent some toxin from slipping in. "He needs to be in bed," Graham finally said.

Charles didn't understand, but he could demand explanations later. He put an arm around Philip and guided him home, walking slowly and stopping every time Philip coughed. It took them quite a while.

Graham stayed on the porch, willing away his tears and breathing loudly, as if he had just emerged from under water. As the adrenaline slowly faded, though his arms and knees were still shaking, he felt the harsh cold on his arms, the hair prickling up against his shirt. And still he felt Philip's breath on his face.

He looked up and there was Amelia on the other side of the window. She had one hand at her breast and the other on the glass, not two feet from Graham. He wanted only to close his eyes and hold her. But he stood there, motionless, terrified, and unwilling to walk through the door.

III

Philip knew it was morning only because Rebecca told him it was. To him it was just the latest stop on this hellish train ride he had been sent on, an overcrowded train car so hot from the press of bodies that he felt the sweat pool on his clavicle and in his armpits and groin, felt the sweat roll from his forehead. The train was unsteady and it swayed back and forth, and the clattering of the rusty metal cars was a booming cacophony in his ears. The motions of the train had turned his stomach, contributing to the weakness that sapped every ounce of vitality from his body. He was standing in the car between two large men who hadn't left him enough room, but when he opened his eyes he saw that he was actually lying down in his bed. He closed his eyes again and things made more sense: his legs ached and his foot throbbed because he was in this dark train car, his toes occasionally stepped upon by others and his leg muscles weary from too many hours of standing, trapped. Where was the train going? Every once in a while it stopped briefly, but only to board more passengers. No one ever seemed to get off the train. It was becoming more crowded, hotter still. His clothes were sticking to his flesh, the sweat was everywhere, and despite this, he shivered. He tried to look out the windows but there were too many bodies in the way. Where was he?

"Mom," he tried to say, but instead coughed. There was something inside his chest, something large and waxy and heavy, something that had attached itself to his rib cage and woven its fibers into his muscles and ligaments. He coughed all over the man in front of him, whose chest was facing him even though his face was not, as if the man's head were turned 180 degrees. But the man didn't seem to mind Philip's coughs, didn't try to move away or demand that Philip apologize. That was when Philip realized everyone was coughing. It was the coughs that were making the train shake back and forth, the force of so many heaves and spasms. Was the train even moving forward, or were they just sitting in the middle of some wasteland?

Rebecca was telling him it was morning and he opened his eyes. The train dissipated briefly and there she was, holding a mug of something steaming and placing it on the table beside his bed. She was wearing a gauze mask. He coughed again and wasn't able to cover his mouth because his hands, balled into sweaty fists, were buried beneath the covers. Rebecca put her hand on his forehead and frowned. Philip closed his eyes and the train kept rocking. He thought he heard someone singing a familiar song. Then he was hit by such an awesome chill that his eyes bulged open and there was Rebecca again, her hands extended above him as she placed a cold towel on his forehead. Every nerve in his body stood up and genuflected with gracious thanks for that beautiful towel, even though Philip knew that in twenty minutes, maybe less, he'd again be wilting from the heat of the train car.

I can talk, Philip reminded himself. So he pulled one of his arms out from under the covers and put his hand before his face as he coughed. He was able to say, "Thank you." Rebecca nodded. There was a grim look in her eyes, and the rest of her face was covered by her gauze mask. She sat down in a small chair she must have dragged in from the dining room, stayed watching him, but eventually, her soft, lined visage was replaced by the faceless heads on the train car, by the shaking and rocking and swaying and all those other coughs, the stale and reeking breath.

Then Philip felt something, and he opened his eyes again to see Rebecca standing up. His left hand shot out from beneath the covers and he grasped her hand, unsure whether he was holding her roughly or barely touching her, so unfamiliar had he become with the way his own body worked. *Don't go,* he said. *Don't leave me. Everyone's leaving me. My father left me before I could even remember and then my mother left me and Frank left me and Graham's leaving me, too. Please don't leave me.* He wasn't sure how much of this he was able to say through the mucus and phlegm, but the look in Rebecca's eyes showed that she understood enough of it.

She sat back down, holding his sweaty hand.

As much as Philip preferred the sight of his bedroom and Rebecca to the image of the men with no faces, he kept slipping back into that scene. The sweat had begun to pour down his forehead again when he felt his hand jostled by something that he couldn't see, something that wasn't in the train car. He opened his eyes and Rebecca was leaving again, this time having already reached the door.

"Don't go," he choked, rearranging his body on the damp pillows.

"I'll be back soon," she said. "I have to take care of your sister, too."

His sister. "Laura . . ."

"Laura's sick, too." Then Rebecca was gone and the train car was swaying more violently than before, Philip's chin whacking against so many shoulders and heads and elbows that he felt he was falling, felt the train car dissolving beneath his feet and the bodies of everyone around him sliding on top of his, piling up, and everything was dark and hot, so very hot.

He opened his eyes later and was back in his bed. How long had he been on that train? Days. He bent one leg and pulled the knee up halfway toward his chest, just to stretch the muscles, just to feel human, and within those muscles he felt some hazy memory, covered in wax paper and dust, of slowly stumbling through the house to the bathroom. Maybe twice a day. How many days? He had completely lost track, since days had no meaning here, no meaning in this bed. Time was a chimera dancing before him to distract him from the only thing that mattered: getting healthy. He realized he hadn't even thought of this, of being healthy, in the longest time. His body dared not consider health—it took all its strength to fight on and stay alive while in this siege. Just as the town had been under siege from all sides. Now the same scenario was playing itself out, but this time the flu-infected world was his body and the safe haven of Commonwealth was his mind. He needed to protect his mind from his body. If his mind could stay healthy, if he could properly quarantine it, then maybe his body would give up this gruesome battle. He thought about that, then realized it made no sense. He was already losing his mind—his brain had already fallen victim to his body. The flu had broken the quarantine.

The door opened and in walked Graham, wearing a gauze mask. Philip was too weak to be confused by this. All the muscles in Graham's forehead and temples were tensed around his eyes, wary of the inevitability of attack and constantly on guard. He was carrying his rifle. In that tiny room, it looked as big as a cannon.

"Hi," Philip said, and amazingly, his voice sounded clear of infection.

Graham nodded.

"What are you doing here?" Even to himself, Philip still sounded weak, and the words were slow. He wanted to ask why Graham had the gun in here, but that would have been too many words.

"Keeping watch." To underscore that point, Graham's eyes darted from one side of the room to the next. Suddenly, the room felt large to Philip, the walls hundreds of yards away from one another, and between those walls were trees and boulders, Douglas fir and fallen branches, uncountable nooks where nameless animals had been born and had returned to the earth, thousands of places where enemies might hide. "Don't worry. I'll keep you safe."

"From what?"

Graham said, "Sshhh." Then he looked into Philip's eyes gravely. "You know."

Philip started to cry. He hated Graham so much yet felt so grateful that his friend was standing here beside him when no one else would, staring down whatever it was that wished to feast upon him. The something in Philip's chest suddenly had company as a thick warmth welled up inside him, and the tears continued to roll down his cheeks until he fell asleep once more.

Philip opened his eyes. The room was dark. How long could you be sick with the flu? Philip wondered.

There was a tap at the window. Was that what had woken him up? Again a tap. With great effort, Philip lifted himself into a sitting position, letting the sheets fall down across his lap, exposing half his body to the room's chill. His fingertips felt almost numb, and although he was used to this feeling since the auto accident, he knew it was a strange symptom to have when sick. Did this mean his infection was moving on to an even more sinister stage? He reached forward, taking the window curtains in his hand. He could feel them, barely. He pulled them apart and looked outside.

Little light trickled in; the outside world was nearly as dark as his room. But he could see, standing only a foot away from the window, Elsie. She held a stick that she'd been using to tap on the window, as if afraid to touch it with her bare hands. Not bare: she was wearing gloves, he saw, and it was cold enough outside for him to see her breath, that thin and quickly dissipating smoke hovering before her. Her scarf was wrapped thickly around her neck, tightly bundled beneath her chin, and some of her curls blew in front of her face, twisting in the November wind. Just above the scarf he could see her mouth, her thin lips pale in the cold. With his parents wearing masks, Elsie's was the first full face he'd seen in days.

She waved. Her face had looked serious and drawn, but she now allowed herself a slightly hopeful look, her eyebrows curving in lieu of a smile, which would have seemed misplaced right then. He waved back. How late was it? It might have been seven in the evening or three in the morning.

He leaned forward, grasping the bottom sill, and was about to pull it open when he saw her shaking her head. She had stepped back as well, apparently ready to flee in case he opened it. She was afraid of him, afraid of his flu, despite having lived in the same house as her sick mother. He pulled his hands away from the window, showing her his empty palms as if he had just dropped a gun. He said, "Sorry," but wasn't sure if she could read his lips. She nodded, though, and stepped forward again.

She breathed on the glass and it fogged between them, tangible evidence of the barrier separating them. Then she reached forward and, with one gloved finger, wrote on the glass. She wrote slowly, as she had to write backward in order for Philip to understand it.

YOU OK?

Philip smiled weakly and nodded, lying to the vision of Elsie before him. She looked so beautiful but forlorn, all bundled against the cold as if waiting for a train she had missed. Her eyes were sad, but beneath this sadness was a tenderness that warmed him and made him wish more than ever that he could shatter the glass and hold her again. He opened his mouth but didn't know what he could say that would be easily readable on his lips. There was no paper nearby for him to write her a note, and the thought of breathing on the glass the way she had, of expelling his germs toward her, even with the barrier, seemed unwise. So he sat there looking at her, hoping that his eyes were conveying all that he felt.

Elsie wiped at the glass, removing her message. She leaned forward and breathed on the glass again, just off to the side of the previous spot, and the fog magically grew before their eyes once more. This time she looked at him for another moment before writing, looked at him closely.

Then she reached out with her finger and wrote on the glass, *LOVE YOU.*

Her face was so serious, as if love and the mere thought of love required her most adult expression. But the sight of those words and the meaning behind them were so amazing to Philip that he couldn't stop from smiling. When she saw this she smiled too, looking down briefly, perhaps embarrassed by what she'd written. Then she looked back at him, and he mouthed a silent "Me, too" and hoped she understood it.

Beneath the *LOVE YOU,* the fog provided more space for her scrawled thoughts, so she wrote, in smaller letters, *GET WELL,* though the second *E* she got backward. He would do anything for her, he knew right then, and it made getting well seem like such an easy task. He breathed deeply.

For those few minutes he had felt strangely freed of the flu's grip, but now everything was coming back. He felt the itching at the back of his sinuses, the throb in his leg muscles, the strangely loud and hurried heartbeat, the something that still lived in his chest and made him cough once again. How long has it been? he wondered. That night at the general store, sitting beside her, kissing her. How long had he been trapped in this room, been in and out of the train car?

Elsie reached out and pressed her palm flat against the window. He wanted to put his hand on the other side of the glass but hesitated. He felt the men on the train stiffen, felt the shoulders and the elbows jostle him, and he felt dizzy, all those faceless heads confusing him about which direction to turn to find Elsie. Where had she gone? His body slumped back; he was startled by how quickly the train was moving. It was rocketing through the empty landscape, the world beyond the windows that he couldn't see. And although he had no idea where it was going, he knew it was hurtling away from Elsie, taking him farther away with every second, every breath.

Philip had never been this sick. The worst he'd felt was after the accident, lying in that foreign hospital bed surrounded by people he didn't know, people who wouldn't tell him where his mother was. Even that had felt different, not a sickness but a recovery, albeit a long and brutal one. Almost like a rebirth, a painful passage from one phase of his life to the next.

He'd been bedridden one other time. He had been eight or so, and he and his mother had been living in some Oregon town when he'd caught a bad case of pneumonia. His mother had nursed him, had been at his side every time he woke up, whether early in the morning or in the middle of the night. She had been working as a secretary for a lawyer who had always made eyes at her, Philip had noticed, but she had stayed home from her job all week. And even though he felt miserable and had honestly wondered if he might die—one boy from his school had already succumbed to the same illness—his memories of that week were somehow happy ones. He had never felt more loved by Fiona. All of the tortured ambivalence was replaced by a calm maternal consistency, and he felt so protected and happy with her bringing him soup or reading him magazines or newspapers. He'd stayed in bed at least one day longer than he'd really needed to, just to prolong it.

The night before he was to return to school, he had woken up when he heard a noise coming from his mother's room. He rose from his bed, the wood floor cold on his feet, and he pushed open the door as quietly as he could. Her bedside lamp was lit and she was sitting at the small dining table, her back to him, her shoulders hunched. The clock above her told him it was past three in the morning. She was crying. Was she as sad as he was that their idyllic time together was coming to an end? Was she as crushed as he was with the disappointment that he must return to school and she to that lawyer? Or was there something else? For one solid week—and for the first time he could remember—he had completely overlooked her emotions, her opinions, her thoughts. He had felt that her whole being revolved around him.

Maybe there was something else making her cry, some other aspect of her confusing adult world. Maybe there had been other reasons why she had chosen to stay home and avoid that lawyer. Philip walked toward her, and she showed no signs of hearing him until he put his hand on her shoulder. She was shaking slightly from the tears, but she put one of her hands on his, squeezing it. They stayed that way for a while, his feet freezing beneath him and the unimpressed clock ticking away the minutes. Eventually her tears slowed and she gave his hand a final squeeze. She told him to go back to bed and he obeyed, never having seen her face.

When Philip next opened his eyes, Charles was sitting in the chair before him, holding his hand. Philip wasn't sure how long Charles had been there but felt from the sweatiness in his father's palm that their hands had been clasped for some time. Charles, seeing Philip's eyes open, began to speak.

"I know you feel at fault for this," Charles said, his voice the slightest bit muffled by the gauze mask. "That's why I wanted to tell you what Dr. Banes told me a few days ago."

Philip gritted his teeth against the ache in his head and the light filtering through the curtains.

"I've tried to tell you that you aren't to blame, but I know you didn't believe me. You've always been willing to own up to the consequences of what you do, and I admire that." Charles smiled slightly, and the look in his eyes was that of a man remembering what he loved about a dearly departed family member. Philip's eyes had been closing periodically—he'd been slipping back onto the train—but now that he knew what was happening, the power of this realization and a deep, innate fear beyond any he'd felt before kept his eyes open.

"But you need to know that this is not your fault. I won't have you think that." Charles's eyes welled up, and he exhaled a few times. "Dr. Banes told me that he was in someone's house—whose house it was, that isn't important. Someone very sick. He noticed a newspaper in the corner of the room, the *Timber Falls Daily.* It was dated a week ago, Philip. Well after we started the quarantine."

Charles paused briefly, then said, "Do you see? Dr. Banes questioned the man's wife, and she tried to deny it at first. But she finally admitted that her husband and some friends of his had sneaked off a few times over the past two weeks, to Timber Falls. To buy alcohol." Charles shook his head. "We were guarding the road, but they took one of the Indian trails. Since then other men have confessed to Dr. Banes, confessed on their sickbeds, confessed that they'd stolen off to Timber Falls for other reasons. To visit girlfriends, to visit . . . prostitutes." Charles stumbled over that word, embarrassed to say it in front of his son. "Not many men but enough. One would have been enough, really." Charles's right hand still clasped his son's. "We don't know how the town fell sick, Philip, and we never will know. There are too many possibilities. I so regret keeping you in that building for those two days."

Charles paused. "I worry now that nothing I've done here has made any difference, nothing at all. But I've tried, and you've tried. You tried so admirably." He squeezed Philip's hand. "So I don't want you blaming yourself, or feeling that you've done anyone in, because you haven't." His voice was now as firm as his grip. "I believe now that what's happened here was simply meant to be, that this is something larger than all of us—larger than each of us individually and larger than all of us collectively. I don't know why God would see fit to do this, and I don't know what lessons we'll draw when it's passed. We can only press on as best as we can, and I intend to do that." He swallowed painfully. "And I want you to be there with me."

Philip had never seen Charles cry and never wanted to again. "Is Laura okay?" he managed to ask.

"She's in bed still," Charles said. "But she'll be better." From Charles's tone, Philip couldn't tell if he had some concrete reason to believe this.

Philip knew that all of this was important—Laura still being sick, some men escaping town to run wild in the disease-ridden streets of Timber Falls—but it seemed to glance off him. Soon Charles was gone, and Philip was back on the train.

The men were still packed so tightly that Philip could barely breathe. He had hoped it was from the emotion in his chest at seeing his father cry, but that had long passed, and still his breaths required great effort. Was it worth this pain? If it would always hurt this way, Philip wasn't strong enough to continue. The flu had him now, its talons so deep in his lungs and heart that it would soon overtake him completely.

"You look bad, kid," Frank said. He was smiling, the smile that had made Philip hate him so much at first—because how could he smile with a gun pointed at him, and how could he smile when he was trapped in a stinking prison? But that smile had disarmed Philip over time; eventually, it had made Philip like him, too quickly and too intensely considering how briefly they had known each other. Perhaps it was the pressure of the situation that had played with his emotions, but the fact remained that when Philip had realized what Graham had done, it was as if Philip's own brother had been murdered.

"I *feel* bad," Philip replied. "I feel horrible."

"This train stinks. You notice that?"

"I can't smell a thing. I can barely breathe."

Frank was riddled with bullet holes, his army shirt in tatters, but thankfully, there was no blood. Philip didn't know how Graham had killed Frank, but the bullet holes seemed as likely a method as any.

"You don't think I was lying to you about the C.O., do you?"

"I don't think so. I don't really know what to think, you know? All I know is I liked you." Philip thought of something. "Do you know where this train is going?"

"'Course. You don't?"

"I guess I hoped I was wrong. What happened to all those other guys?"

"The hell with those other guys. The hell with everyone, is what I say. It's just about you, you know? You can't worry about other folks—you just gotta watch your own back. The hell with everyone else."

"Then why'd you help the C.O.?"

"Look where it got me, kid."

"Doesn't mean it was wrong."

"Didn't say it was wrong. All I said is that if I had to do it all over again, I wouldn't."

Philip nodded.

"What?" Frank challenged, noticing the look in Philip's eyes.

"Nothing, I just . . . That's sad, I guess."

"This whole mess is pretty goddamned sad, don't you think? The hell with sad. And the hell with everyone. The hell with you, too."

"Why?"

"I wish I'd gotten to France. I would've been a hell of a soldier. I would've rounded up hundreds of Heinies, captured 'em with my bare hands. I would've been a madman out there."

"What kind of soldier do you think I would have been?"

Frank eyed him carefully. "You would've saved somebody's life or died trying."

It felt like the greatest compliment Philip had ever received.

"I gotta go now, kid."

Frank was gone. Philip was alone on the train.

Later, he heard singing, the same song he had heard before, a song his mother used to sing to him, a lullaby. He stood there on the train listening intently, swooning at every word, until he thought to turn around, and there she was.

"What are you doing here?" he asked. She was so beautiful, an enchanting loveliness that surely spoiled every man who enjoyed her company.

"Just waiting to get off." She peered out the window. He did, too, but everything out there was black—not an eventide darkness but a void.

"Can I come with you?"

She looked shocked and somewhat amused by his question. "Of course you can." She seemed about to laugh but smiled instead, a wide smile, the one he would always work so hard to win when she was in one of her moods. He would do anything to see a smile like that. "You were always thinking I was going to leave you."

He almost stammered a reply, but his throat felt too tight, not from the something but from love.

"Let's get out now," she said, holding her arm out for him.

He reached out and took her hand. She stepped off the train, through a doorway he hadn't seen before, and he followed.

There was no train then, no featureless men. Everything had dissolved, faded away. The pain was gone and so was the something, the sharpness he had felt when he breathed. He felt his mother's hand in his, and that was all. The train had stopped and there was no world surrounding it, no land and no sky, there was nothing at all except himself and a calmness he had never felt before.

Philip slept.

IV

The flu had laid siege to Commonwealth for more than two weeks when Doc Banes began to believe, cautiously, that the disease was abating. The number of new cases had seemed to be on the decline for four days, though Banes could not be certain, as there was no official way to tally the sick beyond the scrawled and decreasingly legible notes in his journal. The deaths, too, seemed to be slowing: fifty-two people had died, but only seven in the last five days. This accorded with what he knew of past epidemics, that they tended to be deadliest in their earliest days, that those who were exposed to disease first had the most severe cases. If the flu was indeed on the wane, that would be the first hint of good news since they posted guards.

Banes's head hurt that morning as he visited the sick in their shut-in homes. After too many sleepless nights—too many nights of arriving home at three A.M. and being unable to let his mind drift—he had placed his bottle of Scotch by his bedside, had sipped at it until the warmth took him. He had woken up that morning amazed at how little was remaining in his bottle, a dull and dry headache making it even more difficult than usual for him to rise from his cold bed.

Banes was joined that day by Deacon, as he had been for nearly a week. Deacon had come down with the flu the day after Philip; for two days he had been as sick as the most wretched man in Commonwealth. And utterly alone, as no one had known he was ill, no one had knocked on his door, no one had missed his presence at the places he had always haunted more like a spirit than a man. But on that third day in bed, as Deacon lay there feverish and weak, God finally spoke to him. When he heard the voice from his sickbed there was no mistaking it. The Lord told him to rise from his bed, to aid the doctor in treating the afflicted. Suddenly the strength returned to Deacon's body and he felt as youthful and lithe as a teenager. The Lord wanted him to help Doc Banes, and Deacon would obey. The timbre of God's voice and the sound of the wind in the heavy branches above and the gentle roll of the doctor's carriage were all deafening, and Deacon marveled at everything that he had never heard before.

Deacon joined Doc Banes the next morning, though he kept his revelations to himself, as he was still somewhat dazed by their power. Doc Banes was left to wonder how this formerly taciturn man had become the most eager nurse Banes had ever known, how he could sit there beside the dying and look into their eyes with an understanding that Banes dared not attempt, with an empathy that Banes and his years of hardened experience knew enough to run from. Deacon held hands, administered cold towels and pills, cleaned bedpans, and helped strip beds as if doing so were a supreme honor. A fever does things to people, Banes had noticed, and rather than question Deacon's transformation, he simply felt thankful that for once the flu had changed someone for the better.

Everyone else remained a shut-in, whether healthy or not. And even though Banes was the one who'd told people to stay in their homes, he was beginning to realize how badly he missed the sight of women walking on the street, baskets in hand, dresses swaying. How much he yearned for the sounds of children playing, even if they would forever remind him of the children he'd never had. How much he needed—desperately needed—to see even so mundane a sight as two men approaching from opposite ends of a road, nodding as they neared each other and shaking hands. Just that simple touching, the clasp of two unfamiliar hands. Over those past two weeks Martin Banes had seen people die and people mourn and people suffer to unimaginable degrees, but he knew as he rode to the next house that if he were to see two strangers shake hands, he would collapse into tears.

Banes drove his carriage up to the home of a young couple who had already lost their two-year-old and now had a sick four-year-old. The mother had become ill the day before. Banes had already seen three families completely wiped out, like characters in a Bible story most people skipped over, but as he and Deacon approached the door, Banes dared to hope.

The first to see the specters was a little boy. His name was Harmon, and he knew that he wasn't supposed to be outside. No little boys can go out, his mother had been telling him. Why not? The flu. But Harmon had been told that the flu couldn't come to this town, that there were strong men standing guard and making sure nothing entered. How did the flu get in? he asked. Specters, his mother said. The flu was brought in by specters that the guards couldn't see, specters that could slip between trees and move only during the second when the guards' eyes were blinking.

Harmon had stayed inside for what seemed like years. Finally, while his parents slept, he slipped out. He hadn't thought to wear a coat and he shivered in the bitingly cold air. He saw that the entire town was frozen with inactivity, that every street was empty, every door shut, every window covered. Being outside wasn't any more interesting than being inside, he realized to his disappointment.

He passed the last houses and walked to the place where the strong men had guarded the town. Harmon climbed on a big tree stump at the edge of the hill, looking down at the lone road and the huge forest beyond.

He had been sitting there for just a minute when he saw the specters. There were four of them at first, gathered at the bottom of the hill. Then there were eight. Then he lost count. The trees down there shaded them so they were dark, barely more than shadows. That was just how he'd imagined specters looked. They seemed to be talking to one another, but he couldn't hear them, which also made sense, as he'd assumed that specters only whispered, or maybe hissed.

Had they seen him? Harmon was little, so maybe they hadn't. Scared, he climbed off the stump and hid behind it.

He had not thought specters wielded saws, but there they were, sawing into the big tree that lay on its side, blocking the road into town. They used two big crosscut saws, and soon they were pushing the cut tree off to the side, clearing the road. Then the specters disappeared.

Harmon was still scared, so he started walking home. He didn't understand why evil specters would come to clear a road if they could slip through trees.

He was almost at the bend in the road when he heard the specters roar. A white chill ran up his frame at the howling as they stampeded toward him. Harmon turned around and saw the autos and trucks pulling up the hill, then he ran home as fast as he could, the specters licking at his heels.

There were no more books for Amelia to read, no more journals. There was no extra food to can, and it was too late in the year to do any work in the back garden. She had used up all of her yarn and had repaired every damaged garment she could find. After two weeks of being trapped, she felt she had long ago exhausted any potential avenues for enjoyment.

Except her daughter. Millie had a sunnier disposition than Amelia had expected, seemed so much happier than the vision of screaming, colicky malcontent that her father had put in her head. Horace had always complained about how difficult it was to raise Amelia and her brothers, never failing to mention any of the inconveniences that their existence had caused for him and their dearly departed mother.

Millie didn't seem to mind that she hadn't been taken outside in days, but after two weeks of it, Amelia was desperate. The previous night she had dared to voice the suggestion that going for a short walk might do them all some good, but Graham had sternly reminded her that they could run out for vital errands only, and certainly not just for the sake of enjoying the fresh air. The flu was still out there.

Since Graham's strange altercation with Philip, he had left the house only a couple of times, as had Amelia—for quick errands, for emergency trips to borrow needed items from friends. They knew that many friends, such as Jarred Rankle, were ill. They had seen Doc Banes walk into and out of houses across the street, had seen the undertaker follow. They had seen the crape hanging in so many windows, the very houses themselves in mourning.

Amelia had noticed that Graham had been even quieter than usual the past few days. Every time she tried to broach the subject of Philip, he would darken, turn silent.

Amelia desperately wanted to take a walk, to feel the cold air on her face, to hear the wind. But as much as the confinement pained her, she told herself that this she could endure. She had endured her miscarriage and the death of her mother, and Graham had lived through the loss of his finger and the loss of friends in the Everett Massacre, had survived shooting that soldier. When all was well, you assumed that to suffer such a staggering blow would break you, but when such ills actually befell you, you somehow persevered. You didn't survive to prove something to anyone, you didn't press on simply because you wished to, and you didn't endure because of what the preacher in church said. You survived because deep inside everyone was the simple, indefatigable need to press on, whatever the costs. And even if so much was stripped away that you no longer recognized yourself, the thing left was the part of you that you never understood, that you always underestimated, that you were always afraid to look at. You were afraid you'd need it one day and it wouldn't be there for you, but in fact was the one thing that couldn't be taken away.

After Philip had coughed on him those many days ago, Graham had stood out on the porch for a long while, so afraid he was contaminated that he couldn't bring himself to open the door and enter his wife's embrace. He had instead swallowed his pride by seeking out Doc Banes's opinion. Banes had shaken his head at Graham. Graham couldn't remember the last time he had felt so belittled. Banes's eyes, the bags beneath them, and the bit of blood on his shirt collar bespoke real fear, true terror. The doctor simply told Graham to go to his family; there was nothing that could be done. And though Graham still was not impressed with the doctor's expertise, he realized he had no alternative.

Graham was haunted by Philip's accusation. No matter what he did to try to distract himself, he kept hearing the word *murderer* and feeling it in the most tightly guarded quarters of his being. It was there when he slept, it was there when he opened his eyes, it was there when he looked at his wife.

The second soldier had been a sacrifice, Graham reasoned. The man's life was sacrificed, but Graham, too, had sacrificed a part of himself. With each passing day, the cost of that sacrifice seemed to grow beyond his reckoning. Every time he saw the undertaker emerge from a house with a body cloaked in blankets, it looked just like the bloody soldier lying at the bottom of his grave. Graham had killed that man to preserve everyone else, but it hadn't worked. Each death was piled on top of Philip's accusation, giving it the horrible weight of truth.

Millie was taking her morning nap while Amelia sat in her chair, staring out into the street. It had started to snow for the first time that season, and the startling newness of the snow, the beauty of it, dazed her. Her right hand was on her belly, resting near her unborn child.

Graham walked into the room and sat beside her, taking her left hand in his. She wanted to ask if he'd ever seen such a magnificent sight, the unusually large white flakes falling so slowly and straight it was as if they were being carefully lowered from strings. But she found she couldn't speak. She just stared.

"There's crape in the Wainwrights' windows." Graham pointed at one of the houses down the road. The crape hadn't been there the previous day. "I wonder who it was."

V

They knocked on the first door in town, taking a methodical approach. Bartrum had told the men they would need to be careful not to skip over any houses, since they all looked alike. J. B. Merriwhether shifted nervously on his heels, standing in the back with his hands at his sides.

The woman who answered the door was thin and young, perhaps twenty, and appeared to be a few months with child. Her face had a near-ghostly pallor, and her eyes widened at the sight before her: six men on her doorstep, all of them with badges shining on their lapels.

"Morning, ma'am," Bartrum said with a brusque nod. "Can we see the gentleman of the house?"

She nodded without speaking and went to fetch her husband. Since she had left the door open, Bartrum casually strolled inside. Four of his cohorts followed, but J.B., as instructed, stayed at the edge of the porch, keeping watch in case anyone tried to climb out a window.

The young missus returned with a man who looked even younger than she, though he was at least eighteen, of that J.B. was certain. The husband's eyes, too, were blue, and his hair was a light blond.

"Morning," said the young man. "Name's Ils. What can I do for you?"

"We'd like to see your deferment papers." Bartrum tried to say it without smiling, and he was almost successful. He knew this would be a long day, knew the slackers would offer denials and pleas and perhaps even threats.

But this man was no slacker, apparently. He showed mild surprise at the request, but he turned to his wife and asked her to retrieve the papers from his bureau. After she was gone, Bartrum told him, "You're supposed to keep those on you, son."

"I do, sir, whenever I leave the house. We've just been shut in from the flu for so long now, I haven't gone out in a while."

"It's Sheriff, not sir. Sheriff Bartrum."

Ils nodded, appearing more worried. "My apologies, Sheriff. I didn't realize we had a sheriff here in town."

"I'm sure you folks are used to living lawlessly, son, but those times are changing."

Ils's wife returned with the papers, which Ils quickly shuffled through, his hands beginning to shake, before finding the right ones. He handed them to Bartrum nervously.

The sheriff took his time looking them over, but it was obvious they were legitimate. Mr. Ils Bergman had indeed registered months ago, upon his eighteenth birthday, and had been deferred as an essential war worker.

Bartrum handed them back. "All right, son. You remember to keep these on you at all times, understand?" Ils nodded. "And if this war lasts much longer, they say they're going to drop all those worker deferments, so you'd best be ready."

By the time Ils had said, "Yes sir, Sheriff," Bartrum had already turned around, J.B. and the others following.

Miller stood in the middle of the road, leaning against one of the four trucks they had driven into town along with their Fords. It had taken a while to procure the trucks from nearby towns and municipalities, to impress upon the local mayors and assorted panjandrums the need for them, the dangers of having slacker towns hiding in the woods. One mayor was particularly reluctant until Miller mentioned the possibility that Commonwealth was harboring spies, the same spies who had killed those boys at Fort Jenkins. Then the mayor not only lent him a truck but the use of three officers for the raid.

They were twenty men all told, some of them from Bartrum's force but most of them volunteers who had been deputized for the occasion. There were Winslow and J. B. Merriwhether and other upstanding businessmen alongside brawny toughs like Hightower, the muscle that would be necessary when some of the slackers resisted. Miller and Winslow stood out by the trucks they had parked in the middle of the main street, observing the three groups of six men as they began knocking on doors. Bartrum's gang came away from the first house empty-handed, but it wasn't enough to make Miller worry. He'd pored over the deferment records and had seen only a paltry number of men who claimed to be from Commonwealth. Yet he knew the town had a viable mill and therefore had a few hundred able-bodied workers, knew that the town must be chock-full of slackers. The trucks would not be empty for long.

Once the men were in jail, where they belonged, they could be questioned on the subject of spies. Miller had hoped to get information on that matter from Charles Worthy, but since the haughty mill owner had been less than forthcoming the previous visit, it had to be done this way. Miller didn't like getting his hands dirty, but neither was he one to shy away from a fight.

The snow was falling more heavily, and though the first few flakes had melted the moment they hit Miller's jacket, they were beginning to stick as the snowfall thickened. His hat and jacket were dusted with white, the picture of a man blending in with surroundings he wanted nothing to do with. He used his gloved hand to wipe away some of the snow, a black slash cutting across his chest. That was when the yelling started.

J.B.'s group found its first slacker in the next house.

The man who opened the door was perhaps a decade older than Ils, right in the middle of the age range for enlistment. He had a dense mat of thick hair and a prominent wart stood two inches south of his right eye. The type of face policemen probably wished all criminals had, J.B. thought: ugly and full of distinguishing characteristics. The man, Gerry Timlin, moved with a ropy muscularity that surely served him well as a river driver.

"May I see your deferment papers, please?" Bartrum said as his men hung around him, snow draping the air behind them.

Gerry shook his head, confused. "What papers?" His voice was scratchy and weak, like that of a man who had not spoken in days. Then he coughed into one of his hands, and J.B. realized he wasn't just ugly, he was sick.

The flu had abated somewhat in Timber Falls, at long last. Many were still sick, but death was no longer commonplace, which was how Miller had been able to wrangle enough healthy and strong-willed patriots for the raid. If not for the flu, they would have done this two weeks ago.

But here in Commonwealth, J.B. was learning, the flu was still strong.

Bartrum made a loud exhalation, feigning annoyance with an air of practice. "Did you register for the draft, sir?"

Gerry stood speechless. He looked at Bartrum's badge and considered, but he clearly wasn't used to being spoken to this way. "Who's asking?"

"Skip Bartrum, Timber Falls sheriff."

Gerry's eyebrows shifted. "You ain't sheriff of my town."

Bartrum's expression was unchanged. "We're with the American Protective League, smart guy, and that makes us deputized wherever our boots should take us. And unless you have some papers to show us, you are under arrest for failing to register, for shirking your obligation to your country, and for being a yellow-bellied bastard."

Gerry finally seemed to understand the trouble he was in when two of the men sidled up beside him. They were both as big as he was, and he was not at his best. J.B. stayed outside, nervous at the escalating tone.

"Gerry?"

The men looked into the house and saw a woman nearly as tall as her husband. She had broad shoulders, a full bosom, and a mean face that made the deputies grateful they were there for her husband and not her.

Gerry didn't reply, so she walked up beside him. She glared at Bartrum—if his badge impressed her, she didn't show it. "What's going on?"

"I'm sorry to say, ma'am, your husband did not register for the draft," Bartrum replied. "He is under arrest."

He nodded to the two men, who clamped their hands on Gerry's forearms and started leading him off the porch. Gerry was still too stunned to do anything but follow, and he coughed again, this time unable to catch it with his hands and instead spraying it on Bartrum's chest.

"You can't do this!" Pauline Timlin screamed out at them after a moment's shock. "He's a sick man! He's been in bed all week!"

"Rest assured, there are cots in the Timber Falls jail," Bartrum said with a smile as he followed his men and their captive.

The smile reminded J.B. that he was supposed to feel good about this. After all those days of mourning, of being helpless to stop the flu from ravaging his family and his town, finally there was something he could do, a wrong he could right. There were slackers in this town, and he would damn well help jail every last one of them.

Inside the house, the three Timlin boys, aged three to nine, arrayed themselves in the doorway in differing degrees of undress. Then their mother screamed and chased after Bartrum, slugging him in the arm.

"That's enough!" the sheriff shouted at her, rubbing his surprisingly sore forearm. "Get back with your family, ma'am, or we'll cart you off, too!"

But after he turned back around to watch the men load Gerry into one of the trucks, the back door of which Miller had helpfully opened, Pauline let loose a wordless howl and charged forward, her outstretched hands aimed at the back of Bartrum's shoulders. As J.B. stood in amazement, one of the other men interceded, catching her midway, using all his strength to block her charge. He managed to step forward, slinging her onto the ground. Pauline landed roughly on her backside, cushioned only slightly by the growing pillow of snow.

The younger Timlin boys started crying.

Gerry, enraged at seeing his wife so mistreated, lashed out at his captors. He managed to shake off the two men who had been leading him toward the truck, but before he could get any further, Hightower socked him in the gut. The punch seemed to carry all the weight of Hightower's recent pain, all of the agony of his dead sons. Gerry doubled over, gasping and dropping to one knee. Within a few seconds he had been thrown into the back of the truck, wheezing.

Bartrum unholstered his revolver. The gun was pointed only at the ground, but it was threatening nonetheless. "Tie his hands," he told the men.

J.B. didn't like violence but he remembered Bartrum's instructions: they would need to quash any resistance as roughly as possible to discourage anyone from following suit. There were many more houses to check.

The oldest Timlin boy, Donny, ran to help his mother up. As the men tied up Gerry, Bartrum gave Pauline a calm and steady look, then walked to the truck.

"Go run to Mr. Worthy's," Pauline whispered into her son's ear. "Tell him he needs to get over here—now."

Donny ran.

Not every house in town was occupied. As the flu had stretched on and food supplies had dwindled, a number of families and single men had abandoned the town, running from starvation and from the flu. They left despite the fact that Charles Worthy still owed them for their labor the past few weeks, despite the fact that they had once willingly fled from the same towns where they were now returning. But this exodus had not been as large as might have been expected, as so many had become too stricken to travel. Although many knocks were answered by silence, there were still plenty of houses for Bartrum's men to raid.

There was less coughing in the Worthy house that morning. Rebecca was putting water on the stove for tea when she saw an unusual sight: Philip walking into the kitchen.

"Well, hello there," she said, smiling. This was the farthest Philip had walked since his first day with the flu, when he had wandered over to Graham's in a delirium.

He smiled back, looking weak but overjoyed to be standing there, to be coming back to life. She asked him how he felt, and he said hungry. An auspicious sign. She began to heat oatmeal for him, and he sat down at the table.

"It feels good to move around," he said slowly. He seemed to be remembering how to talk, his tongue awkward, his body stumbling its way through the most basic movements. He had been in bed for ten days, they'd told him the previous night, when he'd been well enough to sit up and carry on a conversation.

He had wanted to walk around the house then, but his parents had asked him to stay in bed a bit more, to continue resting. They did not tell him that his recovery was unexpected. Doc Banes had leveled with Charles and Rebecca halfway through the illness: he did not think Philip would survive. The symptoms and their severity were following the same pattern as those of the men and women who had already succumbed. Philip's flu had begotten pneumonia, and he was having trouble breathing. When

Banes gave his dismal diagnosis to Charles, he was expecting that Philip's lips and fingers would be blue the next day and that he'd be a corpse the day after that.

But the good doctor had been wrong. Philip hung at the threshold for so long that his parents weren't sure if this was just the devil trying to wring every last drop of suffering from his victim, or if Philip was actually recovering, albeit gradually. Days later, here Philip was, sitting at the kitchen table, eating oatmeal. Rebecca didn't believe in miracles, but the vision before her left her wondering how to classify such an event.

Philip had never been heavy, but he'd lost even more weight, his jaw and cheekbones more prominent than before, his skin the color of stones at the bottom of a river. He looked like he had emerged from a grave, not a sickbed.

Rebecca carried another bowl of oatmeal past him, heading toward the stairs. "I'll be right back. I have to take this to Laura."

"Is Laura still sick?" His voice was gaining strength, but it sounded small beside the hugeness of this question.

"She's much better," Rebecca said. "She's worried about Elsie."

Rebecca stopped, wondering how blunt to be. She had seen how he acted around Elsie, had seen her writing a letter to him in school once. But after so many near-sleepless nights, after seeing the town collapse around her, she lacked the strength to soften the blow for him. "Elsie's very sick," she said. "The doctor doesn't think she's going to make it."

Long after Rebecca had ascended the stairs, Philip sat at the table, staring off into the space just above his empty bowl.

The world looked different. He couldn't believe how long he'd been ill. Only twelve days had passed between shooting the first soldier and then becoming sick; an entire lifetime had been crammed into those few days, or so it seemed. And now ten days more had passed with no reliable record except disturbing dreams, conversations he wasn't sure were real or imagined.

Elsie's not going to make it. His head didn't hurt anymore; it felt like a too-tight helmet had been unscrewed from his skull. This sensation of newness, of space, of freedom, left him feeling almost dizzy, made the air around his eyes feel fuzzy, glowing. Elsie's sick. He tried to focus on that thought but found it strangely elusive. Elsie. He had seen her in his dreams, visions of her, and although the train he had ridden on had not been real, Elsie was real. She wasn't a figment of his imagination, a hidden longing that was incompatible with the world around him. She was real, she existed. Elsie. She was sick?

He sat there for a good long while, beginning to understand. The oatmeal felt good in his stomach, strengthening him, but a new nervousness unhinged him, starting in his gut and working its way through his depleted frame. He anxiously started scraping his fingernails—they had become so long while he was in bed—against the wood table. He was getting better, he had survived, he had returned to the world that had continued without him, but where was Elsie?

Then there was a frantic knocking on the door, and a child's voice, screaming.

VI

The first truck was full in less than an hour.

More than a dozen had been arrested so far, Miller noted. At this rate they would need to send the full trucks back to the Timber Falls jail and then return for a second batch, even a third or a fourth.

"I'd like to see how he's going to run his mill now," Winslow said to him with a short laugh.

"That has nothing to do with this." Miller's face soured as if he'd been offended by a dirty joke. "I told you this isn't about Worthy's mill—this is about protecting our country, making sure men are following the law. I don't give a damn what this means for his mill or yours."

Winslow's smile could not be erased. "You have your reasons, Mr. Miller, and I have mine."

Miller saw the man's point: if the flu hadn't already crippled Worthy's mill, losing eight or twelve truckloads of men surely would. The Winslows would do quite a bit better without Worthy's mill undercutting their prices and offering higher wages to lure away workers.

And speak of the devil, there he was: Charles Worthy, looking far less commanding and proud than he'd appeared that day by the road into town. He was sweating in the snow, his hair disheveled and his normally pale face gone red with fear or rage or cold.

Charles had driven the old Ford he usually reserved for longer distances; this matter was too urgent for walking. After stopping near the crowded spot where the trucks and autos were blocking the street, he kicked open his door, nearly forgetting to turn off the engine.

He had wanted to bring more men with him, but if this visit was what he thought it was, that wouldn't have been wise.

Charles should have done more to ensure that everyone had registered, he now realized—he should have required every man to prove that he had secured an essential-worker deferment. Instead, he had let his own ambivalence about the war, combined with his wife's hatred for it, allow him to make a poor decision. And this was the result.

Charles couldn't believe the sight before him. He knew all the men locked in the trucks. Some of them looked to be in shock, but many of them were clearly scared. Many were still sick, their faces hollowed from the time Charles had last seen them, their coughs polluting the trucks. Some of the men were young, barely older than Philip, but an equal number were in their late twenties or thirties and had wives, families.

And there the families were, at least some of them: a small crowd had gathered around the trucks, women screaming or crying or pleading, some of them with babies in their arms or children at their side. They stood there in the snow, most having rushed out of their houses without wraps, imploring three large men with badges and holstered pistols to let their husbands go. The APL men stood there expressionless as statues, hands at their sides in case they needed to unholster their weapons.

"What in the name of God is going on here?" Worthy yelled.

Miller waited for Worthy to reach him—he wanted to explain the situation, not holler it down the street. Worthy was irate but alone, no armed guards this time, and Miller was comfortable with the fact that he and his colleagues were firmly in charge.

"These men are under arrest for failing to register, Mr. Worthy," Miller said. "We're knocking on every door in town and will see the papers of every man of draft age. Any man who doesn't have such papers will be sent to jail in Timber Falls to await trial."

"These men are essential war workers, you know that!" Miller could tell Worthy was not used to bellowing like this. It made his own calmness feel like a form of power.

"And you know that all men of age, regardless of their occupation, are required to register. *Then,* and only then, the registration boards decide who is and is not an essential worker. If your men assumed they would be protected, that assumption wasn't theirs to make."

"This is ridiculous! Why arrest men you know would be declared exempt if they had—"

"Because they're breaking the law," Miller interrupted, raising his voice. "Because other men all over the country have registered and been sent to France and are doing their duty, and no one here has any right to shirk those obligations."

Beside Miller, Winslow broke into a smile at seeing the pompous Worthy in such a state. Worthy saw the smile, which seemed to increase the fire in him.

"How much are the Winslows paying you for this?" Worthy asked Miller. "How much are they paying you to cart off my—"

"I am no one's lackey!" Miller stuck a finger in Worthy's face, finally shaken from his calm. "I am doing this for our country, Mr. Worthy, for our *country.* I'm in debt to no one and nothing but that. I don't know how these men of yours can look themselves in the face while other boys are out there risking their lives, but they'll have plenty of time to ask that question of themselves from behind bars. Do not get in our way."

With that, Miller turned around and strode toward one of the trucks, as if to assist the three armed men in keeping back the shrieking families. Really, all Miller wanted to do was put his back to Worthy, to show that their debate was over and that Worthy's presence here was useless.

Charles looked at Winslow, who was certainly of draft age but likely had received his exemption already. Men like him didn't fight in wars.

"You can blame me and my family all you want, Worthy," Winslow said, still unable to control his glee. "You're the one who chose to hire rapscallions and reds. This is what happens."

He too left Worthy to stand there, impotent in the swirl of events larger than himself, larger than his love for the mill, larger than this town and its dreams.

Rankle resisted.

He had been sick for six days but had been recovering, slowly, for the past forty-eight hours. His neighbor, a man named Hunt with whom he had chatted amiably on many occasions but never known well, had died early on in the epidemic, and Hunt's wife, Corinne, rather than subsuming herself in grief, had dedicated herself to keeping Rankle alive.

Corinne had hung crape in her windows the morning after the undertaker had retrieved her husband's body. There could be no funeral, the doctor had informed her, because there could be no public gatherings—a service would have to wait until the flu had passed. That evening Corinne had seen the doctor leaving the house of Jarred Rankle. So the next morning, her husband barely twenty-four hours dead, she had knocked on Rankle's door and, hearing no reply, had opened it herself and brought him hot tea and put extra blankets on his bed; she spoke to him while he lay there, flayed by the fever's lash. She did all the things she had been unable to do for her husband, who had died after only one day of sickness—one day! She had barely had time to put a cool towel on her husband's forehead, to put her lips there and marvel at the heat. By the time she had told him how much she loved him, her husband had already been shaking uncontrollably, already halfway to a place where he could no longer hear her. And then he was gone.

But Rankle's flu was slower, and this time the Lord had given Corinne a chance to help. Rankle spoke little that first day, but he seemed unsurprised to see her there, as if this were the fulfillment of some predetermined arrangement. Hardly anyone in town was helping their neighbors this way, too terrified of bringing infection into their own homes. But with Corinne's husband gone, she was unafraid of death. She slept on the floor of Rankle's bedroom, caring for him when he woke with coughing fits. At night she looked through the windows and saw her own house, empty, desolate.

The day it first snowed—the day of the raid—Rankle had recovered to the point where Corinne's presence was no longer needed. He had slept soundly that night, never stirred by a cough or by nausea, and had woken up with a full appetite. As Corinne cooked for them, she knew it was time for her to return to her house, to the emptiness she did not want to confront. She had offered herself to God, helping this man who she thought would eventually spread the disease to her, but they were both healthy now, and her husband was still dead.

She was giving the kitchen a final cleaning when they heard the knock on the door. Rankle had been in the parlor, finally able to stand without dizziness, to inhale deeply without choking, so he went to the door and opened it. Unlike Charles, who had been hoping this day could be avoided, and unlike Gerry Timlin, who had been stunned when the men showed up, Rankle knew who they were and why they were there the moment he saw the sheriff's face.

"I have no papers," Rankle replied to Bartrum's question. "And I will not fight in Wilson's crooked war."

The two larger men, one of whom was Hightower, stepped into the doorway, flanking Rankle.

"Then you're going to jail, son."

"Don't act like you don't know who I am," Rankle said, staring evenly at Bartrum. "I sure as hell remember you."

"All you slackers look alike to me."

"You used to live in Everett. You ran with McRae's boys." Rankle stepped up a bit, as if to accentuate the fact that he was a few inches taller than Bartrum. "You're awfully big when you've got a pack of men, and you're awfully tall when you're kicking men who are lying on the ground."

Bartrum's face grew even redder, as if Rankle had clamped his fingers across the lawman's neck. "You keep your trap shut and this'll go a lot easier for you."

Rankle shifted his gaze from Bartrum to Hightower and the other man. Both were too old for the draft, but they were strong and lean enough to be fighting in France if they so desired. Rankle thought about commenting on this but chose to say something else.

"I suppose you boys think this is real big of you. You're all a bunch of fools if you think this war's doing anything but—"

Bartrum shut him up by socking him in the gut. Rankle had been bracing himself for something, so even though he doubled over and felt his breath escape him, he was already choosing his spots. Hightower and the other men pulled him upright, ready to drag him to the trucks, but Rankle stepped forward and broke two of his fingers on Bartrum's face, throwing the sheriff back so hard he would have fallen through the doorway had there not been three other men standing behind him.

Rankle didn't know who hit him next, but soon he was on the floor. His face had been struck and likewise his neck and then his ribs. Rather than rolling himself into a ball, he tried to get back to his feet, but someone's boots prevented him. The blows kept coming, and they were so loud he couldn't hear Corinne screaming.

"I *am* tall when I'm kicking men on the ground," Bartrum gritted his teeth as he kicked Rankle a second time. He was gearing up for a third when one of the men behind him put a hand on his shoulder.

"Skip," the man said. "Let's just carry him in."

Corinne ran to the bloody heap on the floor but Hightower grabbed her arms. She thrashed and wailed and to all these men it was obvious that she was the man's wife.

Hightower not only heard her screams but felt them, felt them reverberating through his hands gripping her; the screams shook his shoulders and ran down his legs back into the earth beneath them.

After Bartrum had put a handkerchief to his bloodied nose and spat on the floor, and after the other men had half carried and half dragged the broken and unconscious Rankle out of his house, Hightower released Corinne's arms and she dropped to the ground as if she had been dead all along.

Philip sat on his bed, staring out the window. Ever since the accident, he had hated snow, hated how the world grew quiet as the snow fell around him.

He could still see Elsie's words written in the fog on the window, dim and faded but legible if one knew where to look. *YOU OK?* and *GET WELL* with the backward *E,* and in between them, in taller and bolder letters, *LOVE YOU.* Still he felt unwell. His throat did not burn, but he felt cold inside his head, as if something were missing in there, as if it were all air and the winter chill were freezing his skull from the inside. He found it difficult even to think about Elsie, difficult to fully grasp love and its meaning, impossible to grapple with the concept of loss or death. He just sat there dazed, the world before him shimmering.

Time passed. He heard Rebecca angrily muttering to herself, so he rose and walked into the kitchen, which she was furiously cleaning, as she was wont to do when she needed to distract herself.

"What's wrong?" he asked.

She looked up at him, strands of gray hair cascading across her face. Her cheeks were red, and sweat streaked her forehead.

"They're arresting men who didn't register. Right now. Just carting them off."

Philip sat down. Donny Timlin's panicked visit had seemed to pass like a dream. The moment Charles and Donny had left earlier, it had been like they never existed.

Rebecca slammed her hand against the counter, but the sound didn't hit Philip for a couple of seconds. Then she hugged herself and let out a sound that Philip couldn't quite discern, either a shortened cry or a bereaved sigh or a minor scream, the sound of a fist tightening around someone's heart.

"Who are they arresting?" Philip asked, folding his arms against the cold.

"*Everyone.* Everyone who didn't register."

Philip imagined them dragging Graham and throwing him in a dank prison, something far darker and fouler than the last place Frank had laid eyes on. He saw them hanging Graham after a quick trial, saw Graham's body being thrown into an empty and nameless ditch, saw Amelia in black. Philip tried to remember the conversation he'd had with Graham about the war those many months ago, but it felt like that part of his brain had been scrubbed away by something so abrasive that even trying to think about it hurt.

So he focused on the present: Graham was being arrested. Philip concentrated so hard he had to close his eyes, concentrated on making his mind work the way he knew it could. The Timlins lived in one of the houses closest to the town entrance. But Graham and Amelia lived far to the other side of the Worthy house, closer to the mill. If the men hadn't knocked on the Worthys' door yet, then perhaps they hadn't yet knocked on Graham's.

Philip slowly made his way through the parlor. He gazed out the window, this one adorned not with Elsie's thoughts but with snowy patches in the bottom corners, the whiteness clinging there. He looked out and saw, far to his right, a group of men knocking on a neighbor's front door: Jay Wachowski, the man who'd broken both his hands in a mill accident a few weeks ago. Philip didn't know if Wachowski had registered, didn't know if

Doc Banes had cut open the man's casts yet. Would he be carted off to prison with his hands still bound in plaster?

Philip tapped at the cold glass, remembering the time his hands had been covered in bandages to save them from frostbite. He remembered being unable to touch his own brow, being unable to feed himself, unable to so much as count on his fingers because they were all balled together in the same hideous mash of white. The snow was falling more heavily, growing thick on the roads, which would soon be dangerous, impassable.

But his thoughts returned to Graham. Graham had been the one who pulled the trigger while Philip had just stood there. He had been granted the luxury of seeing what happened to Graham as a result, and that was why he hadn't been able to repeat Graham's act when Frank came walking up that hill. When Philip thought of all that Graham had done, he could not escape the fact that he too might have been forced down the same path if he'd been the one who pulled the trigger. He hated and feared what Graham had turned into, but Graham's actions had saved him from a similar fate.

Rebecca had gone back upstairs, so Philip walked to the closet by the front door. He grabbed his boots and his coat, his hat and gloves. Then he grabbed the rifle.

This was already too rough for J.B. Though Miller had said there was a chance things would get out of hand, he had also said these were weakling slackers and the vast majority would go willingly. He had said that twenty men, a show of such force, would cow the slackers into surrendering, would send them single-file, heads hung, into the backs of those trucks. Men like J.B. were doing what they could for their country, Miller had said: *We may be too old to be out on the front lines, but we're doing our part to keep the home front protected.*

But seeing that first man get slugged by Hightower, with the man's wife and children crying in the background, had turned J.B.'s stomach. The sight of the suffering family reminded him even more of his own wife and his lost children. He did not want to be here. He had made a mistake. He should be back home, knocking on his wife's door, again and again, beseeching her to let him in so they could wrap their arms around each other and try to keep the world at bay.

Many of the APL men with him were young enough to serve in the army but had been deferred for various reasons. Some were essential war workers, some were policemen whose absence their towns could not afford. The rest of the men, like Hightower, were older but still strong enough to defeat any young man who should foolishly challenge them. J.B., though, knew he was just a pencil pusher, a man more like Miller, who had given himself the lightweight role of truck guard. As part of Bartrum's six-man brigade, J.B. stayed in the shadows while the others used their broad shoulders to intimidate and used their thick boots to pound down anyone who tried to resist.

"Kick the sonuvabitch," Hightower told J.B. after the rest of them had subdued a man who had tried to escape, who had spat in Bartrum's face and grazed Hightower with an inept punch. Every other man in the crew had kicked him at least once except J.B., whose lack of gusto had finally, as he'd feared, become suspect.

J.B. didn't look at Hightower, looked instead at the man on the ground, covered in snow. An older child, really, a kid who probably had turned eighteen only a few months ago.

"Kick him for our sons," Hightower said.

J.B. felt that everyone was looking at him, waiting, assessing. What was he doing here? His son, James, wouldn't want him to kick this weakling. James wasn't like Hightower or his roughneck sons. James would want to help this boy up. But James was gone, his shattered body a million miles away and his soul across the impassable void. War changes a man, and J.B. shuddered to think what James may have become by the day he died. Maybe James would have stomped on this young man's face, would have leaped upon him with terrifying enthusiasm.

Hightower and the others were still waiting. J.B. kicked the boy in the back. Not too hard but enough. He exhaled. He would kick the next one harder.

Graham stood up when he heard the shots. He had been sitting beside Amelia, staring at the snow, when they heard the first pop followed by three more volleys. It was a hundred times louder than any sound the town had mustered in days.

Amelia stayed in her chair, looking up at him questioningly. From their vantage point, they could see nothing but a neighborhood being buried by winter's first act, but Graham recognized gunshots. He went to the front door and stood behind it for a moment, afraid to open it, afraid of what he might let in.

He opened the door and stepped onto the porch, shivering in the biting wind. About two blocks to his left, he saw a pile of men, a scrum, at the bottom of which was some whitened rodent flailing about. But it wasn't a rodent, it was a man lying there in the snow, a man being kicked and hit by the surrounding men, at least one of whom held a gun pointed to the heavens.

Then a truck started driving toward them. It pulled up beside them, and a well-dressed man in a derby emerged. He opened the large back door, then the scrum of men picked up the snow-covered body they had been trouncing and carried it into the back of the truck. Graham saw the redheaded mane of one of the Timber Falls men who had tried to enter Commonwealth, the man who had called them slackers and had ranted about his dead sons in France. The sight of the man gradually meshed with that past experience, became bound in a tight net Graham felt closing around him.

The men dusted the snow from their coats and walked up to the house of one of Graham's neighbors, where the crape in the windows should have told them they were entering a death house. They knocked on the door nonetheless, perhaps too enthralled by their bloodlust to notice the telltale signs surrounding them.

Hightower was doing this for his sons. He was doing it because he and his wife had raised their boys right, had produced two strong and right-thinking young men who went to church and had adoring Christian sweethearts. He was doing it because they had proceeded to the registration board on the allotted date, had entered their names and accepted their numbers with dignity. He did not know what had transpired in their rooms behind those shut doors on the last night before they reported at Fort Jenkins, did not know what they had asked of God in their prayers on their last night at home, did not know if fear had yielded to tears or if they had been calm before sleep took them. He knew what they had said to him, though, and what they had written in their letters, knew the looks in their eyes the last time he had seen them, decked out in military fatigues and looking so much older than he had ever realized they could be.

Maybe if every other young man in the country had responded as his sons had, there would have been more doughboys at the front. Maybe the Expeditionary Force would have been twice as strong, would have mowed through France in days, would have beaten the Hun clear through Belgium and back into the primeval German forests where it belonged. Maybe if every boy had been as valiant as the Hightowers, they would be home again, announcing their wedding engagements. Maybe if this damn state hadn't been overrun by slackers and reds, by people who would rather hide from a threat than face it, Hightower's sons would be alive.

His sons were so unlike this weak young man, who'd climbed out of his side window and leaped down into the snow, trying to sprint away through the thickening drifts. Bartrum had fired some warning shots, which slowed the kid a bit, left him debating whether this tactic was the right one. Before he could resume his flight, Hightower had tackled him from behind. The kid had tried to wrestle free and had landed a boot square across Hightower's jaw, but by then the others were upon him. He wasn't even moaning anymore by the time they loaded him into the truck, the last one they hadn't yet filled.

"We're running out of space," Miller said.

"There's still plenty slackers left," Bartrum answered. His nose was broken, and though the blood no longer flowed, it was the color of cooked beets, so much darker than the white snow surrounding his head. The skin around his eyes was also darkening—that slacker from a couple houses ago had clocked him good. "We haven't even been to half the town yet."

"We'll need to come back," Hightower said.

"Not today," Miller replied. "Way this snow's falling, this is the last chance we'll get for a few days. I say we stuff as many into these trucks as we can before heading out."

Hightower nodded. "No argument here." He gazed down the block at the next residence on their agenda. But what captured his attention was a few houses beyond, a man standing on a porch, watching them. "Sonuvabitch," he said. "There he is."

"Who?" Bartrum asked.

Ever since the first day they'd come to Commonwealth, Hightower had been haunted by those eyes. Even though the man had pulled a mask over half his face when Worthy had shown up, Hightower would never forget those insolent eyes. He didn't know the man's name, but he'd been hoping he'd be the one who got to knock on his door.

"Let's skip the next few houses," Hightower said. "I want to make sure we take that bastard in today."

When Charles saw them carrying an unconscious man toward one of the trucks, he lunged forward. He was horrified by all that blood, by the fact that a man had been beaten so badly he could not walk. As they brought the man closer, Rankle's head rolled to the side and Charles recognized his friend.

But as Charles ran, two other men stepped up and blocked his path. They told him he'd come far enough, and as he tried to press past them, they pushed him back until he fell into the snow.

Rankle was tossed into the back of the truck alongside Deacon. Deacon had been leaving a sick house with the doctor when the APL had confronted him and carted him away. He didn't understand why the Lord would speak to him and then cast him off like this, but he had felt no fear as he allowed himself to be carried by God's will. His faith was shaken, however, by the wounds he saw on Rankle's face. He squeezed past the other captured men and took off his jacket, folding it into a makeshift pillow and stuffing it under Rankle's head. He brushed some of the hair from Rankle's forehead and sopped up his blood with a sleeve.

"All right, there, Jarred," Deacon rasped. "You'll be fine. We'll get you to a doctor soon. We'll be okay."

Doc Banes helped Charles to his feet. All around them, teams of APL men were knocking on more doors, emerging with more workers. Many of the workers were sick, but the men from Timber Falls didn't seem to care.

Banes was too tired to rail against them, as Charles had. He knew that these men had lived through the flu in Timber Falls, so perhaps they would survive anything the sick people of Commonwealth could breathe upon them. These were the lucky ones, the ones chosen by God or biology to be immune, or perhaps they had already suffered and survived.

"What can I do?" Charles said emptily, looking at the trucks. One by one, men who had ignored Charles's advice about registering were being led away. By the time the APL was finished, the town would be emptied of most men.

The few who tried to fight were easily subdued, not only outnumbered but also weak from disease or hunger. Even Charles had lost weight. People had stretched their meager provisions as far as they could, and many had been too sick to venture out to other towns for food when the quarantine had been lifted. Everyone looked half starved, unable to defend themselves.

VII

The three knocks were so strong that Graham's door shook on its hinges.

When he'd seen the men coming, Graham had sent Amelia upstairs with the baby. He had pondered his options and found them few and unappealing. The knocks, when they came, were more of an assault, the door nearly giving way to the weight of the men behind it.

There were three men on the porch, all of whom Graham recognized from the earlier confrontation. The redheaded one was eying him especially closely.

"Let's see your deferment papers," the sheriff said.

"You've got no right to be doing this," Graham told the sheriff, whose eyes seemed to be disappearing beneath the puffy blackness billowing from the bridge of his nose. "You boys have already caused enough trouble—go back to Timber Falls before this gets any more out of hand."

Graham's right hand was pressed up against the doorjamb. He had opened the door only halfway, and in his three-fingered left hand, behind the door and out of the men's view, he was holding his rifle.

"We are deputized by the federal government," the sheriff replied, "so we have every right."

"Federal government's got nothing to do with us. We built this town, no help from any of you." The very doorjamb Graham's hand was resting against, he had placed there himself; there was no way he would let some two-bit thugs drag him from it.

The redhead stepped forward to push the door open farther, but Graham's hold was firm, the edge of the door digging into his forearm. He had elected not to brandish his weapon when he opened the door, thinking he could talk them into leaving. Now he was regretting the decision.

When Hightower had pointed Graham out to Bartrum, the sheriff hadn't wanted to skip the other houses, so he sent three of the men from his group to knock on the neighbors' doors. He kept Hightower and J.B. with him. Meanwhile, Miller had walked back to tell Winslow and another man to drive two of the trucks, filled beyond any point where more men could be shoved inside, back to Timber Falls. In only a few minutes, they'd fill the last two trucks and head back.

Bartrum knew how much Hightower had been yearning to bring this man in. The slacker had disparaged Hightower's dead sons, and in so doing had disparaged J.B.'s dead son, disparaged Bartrum's own son, still off fighting somewhere in France. Bartrum did not have the weight of a child's death on his soul, but he saw how such weight pulled down even stronger men than he. He wasn't going to let some yellow son of a bitch keep them from exercising their patriotic duties.

Bartrum reached for his pistol, removed it from the holster at his side. He held it there, pointed at the ground, and made sure Graham saw it. "Son, we bring you in alive or we bring you in dead. It doesn't matter to us."

Graham wasn't left-handed. He would need to back up, let the door swing open, and switch the rifle into his right hand. Shoot the man with the gun first, then the redhead. The four-eyed guy in the business suit would probably run away. Graham looked at all three of them, gauged how quickly they would act.

But Hightower surprised Graham by stepping in front of Bartrum and driving his shoulder into the door, forcing it open. It smacked against Graham's left wrist so hard he nearly dropped the rifle, now plainly visible.

Graham switched it to his right hand, but Hightower was so close Graham couldn't even point the gun at him. Hightower pushed the rifle aside, then punched Graham in the side of the face.

Graham stumbled back, the rifle hitting the ground, and wasn't able to steady himself before Hightower charged into him again. Graham was younger and stronger, but he was back on his heels and off balance. He used his raised arms to deflect some of Hightower's blows; the ones that struck him left him dizzy. Hightower was leaning him back against the couch, and Graham was about to fall when he landed a punch just to the right of the man's chin, feeling the crunch of breaking bone. But Graham fell backward after landing that blow, and Hightower, gripping his aching jaw, stepped forward and kicked him the second he hit the floor.

"Jesus, J.B." Hightower winced through his broken jaw. Finally, J.B. joined in kicking Graham's ribs and abdomen.

Bartrum had leveled his gun at Graham, ready to shoot if the slacker tried to attack again. But that clearly was not going to happen.

Hightower held back once he knew the fight was won. As much as he hated this man, he was already losing his taste for fighting. He reached down and picked Graham up, holding him around the neck from behind.

"Graham!" Amelia screamed. Graham's nose was bleeding, his left eyebrow was badly cut, and his face was becoming redder and redder from the thick arm around his neck. When Amelia reached the bottom crooked stair, she stopped, her face contorted by fear and fury. "Stop it, please!"

"We are stopping." Bartrum silently cursed the fact that every one of these millworkers seemed to have wives.

"Why are you doing this?" she asked, her eyes filling with tears as she slumped at the foot of the stairs. She looked straight into her husband's eyes, and the sight of her caused Graham to struggle again, his fingers digging into Hightower's arms. Hightower tightened his grip.

"Your husband is a yellow-bellied coward, young madam," Bartrum informed her, "and he's going to rot in jail till long after our boys have won this war." The sheriff nodded to J.B. and Hightower. "Let's go."

But as he turned toward the door again something new caught his eye. Emerging from the kitchen was another figure. And he was holding a rifle pointed at Bartrum's heart.

"Let him go," Philip said, walking slowly but steadily through the kitchen and into the dining room. The rifle felt so heavy to his atrophied muscles and hollow-seeming bones, but he would not lower it.

Philip had reached Graham's house too late, had seen the men standing on the porch when he turned the corner. He had stood there a moment, unsure what to do, the thoughts echoing in his cavernous head. The men would take Graham away, would stuff him into one of those trucks. Philip had carried the rifle with him as if heading back to guard duty at the town entrance, as if the flu had not come to Commonwealth. But it had come, of course, and he still felt it inside him. His head was wrong, his thoughts were wrong and his feelings were wrong. He found it hard to concentrate, hard to deliberate. It was so much easier just to act, and so he had walked through the snow to the Stones' back door. Despite his weakness, his body seemed lighter, as if it were being propelled by the wind, by someone's breath, by thought alone.

He had opened the back door silently. He had heard the sounds of fighting but had concentrated on stealth, on gliding through the house and aiming the rifle perfectly. His breaths were quick and he fought the urge to cough. He glanced at Graham just long enough to see his face contorted from the grip of the man holding him, then Philip trained his eyes on the midsection of the man with the pistol. The pistol was pointed at the floor, still aimed at where Graham had lain.

"Son, you'd best put that rifle—"

"Let him go," Philip cut Bartrum off, repeating his command with added force. "*You* put down your gun, and then get out of this house."

Hightower and Graham were still. Hightower had loosened his grip, apparently afraid that further struggle would cause Philip to fire their way. The man's arm was still around Graham's neck but now it was almost an embrace.

Philip coughed despite his attempts to choke it back. The rifle wavered but then returned to its target: the chest of the man before him, the man with the beaten face, with crusted blood and pus pooled beneath his trampled snout.

"Son, you're pointing a weapon at an officer of the law," Bartrum said, his voice calm but serious. "I'm sure you're a sick boy and you aren't acting yourself, but you need to put that down right now." He began to raise his own pistol.

"If you even twitch your arm again—" Philip warned, and Bartrum stopped.

Philip imagined himself firing at the man. Shooting the C.O. had been wrong, and shooting Frank would have been wrong. Graham, too, had done something so wrong Philip still could barely understand it—would probably never understand it. But this, this was not wrong. These men should not be here. Philip would finally be able to do something unimpeachable. He would pull the trigger if he had to.

Amelia was still at the foot of the stairs, paralyzed and mute. Graham was staring at her as if he desperately wanted to cover her body with his, but she was so far away.

The windows and the open doorway behind the men were an explosion of white, the snow falling even thicker than before.

"Philip," Graham managed to squeeze out of his dry throat, but that was all.

Nothing felt real to Philip—the scene was even more dreamlike than his conversation with Fiona on the train. He felt surrounded by death, felt that Fiona and Frank and the C.O. were nearby, felt the heavy spirits of all the people in Commonwealth who had been taken by the flu. The men standing in front of him were probably dead, too. All Philip had to do was knock them down.

"Son"—every time Bartrum spoke, his words came even slower—"I'm sure you think you're doing the right thing. But these men have done wrong, and it's our job to set things right. Now we're going to walk out this door with this man, and then—"

Philip shook his head, and the end of the rifle bounced. "No. You're leaving alone."

The pistol in Bartrum's hand moved again. Whether he was aiming it or moving it away, Philip wasn't sure, but he squeezed the rifle's trigger.

Bartrum disappeared. The shot threw him so far through the open doorway and into the descending layers of snow that he seemed erased into whiteness. Graham drove both of his elbows into Hightower's stomach, less stunned by the gunshot than his adversary had been, and the arm fell from around his neck. Graham turned around and slugged him twice in the face, the second blow barely glancing off Hightower's ear because he was falling so fast.

Philip hastily reloaded his rifle, then turned it toward Graham and Hightower, but Hightower was already on the ground, motionless. Philip looked at Graham, at his bloody face and the sweat that covered his forehead, dripping from his brow.

Bartrum's pistol had landed on the floor between J.B. and Graham. J.B. had just seen one of his companions shot dead and the other knocked out, and he was now outnumbered, and there was the pistol right in front of him. It was out of neither cold calculation nor bold decisiveness but sheer self-preservation that he leaped onto the hard floor, lunging for the pistol.

Graham, too, saw the gun, and he lunged forward. He was faster and less frightened than J.B., and just as the banker's fingers touched the handle of the gun, Graham's larger hand took it from him. They were both on their knees as Graham grasped the revolver, aiming at J.B.'s forehead. Graham's nerves were all firing, sparks running up his limbs and his finger tensed on the trigger, ready to pull, ready to pull. He needed to put this intruder down.

J.B. was so close that Graham could see clearly the look of terror and survival in the man's eyes, eyes that perfectly mirrored Graham's. Despite the adrenaline and the fear, Graham heard Philip's accusation echoing in his mind once more. That and the look in J.B.'s eyes made Graham hesitate.

"Graham, don't!" Amelia shouted.

Graham staggered to his feet, lowering the pistol while keeping his eyes on J.B.

Philip walked forward, the rifle pointed ahead until he saw Hightower lying behind the sofa, conscious but disoriented, blinking again and again. Philip told him to get up.

Graham pointed the pistol at the open doorway. Hightower and J.B. rose, staring at the two men and then at the feet of the sheriff, barely visible at the edge of the porch. Hightower's eyes were already swelling and he was silent. He and J.B. walked through the doorway toward their vehicles, their footfalls unsteady as their legs shivered with adrenaline.

Philip followed them a few steps and looked down at the fallen sheriff, the man's eyes wide open, his eyebrows still arched with surprise. The blood was beginning to seep even through his thick coat. Things felt fluid, one action leading to the next with unusual speed, and Philip felt he could no longer pause between events to try and understand them.

Amelia and Graham were holding each other, the sheriff's pistol sitting on the table. They were crying, and Graham's arms seemed to be shaking.

"Graham," Philip interrupted them, his voice trancelike. "There are men outside."

Graham steadied himself, then stepped away from his wife. "Don't go," Amelia said, making it more of a command than a plea, but he shook his head, wiping at his tears.

He grabbed the pistol. "Please," he told her.

Philip and Graham went onto the porch and saw Miller and two other men standing outside two trucks and a Ford half a block away. Graham led the way and Philip followed. Before the APL men had time to react to the sight, Graham fired a shot into the white sky that was disintegrating all around them.

"Get out of our town!" Graham screamed, his eyes no longer tearing up but still shining, still wild. Miller froze. He had no weapon, nor did the man beside him.

Behind Graham and Philip, four other Commonwealth men—as if they had been waiting all day for the opportunity—emerged from their homes, rifles in hand.

Miller had already sent two trucks and most of the men back to Timber Falls. He was outnumbered and outgunned, but he tried to remain calm. He saw the body on the porch, saw Hightower's beaten face and the look in J.B.'s eyes. J.B. stepped up to him and spoke low in his ear: "They killed Bartrum."

Miller swallowed. "We'll be back, gentlemen," he said to Graham, trying to bite back his fear. "I promise you that."

"You were right about the spy," Graham told Miller, his voice thick with emotion. His head ached from Hightower's blows, his ribs pinched his insides with every breath, and his trampled abdomen screamed at him to bend over rather than standing so tall. "He did come here after you left, and I killed him. And I'll kill you next if you ever come back."

Miller kept his eyes on the gunmen as he walked toward one of the trucks, filled with captured men. He jumped when he heard the pop, and one of the tires before him exploded.

Graham shot another wheel, then two on the other truck. "The trucks stay," he commanded. "The men stay." He was less than ten feet from Miller now.

Philip kept his rifle aimed at Miller's chest, but Graham held his pistol pointed at the ground a few feet in front of him. He couldn't aim at another man.

"You've made a terrible mistake, son."

Graham gritted his teeth. The pistol was heavy in his hand. "Get out while we're still letting you."

Miller stood there another moment, his face white. Then he nodded, turned around and started walking toward the Ford. His compatriots followed.

Graham, Philip, and the men who had left their homes came closer as Miller started the engine, then slowly turned it around. Several blocks ahead and out of view, the remaining group of APL men had climbed into their vehicle, having been told by Miller only a moment ago that they'd done all they could for the day. They didn't know Bartrum had been slain and they would not know it until after the long ride home.

Miller's Ford made its way slowly along the snow-covered road. It passed all those houses with crape hanging in the windows, passed the women and children of the men who had already been trucked out of town, Rankle and Deacon and all the others, some of them still sick with flu and some barely recovered and some worsening, some of them beaten and some of them without a mark. Miller gripped the wheel tightly, his jaw clenched at the townspeople watching him go. He saw Charles Worthy standing at the edge of the crowd and fought off an urge to drive into him, to cut him down in front of all these fools who had followed him here to the ends of the earth. Then the town was gone and they were rolling down the hill, nothing before them but the thick woods that would be all but impenetrable after another hour of snowfall.

Philip bent over and laid his rifle on the soft snow near the abandoned trucks, the men still inside. One of the first faces he'd seen through the windows he had recognized: Alfred Metzger, who, at forty-two, was still three years younger than the cutoff for the most recent, expanded draft. Philip pulled at the handle of the back door until it swung clear.

The men burst out, desperate to be free, but once they were safely on the outside, their movements varied. They dropped to the ground and cried with relief, or clapped each other on the shoulders, or ran to their wives, or swore vengeance upon those Timber Falls bastards. But Alfred Metzger spent only the slightest moment standing among them, looking down at the snow-covered ground, and then he walked away briskly. Philip saw the look in the man's eyes and realized that imprisonment would have been a more pleasant fate than the horrors that awaited him at home.

It did not seem at all odd that Philip now stood in a train station. It was like an inexorable fate, something that had been perpetually on his horizon, something he could not run from. He thought about that, how running away was something he couldn't run away from.

He still wasn't right in the head. He had told his father this in the middle of the street, both of them covered in snow, the rifle by Philip's feet smelling strongly of gunpowder, of metal and blood. Charles had not asked Philip what he had done, though surely he was piecing it together from the expressions on the faces of the men around them. *I don't feel right in the head,* Philip had said, and Charles had nodded and walked him home.

It snowed for an entire day. The storm did more to insulate Commonwealth, to block it off from the rest of the world, than the quarantine had done. The heavy snowfall would keep the invaders from returning, but for how long?

Philip rested in bed for the next two days, sleeping for such long stretches that his parents worried he was slipping back into the flu's icy embrace. But his symptoms continued to fade. He still complained that his head, though no longer aching, felt fuzzy; he said he heard ringing in his ears, found it difficult to concentrate. But Doc Banes assured them this would pass, that perhaps this wicked flu would be particularly difficult to shake, but shake it Philip would in time. Philip spoke little; Charles hadn't heard his son laugh in days, perhaps weeks.

Elsie died late the night of the raid. She never knew that her father had been arrested, nor did she know Philip had set him free. She had been lying in a delirium for the final two days, attended by her father, whose pleas that the Lord take him instead of Elsie were left unanswered. Alfred Metzger never suffered the slightest fever or cough despite standing by his wife's and daughter's bedsides.

It never occurred to Charles or Rebecca that the news of Elsie's death may have contributed to Philip's silence, because his outward reactions paled beside those of Laura, who cried herself to sleep the next two nights. Philip had stared out the window at the blindingly white snow, sharing his thoughts with no one.

Once the roads were passable, a small contingent of men who had registered and secured deferments months ago ventured south, seeking news from the outside world. They went to Pauling, a hamlet ten miles east of Timber Falls, avoiding the larger town. The men returned with as much food as they could buy, as well as newspapers whose emphatic headlines displayed, finally, something welcome: an armistice had been signed, and the guns of Europe were silent. The armistice had been declared the same day Miller and his crew had reached Commonwealth. All those men had been arrested for failing to register in a war that had mercifully drawn to an exhausted close.

Charles was confident the armistice would mean the nineteen imprisoned men would be released. Rebecca had decided she would journey to the Timber Falls jail the next day, would visit the post office and find a phone and reconnect with her political contacts, spread the word that the peace-minded men of her town had been rounded up like common criminals. She would visit Jarred Rankle and the others, demand that the jailers treat them fairly—a woman's presence could go a long way toward getting the men humane treatment, she had learned from her experience in the Everett strike. But she did not share her husband's faith that the men would be released, at least not until the war was more of a memory, replaced by whatever new necessities arose from the vacuum of these violent and fear-addled years.

After the raid, Charles and Rebecca had knocked on every door in town—they no longer cared if it put them at risk—and found out who had been taken by the APL, who was sick, who was starving, who was dead. The looks on people's faces and the stories that Charles and Rebecca heard had kept them up the last few nights, lying beside each other. The Worthys had little food left, but they had shared with those too ill to cook for themselves.

Charles and Rebecca had seen the depths to which some had fallen, and the depths that lurked farther below. But as badly as his faith was shaken, Charles had lived through too many tragedies and busts to concede that the mill would fail. Somehow the town would survive, he believed. Somehow.

Doc Banes's badly kept records showed that 250 people in Commonwealth—over half the town's population—had contracted the flu. Of these, fifty-six men, women, and children had died. Most of the dead were adults younger than thirty, those who should have been hardy enough to survive the infection. Banes didn't know why the children had been spared in favor of those in the prime of life, but it made the aftereffects all the worse, as there were now so many widowed parents, so many orphans.

Mo was dead, as was Lightning. The river chief O'Hare, who had kept his distance from Philip, somehow became infected despite his vigilance; he had died a week ago, as had three of the drivers who worked alongside him. Laura had recovered but had lost her best friend and two other classmates.

Doc Banes never took ill, despite his long hours beside the sick and dying. Like Deacon, he began to feel specially chosen, as if God had conscripted him as a watchman for the dead, a scrivener to mark the passage of their lives. But those memories were abominable, and Banes wanted only to be rid of them. Each night his bottles of alcohol beckoned, and he found no reason to resist their call.

The Stone family had been spared by the flu—Amelia and the baby were healthy, as was Graham. He didn't know how it was that Philip could cough in his face without passing on the infection, but there was much he did not understand. He had barely been able to sleep the last two nights and had twice hid in another room so Amelia wouldn't see it when he broke down.

The shock of the raid and the waning of the flu brought people out of their homes, and friends could tell their stories again. Word of how Leonard and others had been sneaking out of Commonwealth for booze and women spread through the awakening town. Those who heard the news, especially those who had lost loved ones, were consumed by vengeful desires. A party of angry men had gone knocking on the sneaks' doors only to find the perpetrators dead of the flu. The vigilantes were all the more enraged when they realized there was no possibility for retribution; the flu was an evil with no body to beat, no face to spit upon, no neck to string up.

But people had heard what Graham said to Miller about killing the spy, and though some thought Graham had said it only to scare the APL away, others saw a glint of truth. It fit all too neatly with the other stories circulating through Commonwealth, stories of another soldier who had tried to enter town weeks ago and who had been shot by Graham and buried by the town entrance. When the Stones walked through town the day after the raid, Graham had received several fearful looks that Amelia assumed were just reactions to his ugly bruises.

The following day, Amelia had refused to believe it when a friend mentioned the stories about Graham and the spy, and that night she questioned him. So he told her what he had done, but he didn't explain why. He once had hoped that his pure motives would excuse whatever hell and muck he'd had to wade through, but his reasons no longer seemed relevant or justified, even to himself. All that mattered was that he had killed someone, so that was all he said to his wife.

And if she had recoiled from him at first and then proffered her own desperate explanations that he would neither agree with nor deny, and if she had broken down crying and then apologized and walked out of the house, returning only hours later, and if she had acted wary of her own husband, not even asking him to hold the baby when her arms were tired, and if everyone in town was looking at him as though he were some part of themselves they wished would simply disappear, then this, too, was something Graham would have to accept.

The third day after the raid found Philip at a train station in Pauling. After saying goodbye to Rebecca and Laura, he had come here with Charles in the family's Ford. In the backseat was Graham, who had asked to join them.

Philip still did not fully comprehend the need for this journey, but Charles had insisted, explaining that it was the safest thing to do in light of what had happened the day of the snowstorm. Charles didn't know whether those men would return, but if they did, they would be looking for Philip. Regardless of the circumstances, Philip had shot a policeman. Regardless of how sick or confused Philip had been, regardless of what might have happened to Graham if Philip hadn't intervened, Charles knew how Philip's act must have looked to Miller. Whether the European armistice would lead to an armistice here in the Washington forest remained to be seen.

The previous day, Charles had made a quick call to a cousin in Portland from a phone in Pauling. The cousin's family had already suffered through the flu, the children sick in bed for days, but all was now well. Charles had explained to his cousin only that he feared for Philip's safety due to an escalated rivalry with another mill, and he gave Philip a series of half-lies he could feed his new caretakers upon arrival.

It won't be long, Charles promised his son. *Probably only a fortnight.* Just enough time for Charles to communicate with the local powers in Timber Falls, for Rebecca to rally her comrades, for people across the state to fully appreciate the fact that the Great War was finally over, that they were free to reimagine the lives they had pursued before it began. Charles was confident there would be a way to justify Philip's actions.

Charles always used such detached language when discussing the situation, Philip noticed. He never said that Philip had shot someone, killed someone. And strangely, as much as Philip had been haunted by the first soldier, he was not similarly tortured by his memories of the sheriff. To Philip, the man with the broken nose and the black eyes had played the role of villain in a way the first soldier had not. The sheriff had invaded Graham's home, had beaten other men, and because of this, Philip had felt a certainty to his own actions. Though his mind had been muddled that afternoon, he hadn't thought of it as taking a life, but as saving lives.

Still, he wondered if the image of himself shooting the lawman would make some nefarious return, would gradually or suddenly insinuate itself into his every thought. Perhaps once his mind was free of the flu's grasp, he would be forced to wear the same yoke Graham was suffering under.

The ride was mostly silent, and it felt interminably long. The quiet was broken only by Charles's interjections that all would be fine. Philip found even those brief comments grating, saw from his sheltered vantage point the awkward way Charles was struggling against the irrefutable winds of all the evidence surrounding them. Philip was certain Graham saw it as well, and every time his father waxed optimistic, he cringed.

At last they reached the train station, no more than an outdoor platform beside a small kiosk where the heavily bundled attendant breathed on his hands. Charles bought the ticket while Philip and Graham waited by the tracks.

"Thank you for coming for me," Graham said. It was the first thing he'd said to Philip that day, his first acknowledgment of what Philip had done. His face was a darkened blue in the spots where he'd been struck by the APL men, and he took careful, shallow breaths due to the stabbing pain of his broken ribs. "Thank you for helping me."

Philip nodded. "What are you going to do now?" If he was in such danger that he needed to be sent away, then the same probably applied to Graham. Yet Philip couldn't imagine Graham running from anything.

"I don't know." Graham looked down the long train tracks that cut into the thick forest, the product of so many hours of hard labor that their creation seemed incomprehensible. Everything here was the result of sacrifice and pain. He looked back at Philip and his face seemed constricted, the muscles along his forehead and temples taut.

"I'll be back soon, my father says," Philip said.

"I hope the town's still standing." Their eyes met, and they held the gaze, then Philip nodded.

Graham knew from his days of riding the rails how quickly a place like Commonwealth could disappear. Many times he had journeyed past abandoned streets that had been thriving storyvilles, and he had seen that villages where he'd once laid his head were no longer marked on any maps. He knew how violence could not only tear a town in two but tear it so many times that there was nothing left to build upon, nothing left to hold, nothing left even to remember as you grabbed your scant belongings and headed someplace new.

Charles was walking toward them, ticket in hand, but not yet in earshot.

Philip looked down at the ground. "I know you want me to apologize for letting Frank into town. But I can't." He didn't know if Graham had been told about the men who were sneaking out of Commonwealth for liquor or to visit their sweethearts. Nor did he know whether those facts mattered at all, or if they were just so many more flakes of snow tossed in among the blizzard of coincidences and occurrences and accidents over the last month, something so discrete and tiny that you couldn't focus on them no matter how hard you tried. Following them with your eyes was impossible amid the swirl. "I'm not sorry I did it."

Philip could tell Graham was concentrating carefully on what he was about to say. "I know you want me to apologize," Graham said, borrowing Philip's line. He paused, his eyes suddenly red and glassy. He wasn't even looking Philip in the eye. What he managed to say, between labored and painful breaths, was "And I know that I should."

But then Charles was back, handing Philip a ticket and some money, not seeing the look in Graham's eyes. Charles repeated the instructions he'd already given, and Philip nodded, looking at Graham more than at his father. Then Philip asked that they not wait for the train with him.

"It'll feel more like a goodbye if you stay." He stuffed the ticket in his pocket. He wasn't quite recovered, but he was well enough to stand there, boots on the tightly packed snow.

Charles embraced him. Philip forgot the anger and disappointment he had felt over the last few weeks, and for a moment he held on to his father tightly.

Charles stepped back and promised to send Philip a telegram in two days with news.

Graham and Philip looked at each other, and Graham nodded abruptly, clapping him on the shoulder a little too hard. Then they were gone.

Graham and Charles spoke little during the journey home. Graham saw that Charles was affected by sending away his son, so much that he didn't notice how close Graham had come to breaking down. Time passed slowly as the car's tires struggled over the slushy roads, the heavy branches of the white-and-green-striped trees swaying above.

The fact that the roads had been impassable had afforded Graham time to think, to deliberate, but now he no longer had that luxury. Men bent on avenging Bartrum's death were free to return; the red-bearded man with the sons dead in France surely would never forget Graham's face. Graham had chosen not to register lest the war tear him from his family: staying in Commonwealth to await possible arrest would mean running that same risk. Charles sounded optimistic that the situation could be resolved, but to Graham that was like hoping the tornado before you might be just a horribly beautiful cloud crafted by a creative but benign God. Graham knew what those storm clouds meant.

With his right hand, he massaged the knuckles of his left, feeling even through his gloves the contours of his bones and the awkward slope where the final finger should be. Amelia had knit the gloves herself, giving the left only three fingers because Graham had hated the way the empty finger of his old gloves had dangled there, purposeless.

To take his baby and his pregnant wife and run from Commonwealth to some other town would be to start with nothing. Some clothes, a scant amount of money to buy lodging and food for a few weeks, but little else. He would be as vulnerable as he had once been, but a thousand times more so because now he had a family. He remembered how difficult it had been to start over after Everett. But this time, he reminded himself, he would not be alone.

Last night, after telling Amelia about the second soldier, and after her long walk and the many silent hours that had passed between them, he had retired to bed. When she slipped into the bed much later, he was still awake, lying on his side and facing the wall. In the dark, she had wrapped an arm around him. "Rest," she said to him softly, knowing his eyes were open. She put her left hand on his, and his outnumbered fingers interlocked with hers. She kissed him on the back of the neck. "Rest." He lay there for a good while before falling asleep, not because he couldn't but because he wanted to revel in that feeling. Hours later, he woke to the baby's crying, and he left the bed before his wife to pick up his daughter and pace through the cold house. There in the dark the building felt hollow, empty, something that could be abandoned. He was so tired of running, yet so tired of holding his ground. And so before accompanying Philip to the train station that morning, he had told Amelia his decision, ready to hear any objections. But she'd had none, simply expressing the hope that their sojourn would be only temporary.

Outside, the trees shook in the wind. The road curved deeper into the woods and beside them was the river, harsh and cold, but still running.

The wait for the train seemed too long. Philip thought about how back in Commonwealth the recovering men were testing their strength by chopping firewood, and women were visiting neighbors they had not seen in days, knocking on doors hesitantly for fear of having those knocks go unanswered. The undertaker was consulting his list of interned bodies and writing a letter to Inston, requesting the minister's presence for a memorial service, and Doc Banes was tending to those still too sick to leave their beds. Commonwealth was staggering to its feet, and Philip was leaving yet another town.

After years of fearing abandonment, he realized he had never been truly alone until that moment. Yet as he stood there in the stunned silence of the outside world—a world he hadn't seen in weeks—he felt curiously unafraid. Perhaps it was the flu clouding his mind; perhaps he was too dazed to appreciate the uncertainness of his fate. But something about what Charles had said, and his tone, made Philip feel glad to stand there by himself, away from the town and all the disasters that its failed decisions had wrought.

Philip wasn't sure when his head would feel right, but part of him wanted that never to happen. His recovery from the flu seemed to be occurring in another world, someplace wholly separate from Commonwealth, so it felt natural that he had not seen Elsie in days. Once he felt right, he would have to confront Elsie. Perhaps it would be better to never again see those riverbeds where they had collected driftwood, never again visit the lonely general store. Better simply to venture to his next destination and any beyond it, to drift on, stripped of so many things that he thought had defined who he was. And what would be left of himself, and who he would be while he gathered the fleeting pieces as they tried to drift away, was something he would somehow have the strength to accept, and build something anew.

Author's Note

Nearly a decade ago I read a magazine article about an infectious disease expert that briefly mentioned the 1918 influenza epidemic. The article also made reference to the fact that some uninfected towns in the western United States were so terrified of the flu that they blocked all roads leading into town and posted armed guards to prevent anyone from entering. I immediately imagined a scene that would become the seed of a novel: two guards confronted with the dilemma of a cold, hungry outsider seeking shelter.

I read what books I could find on the 1918 epidemic but didn't find many. And I could find no information about any of the healthy towns that had supposedly imposed reverse quarantines. Finally, because I am a fiction writer and not a historian, I decided to stop searching for more about the mysterious towns. The fact that I was unable to unearth anything was probably for the best, as it released my imagination from any historical shackles.

Only as I was nearly finished with my rough draft was John M. Barry's definitive work, *The Great Influenza,* published. He reports that Gunnison, Colorado, was one such town that emerged unscathed from the epidemic by completely isolating itself from neighboring towns in the San Juan Mountains. Some other towns' similar attempts were not so successful, he notes.

Although Commonwealth is a fictional creation, had it been real, it would not have been entirely unique in its progressive mission. The vast forests of Washington sheltered numerous communes, collectives, and other gathering places of the radically inclined. Half a thousand socialists lived at the Equality Colony, founded in 1896 on the banks of the Skagit River; Whidbey Island was home to a farmer's cooperative known as Freeland; and across the Sound from Tacoma's paper mills was Home, an anarchist community gleefully practicing free love.

Graham's character was fleshed out by research into the labor violence of the era. The tensions between business owners trying to carve out an existence in the forbidding West and workers trying to earn a solid enough living to settle permanently created an often combustible environment. Though the labor needs of wartime and the coming red scare would soon put most unions on the defensive, the prewar era was rife with violent strikes. The so-called Everett Massacre of 1916 was the apogee of a bitter timber strike, as a gunfight broke out when two vessels carrying strikers and sympathizers from Seattle attempted to dock at an Everett harbor. Although many members of the Industrial Workers of the World were put on trial, they were ultimately acquitted, and historians have been unable to establish who fired the first shots: Wobblies, strikers, McRae's deputies, or town vigilantes. At least seven people (five strikers and two deputies) died in the massacre, though some sources believe an even higher number of strikers may have perished.

Few people today realize it, but World War I had its own strong antiwar movement. President Wilson realized that the war would be a hard sell to a nation in which nearly one quarter of the citizens were of German ancestry. To that end, he formed the Committee on Public Information, which launched a propaganda campaign unprecedented in size and scope. The character of Uncle Sam was born, and countless patriotic tunes hit the airwaves ("Save Your Kisses till the Boys Come Home," "Hello Central! Give Me No Man's Land") and Four-Minute Men unleashed their impassioned oratory in movie theaters and taverns.

Many on the political left felt betrayed by President Wilson—who had campaigned on an antiwar platform—when he decided to enter the Great War. Unionists called it a rich man's war, arguing that America was only fighting because its wealthy bankers had lent so much money to Britain and France that, if those countries fell, America's financial markets would be in peril. To silence such critics, Congress turned its back on the First Amendment by enacting laws that criminalized criticism of the war or the government. This was war, after all; surely the citizens wouldn't mind giving up a few civil liberties as they sacrificed for victory. Rebecca stands in for the thousands of Americans who felt muzzled during that time, who loved their country but felt unable to debate or rectify its policies for fear of imprisonment.

"Everybody is either loyal or not loyal at a time like this," one government announcement explained. The Department of Justice therefore sponsored the American Protective League, a group of patriotic civilians who rounded up draft dodgers, looked for suspected spies, and made sure their fellow citizens were acting with sufficient loyalty. APL branches spread across the country, encompassing a membership of 300,000, and some vigilante "superpatriots" were known to break into immigrants' homes and demand they kiss the flag or buy Liberty Bonds.

Secretary of War Newton Baker did allow men to declare themselves conscientious objectors if they had "personal scruples against war," and approximately sixty-five thousand men requested noncombatant service, such as driving ambulances, serving as orderlies, and performing electrical or agricultural work. But such C.O.s faced enormous pressure to recant—including outright torture at army cantonments—and as many as 80 percent folded under the pressure, agreeing to bear arms. At least seventeen C.O.s died from the treatment they received for expressing their beliefs.

The 1918 influenza epidemic killed as many as 100 million people worldwide in one year. It would ultimately kill more people—and five times as many Americans—as the Great War, which drew to its close in November 1918, while the flu was still raging.

The flu had an amazingly disabling effect on nearly all societies that suffered it, and it left its mark on the outcome of the war. Some historians believe that had the flu not infected so many German soldiers, a massive German offensive in the spring of 1918 would have forced France to capitulate before American aid arrived to turn the tide. Others believe that President Wilson, sick before the conference at Versailles, was slowed by the curiously lingering mental aftereffects of the flu. Some speculate that had he been his steadfast self, the European Allies wouldn't have imposed the harsh conditions on Germany that Hitler later used to rally his citizens to the Nazi party.

Fear of spies at home, the loss of loved ones overseas, and the sense that the country's very way of life was under attack combined to form a volatile environment eerily reminiscent of contemporary times. Into this tense mix the flu appeared. Newspapers cowed by the government into reporting only good news initially denied or downplayed the flu's existence, yet citizens could see their neighbors' bodies being carted off, could hear the baleful church bells. Radio jingles told people to be brave, mayors reminded everyone they need only wash their hands to avoid infection, yet the corpses piled up on street corners.

This is the world, in all its tensions and complexities, that slowly formed itself in my imagination as I sat down and began to write *The Last Town on Earth*.

Thomas Mullen
January 2006

Notes and Acknowledgments

This is a work of fiction. Although some uninfected towns did endeavor to fend off the 1918 flu pandemic by means of reverse quarantines, this book is not an attempt to retell their stories.

I am indebted to several historians in the research for this book. Anyone wishing to learn more about the 1918 pandemic should read John M. Barry's *The Great Influenza*. Alfred W. Crosby's *America's Forgotten Pandemic: The Influenza of 1918,* Allen Churchill's *Over Here! An Informal Re-creation of the Home Front in World War I,* Frances H. Early's *A World Without War: How U.S. Feminists and Pacifists Resisted World War I,* Meirion and Susie Harries' *The Last Days of Innocence: America at War, 1917–1918,* Robert H. Zieger's *America's Great War: World War I and the American Experience,* and Howard Zinn's *A People's History of the United States* all were helpful in re-creating the tenor of the times.

Patrick Renshaw's *The Wobblies: The Story of the IWW and Syndicalism in the United States,* Len De Caux's *The Living Spirit of the Wobblies,* and Joseph R. Conlin's *Big Bill Haywood and the Radical Union Movement* provided details on the labor movement and violence of the era, and the author could not have done without William S. Crowe's *Lumberjack* or Norman H. Clark's *Mill Town: A Social History of Everett, Washington, from Its Earliest Beginnings on the Shores of Puget Sound to the Tragic and Infamous Event Known as the Everett Massacre.*

Big thanks to several friends who read past drafts of this and other works:

Brent Wincze, Demos Orphanides, Rick Runyan, Erin Core, Matt Power, Brad Dececco, Geoff Sharpe, Deneb Meketa, Brian Dawson, Hadyn Dick, Candace Sady, Chetan Rao, Shauna Sutherland, and Becky Givan. Overdue thanks to Gus Muller and Dom Ambrose for early encouragement.

My agent, Susan Golomb, provided sound advice, tirelessly edited rough drafts, and encouraged me to tackle a book I initially intended to put off for a few years. Thanks also to Rich Green, Amira Pierce, John Mozes, Anna Stein, and Casey Parnell.

My editor, Jennifer Hershey, and Laura Ford, Janet Wygal, and everyone else at Random House helped make a lifelong dream into reality.

Grateful and loving thanks to my parents and family, who never once suggested I might want to abandon the whole novel-writing idea in favor of something a tad more practical.

And, of course, Jenny, for everything.

Ideas, interviews & features …

About the author

About the book

Read on

A Rewarding Struggle:

Thomas Mullen talks to Louise Tucker

What did you want to be when you grew up and how, if at all, did your family background influence your eventual choice of writing?

I've wanted to be a writer for as long as I can remember. I wrote my own versions of certain kids' books as a young boy, I scribbled away at mysteries when I was in secondary school, and I've been seriously writing fiction since college. I've been extremely fortunate in that my family always encouraged me to pursue my writing. I have many friends with artistic aspirations whose families have soundly discouraged them from pursuing these goals, and they wind up attending medical or law school and wondering whether they're chasing their own dreams or those of their parents. I feel lucky indeed not to have faced such an obstacle – success in fiction is hard enough to achieve without having to jump hurdles placed by well-meaning loved ones. The fact that my mother is an art teacher, my older sister was an art student, and my father is an inveterate reader certainly didn't hurt.

What tempted you to cross the continent, in literary terms, to write about the other Washington?

I was inspired to write this story when I stumbled upon the little-known fact that some towns in the Pacific Northwest did indeed enact such reverse quarantines, going so far as posting armed guards to prevent outsiders from entering. As a New

Englander, I did consider transplanting the story to areas I knew better, but it wouldn't have worked. Even in 1918, most of New England was so thickly settled that it would have been difficult to imagine a town being sufficiently cut off from its neighbours that it could have accomplished what Commonwealth set out to do. The Pacific Northwest of that era, however, was very much a frontier, and the dense forests provided ample cover for the creation of my little world. Indeed, Washington State, which remains a very progressive area, was a haven for radicals in the 1910s, so it was easy to imagine a utopian community like Commonwealth hiding in its dense forests. Coupled with the volatile labour environment of that time and place – the logging and mining industries were particularly plagued by strikes and armed conflicts, and their mostly itinerant workers were represented by the militant Industrial Workers of the World – the setting provided plenty of material that fitted in well with the themes and ideas I was already interested in exploring.

‘I was intimidated at the prospect of historical fiction so I filed away the idea for *The Last Town on Earth* while working on other fiction. But the idea never went away’

Your author's note mentions that you first read of the reverse quarantines of the 1918 flu epidemic nearly a decade ago. Did the book take you a decade to write or was the idea buried until more recently?
I had the idea for a very long time before I set out to do anything with it. In my head was a very rough outline, but for some ▶

A Rewarding Struggle *(continued)*

◂ reason the book seemed like something I should tackle as a third or fourth novel and not as a first. I was intimidated at the prospect of historical fiction, and was worried that the various themes and characters necessary to tell this story would overwhelm a first-time novelist. (Perhaps I was overly influenced by the fact that so many first novels tend to be about young people complaining about their jobs or lovers or parents.) So I filed away the idea for *The Last Town on Earth* while working on other fiction. But the idea never went away, and after I began working with a literary agent, I mentioned the idea to her and she encouraged me to tackle it sooner rather than later.

How did you learn to write? And what was the most helpful lesson you learned en route to becoming a novelist?
I never took classes on creative writing and can't claim any mentors beyond some encouraging secondary school teachers. Most of what I learned about how to write I learned by reading. You need to immerse yourself in great writing to have any hope of creating some yourself. Reading great fiction allows you to see what has been done and what remains unwritten, what works and what doesn't, what you admire and what you want to improve upon.

What, or who, inspired you to write historical rather than contemporary fiction?
I never would have predicted that my first novel would be a historical one; it's solely the result of my discovering that historical

footnote about the reverse quarantines and imagining a situation in which the guards were presented with the quandary of a tired, cold, possibly ill traveller seeking food and shelter. Would they shoot him or shelter him? That moral dilemma, and the many conflicts it could lead to, took me down the path of historical fiction, almost despite myself.

Do you ever wonder what you would have done? Pull the trigger like Graham, or try and find another solution like Philip?
Part of why I chose to write the book is because I honestly don't know the answer to that question. If you seek to write a book about a troubling issue about which you already have rock-solid, unbreakable opinions, your book will probably come off as didactic and preachy. I hope that one of the strengths of the book is that I sought to portray, with great sympathy, the perspective of characters who disagree strongly about how this situation should be handled. If I had thought one character was fully right and the other fully wrong, the result would have been slanted and unfair – and uninteresting to read.

I would hazard that most people would like to think they would act like Philip, but, the fact is, no one truly knows how they would act in such an extreme situation until it happens to them. The way in which society as a whole reacted to the 1918 flu – and the way it has reacted to other threats, be they medical or military – shows that human nature does not always fit into the ▶

‘You need to immerse yourself in great writing to have any hope of creating some yourself’

A Rewarding Struggle *(continued)*

◀ ideological belief systems or moral codes that we would like it to.

The town of Commonwealth, like many towns in the world both then and now, was ill-equipped to deal with an epidemic, and the forethought of someone like Charles could not encompass the weakness of those like Leonard. Do you think that Commonwealth's experience was inevitable, because humans won't pull together, or avoidable, because they have it within them to do so?
Another difficult question to answer. I would like to think that humans can pull together, as you say, but the reality of our many conflicts suggests that this is not something we are particularly skilled at. I would hope, however, that Commonwealth's situation is not read as an indictment of mankind's ability to act cooperatively so much as an analysis of why certain problems tend to plague us. Great tensions can derail the best of people and the best of societies, which is part of the reason writers – and readers – have been so interested in studying tragedies, for centuries.

On a similar note, the book is very engaging but it also raises difficult moral debates. Does fiction have a particular purpose for you, whether asking questions, entertaining or teaching us about a relatively unknown event in history?
Fiction can accomplish multiple goals: posing moral debates and/or thought-provoking themes, introducing a new and fresh writing

style and/or narrative perspective, creating engaging and realistic characters, and telling a great story. Some books and authors focus on one or two of these goals to the exclusion of the others, and though the result can be rewarding, I find that my favourite novels hit on most or all of these points. If *The Last Town on Earth* had posed its moral debate without placing it in the context of a page-turning story, the result would have been pedantic. Alternately, a fast-moving plot that isn't animated and coloured by challenging themes and difficult personal, social, or political questions is something I myself wouldn't care to read.

The detailed historical and physical landscapes are very important to the sense of time and place in the book. Where did you start your research and how long did it take?
I conducted research for a little less than a year, and I was writing early chapters during some of this time. One of my younger brothers had attended college in Washington State, so I had visited the area, hiking in both the North Cascades and the Olympic Mountains. I had been enchanted by Washington's striking physical beauty but also by the unmistakable sense of the forbidding, the seeming endlessness of the forest and the darkness it throws upon those wandering in it. These days, people think of nature as quaint and relaxing, or as the rustic setting for adventures like kayaking and hiking – as if the natural world has become a theme park. In 1918, however, the forests and mountains were obstacles that ▶

‘This sense of being surrounded by a beautiful but at times malevolent land worked well with the idea of the invisible flu lurking in the outside world’

A Rewarding Struggle *(continued)*

◄ needed to be overcome in order to survive in such harsh locales. I felt that this sense of being surrounded by a beautiful but at times malevolent land worked well with the idea of the invisible flu lurking in the outside world, adding to the characters' sense of dislocation and siege.

Did the historical realities ever hinder the narrative? And were you ever tempted to take liberties with some of the facts?
As a novelist, my first job is to tell the story well. Well can mean using historical facts to provide a foundation for a situation or character, and many readers particularly enjoy novels that are rich with such detail. Certainly, the fact that this time period included violent strikes and a fear of radical unionism in America (exacerbated by the recent Bolshevik victory in Russia), war in Europe, and suppressed free speech for political dissidents back home gave me much to work with. But telling a story well can also mean relying on my imagination to create scenes and episodes that tie elements together or bolster existing events. I don't believe there are any historical facts that I altered – apart of course from the existence of all these characters and the main settings of Commonwealth, Timber Falls, and Fort Jenkins – but if facts had ever gotten in my way, I would have gleefully brushed them aside as necessary. As a novelist, you don't get bonus points for having an extra historical fact on page 27 – indeed, some stories can be dragged down by the ponderous accumulation of irrelevant information as

authors show off the fruits of their research. A novelist needs to get the facts straight enough so that readers won't stop and say, 'wait, that's not right', or 'but what about X?', because that would ruin the reading experience. But beyond creating a believable framework for the tale, I feel that everything is fair game.

***The Last Town on Earth* is your first novel. How did writing it change you?**
Publication of the novel has certainly altered my day-to-day life, as I'm now able to devote all my energies to fiction, whereas when I wrote the book I'd held another job and thus had to squeeze fiction into the weekends.

On the one hand, writing *The Last Town on Earth* has helped my confidence – particularly because it was in a genre that I initially found so intimidating – but at the same time, there's always a degree of uncertainty when facing the challenge of a next book. Writing is what I love, and I consider myself extremely fortunate to have this career, but it is still work. It's the struggle that makes the rewards of completing a book so great. ■

LIFE
at a Glance

Thomas Mullen was born and raised in Rhode Island and graduated from Oberlin College. He lives in Washington, DC, with his wife and son.

Ten Inspiring and Wondrous First Novels

in no particular order:

The Known World
by Edward P. Jones
Jones takes a staggering, little-known historical footnote – that in the years preceding the US Civil War, some freed blacks owned slaves – and uses it to take a fresh look at the myriad ways slavery impacted Americans of every colour, class, and creed.

The Virgin Suicides
by Jeffrey Eugenides
A group narrator – men looking back on their adolescence – tells the tale of the five sisters whose incandescent lives and tragic deaths beguiled them then and haunt them still. Lyrical, lovely, lonely, and unlike anything else.

Carter Beats the Devil
by Glen David Gold
What if 1920s magician Charles Carter had been suspected of playing a role in President Harding's mysterious death? A fun, thrilling ride through a tumultuous time.

The Commitments
by Roddy Doyle
The greatest novel about music ever written, because it captures how music *feels*.

Bringing Out the Dead
by Joe Connelly
Based on the author's experience as a medic driving the streets of New York's then-seedy Hell's Kitchen neighbourhood in the 1980s. Haunting and hallucinatory.

The Bluest Eye
by Toni Morrison
For some reason, I didn't read Morrison's devastating first novel until I'd read all her other work. I deeply admire everything she's done, and this was quite a start to her illustrious career.

Bright Lights, Big City
by Jay McInerney
Expertly capturing the manic folly of a young man trying to make it in New York, this novel is as well written and deeply felt as any debut.

The Intuitionist
by Colson Whitehead
Combines a noir detective story, racial allegory, and an absurdist premise – a world in which elevator inspectors are as important and revered as master sleuths – into a brilliant and thought-provoking creation.

Ten Inspiring and Wondrous First Novels *(continued)*

Gun, with Occasional Music
by Jonathan Lethem
Maybe I'm a sucker for books that combine the noir genre with other elements – in this case, a science-fiction future in which kangaroos carry guns, the asking of questions is illegal, and narrator-detectives pack wry laughs into every line. I love how Lethem takes such risks with his writing.

The Russian Debutante's Handbook
by Gary Shteyngart
The hilarious account of a young Russian immigrant's misadventures in New York, and in a fictionalised Prague, and in the enraging, mutable thing we call language.

A Writing Life

When do you write?
When I wrote *The Last Town on Earth* I had a full-time job, so I did most of my writing on the weekends. I usually began in the morning and tried to write until dinner, though my productivity tended to fall off somewhere in the mid-afternoon.

Where do you write?
Mostly at home, but sometimes I take the laptop to a coffee shop just to get out of the house.

Why do you write?
It's what I love, it's the thing I'm best at, it's what I think about, it's how I define myself, and if too much time goes by and I haven't written anything, I get cranky.

Pen or computer?
Computer. What's a pen?

Silence or music?
Silence.

How do you start a book?
I've found that it's best to have a rough outline of at least the first half of the book; otherwise I meander and/or write something that lacks forward momentum, thus requiring so much tinkering (or outright abandonment) that I should have just outlined from the start. But I'm not an extremely detailed, scene-by-scene outliner, and my outlines tend to morph as today's writing leads to new possibilities for tomorrow.

A Writing Life *(continued)*

And finish?
Usually I reach the end and know full well that there are flaws I need to address. So I reread the book and edit as I go, spending special attention to these problem areas, and in rereading I also discover countless other things that embarrass or horrify me, necessitating revisions, rewrites, excisions, etc.

Do you have any writing rituals or superstitions?
I do seem to be drinking entirely too much coffee lately, but that also owes a lot to having an infant in the house.

Which living writer do you most admire?
Toni Morrison and Cormac McCarthy write perfect sentences, craft surprising stories populated by fascinating characters, and create intricate moral universes – book after book, decade after decade. And I admire – and hope to emulate – the way in which Michael Chabon and Jonathan Lethem have been able to build their careers and engage their audiences by writing very different novels from one book to the next.

What or who inspires you?
Great music, beautiful films, amazing stories both true and fictional.

If you weren't a writer what job would you do?
If I knew the answer to that, I probably would have earned more money in the years preceding publication of this book.

What's your guilty reading pleasure or favourite trashy read?

I spend far too much time watching sports and therefore reading about them in the newspapers and online. Even the best sports-writing devolves into cliché after cliché, filled with quotes from men who are not terribly well spoken, and it pains me to think of all the other books I could have read if I weren't a sports fan. But it's how I was raised, and I cannot purge it from my blood.

'But They Never Talked About It'

by Thomas Mullen

One tip an aspiring novelist often will hear is 'don't try to write something trendy or marketable'. The reason for this is that novels take so long to research, write, edit, and publish that by the time your book hits the stores, the trend that you were hoping to capitalize on will be last year's news – or, more likely, news from five years ago.

So I thought I was safe from this quandary by writing about the 1918 influenza, a historical footnote that few Americans other than historians, virologists, and public health officials seemed to know about as I began my work in 2002. Indeed, one of the only books I could find on the event was titled 'America's Forgotten Pandemic'. I myself had been a history major in college and had even focused on Twentieth Century history, yet I'd never heard of the 1918 flu until I saw mention of it in a long article about an AIDS virologist who had once studied the fatal flu strain. What truly got my attention was the striking fact that some uninfected towns in 1918 had posted armed guards to keep outsiders away – the novel's opening confrontation took form in my mind immediately – but I was equally amazed that such a horrific and worldwide event could have become, as the book's title suggests, forgotten.

Why had this major catastrophe been swept under the carpets of history? Possibly because it had occurred during World War I;

history texts from this era spend all their ink on the war and can't be troubled to mention the flu – it merits a sentence or two if it gets mentioned at all, even though it killed *as many as 100 million people* worldwide, far more than the war itself.

I was further intrigued by the fact that, although the 1918 flu took place during the formative years of such literary giants as Hemingway, Steinbeck, Faulkner, Fitzgerald, and Dos Passos, none of them had written about it. Many writers of that golden literary age found war a weighty topic to expound upon, allowing exploration of such themes as manhood, patriotism, and courage. (Indeed, many proponents of America's entry to war – the so-called Preparedness Movement – had argued that war would provide chivalric meaning to the younger generation, which was believed to be cast adrift in an amoral society of wanton materialism and inhuman industrialization.) But a senseless illness that killed so many without discrimination did not appeal to these writers the same way, apparently. Perhaps it was too reminiscent – albeit in much greater form – of past typhoid or yellow fever or cholera outbreaks, a reminder of pre-modern times that was best ignored by young writers hoping to forge a bold new artistic path. Perhaps people had so internalized the incessant propaganda of World War I – to be strong and patriotic and never ▶

' Although the 1918 flu took place during the formative years of such literary giants as Hemingway, Steinbeck, Faulkner, Fitzgerald, and Dos Passos, none of them had written about it. '

But They Never Talked About It *(continued)*

◀ admit fear – and as a result it would have been unseemly to write about the lives lost to the flu, to stare in the face of such issues as failure and helplessness, to recount such undignified deaths.

Or perhaps the flu was a bitter memory they just wanted to forget.

A number of readers have approached me after reading *The Last Town on Earth* and told me that its subject reminded them of a great-aunt or a great-grandfather who lost a spouse or parents or children to the epidemic. I have been struck by the fact that their stories ofter end with some variation of the line: 'But she never talked about it.' There seemed to be a wall of silence surrounding survivors' memories of the 1918 flu, which, after the passing of many generations, was quickly leading to the very erasure of those memories. I can only imagine that this is due to the unimaginable horror of the time, the mind's inability to fully grasp what it had experienced and what it had lost. In our current age of psychoanalysis, talk shows, and tell-all memoirs, it is argued that the best way to recover from traumatic events and difficult pasts is to dredge up those memories, to 'come to terms' with the fact of those wounds and their effect on our present selves – only then, the theory goes, can we achieve 'closure' and become a healthier person. But the mindset in the 1910s was very different indeed, and perhaps survivors felt that the only way they could possibly recover from such an event was if they built a wall around those memories and tried, ever so slowly, to walk away from them.

One of the reasons I wrote *The Last Town on Earth*, then, was that it felt needed, that it would not only fill a gap in the literary canon but also, hopefully, would help retrieve some of the memories that were fading, and would provide a new echo for stories that had not been voiced in many years.

By the time the book was published, of course, fear of bird flu – and virologists' warnings that mankind was overdue for another major influenza outbreak – had brought the 1918 flu out of history's dustbin and onto the front pages. Suddenly I was being told that the novel that I thought would be most interesting due to its unknown setting was now 'timely', though such timing was unintended and certainly unexpected.

Although the 1918 flu was largely a natural disaster, human actions certainly exacerbated the situation. Governments were too distracted by war to devote sufficient resources to protecting public health, newspapers were cowed by censors into reporting only good news, and citizens showed distrust and suspicion toward neighbours most in need of aid. People, quite simply, did not know what to do; they had neither government nor media nor family legends and stories to guide them. Even today, despite our many medical advances, it is sobering to realize how much more vulnerable our globalized world would be to such an outbreak. ▶

‘By the time the book was published fear of bird flu had brought the 1918 flu out of history's dustbin and onto the front pages.’

But They Never Talked About It *(continued)*

◀ Eighty-nine years since that most awful epidemic, perhaps now is the time to remember what those before us have endured, to understand how the earlier versions of our societies reacted, and to talk about how we might respond if cast in a similar crucible. ■

If You Loved This, You Might Like . . .

Cold Mountain
Charles Frazier
Inman, a soldier wounded in the American Civil War, decides to turn his back on the battlefield and try and reach Ada, the woman he left behind before the war. Whilst he struggles to reach her, she struggles to survive. The story has now been made into a film starring Jude Law and Renée Zellweger.

March
Geraldine Brooks
In Louisa May Alcott's *Little Women*, the father figure was rather surplus to requirements and in this historical novel set during the American Civil War, Geraldine Brooks imagines his life, and love, away from his more famous daughters.

The Plague
Albert Camus
An obvious comparison, but no less a recommendation for that. Camus's classic allegorical novel is set in the city of Oran, in Algeria, where a mysterious plague of dying rats and a subsequent deathly fever eventually forces the residents to live, and die, under quarantine.

The Colour
Rose Tremain
The Blackstones, Joseph, Harriet and Joseph's mother Lilian, emigrate from England to New Zealand in order to start ▶

If You Loved This, You Might Like . . . *(continued)*

◀ a new life. But the shock of the unforgiving land they arrive in threatens to destroy their dream.

The Tenderness of Wolves
Stef Penney
Set in nineteenth-century Canada, this first novel combines aspects of murder mystery, historical fiction and the pioneer spirit and adventure of westerns. Mrs Ross has left Scotland for Dove River, Canada, where, fifteen years into her new life, a murder tests the morals of both new settlers and older residents.